Papa's Obsession

Papa's Obsession

By Philip Iovino

Belle Isle Books
www.belleislebooks.com

ISBN: 978-1-9399305-0-7

Library of Congress Control Number: 2015945089

Printed in the United States

Published by

BELLE ISLE BOOKS
www.belleislebooks.com

Belle Isle Books, an imprint of Brandylane Publishers, Inc.

To Christina, my wife
The Mama in my life

Table of Contents

Chapter One

Meeting Natalie

My father is not the easiest man in the world to love, but I do love him. During those years when I was growing up, it seemed that he was more critical than he was encouraging. I always felt that he was disappointed in me. Now that I am older, I have come to realize that he is just a sonavabitch with a heart as big as the moon when it comes to his family. Let's say that sensitivity is not his strong suit. What he lacks in sensitivity, he more than makes up for in obsessiveness.

He collects music like crazy. I could understand if he collected vinyl albums or 45s – that would make some sense – but he collects digital music and categorizes it. In today's world, the music is there in cyberspace and readily available. Why he wastes the precious few years he has left spending hours a day amassing all the top 100 songs dating back to 1955 boggles my mind. Now he is collecting or making all Academy Award nominated soundtracks from 1934, the first year this was a category. For those years when commercial soundtracks did not exist, he sits through the entire movie and rips his own soundtrack, dialogue and all. Then he makes his own compact disc and CD case with artwork included from the movie poster. He says this relaxes him. By this point, he should be so relaxed that he approaches unconsciousness. Now he has made it his mission to watch every movie that was ever nominated for an Academy Award dating back to *The Jazz Singer* and *Wings*. He has discovered that many movies are out of print. I wouldn't be surprised to hear that he crossed the country to visit the UCLA visual arts library. He says that there are out-of-print movies he may be able to watch at the library. He has not checked on that yet, but just give him time.

Though he is obsessive, I really do not think that he is OCD. He does show signs of normalcy at times. He does not break out in a sweat or act irrationally if he is suddenly forced to shut his computer down. But at his first opportunity, he would be right back in front of that keyboard.

From what I can tell, Grandma may have caused his obsessiveness. Papa has told me more than once how Grandma traumatized him by throwing away all his stuff after he went off to college. I think I knew Grandma quite well before she died, but do you really know an older relative? I am sure that when she was young, she was quite a different person. In fact, she was not really that young when my father was born. It was fortunate for me that she lived to be ninety years old and I got to know her. Even in her old age, Grandma had a pretty good mind, except that she would tell you the same story about ten times. I can only assume these events were very significant in her life.

My father grew up in the fifties and Superman was big back then. I can remember when he told me the story about the time he was watching Superman with his brother and the show was interrupted to report that the Russians had launched Sputnik, the first man-made satellite to orbit Earth. At nine years old, he could not understand why Superman was being disrupted for this nonsense. His brother nearly punched him in the mouth trying to shut him up. His brother was really upset by this news and Papa got the sense this was really important. This, of course, happened in the middle of the Cold War, a time when Papa and his peers had to duck and cover under the desk for air raid drills.

Getting back to *Superman,* Papa told me he collected all the Detective Comics he could afford and carefully stacked them on the vestibule in the basement. It was just a place to store old clothes and not used for much else. He thought his treasure trove would be safe there for eternity. One pile had *Superman's Pal, Jimmy Olsen*. Another pile had *Superman's Girlfriend, Lois Lane*. He also had a pile for *Superman, Batman, Action Comics, Adventure Comics*, and *Superboy* comics. Add to this the *Justice League of America* and *Showcase* and Papa collected nine comic books each week totaling $1.35 per week. This was a handsome sum on a paperboy's salary. Papa religiously collected these comics for years. Added to this were some older comics from the 1940s his older cousin did not want anymore. Not even thinking about the fortune he had collected as an investment, Papa said he just loved his comic collection.

As if that was not enough, Papa was also an avid collector of Topps baseball cards. Papa said for five cents he could buy a pack of cards with a flat piece of bubble gum inside. He told me that he loved the smell of the gum-odorized cards almost as much as the cards themselves. He would flip cards, matched or unmatched, where the flipper would need to match the color of the background or border of the card to win it. Or he said they would simply flip the cards, heads being the picture and tails being the statistics side. Other times they would toss the cards nearest to the wall to determine a winner. The duplicates and triplicates would end up in the spokes of his bike to create a motor sound. That was, of course, unless they were Red Sox or Yankees players. All his cards from several years of collecting were placed in many shoeboxes. I suppose this is a big reason why Papa's teeth are loaded with fillings and more fillings.

Papa is now into his sixties and the traumatic event of his mother throwing away all his comics and baseball cards has not totally left him. Now he guards his precious digital collection of totally valueless mp3 files by backing them up to his hard drive, a large-capacity thumb drive, and an external hard drive, *and* he subscribes to an online backup service to boot.

I paint this picture to help you understand that Papa's obsessions are very real. I will leave it to you to decide if they are irrational. I intentionally omit Papa's confrontation with Grandma upon learning that she threw out all his stuff. Just picture the worst tantrum you can imagine and triple it – this approaches the scene on that fateful day. Grandma, bless her heart, never enjoyed confrontation and, from what I heard, she did not take Papa's rant unemotionally.

Let us leave Papa for the time being. Papa will play an instrumental role in the following events. However, we must now introduce a young lady who, at the outset, has absolutely no connection to Papa whatsoever.

As this story begins, Natalie Romano, a beautiful young coed, was in her last year of her undergraduate studies and planning to receive her bachelor's degree in nursing. Her shimmering cinnamon-colored hair had certainly been inherited from her mother's Irish ancestry. Natalie's parents were both devout Catholics and made certain that Natalie was raised in the strictest tradition of the faith. In fact, Natalie was one of a dying breed of women who attained the age of twenty-one with her maidenhood unmolested by gentlemen admirers using all the tactics employed by that wily sort.

This fact was becoming more and more frustrating for Jeremy Quinn, a very respectful but red-blooded American boy, three years her senior. Jeremy was about to complete graduate school and already had a job offer in the field of radiology. Natalie and Jeremy expected to marry – it was an engagement of understanding long intended minus the announcements and diamond ring. These two were inevitably fated to be together forever. Jeremy and Natalie just seemed to fit well together. He carried a six-foot, well-constructed frame ideally suited for most of life's challenges. His prospects in life and his charming smile and wavy dirty blond hair assured him that he would never be at a loss for female companionship. And yet, Jeremy respected Natalie's values, having himself been brought up a Catholic in a not-nearly-so-dedicated manner.

Jeremy had the luxury of living a bachelor's life minus the obvious benefits. His apartment was small, but it was his alone. One evening Jeremy was in an especially romantic mood. Natalie was no stranger to Jeremy's apartment. Neither was she disinclined to bring Jeremy to the point of sexual relief, though always forbidding herself the same pleasure.

"Natalie, don't you feel this game we play has run its course? Do you think I'm going to lose respect for you and leave you if we make love?" Jeremy asked, pulling her close. "Two years seems to be a pretty good indication that I am here for the long haul. I love you and I miss that complete and total intimacy that we never had."

"It's not about that, Jeremy," Natalie replied. "We've been all through this a million times. I love you, too. I try to make you feel good and make you happy." She sighed and put her hand on his cheek. "There is just something inside me that tells me it is wrong to let you or anyone take my purity before we are one before God. You've always understood that. What's so different about tonight?"

"Tonight you look so damn beautiful I just can't stand it." There was practically a whine in Jeremy's voice. "Please give it up!"

Natalie was tempted. She had been on the brink of ecstasy many times before but always found the strength to stop just short of abandoning her promise to God and herself. But on this night, Jeremy's determination and persistence were more powerful than ever.

"Natalie, I swear, if you don't make love to me tonight, I will find someone who will!"

As soon as the words left him, Jeremy feared he had opened his big fat mouth wide enough to stick a truck inside. It's not that he didn't mean wanting the sex part, but the risk of losing Natalie over a moment of frustration was not what he intended. A young man in the sexual peak of his life has no clue about having a lifetime of lovemaking ahead of him. That doesn't help in the moment.

The silence was deafening. All Jeremy could think about was the first time he ever saw Natalie at a mutual friend's apartment. She had perched herself up on the sink counter while everyone else was sitting around the kitchen table. He thought she was the most beautiful girl he had ever seen. And now, two years later, he still could not believe this gorgeous creature was actually his girl.

If Jeremy had followed his first instinct, he would have apologized immediately and begged for Natalie's forgiveness, but his manly pride got the best of him. He figured that either Natalie would give in to him or, if she did not, he could get her back after a day or two. He never once believed that this episode would be the final blow to their relationship. It would be different if they hadn't fought, broke up, made up, and played that whole game a few times. Many of his friends had numerous breakups and always got back together with their girls. As the song says, "Break up to make up … that's a game for a fool."

Natalie sat there stunned for a moment at Jeremy's words. When she composed herself, she started to leave the apartment.

"Where are you going, Natalie?"

"I just heard you say that you were about to find someone to give you what you need. Obviously, that person is not I."

"Do you think I would let you leave here by yourself to get home?" he asked, jumping to his feet. "I'll take you. If you got hurt or hassled on your way home, I'd never forgive myself."

Natalie was happy that she did not need to find a ride home, and Jeremy figured this was just a cooling off period. Tomorrow would be another day.

Both Jeremy and Natalie waited for the phone to ring, each expecting the other to make the first move. It was not unlike the Democrats and Republicans waiting for the other side to blink first on some hardened principle from which they refused to bend. It always amazes me how seemingly mature people put common sense and heartfelt feelings aside for the sake of pride. After a week of this standoff, Natalie wondered if she had misjudged Jeremy's love for her. She felt used and betrayed by Jeremy's lack of sensitivity. Even so, she loved Jeremy and felt things would get back to normal.

Jeremy, on the other hand, took this time to feed his basic needs. He tried not to be too obvious because he did not want to flaunt his infidelity before Natalie, nor did he want to hurt her by having word of his new conquests somehow reach her ears. It wasn't difficult for him to find girls willing to share intimate sexual encounters with him. After several such experiences, he came clearly to the realization that sex and love were not really the same thing. Sex without love feels good, but it's unfulfilling after the moment is over. Love without sex is much different. For Jeremy and Natalie, it was love based on a promise of forever. It was a promise that both truly expected as an unspoken inevitability.

Jeremy should have known that eventually his secret would reach Natalie. I suspect that he always believed deep down that he could avoid the fate of losing Natalie forever. This had to be the future since Natalie and Jeremy were destined to be together regardless of what life threw at them.

Natalie's friend Regina saw Jeremy at a club with someone who was definitely not Natalie. And Regina happened to know who Jeremy's someone was because that someone told Regina's friend about this terrific, good-looking guy who was very exciting (if you know what I mean). Regina, having less than half the story, felt it was her responsibility and duty to tell Natalie about her two-timing boyfriend. Maybe Regina felt that Natalie had it too good for too long and needed to feel the heartache that everyone else had to endure. I happen to know that Regina had endured her own share of heartache.

When Natalie heard Regina's vivid and embellished story about Jeremy, she was devastated. I think Regina enjoyed playing the part of the wiser, comforting friend. She didn't realize that resentment and not gratitude probably awaited her somewhere down the road. But I can at least thank Regina for one thing. It was because of her meddling that providence provided me the opportunity to meet Natalie.

"Why have you been moping here in this room staring at your cell phone?" asked Regina. "I know Jeremy is not staying home night after night."

"I just can't believe he hasn't called in all this time. It's been more than three weeks since we argued. Jeremy and I have never stayed away from each other this long."

"Natalie, you're twenty-one years old. Why in the world did you argue about having sex? Shit, girl – you've been going out with him for two years. Are you made of porcelain? Haven't you been excited enough in all that time to please your man?"

"It's not like we haven't done anything, Regina. I've gotten him off and he's gotten me off. It's only when he pressures me to go all the way that things get tense."

"Having sex is as natural as breathing. I'm not saying sleep around with everyone you meet, but you've really got a hang-up. Your folks or somebody have really laid a guilt trip on you. If people today only married virgins, David's Bridal would go out of business. Hell, you've already felt, tasted, and exploded the merchandise. How is seeing if it fits any different?

"Regina, I guess there's no making you understand the difference. There just is! So what do you suggest I do? Should I call him up and give in to his primal urges?"

"Do you really want to know what I'd do?"

"Sure I do."

Regina got quietly devilish. "I would take him back all right, but on my terms. You know he is out there right now doing God knows what. Why shouldn't you do the same? What gives him the right to make demands on you? You should have your first sexual experience with someone to whom you are not emotionally attached."

"What?" Natalie exclaimed.

"See, this way you get experience for Jeremy and you'll know what to expect when it happens. Besides, you never need to tell Jeremy about it. Girl, you better *not* tell Jeremy because he never could handle that! If you're determined to be a virgin, you'd better be Jeremy's virgin – at least in his mind."

"Your thinking is really convoluted, Regina. Why would I even want to give my virginity away to anyone *but* Jeremy? I especially wouldn't want to do it with a stranger."

"There you go again. You keep confusing love and sex. They are totally different."

Natalie tried to make sense of Regina's logic. "OK, they're different, I get it. But I still don't want to do it with anyone but Jeremy and especially not with a stranger."

"Having sex solely for pleasure is liberating. I'm not suggesting that your first time be with a toothless old man. Look for someone who excites your juices. You'll enjoy it way more this way. Then when you finally have sex with Jeremy, it will be for love. That is an entirely different feeling. It's more spiritual – the physical part just goes along for the ride. I should know. I've had lots of physicals and a few spiritual lovemaking experiences. The spiritual is a totally intense serenity." Regina continued, ignoring Natalie's befuddled expression. "I want you to plan having a girls' night out this weekend. I do not want to hear any more excuses."

Natalie did end up going out with the girls that next Saturday night. I know because I was at the same club that night. I was playing the games the other guys play: trying to act unaffected while covertly checking out all the girls. I enjoy watching the young studs steal up-and-down glances at the babes almost as much as I enjoy checking out the babes myself. When Natalie walked in with her pack of girls, she was a game-changer. The stares from all the prowling hounds were embarrassingly obvious. They were so obvious that Natalie could not possibly have missed their gaping. I suppose when she had been in the company of Jeremy, the hopeful gentlemen kept themselves somewhat in check. But now, it was open season and the contenders came out swinging. I wanted to throw my hat in Natalie's ring, too, but I am not twenty-eight and single for nothing.

Sure, I've had my share of dates and even some longer-term girlfriends; but my insecurities always convinced me that I would screw it up in the end. And I always did. One of my biggest problems is the classic insecure guy syndrome. I would embellish to the point of humiliation. I remember the time after drinking Scotch whiskey for about five rounds, how I blurted out that this was the best bourbon I'd ever had. Everyone else knew what we were drinking. I just proved with that one comment that I really was not cool when it came to hard liquor. The truth is, I am not much of a drinker and when I imbibe too much I become ridiculous. I find myself at times talking too much about my accomplishments when the truth is they're just normal things. It took too long to learn that it is not necessary to build yourself up. If others can't see the good traits and strengths in your makeup, then your own talking about them won't convince anyone otherwise. I had convinced myself that Natalie would not give me the time of day so I pretty much did what I always do: for fear of rejection, I rationalized she was just a stuck-up, rich college girl that I would have no real interest in meeting.

But her beauty and infectious smile told me I was lying to myself. The way her eyes gleamed when she smiled incited me to take some action and stop making excuses to myself. And again, in typical fashion, I waited too long. Someone else made the first approach on my goddess.

From afar I studied every move Natalie made. I never saw her show the least bit of interest in any of the guys ogling her. She sat with an unidentified drink in front of her. Most of the time she spent laughing and talking to the three other girls who accompanied her to the club. I observed her reject four invitations to dance. One guy was a body-builder type and not totally unattractive, if I am any judge of a man's looks. Another guy was rather flamboyant, and his gyrations led me to believe he fancied himself a *Dancing with the Stars* star. I laughed to myself when I saw him boogie away quite a bit faster than he had sashayed over to the table. In between, Natalie would take very small sips of her drink through one of those small, thin white straws. At the rate she was going, I figured two drinks would last her the entire evening.

Then I saw two other fairly normal-looking guys come over and mumble something to Natalie. I assume the soft movement of Natalie's lips said "no, thank you," because both guys sheepishly sauntered off to look for another conquest. I sensed Natalie was enjoying the music, her friends, and the atmosphere. It was later that I learned that the feeling of going solo was still quite new to her.

And then something happened that totally changed Natalie's demeanor. I wasn't able to detect what happened until I was able to follow the path of Natalie's glare to a couple standing close to the bar, buried two rows deep behind those ordering drinks. I subsequently discovered that she was staring at Jeremy.

Jeremy's current escort was Stacy, but he did not call himself her boyfriend. He wasn't interested in jumping into another long-term relationship. He was currently attracted to the type of girl who was looking to have some "fun."

I watched as Natalie's mood fell from happy and upbeat to sullen and despondent. Her reaction was to immediately down the drink in front of her and order another from the waitress. As she followed Jeremy's movements, her pace of drinking picked up substantially. Before much longer, she was on to drink number three. I suspected from her initial approach of babying that first drink, this rapid imbibing was anything but the norm.

It was at this point I decided to very casually and coolly enter the immediate space of Natalie's table. My curiosity over what had precipitated this sudden change in Natalie's behavior was keenly piqued. I was not too proud to do a little eavesdropping if I could convert any chatter into information I might use to my advantage. This is when I learned who Jeremy was and why daggers were being delivered in his direction from those beautiful green eyes.

I overheard Regina tell Natalie that she must not let Jeremy see her all by herself while he's out there prancing around with some bimbo. "Natalie, my darling fool," Regina said, "you've had all these guys dying to be with you. Go pick one out and stay with him as long as Jeremy's here. It's just a matter of time before he sees you. Do *not* give him the satisfaction of thinking that you're sitting home by the phone waiting for him to call or looking to have a chance meeting with him – here, for instance. Remind him of just what a catch you really are! What the hell do you think he's doing here with Miss Jeans So Tight You Can Read Her Lips? This is just his foreplay for what comes next."

I was pleased with Regina's instructions and saw my role in this drama forming before my eyes. I saw Natalie's mind actively digest what Regina was saying as she ordered her fifth drink. Her other two friends were supporting the "screw that bastard Jeremy" stand that Regina was pounding into Natalie. I am no suave bon vivant, but you don't have to hit me over the head to realize that this was my one and possibly only chance. Maybe my mother was right. Maybe I really am handsome only I didn't realize it with all of Papa's put-downs. Hell, I decided to make my move. The timing would never be better and there was a rare slow dance being spun.

I do not believe that I ever formally introduced myself to you. My name is Ricky Santo. I have an older sister, Connie, and a terrific mama and papa. My mother has spent my whole life defending me against any brutality imposed upon me by Papa. This has not been physical brutality –

well, maybe one time – but it's just as frightening. I am twenty-eight years old and fairly well educated. In fact, I have a two-year master's degree from a respected college near Boston. No, it's not Harvard. Papa would have paid for me to go to Harvard if he'd had the money, but he didn't. I could have earned a scholarship to Harvard if I'd had the credentials, but I didn't. Even now Papa helps – well, maybe more than helps: he pays my monthly college loans. As long as he sees that I am working hard and not taking the year off to go hiking in Europe, I believe he will continue to support me. That's just the way he is made. I do not want to test his munificence by becoming a slacker.

Just then I noticed Jeremy and his new passion step onto the dance floor. I also felt the daggers shooting across the room in his direction. This was my moment. I softly asked Natalie as I extended my hand, "Do you want to dance?"

Without hesitation or saying a word, she came with me.

My mama didn't raise no fool. I knew that Natalie was only using me, but, as Billy Withers said, "... Just keep on using me until you use me up." I could feel Natalie gravitate toward Jeremy as we danced. I was not certain whether she wanted him to see her or if she wanted to get a better look at the other woman. In any event, she became silly and giddy, holding me tighter with each step we took closer to them. When Jeremy and Natalie's eyes met, I suddenly became the most charming and humorous guy in the room. The funny thing is, I was not saying anything.

When the dance ended, Natalie asked *me* if I wanted to sit. I was only too happy to oblige. I escorted her to a two-seat table where my friend Raymond and I had been sitting. When Raymond saw us approaching, he furtively slipped away to allow us to sit together. Raymond has always been a good friend. All I could notice was that Natalie would stare off, apparently seeking Jeremy's whereabouts. I think I played this whole thing out correctly. I knew that talking too much or trying to impress her would not be the way to win her over. She was still on the rebound and not much interested in anything but her personal angst. So I did the only gentlemanly thing I could – I bought her drink number six. Natalie was at this point leaving giddy and entering the introspective stage.

As I listened to Natalie ramble, Regina and Natalie's two other bodyguards bounded over to our table. "OK, let me see your driver's license!" Regina demanded of me.

This took me aback. "What in the world –"

But before I could finish my sentence, Regina stopped me. "If you expect to take Natalie home, we've got to check you out."

Neither Regina nor Natalie had any way of knowing that I was aware of the whole situation, including knowing that I was being used. This may have been my opportunity to escort Natalie home. Of course, this whole show would be wasted unless Jeremy saw us leave together. I expected that Regina would see to that. She seemed to be a very efficient agitator.

"OK, here it is."

Regina checked my picture, birth date, and address. Then she took a photo of my license with her cell phone.

"You don't look twenty-eight. OK, what's the plate number of your car?"

I complied. At this point, I was starting to enjoy the attention. "It's KHJ 323. It's the blue Malibu parked right under the second lamppost headed toward the overpass."

"Sherry, go outside and check it out." Regina ordered. And Sherry automatically obeyed.

"Where does your mother live?" inquired Regina.

I wondered if she would have been embarrassed if I had told her my mother had died or met some otherworldly fate. Somehow I doubt it. "She lives in the city."

"Give me her phone number," Regina commanded. And I did.

Regina immediately whipped out her cell phone and dialed the number. "Hello, Mrs. Santo," Regina said in a saccharine-sweet voice, which was totally foreign to my ear. "My name is Regina. I'm sorry for calling after nine, but this is important. Ricky is here with my best friend and I am checking with you on my friend's behalf. I am worried that he may ask her to leave with him."

Regina held the phone out so everyone at the table could hear my mother's response. I could hear the smile in her voice and felt the heat creeping up into my face. "Why worry? Can't you tell that my Ricky is like an angel? He wouldn't hurt a fly. There's not a violent bone in his body. He has always been a gentleman whenever he escorts a young lady. I only wish he would find a nice young girl and settle down. I must say this is a most unusual call, though. Did you expect me to say that he was a serial killer?"

"No, Mrs. Santo. I was really listening more to how you said it and not so much what you said. I can see that you are sincere. I think that when a boy loves his mother and a mother loves her son, that says it all. Well, good night. It was really nice talking to you."

Sherry returned to the table and Regina, the sergeant, turned her attention to her. "Did you find the car?"

"Yes, the license plate checks out," Sherry assured her.

Regina took Natalie into the restroom, promising she would be back. It was clear that Natalie was beginning to crash. I suspected that this was the biggest drinking night of her young life. After all, Natalie had not been of legal drinking age all that long. She did not even appear to me to be a drinker – but what did I know?

I daresay their trip to the restroom included a strategy session. Even though I was not in on the plan, the whole thing was so obvious. I just had to play along. I was really enjoying the way this whole night was turning out.

Regina escorted Natalie back to my table, guiding her to the seat beside me, leaning over to whisper in her ear. Given the background noise of the bar and the tension of the moment, Regina's attempts to whisper were fruitless – or perhaps that was part of her strategy. I heard every word she said.

"OK, Natalie," said Regina, "don't forget the plan. You sit here with Ricky, but watch me, too. On cue, you and Ricky get up and leave. Remember, this could be your night to leave your childhood behind!"

"Poo to that," replied Natalie.

Natalie's friends returned to their table, leaving the two of us alone. I noticed that Natalie was only half listening to me, looking past me rather than at me. Soon I saw Regina walk towards Jeremy and his new girlfriend. Regina made a point of bumping into Jeremy, and then struck up a conversation with him. I could only guess the subject of Natalie came up. As they were talking, I noticed Regina pointing to our table. Then she suddenly turned to wave at Sherry and Monica. At this same moment, Natalie jumped up and said, "Come on, Ricky, let's get out of here."

This was definitely an orchestrated performance for Jeremy's sake and I was the pawn. Imagine. I knew I was being used to make this other guy jealous, but I was also getting a terrific girl on my arm, if only for one night, and I was having a hell of a good time being in on the joke.

I only hoped that Jeremy was not the crazy type. I don't mind being in a good fight if it's for a good cause. I did not consider being used as a patsy a very good cause. As it turned out, Natalie and I left unmolested. I know that Jeremy saw us leave, because Regina was yelling, "Where are you going, Natalie?"

As I escorted Natalie to my car, I really did not know what would transpire. I wanted to take her to my apartment and make passionate love to her at least three times. I knew the chance of that happening was less than winning the Powerball jackpot. Now that we were alone and out of Jeremy's orbit, Natalie was able to be herself, albeit a somewhat intoxicated version of herself.

"Ricky, where would you like to go?" Natalie asked.

This question startled the hell out of me. I expected her to instruct me to take her home, or maybe if I were lucky she would ask to stop off and get some coffee. Instead, she actually asked me where I would like to go. Knowing the entire situation, I felt that I was playing with house money. I had very little to lose since I was basically a warm body being used to make her boyfriend jealous. Was there a chance that she was considering Regina's advice to leave her childhood behind? I figured, why not? Columbus took a chance. I knew, even if Natalie didn't know it, that I would never force myself upon her. I had too much pride to do that. In fact, when it came to sexually forcing oneself upon another person, I was a champion of women's rights. But I kept asking myself why this stunning young woman would put her fate in the hands of a stranger. The alcohol was part of it, but I sensed it was much more than that.

"Well, Natalie," I finally replied, weighing my words carefully. "I've had enough loud noise for one evening. Would you object to one nightcap at my place? I assure you that it is very quiet and I am quite harmless. You can call my mother if you don't believe me."

Knowing that Regina had called for a reference, Natalie laughed. And what a laugh it was. It was a melodic enchantment that made my mind race.

"It's still fairly early for a Saturday night," said Natalie. "I suppose one more drink at this point would be all right."

"That's terrific. It's not too far from here."

I cannot pretend to know what possessed Natalie to accept my invitation. Even now, I can only speculate. Maybe it was the thought of Jeremy running around getting laid while she was sitting at home waiting for him to call. Maybe it was Regina constantly taking her to task for being a girl of the 1600s in old Massachusetts Bay Colony that finally got to her. Maybe she'd had too much to drink. I suspect it was all of these things.

When we got to my apartment, I turned on some music and fixed us both one more drink, as if Natalie hadn't already had too much. Natalie would now enter stage nine of drunkenness. This is the stage where you become invisible. You can pee in the street and it's no big deal because no one can see you. Personally, I have always believed that even in the worst stage of drunkenness, the person knows what he or she is doing. If someone has less inhibition and does something they would not normally do, it's probably something they wanted an excuse to do in the first place. I was hoping this was Natalie's state, because although I would never force myself upon her, I was not beyond taking advantage of the situation. I kept looking at Natalie, and she was breathtaking.

We sat on my sofa and Natalie did not seem to mind me putting my arm around her. As I took her drink from her hand, I slowly brushed her soft pink lips. Her lipstick was less pronounced after hours of drinking, but her natural color was more beautiful than any chemist's creation. Her soft lips almost molded into my own, creating an erotic sensation my body could not disregard. In fact, I could not remember when a simple kiss had caused such excitement in me. I was hoping not to blow the whole night after one tender moment. Natalie did not resist my sexual advances, so I continued. I took her hand and walked the short distance to my bed.

The room was dark and Adele was singing in the background, the volume turned down to one notch above barely audible. The whole seduction, if I may call it that, seemed surreal and trancelike. Natalie never really resisted, nor did she seem a cooperative participant in our lovemaking. I had the sense she was making love to Jeremy and I was his proxy. Every aspect of being intimate with Natalie was as if it was my own first time. I truly felt a unique sensation, triggered by her silky presence. I could feel her warm wetness indicating that she too was electrified by the moment.

As desperately as I wanted Natalie in that moment, I knew she was using me to lash out at Jeremy. I knew that too much booze had lowered her defenses. I felt ashamed of myself for taking advantage of her situation but was so enchanted by her captivating being that I convinced myself that making love to her was the right thing to do.

I found the strength to suppress my natural urge to continue and asked, "Do you want me to stop?"

I listened carefully for her response, hoping she would give me permission to continue. I heard only soft sighs and gentle moans but no words left her sweet lips.

"Did you hear me?" I repeated tenderly.

"Did you hear me say I wanted you to stop?" she finally whispered.

She answered my question with another question, which implied her tacit permission to resume. When I finally entered her, I had to imagine all sorts of unrelated happenings to take my mind off of the ecstatic pleasure my body and mind were feeling. I fought to prolong the rapture. When I felt Natalie's tightening grip around my neck and her body's quivering, I could no longer hold back. My climax was violently subdued from fighting the feeling. My body became sedated and I lay close to Natalie's warm body for probably the next hour.

Usually your first love happens when you are a teenager. In my case, Natalie would be my forever memory. She would become the standard by which every other woman would be measured and which none would ever attain. In a short three hours, I had fallen desperately in love with a young woman whom I knew was only using me, who allowed me in only when she lost control in a moment of sullen weakness. I was a blissful cad, detestable to myself without regret.

Natalie woke up slowly during the second hour of our afterglow slumber. She straightened herself up in my bathroom and asked if I would drive her home. Without exchanging any words except directions, we rode. Natalie poignantly said goodnight. I did not kiss her or ask for her phone number. I was passionately distressed by the idea that I would be Natalie's one-night stand.

Chapter Two

The Romanos

Natalie still lived at home. It was her own practical decision. Her campus was only ten miles away. Her parents, Harry and Kathryn Romano, would foot the bill for her to live on or off campus in order to experience the college life. Natalie knew her parents could afford this, but she also knew they could put this money to much better use. Instead, Natalie's parents bought her a new car after high school graduation that she would use for the four years she attended college. Natalie had her freedom and was treated as an adult without restriction while living at home. There were nights when Natalie stayed with friends as a guest. She even spent an occasional night at Jeremy's apartment. Natalie's parents trusted their daughter to make good decisions. Until last night, she did.

When Mrs. Romano went in to wake Natalie for church, she found Natalie in a coma-like sleep. Upon closer examination, she found Natalie's breath was foul with the smell of alcohol. Instead of waking her, Mrs. Romano let her sleep it off. This had been the first time she ever found Natalie in this state and she debated with herself what to do about it. In the end, Mrs. Romano did nothing. This was not a common occurrence and Mrs. Romano decided it would be better not to impose herself into her daughter's night of adventure. Natalie's hangover would probably do more to moderate her drinking than any lecture she might deliver. This was the strategy, at least for the time being.

Even though Mrs. Romano was a devout Catholic and raised her daughter in the strict tenets of the church, she was a modern woman with her own mind. She was not a prude. Mrs. Romano was still a beautiful woman at forty-four years of age. Her husband, seven years her senior, was much more proper and pretty much ruled the home. But he only ruled over Mrs. Romano to the degree she would permit it. His power was far more ominous over his children.

Mr. Romano inquired, "Where's Natalie?"

Kathryn Romano said, "Let's just go to church, Harry. Natalie isn't coming this week."

"Not coming? Natalie never misses church. Is she sick?"

Mrs. Romano considered how to reply to the seemingly simple question. She knew that her husband was not the most understanding man in the world. The fact that his precious little girl was out carousing all night in an apparently intoxicated state would not make him happy.

"Not actually sick," said Mrs. Romano. "She was so sound asleep, I decided not to wake her. I think she came home very late last night. Let her sleep. She's worked hard to get where she is. If she lets her hair down one Saturday night, what's wrong with that? She's young. In case you haven't noticed, since Jeremy and Natalie stopped seeing each other, she has been a depressed blob around here. Other than school, she hasn't left this house in weeks. Is it possible that you are not aware of this?"

"Well," Mr. Romano said, stumbling with his words, "I've been preoccupied with work things. Those two will kiss and make up eventually. If not, your daughter has her first heartache. It happens to everyone."

"That doesn't mean you need to get all huffy about Natalie missing church once or twice. I swear, I just don't believe you sometimes. Come on, Harry, let's go. We'll be late."

During the drive to church, Kathryn could tell that her husband was stewing over Natalie missing church. "Harry, you're a damn hypocrite," she finally burst out. "Before we were married, you screwed anything wearing a skirt. Then you have a daughter and you want to pretend you're a saint. You scared Natalie into believing that you would be devastated if she ever let you down after all you've done for her. I don't know what happened last night in Natalie's life – but don't you say anything. You are lucky she is still living at home. I can only imagine that you would be blubbering like a baby if your precious little girl left home. Get used to the idea, Harry. The time is fast approaching and then it's just you and me, sweetie!"

"Natalie misses church and stays out all night and you want me to forget about it?"

"Yes!" Kathryn snapped back. "Natalie is twenty-one and a woman. You're not her father! Well, you are her father, but you're not her moral policeman – that role you've done with intimidation for far too long. It's time for you to retire the policeman and become just her father. Help Natalie. Comfort her when she's sad; advise her when she needs her daddy. Other than that, just shut up."

"Kathryn, do you hear the way you're talking to me? If you were trying to piss me off, you couldn't do a better job!"

"I'm just tired of you trying to be the big boss over everyone else's life," said Kathryn. "I'm really sick of you trying to be Saint Harry around this house. Do you think I am so naïve, not knowing what you do with your time when you are supposed be working late at night or on weekends?"

This statement really put the brakes on any conversation having to do with Natalie. Harry Romano fancied himself to be the soul of discretion. He never considered that his own secret life would be questioned. Kathryn knew her husband's moods, habits, gestures, movements, body language, and every other nuance that would reveal when he was lying. For her own personal reasons, she allowed things to continue. She knew her husband would never leave her. He was a strict Catholic, even though he picked and chose which commandments were worth keeping. He did not believe in divorce. He had an image to uphold and would not allow a scandal. His children had to respect him and he could not be found to be a charlatan. But even beyond all these things, Kathryn was a devoted wife and Mr. Romano loved and respected her beyond what words could express. The fact that she saw right through him was his own personal wake-up call.

Instead of challenging his wife's most damning allegation, Harry wisely decided to diffuse the entire conversation. He never mentioned Natalie's late night again nor did he try to refute his wife's contention. "You're nuts, Kathryn. I work like a dog and you accuse me of who knows what. Let's calm down. We are about to visit the house of the Lord."

Kathryn knew she had won that battle. She usually did.

Natalie arose about one o'clock that afternoon. Not bad really, considering the amount of alcohol she had consumed. For someone used to drinking or for someone with a bigger frame to absorb the drinks, it may not have been all that much. For Natalie, it was way too much. She had all the classic signs of a hangover. The sunshine was blinding and sounds were all explosions. She had a cottonmouth and the sight of food nauseated her and yet she felt very hungry. Slowly, she would adapt to her environment. She moved tepidly and drank hot tea painstakingly. A bit later she would be able to handle some crackers and celery sticks. The idea of having a drink revolted her.

Regina just had to hear all the juicy details. She felt this needed a personal accounting, not simply by telephone. Fortunately for Natalie, Regina came by much later in the afternoon, and by that time Natalie was somewhat able to function.

"OK, lady, give me all the sordid details," said Regina with a grin. "Where did he take you? I hope you didn't go straight home. Oh, wow, you should have seen Jeremy. Right after you left with what's-his-name, he bolted to the door. I know he saw you get into the car. I guess he was either too late, too stupid, or too embarrassed to run after you."

"Well, I never saw him follow me out, and if I had, I wouldn't have given him the satisfaction of saying goodbye," replied Natalie. She folded her arms across her chest and spilled the details in a rush, frowning as she talked. "His name was Ricky – don't you remember? We went to his place because I was too wasted to go home right away. But after we got there, I was so blitzed, I think I crashed on his bed. What's worse, I really think we had sex. I mean, all-the-way-come-inside-and-do-what-you-want sex. Can you imagine that? I've been going with Jeremy for two years and I love him and denied him sex. I meet this perfect stranger and in a few hours I screw him. How sick is that?"

"Are you sure? You don't sound like you were participating," said Regina. "Did he force himself on you?"

"Not really. I couldn't say he raped me, if that's what you mean. After all, I agreed to go with him. I was drunk. I have no sense of his forcing himself on me." Natalie paused, searching her mind for memories. "Most of what happened was like a dreamlike blur. I do remember feeling excited. I also remember wanting to tell him to stop – but I just let it happen. Now I feel I've been robbed of something I waited so long to experience. It was a semiconscious loss of my virginity. I know I can blame no one but myself."

"He was kinda cute," said Regina. "His mother loves him. He took care to see that you were safely delivered home. I don't think he is a bad person."

"Maybe not, but he's a stranger that I let screw me. He must think I am a total tramp."

Regina asked, "Do you care what he thinks?"

"Not really," Natalie replied. "I'll never see him again anyway."

That Monday, Natalie went to her classes. Mr. Romano went to work as usual, and Mrs. Romano had her weekly errands to perform. Mrs. Romano only worked part time and had Mondays off. About eleven that morning, a lovely bouquet of roses arrived from Ricky. The card simply read, "Beautiful roses for a more beautiful lady. Ricky." Mrs. Romano probably should not have read the card, knowing that the flowers were being delivered to Natalie, but curiosity got the better of her. After all, her daughter comes home late Saturday night stinking drunk and now these flowers. After seeing that these were not make-up flowers from Jeremy, it did not take a genius to figure out that Ricky was probably the one who kept her daughter out late that weekend.

It was not unusual for Natalie to come home after six p.m. Once she arrived on campus, she tried to stay there until all her work was finished.

On Mondays, she had three classes, and the last one ended at 4:50. After she had a small bite to eat, Natalie remained in the library finishing up a paper that was due and studying for an upcoming exam. This was her last semester, and her load was lighter than she'd had in previous years. She had planned it this way to make certain her final semester would be less stressful. With most of her courses completed, Natalie had one last required course and two undemanding electives plus an internship at the hospital on Tuesdays and Thursdays. With her high grade point average, graduation was simply a matter of time.

Mr. Romano arrived home for dinner before Natalie arrived home from school. This was typical. Only on her hospital days did Natalie make it home for dinner. On her class days, unless Natalie told her mother she would be home for dinner, Mrs. Romano and her husband planned on dining alone. Dining at the Romano home usually meant Kathryn fixing something for her husband and herself and sitting down with some snack trays to watch the news and a show or two.

"What's the occasion with these roses?" asked Mr. Romano. "Do you have a secret admirer, Kathryn? Should I be jealous? I hope you're not trying to tell me something."

"Look at the card, Harry. You'll see that these are for Natalie."

"Who the hell is Ricky? Whatever happened to Jeremy? I thought those two were getting married after Natalie graduated."

"I told you – and you should have noticed anyway – Natalie and Jeremy had a fight. She has not seen Jeremy for close to a month."

"Oh, I knew that," bellowed Mr. Romano. "I just never expected that breakup to last. What the hell happened there anyway?"

"Natalie has never confided in me about that. I really suspect that it's about sex. You know, Harry, as far as I know, Natalie is still a virgin. Your proselytizing has really paid dividends. Although I must say, considering our own X-rated courtship, I have always found it to be a bit hypocritical. Don't you agree?"

"Absolutely not," Harry Romano balked. "This is our baby girl we're talking about here. And anyway, you were much older than Natalie is now."

"Actually not, Harry. I think your overprotectiveness is sweet. But maybe now at twenty-one, Natalie is conflicted. I hope that you will be tolerant, compassionate, and understanding."

When Natalie got home, she was surprised to see the roses.

"Why would this guy send me roses?" she wondered aloud. "I only just met him and do not expect to see him again. I made that clear to him when we said goodnight."

"Apparently you made a big impression on him, Natalie," stated her mother. "Is he the reason you came home so late on Saturday?"

"I wouldn't say he's the reason, but I did spend quite a bit of time with him Saturday. We met at a club. He is a perfect stranger to me. I guess seeing Jeremy Saturday night with somebody else just ticked me off. I latched on to this Ricky for spite. I never expected him to become my new boyfriend or anything like that."

"Well, young lady," her father chimed in, "if you go out to clubs unescorted you can expect guys to be after you. After all, you are the most beautiful woman in New England."

"Oh, Daddy, I think you are a bit prejudiced on that subject."

Natalie promptly placed the roses in her room and out of sight. She did not want to continue the discussion about Ricky. In truth, Ricky was a hazy recollection. She struggled to even remember what he looked like. She struggled even more to put her own humiliating behavior behind her. Ricky was a reminder of something she desperately wanted to forget.

While all this was going on, I was desperately trying to get Natalie's phone number. Fortunately, I had a not-so-bogus reason for trying to get Natalie to contact me. She left an earring in the bed the night we had our impromptu rendezvous. I knew where Natalie lived from dropping her home that evening, but I didn't know her cell phone number. This she refused to give me when I requested it. Then I remembered that Regina called my mother that evening seeking a character reference. Knowing Mom, she never clears the last-call queue and I was able to get Regina's phone number. I explained to Regina that Natalie had lost an earring at my apartment and I wanted to return it. She would not give me Natalie's cell phone number, but she did agree to tell Natalie that I called. I thought this was kind of dumb, because once Natalie called me I would have her phone number on caller ID anyway. Maybe Natalie wasn't thinking or maybe she never worried about my having her phone number, but she did actually call me.

"Hello, this is Natalie." Hearing the soft melody of her voice excited my senses, despite the chilly monologue that followed. "I understand you have an earring of mine. I know you have my address, so please drop it in an envelope and mail it. And thank you for the beautiful roses. I wish you hadn't sent them, though. I told you, that whole evening was a big mistake. If you think we will be seeing each other again, think again. Things have not changed since that night. I am still embarrassed by my behavior. You took advantage of my state and that was not a gentlemanly thing to do."

"I'm sorry you feel that way," I replied. "My being there to pick up the pieces was not an accident. I was actually watching you all that night. You are poetry in motion. I think you are beautiful."

"That's nice to hear, but it makes no difference. I am not looking for a new boyfriend. Please mail the earring, and thank you."

If nothing else, at least I had her cell phone number now. I decided that I would wait a few more days before I called her. She seemed pretty adamant about not wanting me to call. My ego told me that she found me a little bit interesting. After all, Natalie was not going to be alone for the rest of her life simply because this Jeremy guy dumped her. She was still in denial about that. Natalie's being with me that one night was proof enough for me that she would not wait forever until Jeremy came to his senses. Not many girls are worth waiting two years for, but Natalie was the exception.

My thoughts were so consumed with Natalie Romano, I just had to invent ways of seeing her before I totally gave up on what I felt was the love of my life. Now it is only right that I confess to some unusual tactics that many may consider fixated or possibly even neurotic. I assure you that I am neither, but merely a guy madly in love with a dream.

My position as a public relations officer allows me some flexibility in my work schedule, which I took advantage of one morning. I parked near Natalie's home, slightly out of sight, and waited, recalling her telling me she was in her last semester of nursing school. I carefully followed as she drove to campus. I watched her enter a classroom. I took note of the building name and the room number. Through the magic of online search, I combed the school of nursing catalog and learned that Natalie was attending an anatomy class instructed by Dr. Lewis Davis. I made an appointment with Dr. Davis during his office hours and told him that I was considering a career change and asked permission to audit one or two of his classes to help me decide. Dr. Davis was very open to my request and graciously invited me to sit in on any of his classes. I thanked the professor and told him I would likely attend a class or two during the next couple of weeks.

At the very first opportunity, I arrived at Dr. Davis's class and situated myself in the back row toward the middle. I watched as the students took their seats, but my heart pounded as I saw Natalie gracefully take hers. She was not aware of my presence. I sat through seventy-five minutes of grueling graphic detail about the inner workings of the digestive system with special emphasis placed on the lower intestines and the maladies the human body is prone to attain if one lives long enough or recklessly enough. The nursing students, during their practicum, would have the opportunity to see firsthand how to assist the patients with these unfortunate medical problems. It is a testament to the dedication these nurses have that they can perform this work while still maintaining the patient's dignity.

As class ended, I moved toward the aisle and made a point of making my presence known to Natalie. She displayed an expression of surprise at seeing me, and I did not sense it was one of happiness.

"Please forgive my abruptness," I apologized. "I just had to see you again to understand your reasons for writing me out of your life. May I sit with you for lunch? I know it's probably not the best time to eat after that lecture, but it's lunch time, after all."

Natalie paused before replying, her jaw clenching slightly.

"Well, I normally eat lunch after this class," she said finally.

We walked towards one of the campus cafeterias.

"I'm only doing this to set the record straight," she said. "The problem is you remind me of the most embarrassing night of my life. Not just that, it's a night I wish I could take back, but I can't. I don't know what you must think, but I do not go to bed with someone I just met. In fact, I haven't done that before – ever – and that includes my boyfriend of two years. You caught me at a moment of despair and weakness."

"I have my own confession," I said. "I knew you were in the middle of this breakup because I purposely listened in on your conversation with your girlfriends that night. You were so beautiful that I was hoping to get to know you. I was discouraged when I saw you turn down many invitations to dance. But I did overhear that whole episode when you saw your old boyfriend."

Natalie frowned, but I wasn't through.

"I swear that I didn't know about your sexual history," I continued, "and I admit that surprises me somewhat, but not really. I saw you as the image of goodness and purity from the beginning. I do not judge you for what happened and if you see me again, I promise not to expect more of the same."

Natalie couldn't know if I was sincere or giving her a bullshit line, though I believe her natural defensiveness made her take the cautious route. She again told me that she did not want to see me. She was polite but very convincing.

It broke my heart to think that I had lost the love of my life before it even began, but I told her that I understood.

"Natalie, you have my phone number. If it takes forever, I will wait for you. Call me after you come to grips with what happened that night. Call me when you realize that your old boyfriend is not worthy of you. Just know, I meant no harm, only love and tenderness. I would never hurt you or force you to do anything you didn't want to do. I will be praying that you call me."

"I'm sorry, Ricky. You seem like a decent guy, but don't wait for my call. It's not happening. Goodbye, and thanks for lunch."

With that, Natalie left. I was anguished at her departure, thinking this could be the last time I would ever see her. I knew even then that I could not give up so easily. I simply felt that Natalie was my destiny.

Later that evening, Natalie stopped by Regina's apartment for some girl talk. Since Regina was mainly responsible for Natalie's going out that night, planning the whole jealousy scheme, and leaning on her to do all kinds of things she had no intention of doing, she felt Regina should at least be her confidante, to endure her torment vicariously.

"Regina, can you believe this Ricky person actually sent me roses and then shows up at my anatomy class? This guy is creepy!"

"Has he seemed too intense or, well, deranged in any way?" asked Regina.

"Well, not really," Natalie admitted, "but what kind of person does something like that?"

"Did you consider that he might actually like you? What's not to like? You're smart, beautiful and have sex on the first date. You're every man's dream date."

"Very funny. We actually discussed that whole humiliation. I think he believed me. He said if we go out again, he would not expect sex nor try to pursue it. He just wanted to be with me. What a line! This guy is pushing thirty. He's after sex and maybe marriage at his advanced age. I do not plan to provide him either one."

"It's your life," said Regina. "But he has a decent job and is good looking and his mother loves him. He can't be all bad."

"Listen to yourself, Regina. This is a guy who picked me up and took advantage of my weakened condition. That doesn't say very much for his character."

"Bullshit. This was a guy who wanted to get laid and took his opportunity with an inebriated willing woman. I'd say he showed quite a bit of initiative."

"Why do I even talk to you?" exclaimed Natalie. "I look for confirmation and all you give me is your distorted view of a very uncomfortable evening that stole from me something I had been protecting for years."

"You should be thanking me, Natalie. Why you insisted on protecting some Puritan belief from the 1600s is beyond me. Now maybe with this monkey off your back you can actually go out and enjoy yourself. Sex isn't a sin or a crime – it's a natural human function."

"I should know better than to debate this with you," Natalie replied with a sigh. "You have been a free spirit since high school. To me, making love is a spiritual act to be entered into with affection and devotion. Those two conflicting beliefs cannot be reconciled. Beliefs are nurtured over years and you can't expect me to abandon them simply because Regina Sullivan says it feels really good with the right dude!"

"So I guess that means you won't be seeing cute Ricky again. You silly fool."

At that, Natalie groaned a sigh of exasperation and hugged Regina goodbye. The two lifelong friends never stayed mad with each other for very long. They had shared too much growing up to let any little disagreement ruin their friendship. Both Natalie and Regina respected each other's opinions and were swayed by them more than either would admit.

The very next week, Natalie received another dozen roses in a beautiful arrangement. She naturally assumed that Ricky was still wooing her.

"You know, Mom, this guy will go broke if he keeps sending me a sixty-dollar arrangement every week."

"Did you even read his card?" Mrs. Romano inquired. "Maybe he has something inspiring to tell you."

When Natalie read the card, she couldn't believe her eyes. "This is from Jeremy, not Ricky!" she exclaimed. "It's been over a month without hearing a word from Jeremy and now he sends these. I'm sure he expected me to give in and beg him to take me back. The nerve of that guy! He must think he's God's gift to women."

"There was a time you thought so," said her mother. "It was Jeremy this and Jeremy that. You were seriously thinking about marriage after graduation. Then it's over and I never really got into it with you. Your father and I expected this was a short separation. This happens to lots of young couples. Now it looks like things will get back to normal."

"Not so fast," Natalie exclaimed. "You really don't know what happened, Mother, and it's not something I can just get over."

"What can be so bad?"

"He wanted sex from me and I refused. And the next minute he's out and about with every tramp he can lay his hands on. Is that enough of a reason for you?"

"And you can't forgive him now?"

"Could you?" cried Natalie. "I was saving myself for him. His behavior says it all. I was not worth waiting for."

Her mother shocked Natalie with what she said. "Natalie, you're a woman now and Jeremy is a man. It's only natural that he has these strong feelings for you."

"Are you saying that I should forget all the things the church and you and Dad have been telling me all these years? I can't believe my ears! I know that you and Dad would never have behaved that way. Weren't you glad you waited until you were married?"

"I'm glad you waited," said Mrs. Romano. "Too many young girls mess up their lives by having babies when they are not ready. That's why we preached abstinence to you. I am just saying that you're a woman now and not a young girl."

"Now I'm really confused," cried Natalie. "Between you and Regina I guess I'm ready to go out and start screwing everyone."

"You know that's not what I'm saying. You're a smart girl. Just use your head and the God-given judgment you have developed over the years. I have faith that you will always do the right thing."

Natalie was now perplexed. What should she do about Jeremy? She had quite a bit of soul-searching to do.

I must laugh at myself. I call Papa obsessive, but I became totally consumed by the very idea of Natalie Romano. And from every indication, Natalie wanted absolutely nothing to do with me and possibly loathed me. I promised that I would not pursue her. I am not a stalker. I would never intentionally scare or hurt Natalie. But I must admit that the possibility of never holding her again tormented me to my soul. So I decided on a plan to circumvent my promise. I called Natalie's mother and asked to see her instead. She knew who I was from the flowers I sent Natalie. Apparently, I was the subject of some brief discussion between mother and daughter. To my utter surprise, she agreed to see me. Doing some marriage research on Natalie's family, I discovered her mother had an Irish surname. I decided to bring her a CD of Irish traditional ballads and love songs as a gift. Mrs. Romano seemed pleased to receive it.

"Where in the world did you ever find this?" Mrs. Romano asked. "Bing Crosby, Dennis Day – do you even know who these singers are at your age?"

"Sure, I've heard of Bing Crosby. He sang 'White Christmas' and I've seen some old movie he was in. I think he played a priest. Dennis Day, I really don't know him," I confessed.

"Dennis Day was a regular on the *Jack Benny Show*," Mrs. Romano instructed.

"Who's Jack Benny?" I asked.

"You know what? Never mind about that, Ricky. So tell me about yourself. I am intrigued by the fact that you took Natalie out the one and only time I ever saw her come home stinking drunk. You must be quite a powerful influence."

"Now, wait a minute, Mrs. Romano. The evening I met Natalie, she was already well on her way to drunk. I will confess that my buying her another drink or two did not help the situation. But I am not a drinker myself. Maybe a beer once in a while, but please don't think I am a drunk or a bad influence."

"What do you do, Ricky?" asked Mrs. Romano.

"I actually work for the city of Boston putting out stories and press releases about what's happening in the government. As you can imagine, the job can be highly political at times, but I enjoy the troubleshooting and the fast-paced excitement that comes with the territory. I would rather be doing this than sitting around bored most of the day."

"I'll bet you have some stories to tell."

"I certainly do, but I am the soul of discretion both at work and in my personal life." I said this as if I was pleased with myself and hoped I didn't come across as boastful or arrogant.

"So tell me, Ricky, did you come here to give me a CD of Irish love songs? Somehow, I doubt that was your main reason."

"This is exactly how I thought you would be, Mrs. Romano. You're too sharp for your own good. Not only that, Mrs. Romano, I see now where Natalie gets her killer good looks. I always thought that my own adorable mother was the most beautiful woman in the commonwealth. I hate to put my own mom in second place, but the truth is the truth."

"Okay, Ricky, stop the blarney," Mrs. Romano said with a short laugh. "Let's get down to business. I confess that I permitted you to see me because I was curious about the person with whom Natalie spent that night. What do you really want?"

"Mrs. Romano, I have no plan. I don't know what I expected by seeing you. I guess it's because Natalie wanted nothing to do with me. Meeting her mother sounded like a good idea at the time. I'm going to leave now. If it ever comes up in conversation, I wanted you to know I have no ulterior motive except to please Natalie. I know all about Jeremy. I know that she loves him, but that right now things are shaky between them. I wanted you to know that I would never hurt Natalie in any way. I think she is the most terrific lady I have ever met. That's all I wanted to say. I am not a creep or a nutcase. Talk to my mother if you want, everyone else seems to use her as a reference. Talk to my boss. He will tell you that I am conscientious and hard working." I shrugged and smiled. "Okay, that's about it. Thank you for seeing me. It was certainly a treat for me."

With that, I left. There were no hugs or kisses, just a shy little wave and an awkward exit. I think she liked me. I know that having Natalie's mother on my side doesn't really count. But if her mother likes me, then winning Natalie will be less onerous. I wasn't kidding myself. I had two chances: slim and none.

Chapter Three

Make Up to Break Up

The day after the roses arrived, Jeremy called Natalie for an old-fashioned date. By this time, he realized that Natalie would never make the first call. This somewhat surprised Jeremy since he figured she would abandon her archaic principles and give in to his appeal.

"Natalie, it's me."

"Hello, me," said Natalie. "I received your roses and they're beautiful. But I wondered why you would send them. Are you finished cruising?"

"This is not really something I want to discuss with you on the phone. After all the time we've been apart, there are things that we should discuss. How about dinner? You name the place and time and I will make the reservation. Or if you prefer doing something else, that's fine, whatever. We just need time together to talk."

"Dinner is OK by me," said Natalie. "Friday night will work. Surprise me – pick a nice place we've never been before, like a fresh start."

"Sure, that'll work. I'll call you, Natalie." Jeremy hung up without saying his typical "I love you," but he felt that his actions screamed it. He knew it would take him some time to win Natalie's trust and he did not want to assume things were immediately back to normal.

For the past two years, Natalie had been deeply in love with Jeremy. It was that Sunday kind of love that she expected would end in a trip down the aisle. It's not that her plans were crushed, but, after all, Jeremy had profoundly hurt her. His actions told her more than his words could ever say. She questioned whether this was a glimpse of the future with Jeremy. Natalie rationalized they were not officially engaged, but that was a mere formality. She and Jeremy were a steady one-guy/one-girl couple. She needed to be with Jeremy again if only to know if that same passion was still there. She wanted that feeling back desperately, so it was worth the effort.

Natalie told her mother that she had a dinner date with Jeremy on Friday night. For some reason, this did not sit well with Kathryn Romano.

Ever since Natalie told her mother why Jeremy stopped seeing her, Kathryn's displeasure over the prospect of Jeremy returning to Natalie's life grew stronger. Mrs. Romano felt a couple of things could happen, and neither was good. Natalie would ultimately give in to Jeremy's sexual desires or Jeremy would continue to seek his manly rights elsewhere. Mrs. Romano felt that if Jeremy had any character or genuine affection for Natalie, he would have stayed by her and supported her wishes until she was ready.

Mrs. Romano was at a loss as to what to do. She did not want to express her feelings to Natalie. Kathryn was wise enough to know that Natalie herself must make her own decision in regard to Jeremy. Her meddling could eventually cause a rift with Natalie. So she decided to do the next best thing. She would covertly meddle. Also, as a much more dangerous strategy, she would enlighten her husband as to Natalie's situation. Harry Romano is an overprotective, loose-cannon-type of father, but Kathryn decided to risk it in favor of securing her husband's support. Before she involved Harry, however, Kathryn made sure to lay down the law and the ground rules. She definitely did not want her husband to confront Jeremy, nor did she want him lecturing Natalie about her life choices. She would, instead, work to subtly and furtively influence her daughter's path.

"Do you have a clue as to what's going on in your daughter's life, Harry?" asked Mrs. Romano.

"I know she's about to graduate in a couple of months. I know she broke up with her boyfriend. I know she's healthy and here most every night. What's to know?"

"Do you know why she broke up with Jeremy?"

"Why does anyone break up? There could be a million reasons. After two years, I suppose they started getting on each other's nerves."

"No, you blind fool! She loved him and was waiting for a marriage proposal. She left him because he gave her an ultimatum: put out or I'm leaving. You know that Natalie cannot be backed against a wall without lashing out. So she left him. He had his fun and now he wants Natalie back."

"Why that sonavabitch," yelled Mr. Romano, "I'll break his back!"

"Now that's exactly why I avoided telling you, Harry," Kathryn Romano exclaimed. "That's the exact wrong thing to do. If you forbid Natalie from seeing Jeremy or if you confront Jeremy, you will probably push her right into his arms!"

Kathryn knew young women in general and her daughter especially – they maintain just enough rebellion in them to make their parents miserable. At least Natalie's teenage years were behind them, and the worst was seemingly over.

"So what is your brilliant plan, Kathryn?" inquired Harry.

"I know that Jeremy invited Natalie to dinner on Friday. Let's ask them to eat here at home together. I will fix a good meal."

"What good is that?" questioned Harry. "That will only force me to keep my mouth shut instead of ripping into young Jeremy."

"I am not telling Natalie, but I am also inviting another fine Italian-American young man that you'll probably like, Harry. Even though introducing another Italian to this family is probably a bad idea, I think it's better than the alternative. His name is Ricky Santo. Ricky knows Natalie, although she is probably not going to be happy to see him. Ricky met Natalie that night she came home very late. I have no idea what happened that night, but I do know Ricky really likes our daughter. He introduced himself to me one day and carried on about Natalie. He even brought me a gift and invited me to call his mother for a reference. He probably said that jokingly, but I actually did call his mother. Apparently, Mrs. Santo is used as a reference for her son quite often. Anyhow, I really enjoyed talking to her. Any mother who loves her son as much as she loves Ricky says something about the boy – I mean, about the man."

"This is the nuttiest thing I ever heard," exclaimed Harry. "You are inviting a third wheel to a reconciliation dinner for your daughter and her boyfriend. Don't you think this will piss off Natalie? Does Jeremy know this other man? This ought to be quite an evening."

"I doubt seriously whether these two men know each other, but you're right. Neither Jeremy nor Natalie will be happy I invited Ricky. I will concoct some story for inviting Ricky. It may fool Jeremy, but I expect Natalie will see right through me."

"So why do it?" asked Harry.

"This will send a very powerful message," Kathryn replied. "We are inviting Ricky and accepting him into our home. This will speak volumes for our support of Ricky and we won't even need to badmouth Jeremy. Believe me, Natalie will get the message."

"And you call me nuts. This has a ninety percent chance of blowing up in our faces," calculated Harry.

"Leave that to me. I will ask Natalie to invite Jeremy here for six o'clock. I will invite Ricky to dinner for a quarter past six. Let's just see what happens. Who knows? It may be a very interesting evening."

So out of the blue I got a phone call from Mrs. Romano asking if I could join them for dinner on Friday. Keep in mind, the call was made on Wednesday. Did she think I had no plans for Friday night? I am a young, attractive, healthy male in the prime of my life. Did she think I was so enamored with her daughter that I would give up a sure thing on the chance that Natalie would express an ounce of interest toward me? I said yes immediately. My past visit with Mrs. Romano convinced her that I was sincere and maybe a bit bonkers over Natalie.

There were other questions. Why did she invite me? Did Natalie know that I was coming for dinner? What did Mr. Romano think? At this point, I did not know the answer to these questions. I also did not know that Natalie and Jeremy were again talking to each other. I certainly did not know Jeremy would be there, too. However, it would not have mattered if I did know. An opportunity to see Natalie was all I cared about. I further pondered Mrs. Romano's motives. Could she be matchmaking? I must have made a really good impression on her. It was painfully obvious that she had no idea I was the one, the first one, to deflower her daughter.

It was only later, when I saw Jeremy at dinner, that I surmised this was probably her calculated move to get Jeremy out of her daughter's life. Apparently, she must have discovered the reason why Natalie and Jeremy were on the outs for so long.

Then I wondered how she got my phone number. It's not like I'm in the phone book. My parents are in the phone book, but how many Santos did she call before she got the right one? Did she actually ask Natalie? I doubted that. I later found out that she actually spoke to my mother. I was shocked but somewhat pleased that she would go to the trouble.

Then the big question was what to take for dinner. Should I take wine? I hate getting wine so I have a natural tendency not to gift it. I considered Italian pastries. This is always a great dinner offering, but then I figured so many people are diet conscious these days. I wouldn't mind eating a cannoli or La Sfogliatella myself. I resisted the temptation. Then I thought a good house-warming gift might be appropriate, like a fragrant Yankee Candle. But then, this being Red Sox territory, this gift may cause some unintended animosity. I finally settled on a nice fruit basket.

At the scheduled time of 6:15 p.m., I promptly arrived at the Romano's house with grapes and apples in hand. Mrs. Romano greeted me, told me I should not have brought anything but thank you. She may have meant you *really* shouldn't have brought anything. Coming to this dinner empty handed was not an option. There, already seated in the living room having an aperitif, were Natalie and Jeremy. Natalie's older brother Rob was also there. I figured this was in order to balance both sides of the dinner table. Natalie looked absolutely shocked but refrained from saying, "What the hell are you doing here?" Jeremy looked puzzled, but he didn't recognize me from the dimly lit club the night I left with Natalie. Her brother basically didn't care if I was there or not.

Mrs. Romano introduced me as if I was a stranger to everyone but herself. She explained that I was invited to dinner with my mother, her good friend. Mama had questioned me about the call she received from Mrs. Romano. I think Mama found all these mystery calls about me from strange people very amusing. She was a good sport and played along without missing a beat.

"Mrs. Santo is feeling a bit under the weather," she explained. "I'm glad you were able to make it, Ricky." Natalie obviously knew this was a bunch of malarkey. Natalie's brother and Jeremy were indifferent to my appearance. I believed that Mr. Romano was part of this whole scam. So I was at dinner with no apparent suspicion save the daggers directed at Mrs. Romano and me by Natalie. To her credit, Natalie played it cool, though she barely spoke to me.

Mr. Romano said that he was very glad to see everyone. His wife had placed him on a low-calorie diet since his weight kept slowly working its way to infinity. Before Mrs. Romano prepared dinner, she had called me just to be certain I wasn't a vegetarian. I assured her that I could eat a horse or a cow.

Mr. Romano exclaimed, "It is a treat for me to have this pot roast and potatoes with gravy. My wife has placed me on a strict healthy diet and it was about to kill me." Mr. Romano said grace, and we all followed his lead.

I carefully studied the dynamics of the table. Natalie's brother ate heartily but barely spoke a word. He did not actually live with his family and I got the impression this whole dinner was forced upon him and he accepted only to be a dutiful son. Mr. and Mrs. Romano spoke to everyone, including me, and asked how things were going. I found myself rehashing my week as public relations officer. Jeremy mentioned that grad school would conclude for him in a couple of months and he had a position already lined up at Brigham and Women's Hospital. He did not appear all that interested in educating those of us at the table. I suspect that radiology is not a subject most people relish discussing at the dinner table.

As for me, most of my attention was focused on Natalie. I tried to be inconspicuous. I did not want Jeremy to catch me ogling his girlfriend, if only to avoid any kind of macho argument in Natalie's home. The truth is that I wanted to snatch Natalie away, take her in my arms, and kiss her passionately right there in front of God and family. Instead, I stole glances whenever it was opportune. I think Natalie caught me a few times, but she was on guard since she already knew I was fixated on her. Jeremy, on the other hand, was oblivious. He obviously felt that being here with Natalie meant she was ready to forgive him his month of romping and resume their romance as if nothing had ever happened. I was hoping that Natalie had more sense than that. We had some coffee in Mr. Romano's den and Mrs. Romano made a point of positioning Natalie in the middle of Jeremy and me on the leather sofa. This was terrific, since I could now actually feel the warmth of Natalie's body and rub up against her very innocently while reaching for a piece of chocolate.

There came that time when dinner and coffee were over. Hanging around longer became awkward, since Natalie and Jeremy were discussing their plans for that evening. I felt my presence was unwanted, so I graciously thanked Mr. and Mrs. Romano. I wondered if this whole evening and my presence had any real purpose. I said goodbye to everyone without shaking hands and left.

Jeremy and Natalie left for their first date in many weeks. The comfortable feeling they previously shared had been harmed by Jeremy's recent conquests. He had damaged their relationship with his unfaithfulness. To Jeremy, his time away from Natalie had not changed his love and devotion for her one iota. For Natalie, however, it was a struggle to understand how she could recapture the feelings she'd had for Jeremy knowing that only a few days ago he was kissing, fondling, caressing, and bringing himself to orgasm with another girl. She now imagined Jeremy having intimate lovemaking with someone other than herself. He was moaning, whispering "I love you," and then exploding passionately, gasping for air. The image haunted Natalie, and she didn't know if her love for Jeremy could wipe this picture from her mind. She really wanted to start over fresh. She loved Jeremy deeply but seriously questioned his forever commitment to her. She told herself that they were not actually married or even engaged. This to her was only a matter of time, believing that a ring was not needed to cement their devotion.

Jeremy thought better of pushing Natalie into anything remotely related to sex. He knew if he was going to work himself back into her good graces, it would need to be done slowly. His behavior was the thousand-pound gorilla in the room, so he felt he needed to apologize and ask for her forgiveness. This he did profusely, to the nauseating point of enough already. Natalie got it. He was sorry. That really was not the issue. Natalie had to decide for herself if Jeremy could be trusted and whether she wanted to resume their previous level of intimacy. Natalie always felt intimate with Jeremy by sharing her dreams and her feelings and by giving him everything he wanted, short of penetration. Jeremy shared that intimacy but never understood why two consenting adults had to limit their expressions of love. Jeremy learned by being away from Natalie that he needed her no matter the sacrifice.

I was the odd man out. I know I let my imagination run wild. Natalie never loved me. She actually never really knew who I was. I had been an object to be manipulated in order for Natalie to get Jeremy back. Now he was back, so I supposed her scheme worked. I always believed that if you wanted something or someone badly enough, that if you applied all your energies to that end, it would happen. This theory works much better for goals and acquisitions than it does for matters of the heart. I just think that if a woman like Natalie loved me that much, it would be hard to dismiss her from my life. Here I am, twenty-eight years old, pining over a girl with whom I spent one night. And she was oblivious a good part of the time. I felt I needed to release my pent-up anguish. I needed a confidant. I thought of confiding in my good friend Raymond, but Raymond is not actually the mature sensible type with years of experience from which to draw upon. In fact, he's probably had fewer relationships than any guy I know that has attained his age. I hated to admit it, but the best person for this task was a person I have never shared my feelings with ever before. It was my papa. Papa is always trying to counsel me and give me the benefit of his wisdom and I always come up with an excuse for having to be somewhere else. Now that I am older, I have discovered that Papa is not so archaic-minded and stupid after all.

At our weekly dinner together, I had an opportunity to discuss life with Papa. This is totally and absolutely a foreign experience for both of us. Typically, Mama will chew my ears off with a million questions and Papa goes into the den to watch his sports or a movie. After Mama finishes her interrogation, I usually join Papa in silence while Mama continues to serve us snacks and drinks. This is how it's been since I left the nest. I enjoy the routine and cherish this time, knowing that both my parents will not be here forever.

This time was different. I told Papa that I had something to discuss with him and asked him if he wanted to join me for a drink. I was shocked when he said, "Let's go," as if he sensed this was his opportunity to educate me to the ways of the world. He had tried numerous times but was always hampered by my blatant display of disinterest. It was Sunday afternoon, so the bars were fairly quiet and empty. There were no big games this day and the small sports crowd congregated together. Papa and I took a more remote booth.

"So, what's so important that you drag me out of my Sunday castle?" Papa intoned.

"What Sunday castle?" I said. "That's your everyday, every-minute castle."

"OK, I confess my life is not the epitome of excitement, but I had my day. If you've got a life question, I've probably been there. So let me have it. Man-to-man or father-to-son – either way, it will probably be the same answer."

"OK, Papa. Here it is. How will a woman deal with a guy who cheated on her?" I asked. "And I'll tell you why I'm asking. I found the most beautiful and desirable woman imaginable. She's even half-Italian on her father's side, Papa. She has been in a steady relationship for two years with a guy she expected to marry. He left her last month because she refused to put out for him. He spent this month screwing anybody he could and then realized that Natalie – this is her name – was really the only girl for him. I met Natalie on the rebound during this time and she knocked me off my feet. Now, he's back in the picture and she actually went out with him again a couple of days ago. What do you think this means?"

"First of all," Papa started, "I'll state the obvious. The number of ways that women will deal with this knowledge equals the number of women receiving this knowledge. Having said this, I will attempt to give you a generic answer and then I will educate you on the whole subject of infidelity."

Papa cleared his throat, took a sip of his drink, and continued. "This boyfriend, hereafter referred to as *this guy,* is a healthy American boy needing to get laid. So he has a decision to make. He can continue to work on his girl, Natalie, until she gives in. Or, he can stay with Natalie and secretly screw on the side. This will spare Natalie's feelings – unless, of course, he gets caught and then she will be devastated. In this case, he apparently did the honorable thing by being honest and leaving Natalie to have his fun."

Gazing at the bottles lined up behind the bar, Papa got a thoughtful look in his eyes. "The fact that she even took him back tells me that she must have had a great deal of love for him. Now she's in that transitional period trying to come to grips with her own feelings. She must be questioning whether he can ever be trusted again. From my vast experience, I can almost guarantee that this guy will wander again. If he will cheat on Natalie now when he's in the throes of love, it's only a matter of time before he'll do it again. Most men – and I will emphasize 'most' – will look for a change of scenery. After years of being together, the intrigue of having a new woman bubbles up inside. Sometimes, this feeling becomes all-consuming and forces men to do things that are totally asinine, bordering on self-destructive."

Papa looked me straight in the eyes. "What about women, you may ask. Do women have that same need for a change of scenery? And again, I am speaking on the general or global perspective. There are exceptions to the rule. Some women are very aggressive, but there are some men so naïve that they don't even recognize the signals these ladies broadcast. But let us return to the global perspective. Most women, unlike men, do not naturally seek extramarital affairs. They sort of gravitate to this situation after years of dealing with their unromantic, insensitive husbands and being trapped in the humdrum of everyday life. Mostly these women have been shackled sometimes by years of childrearing and further saddled with work on top of that. These are the very women ripe for the picking. In fact, most men will feel a lot safer with a married woman than a single woman. A single woman for a married man is like a loaded cannon ready to explode." Papa chuckled. "But I realize that I digress from your original question in an attempt to educate you in the ways of the world. It seems like I have your attention and I may never have it again. Your quest for Natalie has forced you into desperate measures – like seeking my advice. I tell you all this to prepare you for the future I hope you will soon have as a married man."

"I don't know, Papa," answered Ricky. "It sure appears to me that you speak from a great deal of personal experience on this subject. I would hate to believe that you have been screwing around on my own sainted mother."

"You don't have to get burned in a fire to feel the heat, mister. I've had my opportunities, known guys and their stories, and may have been on the precipice of jumping in once or twice. But in the end, thoughts of hurting your mother, mostly, and losing the love and respect of my children have always stopped me cold."

I wasn't really certain that Papa was totally honest about his own experiences but I really did not want to press him on this subject. What good would it do me to know he cheated on Mama? If he did succumb to the call of the wild, I was not interested in learning his secrets. In the end, it would only lessen my lifelong respect for Papa and probably affect the way we acted around each other for the rest of our time together. I was content believing that Papa was just expressing the wisdom of his years. In my mind, both my parents have loved each other through good times and bad.

Papa continued. "And this is the very point that leads me to the essence of this talk on infidelity. It may feel good in the moment, but it nearly always ends up badly. There are so many ways for this whole escapade to end and most of them are bad. Remember what I said. The man is looking to get laid with a different set of knockers. The woman has a totally different mindset. It will probably start out very hot and heavy. The two new lovers will be obsessed with 'the next time.' Actually, after the guy gets his rocks off, he'll be ready to go home. But then the excitement builds up again. It's not unlike a drug addict getting his fix. And no, I have never taken drugs either. Then the two will scheme and plan for the next rendezvous. This can go on for a very long time, but it almost never lasts. After a while, the novelty wears off, and then what? Oh sure, sometimes the marriage breaks up and the lovers marry each other. But how the hell would you feel being married to a woman who cheated on her husband? How do you suppose she will ever trust *you* to be faithful? It's not the most solid foundation for a new marriage."

Papa frowned, taking another sip of his drink before continuing. "Most men are really far too weak to stay committed to one woman. It's human nature to seek excitement and change. But everything has a cost. If you can somehow stick it out with the woman you fall in love with and marry, you will find that in the end, you will end up in a much better place. Think of it: you work your ass off to raise your kids; you struggle to provide them love, support, and guidance. But I assure you that if you are committed to your family, the end result will be a fine man or woman – like you, Ricky, or your sister."

I smiled, pleasantly surprised by the praise.

But Papa wasn't through imparting words of wisdom yet. "I'm not saying that every child from this type of home grows up 'right' or every child from a broken home grows up 'wrong,'" he continued, "but the odds favor the family that stays together. And here's another thing. After all these years with your mother, I could never repay her affection by hurting her. Sure, I have my moments of insensitive stupidity, but I'd never want to disappoint the girl who devoted her whole life to our children and me. You cannot find this kind of love by jumping into bed with a woman in search of a thrilling adventure."

"Papa, I think you may have taken a simple question and made it into a life's lesson," I said. "The answer as it concerns Natalie, I think, is who knows how she will react to her boyfriend's cheating? You are telling me that in general, cheating can only lead to problems and sometimes hurt people beyond healing and forgiveness. I get that. I also heard you say that her boyfriend will cheat on her again if they stay together. OK, I can see how you would conclude this. My dilemma is accepting the fact that Natalie is not interested in me. However, Papa, as long as she is still available, I think I will continue to stay in the picture. At least her mother seems to like me."

"That's fine, Rick. I wouldn't expect you to be a quitter. You know that I feel it's time that you settle down. I want you to have a family of your own. Being married with children makes a person whole. Life is really short and none of us are immortal, but family can be. I truly feel that it is family that makes a person immortal. Corny as it sounds, that's what I believe."

Chapter Four

Upsetting News

As we entered the month of April, Natalie's graduation was only five weeks away. This should have been a time of great relief and joy. Four years of classes, labs, tests, observations, and an internship were almost at an end. Yet Natalie steadily became more stressed, and it had nothing to do with her school situation. Natalie confided in Regina about a very personal issue that had increasingly been troubling her.

"Regina, I didn't get my period in March and I'm really worried. I'm usually very regular. I've waited, thinking maybe the stress of Jeremy and school has affected my cycle, but now it's several weeks late."

Regina wanted to be reassuring, but she didn't want to give Natalie the "don't worry" speech when there was a possibility of there being something to worry about. "Is it possible that you could have gotten pregnant from your one night with Ricky?" asked Regina.

"I'd be lying if I said this wasn't my main concern. It would be ironic that I spend my entire life protecting my innocence and the one time I let my guard down, this!"

"OK," comforted Regina. "There is no sense getting all panicky until you find out for sure. We'll get a pregnancy test today and then you'll know one way or the other."

Regina took charge of the whole ordeal. She was the one to buy the pregnancy test using an out-of-the-way pharmacy. She read all the directions on the box from top to bottom. She took Natalie to her apartment, making certain they were not interrupted by any distractions. The only thing she didn't do was to take the test herself. After all the preparations, Natalie's anxiety was sky high. She solemnly strode into the bathroom and proceeded to urinate on the little stick that could forever change her life. Natalie was not able to face the truth alone, so she and Regina read the results together.

Her worst fears had been realized. Natalie was pregnant – at least according to this one initial test. This was not welcome news, but Regina cautioned her not to go berserk quite yet. "We need to have another test later, let's calm down," assured Regina.

"Easy for you to say," said Natalie. "I'll take another test later. After that turns out positive, I'll have a doctor confirm the results. Nothing will change. I am pregnant from one dumb night of drinking and hooking up with a complete stranger. What really kills me is that I let it happen. I let Ricky do what I wouldn't do with Jeremy. I was totally unprepared. I had no birth control. Why should I? I had the best birth control possible, called abstinence. Some abstinence!"

"Now don't go ballistic and start making stupid decisions," ordered Regina. "You will not show for several months. By that time, graduation will be over."

"Graduation is next month and Jeremy and I were just starting to mend fences. This is the worst possible time for this to happen."

"When is it a good time to get pregnant from a person that you hardly know?" asked Regina. "Now, you will need to make some decisions, and you know I'll help you. It seems you are stuck with me, since I am the only one you can talk to about this." Regina smiled, trying to ease her friend's tension. "You have lots of options to think about, Natalie. Since your brain is probably numb about now, let's review them one by one. The first option I feel is the best option. You're not a virgin anymore and you want to marry Jeremy, so go out with him tonight and screw the hell out of him. You'll have fun and set in motion the pregnancy that you will announce to Jeremy in about a month's time. Believe me, when it comes to the male ego about making babies and the fun of doing it, men have zero math skills. Seven months, eight months, nine months – it makes no difference to them as long as they think they made a baby. You will have a built-in father for your baby and can avoid all the other options, which I feel are far less attractive than this one."

"How do you think, Regina?" Natalie asked, a mixture of anger and despair in her voice. "First of all, that's the most dishonest thing I ever heard. What if something should ever happen to make Jeremy question his paternity? Who knows what the future may bring? Maybe it will be the way the child looks, blood type, or some other hereditary thing. Could you imagine the damage this could do to the child and Jeremy if after twelve years they discover the truth? It would be devastating!"

"Come on, Natalie," Regina replied. "What in the world are you worried about? Ask the next five hundred fathers you meet and ask each one if they ever had a paternity test for any of their children. I bet you won't find one. Do you plan to appear on *Jerry Springer* or *Maury* in the near future? This is the answer to all your woes! And if Jeremy marries you, as I am certain he will, then all will be well. Your parents will be ecstatic having a grandchild. You'll have the husband you've always wanted, and I'd bet that Jeremy will be fine with this whole idea after the initial shock of fatherhood hits him."

"That doesn't work for me at all, Regina. What's your second option?" Natalie asked.

"OK, Natalie," offered Regina. "This one is much more dangerous, but it does have long-term rewards if you can pull it off. It also involves Jeremy. I am assuming you still want Jeremy to be your soul mate. Am I wrong about that?"

"I'm still trying to decide that myself, Regina. His month of lovemaking has really been a tough one for me to get past. Never mind about that. Give me what you have."

"Well, confess to Jeremy about the whole thing. He spent one entire month screwing around and you had one drunken night doing the same. Tell him how much it hurt you seeing him at the club with somebody else. Tell him you wanted to make him jealous but you drank too much because you needed the courage to be with someone else. Appeal to his love for you. Tell him you need him to step up and be the baby's father. Explain to him that everyone would believe it is his child. How does that sound?"

Natalie sat, quietly assessing this strategy. She somewhat preferred it to the lie she would perpetuate under plan one. Having Jeremy be part of the deception would make a world of difference. If Jeremy would accept this child as his own, then nothing else really mattered. But there's the hurdle. Natalie knew Jeremy far too well.

"I rather like that idea," Natalie finally replied. "Unfortunately, it works for me and would be great for the child, but Jeremy would never, and let me emphasize *absolutely never,* raise a child that was not his own. I have had too many rhetorical arguments on this very subject with Jeremy. I have pointblank asked him what he would do if we got married and I couldn't have a child. Do you think he said 'That's all right, baby, we could always adopt'? Not on your life! He said, 'I'll find a surrogate mother and we can raise my child together.' Does that sound like a man willing to raise someone else's child? I think we need to move on to option three. I hope you have lots of options, Regina. Maybe you will hit on a good one by accident."

"OK, Natalie," Regina continued, "I will lay out option three, but I do not hold out much hope of your liking this one! Who is totally gaga over you? Who would accept and love this baby unconditionally? Who worships the ground you walk on and would do anything to make you happy? This is a person any woman would kill to have."

"I know you are not suggesting that I marry Ricky after a one-night stand where he took advantage of my vulnerable condition," Natalie answered, her tone a mix of shock and dismay.

"Come on, Natalie. Ricky is a man who picked up a girl at a club. They're all out on the prowl to get laid. Why does this surprise you?"

"I've told you and him," said Natalie, "I am more disgusted with myself for letting this happen. What happened was my own fault caused by my failure to prevent it from happening. I do not want to start a relationship with a man on this basis. OK, he is sort of good-looking and he is attentive and seems pleasant. If we had met under different circumstances, maybe I wouldn't think he was such a degenerate creep."

"Must I remind you that it was your own loving Jeremy that made all this possible? And isn't this man you love a bigger degenerate creep plus unfaithfully predisposed? You now have three options, all of which involve a man and marriage and you dismiss all of them. Maybe it's the marriage thing that's causing you grief and not the baby."

"Wrong! It's totally the baby! It's just that the baby's due date and my marriage date do not coincide. I would have been happy to marry Jeremy before all this happened and to marry him immediately. But now you are asking me to choose between a virtual stranger and a man in whom my trust is seriously shaken. I am afraid that marriage is not going to happen. It saddens me to think that my first child will be born to an unwed mother."

"That leads us to option four," Regina continued. "Have the baby and don't marry either of them. It sounds like Jeremy will dump you like a lead balloon once he finds out that you are pregnant. Now, of course, your parents will learn the dirty little secret. Daddy's angel will no longer have wings. All his sermons over the years will have been for nothing. I believe your mother is cool enough to deal with this whole thing with some degree of composure. Who knows, she may even turn out to be your best advocate. Parents have a tendency to rally when it means a new life in the family. You know, blood is thicker than water and all that stuff."

"This is killing me." Natalie was outwardly distressed by Regina's fourth option. "I'm not ready for a baby now, especially without a husband! Even if I work immediately after graduation, it won't be long before the baby is born. Then what? Find someone to care for my baby or quit working? If I quit working, I will have no money and be forced to live at home. That really sucks. I was looking forward to finally being on my own. If I continue working, I will be paying for an apartment, my car, childcare, food, and everything else in the world!"

Natalie put her head in her hands. She was on the verge of tears. "This really sucks. I refuse to involve my parents in my child's upbringing. Sure, they will probably say they would help me, but is it fair that I impose my mistakes on them? They have their own lives. My mother wouldn't want to disrupt her daily routine to raise my child while I am off working. She is always saying how good things are for her now that my brother and I are old enough to give her the freedom she sacrificed all those years we were growing up. How could I ask Grandma to be mother-in-charge? She might not say so, but she'd hate that. Babies can be a blessing, but they really can mess up your life."

Regina was down to her last two options. "What's left, Natalie?" asked Regina. "You either have the baby or not. You don't want to marry Jeremy or Ricky. You don't want to keep the baby. How about adoption? You must know that there are lots of couples dying to have a baby, especially a beautiful Natalie baby." Regina shrugged. "There you go. This is all I have left for you. Other than that, the only other option left is abortion and I know you wouldn't do that."

Natalie was confronted with the reality of her situation. Have the baby and keep it or have the baby and give it away or abort the pregnancy. No good choice as far as Natalie was concerned.

"You think you know me that well, Regina. I'm a good Catholic girl who never even had sex before, so how could I ever think about abortion? How do you think I would feel carrying this baby to term only to give it away? I am not strong enough to do that. I have given all the reasons why I can't have this baby. I can understand why so many women have abortions."

"Natalie, forgive my blunt honesty, but all your reasons for not having this baby are truly bullshit! You are over twenty-one and not a kid in high school!" Regina softened her tone and continued. "Sure, your father will be distressed to learn that his little girl is actually a woman with sexual desires. You underestimate the love he has for you, and I guarantee that he wasn't born yesterday. I suspect that your father has been around the block. The men who preach the loudest usually do it because they have been guilty themselves of some hanky-panky. And you worry about your mother taking care of the baby. How in the world would she feel if you killed her grandchild? Your mother is no dummy. She would always have a nanny around to relieve her, but I think she'll enjoy her grandchild more than you imagine. You don't want to marry anyone next week, so don't."

Regina presented a convincing argument, but Natalie was fixated on the disruption to everyone's life. Natalie felt guilty knowing that she was seriously considering having an abortion. She knew it was a selfish and immature solution to a very huge problem. She considered that in months and years hence she would likely have moments of deep despair and regret over the decision. Not the least of her predicament was the religious question. She truly did not believe in abortion, although not in the fanatical way some people approach the issue. She felt that she would knowingly commit a sin in the eyes of God and the church. And yet, all these things still had not changed her decision to abort the child. Thinking about an abortion and actually going through with it were two different things. Then Natalie thought about carrying the baby for nine months. This was not a condition a new graduate scheduled to begin her first job was relishing.

"I need to think some more about this, Regina. I'm going to trust you to keep my secret. We have been best friends since grade school and I know I can rely on your discretion. Can I also count on you to hold my hand if I decide to have an abortion?"

"Natalie, why must you even ask that? I will always be there for you! Just don't expect me to agree with that decision. You know how I feel. You should have this baby. It's a living being and part of you."

Graduation was fast approaching, and Natalie had to make some quick decisions. She made an appointment on Friday of that same week to speak to a counselor at Planned Parenthood at the Greater Boston Health Center. She decided that she would go there alone, since it was only for counseling. She knew where Regina stood on this abortion and didn't need any undue pressure.

Natalie was greeted at the reception desk and asked to fill out paperwork listing her contact information and medical history. She also received a medical intake session and lab work. She received a pelvic exam to determine her stage of pregnancy. The counselor was very supportive, but she sensed that the steadfast commitment to this procedure was absent in Natalie. Natalie assured her that she was committed to having this abortion but agreed to give it some more serious thought before she had the procedure. Natalie was scheduled for Friday of the following week.

But fate was against Natalie. I saw her coming out of the Planned Parenthood building while I was walking out of Shaw's with my lunch. From her reaction, she was not pleased to see me.

"I told you to stop following me," shrieked Natalie. "Do I need to file for a restraining order?"

"For what? Am I not allowed lunch because you may be in the vicinity? I wasn't following you! I'm in this area for work. You need to get a grip. But tell me, why in the world would you be walking out of Planned Parenthood alone?"

I did some quick math and realized that the timing was about right. Since Natalie was a virgin before that night, or so she claims, this chance meeting might have a lot to do with our first meeting. Since she only recently started dating her boyfriend again, I felt a strong sense of destiny in meeting Natalie like this.

"What concern is this of yours? I am here on business. I often come here for my practicum as part of my nursing program. OK, so hello and goodbye."

Natalie appeared to be defensive. Her spontaneous response to my question made me half believe her. However, her tone was more hurried than convincing. I blurted out, "Are you pregnant?"

"You make me laugh," snickered Natalie. "You add one and one and come up with three. I told you what I was doing here."

"Let's go back and talk to your practicum supervisor," I suggested.

Natalie became indignant, which only made me more suspicious.

"Like I need to prove something to you! Get a life, Ricky!"

Natalie clearly did not want to pursue this conversation any further. She hurried off without any word.

I thought about going into Planned Parenthood myself, but I realized it would be a waste of time. People at these places are very guarded. They guard against the presence of anti-abortionist crazies and really protect a woman's right to privacy. I didn't want to follow Natalie around again, but I was very concerned that she would abort my child. The sad thing is, I had absolutely no say in the matter and no rights.

I decided to get the opinion of my new confidant, Papa. I had spent most of my life avoiding Papa's counsel because I felt a bit intimidated by him. Maybe it was my own insecurity or maybe it was Papa's dominant presence around me, but I rarely went out of my way to ask him a question. But on this point, my suspicions about Natalie's pregnancy, I knew that Papa would have a keen interest. After all, if this was my child, it was Papa's grandchild. Papa made no secret of the fact he was waiting for a grandchild. My sister Connie had been married for years and was well into her thirties and still no grandchild. I myself was approaching thirty with no prospects of a special woman in my life, never mind marriage and a child.

I won't bore you with the details of our conversation. You already know how I became suspicious. I told Papa that whole story. What fascinated me was witnessing Papa's reaction to this whole thing. Not knowing if Natalie was really pregnant or if the child was even mine, Papa began to embrace the possibility immediately.

"Well, Ricky, if she was pregnant and at an abortion clinic, we had better move quickly!" exclaimed Papa earnestly. "Who knows when she will do this thing? I know you can't be seen around her. She'll probably try to have your ass arrested the next time she sees your face. But I have an idea that just might work if we want to get to the truth."

"And what's that, Papa?" I asked.

"Let me keep this to myself just for now. You will know soon enough. I hate to jinx the idea, knowing it could backfire as easily as it could work. I will need for you to give me this girl's phone number."

"I can't believe that you would call her and tell her you're my daddy at this point in my life?" I quipped.

"How long must I be with you? Give me just an ounce of credit for not being a total fool," Papa responded.

I gave Papa the phone number and trusted him not to embarrass me out of any sense of pride I might have had left. What happened next I relate to you from the certainty of truth that only time has provided me.

The first thing Papa had to do was solicit the assurance from my sister Connie that she would support his scheme. Understand that Connie is a decent and moral person, not usually swayed into doing underhanded or outright dishonest acts. However, when it comes to Papa, Connie can be persuaded to do things solely because it is Papa asking. Connie has always adored Papa. Connie was and still is Daddy's little girl. He would take her wherever he went and would always spoil her.

Without rehashing the whole story Papa told my sister, since you already know that, let me simply say that Papa explained the possibility that this young lady might be carrying Connie's niece or nephew. Papa always blamed Connie's husband, Thomas, for the fact that Connie never became pregnant. The idea that one of his children might have a fertility problem was an absurd notion to Papa. He confessed to Connie that what he was proposing might be based on totally false information, but the cost of being right and doing nothing would be tantamount to murdering his grandchild.

Clearly, Papa was overly dramatic, but his passion was truly genuine. He wanted to know if Connie would raise my child as her own if it should ever come to that. Never mind that Papa was not certain if Natalie was even pregnant. Never mind that Papa had absolutely no control over Natalie's decision to abort this child if she were pregnant. Never mind that Natalie never expressed any intention of giving away her baby, even if she were pregnant and delivered the baby. You see where I am going. Papa had imagined a whole life for his grandchild without paying one bit of attention to reality. But this is Papa.

After listening to Papa's impassioned pleas for nearly half an hour, Connie agreed to raise the child. This was a very easy decision for Connie, since she felt this whole thing had a snowball's chance in hell of coming to fruition. Anyway, Connie would have raised my child even under more normal circumstances, like if I happened to find myself responsible for a child as a single parent. Connie always wanted a child, but she never expressed a compulsive desire to become pregnant by using fertility drugs or surrogacy or anything like that. Connie would make a terrific mother, because she had a terrific mother as a model.

What Papa did next surprised even me. I have always known that Papa was compulsive, impulsive, and obsessive. But when you add deceit to these traits, there is no telling what kind of scheme might hatch. It's not that Papa did anything physically harmful to Natalie. I mean, he didn't abduct her or torture her or anything like that. Let's just say that he devised a deception that Columbo might have employed to trick a murderer into exposing himself.

To add a degree of authenticity, Papa persuaded my sister Connie to call Natalie announcing herself as Dr. Valentino's nurse. "Is this Natalie Romano?"

"Yes," answered Natalie.

"I'm calling for Dr. Valentino," Connie stated.

"Who's Dr. Valentino?" asked Natalie.

"The doctor will answer all your questions. Please hold." Connie handed Papa the phone.

"Hello, Natalie, this is Dr. Valentino calling from Planned Parenthood at the Greater Boston Health Center."

"Hello, doctor, I am very surprised to hear from you. Is there a problem? And why is your caller ID blocked?" questioned Natalie.

"Our caller ID is blocked for obvious reasons, Ms. Romano. In case the wrong person answers the phone, we would not want to risk your confidentiality."

"Oh, I suppose that makes sense," responded Natalie.

"The reason I am calling is standard operating procedure for me. I realize you had a counseling session about your abortion at the clinic, but this is such a monumental decision that I make it a practice to have a pre-meeting with all my patients prior to the procedure. You are scheduled for the end of the week. I believe we are scheduled for Thursday," stated Papa nonchalantly.

"No, Friday," Natalie corrected the doctor.

"Oh yes, it is Friday. I thought the sixteenth was on a Thursday. I need to use my calendar. Are you free either Wednesday or Thursday to have a brief appointment with me?"

I'm sure Natalie figured she had to respond positively or risk the doctor canceling the procedure. I know Papa can come across as very sincere and yet stern and businesslike.

"I would be free anytime after one o'clock on Wednesday," replied Natalie.

"That's wonderful," said Papa as the doctor. "Hold the phone and the nurse will schedule a time."

Connie took the phone, once again becoming Papa's nurse. "How is two-thirty, Ms. Romano?"

"That will be fine," said Natalie.

Connie gave Natalie the address of Papa's insurance company. Papa was an independent insurance agent and had two days to turn his office into something resembling a doctor's office. Getting the shingle for Anthony Valentino, M.D. was the most challenging part of the ruse, but in today's world of instant products, a few extra dollars can get you most things on fairly short notice. The risk Papa had to take was arousing any suspicions Natalie might have. He actually chose the name Anthony Valentino from a web listing of Boston doctors. He only hoped that she would never call the doctor's number. He felt having a real doctor's name would generate less suspicion than a bogus doctor's name.

Connie was absolutely totally blown away. She wondered how in the world Papa had been able to pull this off. With just a hint of suspicion and a gambler's bluff, Papa had managed to elicit confirmation of Natalie's pregnancy and the actual date of her scheduled abortion. And now, she had to face the possibility that he might even be able to talk Natalie out of having an abortion. Connie lived about thirty miles outside of Boston in the town of Chelmsford, Massachusetts. In order to continue Papa's deception, Connie had to take a personal day from work and drive back to Boston.

Papa hired a man to secure his doctor's shingle to the front of the building and to replace his insurance business sign on the office door with the doctor's name. He converted his front office into a physician's reception area and used his personal rear office to meet with Natalie, replacing insurance certifications with false medical credentials. If Natalie had been suspicious about this whole situation, she could easily have uncovered Papa's scheme, but the phone call from Nurse Connie and Dr. Valentino was totally credible. Who else would have called her about such an intimate detail of her life?

As difficult as this planning was, it was a piece of cake compared to the real mission. How could Papa convince Natalie not to kill this baby? He knew that Natalie was basically a God-fearing Christian woman. He knew she was not promiscuous and that this pregnancy resulted from her first sexual encounter. Papa knew that as a nurse practitioner, Natalie was all about caring for people's needs. He knew all these things from the way I had painted Natalie as a beautiful, caring young woman caught up in dire circumstances. Now he hoped that with his lifelong skill as a salesman, his personal charisma, and his compelling need to save the life of his unborn grandchild, he could pull off the greatest feat of his life.

That Wednesday afternoon, the hands of the clock slowly crept toward two-thirty. I had never seen Papa as anxious and worried as he was on that day. I had to stay away from the area, not wanting to arouse Natalie's suspicions. Connie rented a nurse's uniform and Papa decided that this occasion called for a suit and tie as opposed to a white lab coat.

Natalie entered the office, seemingly unsuspecting, and sat down in one of the chairs. Connie explained to Natalie that this was Dr. Valentino's satellite office, used almost exclusively for consultation, and no procedures were performed here. She hoped this would ease any lingering thoughts about the non-medical appearance of the office. Connie also told Natalie that she was Dr. Valentino's last patient of the afternoon. Then she escorted Natalie to the doctor's office.

I know from talking to Papa later that day that Natalie's first appearance in his office struck him as an awesome spectacle destined to bring uncontained joy into his life. Of course, knowing Papa as I do, I received this information with restraint. But no matter, the facts speak for themselves.

"Hello, Natalie," said Dr. Valentino in greeting. "Please make yourself comfortable. How are you feeling?"

Natalie was noticeably uncomfortable, but she tried to act the professional mature woman. Natalie believed that being an unwed pregnant woman cast a sense of ignominy.

"Well, thank you, Dr. Valentino. I am glad to meet you before we actually have this procedure."

"I know that you had your counseling session, but I wanted to make absolutely certain this is your firm commitment. We both know the consequences of this procedure and are aware that possible guilt after the fact that may last for years. Do your parents know what you are planning to do?"

"No, sir. I am twenty-one and have decided this on my own."

"Does the father of your child know of this pregnancy?" asked the fake doctor.

"The father does not know, and I intend that he will never know," said Natalie.

She crossed her arms over her chest. My father wondered later if she was beginning to feel suspicious or intimidated, so he chose his words even more carefully.

"Would it not be better to let him know? If the father wanted to raise this child, would you accept that? In fairness, is this not his child, too? Would you agree to keep this child under those circumstances?"

Natalie was shocked at the degree of pressure the doctor was imposing. She would not expect the doctor to try to talk her out of having the abortion. She was trying to maintain her composure, as she did not want to jeopardize her abortion by antagonizing the man who, she thought, was doing the procedure.

"Dr. Valentino, I have considered all these things you are telling me and actually much more. I considered the father's position. I considered my parents' position. I considered my religion and its teachings and I severely struggled with my own guilt about taking a life. You are upsetting me all over. Believe me, this is not a decision I made lightly."

"I understand, Natalie, and never intended to upset you. This is such a permanent solution that I had to be certain that we were absolutely unwavering."

"I'm sorry. I know that you must argue on the side of life. My becoming a nurse and being a Catholic has caused me a great deal of conflict. Ultimately, I am resigned to this decision. So, I will see you on Friday. Is there anything else?"

Papa knew that he could go no further with this ruse. If he could not reach Natalie as a doctor, his only recourse was to plead his case as the grandfather. He only hoped that when Natalie realized that Ricky and his family knew of the baby she could be swayed. Her secret would no longer be buried by concealment. She would see firsthand the devastating impact her decision had on others. Papa hoped this last realization would finally break Natalie's grip of obdurate attachment to this unprincipled principle.

"Natalie, you must forgive my deception. It was the desperate and futile act of a very hopeless and distressed man." Papa looked from Natalie to his office door. "Connie, please come in here!"

Connie stood in the doorway and Papa continued. "You see, Natalie, I am not Dr. Valentino and this is not a doctor's office. Ricky told me that he suspected that you might be pregnant. And if you were, the baby might even be his and yours, of course. Connie is Ricky's sister and I am Ricky's father."

Papa waited for Natalie to process what he had said. He could see that she was visibly shocked as she sat in her chair motionless and speechless.

After she had composed herself, she addressed Papa with respectful indignation. "How could anyone be so underhanded as to perpetuate this charade?"

Papa answered, "I do not think that you should be asking me such a question in light of your own decision. Did you feel that your pregnancy only affected your life? Did you consider how Ricky and his family would feel? You must know the child would be part of Ricky and all of us here. Do your parents know of this situation?"

Speaking through a restrained sob, Natalie replied, "Of course I thought of Ricky. I thought about my parents and I especially thought about my God. This decision was not made lightly or in haste. In fact, this decision has caused me much anguish. But the truth is that this ultimately is my decision and my decision alone!"

Papa was wise enough to know that he needed to tread carefully, not wanting to alienate Natalie to the point of her totally discounting his position. He waited for her to bolt out of the office altogether, but, surprisingly, she remained to hear Papa's pleading. She may have wanted to hear more of Papa's next step, since he planted the seed about her parents' absence from this decision. One of the primary reasons for Natalie's wanting this abortion was to prevent her father from knowing about her dilemma. "And I do not want you to involve my parents in my personal and private problems!"

"Natalie, I am not here to cause problems for you and your parents," Papa explained tenderly. "I am here to save the life of my grandchild. This is all and this is my sole motivation. I feel I know you well enough from Ricky to believe that you also want to do what is right. Ricky loves you because he saw in you a beauty that shines from within. Sure, he knows you don't love him. He knows you have another life that totally excludes him. Ricky has sadly resigned himself to this. But this is not about Ricky. This is not about you and your boyfriend. This is about a child not having the chance to live. This is about a child – my family's child – not having the chance to live."

Connie was a bystander during this whole heart-wrenching dialogue but decided to speak. "Natalie, I have been trying to have my own baby for the past ten years. There are no guarantees in life. This baby you are carrying may be the only one you ever have. This baby may be the only child Ricky ever has. Why do you think Papa is so distressed? He knows this may be his only link to the future. I know that sounds ridiculous and probably self-centered, but I know my Papa is sincere. He is a bit dramatic, but his words are heartfelt."

Natalie remained seated and seemed stunned. The pressure put on her by the family most affected by the decision overwhelmed her. She knew in her heart that her own family would feel this exact same way. Add to this the hassle Regina gave Natalie about her misguided decision and Natalie had to reevaluate all that she had so firmly believed. But she could see no good way out of her predicament.

Papa took Natalie's silence as an opportunity to present a solution. "Natalie, I know that next week you will graduate. I believe you may even have a job waiting for you. I do not think it would be a stretch to convince your parents that you will want to spend six months doing humanitarian service in Italy for the refugees from Libya and Tunisia. You could convince them that in this way you could learn some valuable on-the-job experience and reconnect to your Italian roots. Hell, I could even meet your parents as Dr. Valentino and present the whole mission. I can be very convincing. You can tell them I am a visiting professor this term. I'll even throw in some Italian for authenticity."

"Don't get stressed about the idea of actually living in Italy. We have that problem handled," Connie reassured her.

Chapter Five

Grim Decision

Natalie left the fake doctor's office very unsettled. She had overcome Regina's barrage of reasons why she should keep this baby. She had won the hard-fought battle against her own religious teachings and values and was determined to abort this ill-conceived pregnancy. She rationalized that this was not a baby conceived in love or with her intention. She viewed the whole pregnancy as an accident needing to be rectified. But now she had been confronted directly by the family who actually wanted this child. She wondered how she could ever live with herself knowing that she would be killing Papa's grandchild and that he knew it. Natalie, as she always did, brought Regina into her problem.

"Regina, Friday my abortion is scheduled."

"Are you telling me something new?" said Regina. "If I thought I could change that mule head of yours, I would spend the next two days convincing you what a mistake you are making."

"What you don't know, Regina, is that Ricky's father tricked me into telling him about the abortion." Regina listened entranced as Natalie gave her a blow-by-blow description of the bogus counseling session she had with Dr. Valentino.

"The thing I am most agonized over is the reaction of Ricky's father. He didn't come across as angry or threatening, but I actually felt the pain he was suffering because of my decision. His passion was so genuine, I actually felt like the worst person in the world when I left him. I told you what he said, but my own words could never express the emotion and helplessness he conveyed in beseeching me to keep *his* grandchild."

Regina interrupted. "I tried to tell you that, but it wasn't real to you. Your secrecy protected you from the hurt you would cause other people. If you'll remember, I especially told you that your parents would be devastated if they ever learned the truth."

"Mr. Santo will not tell my parents about the pregnancy. He gave me that reassurance and I believe he will keep his word."

"So this has now changed your mind about the abortion?" asked Regina.

"Well, I told you about the sham counseling session, but I didn't tell you about the scheme Papa devised to conceal my pregnancy from my parents. He asked me to call him Papa. He probably wanted me to be on more familiar terms with him to make my decision tortuous. He plans to concoct a story where I go to Sicily for six months on a humanitarian mission to work with poor families. In fact, I will really be going to Chelmsford, Massachusetts to live with Ricky's sister, Connie, until the baby is born. Then, Connie and her husband will adopt the child as their own."

"Isn't that a little too close to home?" asked Regina.

"No one I know ever goes to Chelmsford, especially not my parents or Jeremy."

"And what about Jeremy?" inquired Regina. "If you are away that long, you know Jeremy will be out booty hunting."

Natalie replied without hesitation. "I'm not sure I give a shit what Jeremy does. If he loves me, like he says he does, he will wait six months for me. I would rather he cheated on me now than waiting until we are married. Anyway, I have really been asking myself if trusting in Jeremy's fidelity is worth destroying Papa's lineage. Regina, Papa got to me, and I'd never met him before this afternoon. I have a sense that hurting Papa is something I would regret forever. It's not that I fear he will torment me if I have this abortion. It's living with myself knowing how much I hurt him and the rest of his family."

"It sounds to me as if your mind is changed. Right?" asked Regina.

"I still have until Friday. Let me sleep on it. There is no getting around the obvious truth. Whether I have the baby or not, my life will never be the same. The difference now is that the right thing is no longer personal. They say what you don't know won't hurt you, but Papa and his family do know. And that hurts me more than I ever imagined."

The next morning, Thursday, Natalie called Papa to discuss his proposition. She wanted to know every little detail in order to convince herself that this crazy idea could actually work. Her graduation from nursing school would be on Saturday two weeks away, and she needed to leave shortly thereafter to prevent everyone from seeing the natural changes occurring to her body. Papa met Natalie at the same bogus office. Connie, having spent the night with her mother and father, was also there. Natalie took Regina along for moral support. Natalie explained to Papa that Regina was the only person in the world who knew her secret. Well, she was until Papa's chicanery. Papa greeted both women with the charming manner that one would expect from somebody wanting something from somebody else.

Papa, as usual, took charge of all aspects of the plan. He took the fact that Natalie was listening as a terrific sign. He believed he would soon have a grandchild and tried to conceal his excitement by speaking calmly and with conviction.

"The first thing is to handle the trip to Sicily. There is a flight from Kennedy Airport to Catania on May 5. I will book us both a ticket to New York. You know your parents are going to see you off so we will need to actually get on a plane and go somewhere. We will also need to check the flight number from JFK to Catania. If your parents are like me, they will be checking the flight online until the second that plane lands. No one in your family knows who I am, so my presence at the airport will be totally ignored by them."

Natalie inquired, "Why would we want to go the New York when we can get a flight from Boston?"

"You know, we can't actually fly to Sicily and back from Boston. That would be too long a trip, even if it is part of the cover. Tell your parents that you checked airfares and flying out of New York was the best price. Since this is funded by the charity, you are trying to keep costs down. Believe me, they will not check rates. They have no reason to question you on this. Anyway, rates change all the time. You just happened to find a good one for that day."

"OK," said Natalie. "That'll work."

Papa continued. "When we get to New York, I will rent a car and drive back to Chelmsford. If you wanted to do some sightseeing in New York while we're there, that would be fine by me. It's good that Regina knows of your situation. She might come and keep you company in Chelmsford once in a while. Connie has enough room for a small army."

Regina jumped in. "Sure, Natalie knows that I will be there for her. Don't take this wrong, Mr. Santo – I'm thrilled that Natalie is having this baby. Only I wish she had just told her parents and had this baby here in Boston. It makes no sense that she is concealing this from everyone. Anyway, Natalie and I had that argument already and I'm just glad she has decided not to have an abortion."

"Is that right?" asked Papa. "You've decided to have this baby, Natalie?"

"I'm leaning that way," said Natalie. "How could I not with everyone ganging up on me? Anyway, Mr. Santo, I couldn't live with myself knowing how strongly you feel about having this child."

Papa sighed. "This is a great relief. Thank you, Natalie. And when this baby is born, you will thank God you made this decision."

"What's next?" asked Natalie. "What if my folks want to call me in Italy? How about letters? You know my parents will expect letters and pictures. They will want to have pictures of me in Italy. How will we pull that one off?

Connie was prepared for this contingency. "We will be doing lots of Skype calling. Tell them because of your schedule, you will call them at a certain time. You should try to call them as much as possible on the computer. We have spoken to Papa's cousin Rocco in Scordia and he has agreed to get a cheap cell phone. You will give that number to Jeremy and your parents. If they should call, Rocco will not answer but he'll call you and let you know someone called. You can call them back. We've also looked into you having a spoof ID. When you call, the phone number appearing will be a spoof number, which will show up as Rocco's number. It is a bit tricky, but there is a company that actually does that stuff for a fee. You will want to emphasize with your parents that you should initiate most of the calls because of your schedule and also the charity will pay for these calls since you are volunteering to work in Sicily."

"This will not be easy to pull off," said Natalie.

Papa reassured Natalie. "You need to remember, Natalie. Everyone expects you to be in Italy. They will not be suspicious if calls are delayed or dropped, etc. You should let them know you will only be able to call once a week or so. They will understand that international calls are expensive and you are busy. That's what you will emphasize."

Connie added, "Rocco will set up a mailing address in Catania. Whenever he gets a letter, he will fax it to you and you can reply. Anyway, no one writes anymore. You will be using e-mails just like you were home. You can attach pictures of Sicily. Rocco has lots he can send you. We will find someone to Photoshop you in a few of them to add some authenticity. You will have lots of time while you are waiting for the baby to do all kinds of creative things to make yourself appear to be in Sicily."

"You make it sound so easy," said Natalie.

"You know what?" Papa replied. "This is all wrong. Natalie is giving me the greatest gift of my life and here I am pinching pennies. Why not actually fly to Sicily for two weeks? We could visit cousin Rocco and take lots of pictures that we could leave with Rocco in Italy. We could have a terrific vacation before your baby slows you down. You could write out some letters in advance and Rocco could mail the letters and the pictures a little at a time. And you could still attach some as you please in e-mails. You never met Ricky's mother. She is not at all like me. In fact, she's fairly normal except that living with me for forty years has taken some of the edge from the sweet disposition she has. But don't let that worry you. When she is around other people, she always reverts back to that sweet young girl I married years ago. She will be great company for you in Italy and I know she has been dying to go there since forever."

Natalie liked the idea of a vacation after four hard years of nursing school. She thought about seeing places that her great-grandparents came from. She started getting excited about the idea. She and her father could go over the family tree. She could do some research on her visit. Papa would be only too happy to serve as her interpreter. Papa's grandparents on his father's side came from Sicily and his grandparents on his mother's side came from Naples.

"OK, Papa, let's do it! I will cancel my appointment for tomorrow. You can make all the travel arrangements."

Looking back, I cannot remember ever seeing Papa so happy. Natalie had already become his second daughter, and he could see firsthand how easy it was for me to fall in love with her. Now, ironically, Papa and Mama will get to spend the time with Natalie that I wished was mine. I shouldn't complain. Natalie will have my baby and Connie will raise the child. Things certainly could have turned out much worse.

I haven't really said much about Connie and Thomas. Their role cannot be understated. They were to be the parents of my child. Both Connie and Thomas worked as educators. Connie was a special education teacher, which gave her great insight for raising a child, even if she'd never had her own. Thomas was a school psychologist. I figured between the two of them, the child would either come out totally well adjusted, ready to cope with all the problems of the world, or be totally messed up beyond repair. Knowing Connie, I felt certain it would be the former. I only hoped that the grandparents wouldn't spoil the kid too badly.

Thomas was surprisingly on board with adopting my child. Both he and Connie wanted a child but had never been able to conceive. Medical tests revealed no medical reason why they couldn't conceive. After twelve years of marriage, Connie and Thomas had not given up trying to have a baby, but they were excited at the prospect of raising their niece or nephew. I assured Thomas that he would be the baby's father in every sense of the word except biological. I had no inclination to raise this child by myself and did not want my parents to be overly involved during their golden years. I promised Thomas that I would never interfere in any of their decisions on raising the baby. I know Thomas believed me and was comforted by my words. Thomas knew that I was just a big kid and not interested in any power trip. All the pieces were falling nicely into place.

The next morning, Natalie called Planned Parenthood at the Greater Boston Health Center and canceled her procedure. Then she called Papa and told him to book the tickets. Papa purchased three tickets from Boston to Catania-Fontanarossa Airport. Cousin Rocco's home in Scordia was about seventeen miles from Mineo.

Just in case anyone bothered to check, Mineo was the site Natalie told her parents she was working. She prayed her parents would call her directly and not the Mineo refugee center if they needed anything. Thousands of people undertook dangerous voyages across the Mediterranean Sea from Tunisia and Libya to seek refuge in Italy. Most people were fleeing violence in those countries. Many were sub-Saharan Africans who came to Tunisia or Libya in search of a better life. When conflict broke out, thousands of people risked their lives to reach Italy, crossing the sea in overcrowded, unseaworthy boats. Many of these people were treated in Mineo.

Doctors Without Borders offered assistance to people as they arrived on shore, giving out blankets and determining who needed priority medical treatment. The most common complaints were gastrointestinal, pulmonary and respiratory infections. The center also treated patients who had suffered from violence.

Jeremy couldn't believe that Natalie would just leave for Sicily without even discussing the matter with him. He realized that Natalie didn't treat him the same way she did before he decided to play the field. Natalie, even though she still loved Jeremy, had to keep up this pretense. She probably wanted to keep the knowledge of her pregnancy from Jeremy even more than she wanted to keep it from her parents.

Natalie spent the next two weeks preparing for her trip. She packed mostly summer clothes, since most of her pregnancy would take place in the summer and fall. Anyway, Sicily is a warm climate throughout the year. The clothes she needed while living in Chelmsford either Papa would buy for her or Connie would let her use. Coats and jackets were no problem. Connie had plenty of those and she was close to Natalie's size. Connie would enjoy shopping for maternity clothes as Natalie's shape outgrew their wardrobes.

As you can imagine, Jeremy spent every night with Natalie until she left for her trip. He continued to push the envelope with Natalie, but he never again gave her an ultimatum. Natalie could not even pretend that Jeremy would be faithful to her while she was off having her baby. Natalie's priorities had changed now. If Jeremy could wait for Natalie and convince her that he truly loved her, they might actually have a chance. With Jeremy's recent track record, Natalie doubted this. I suspect that Jeremy viewed Natalie's mission as an opportunity to continue his own pursuit of happiness.

Jeremy treated Natalie with an almost reverent kind of love reserved for much older established couples. He asked, "Natalie, why would you leave me and your new job just when things were good? Are you trying to test me?"

Natalie replied, "Jeremy, not everything is about you. I can't really explain this, but going to Sicily is something I feel compelled to do. This is an opportunity presented to me through my professor's contacts. I would be returning to the land of my great-grandparents and helping unfortunate people, mostly younger people, fleeing an oppressive existence. I would learn more about nursing there than I could ever learn at the clinic. Please understand that I am not punishing you or testing you. I hope that when I return, we will be able to plan our wedding. It's really not that long. Young men are deployed for combat duty longer than the six or seven months I will be gone."

Jeremy seemed to answer sincerely. "Of course I will be here when you return. I could never find another woman to compare to you. You have been my soul for years. I beat myself up over having hurt you. I don't want to discuss my time away from you; it's too painful for both of us. Just know I only proved to myself that I could never live my life without you."

Natalie and Jeremy kissed with a passion seizing both of them. Natalie was totally conflicted. She did love Jeremy but now was committed to having a stranger's baby. Could she ever live a life with Jeremy founded on lies? Would Jeremy want Natalie if he knew her secret? She knew that Jeremy would not be able to overcome her betrayal. The choice was fairly simple. Marry Jeremy and keep the secret buried forever or leave Jeremy as punishment for the sin that she, herself, had committed. It was a lose-lose situation born from her moment of wantonness.

The other problem confronting Natalie was explaining to her parents why she had suddenly decided she had to leave right after graduation for a foreign country. Natalie used the same pretext, knowing her parents would never check with her professor. Having Papa posing as a doctor boarding the plane to Sicily with her lent credence to the deception.

Mr. Romano was especially interested in Natalie's trip. He saw it as an opportunity to visit both Natalie and his grandfather's family. Natalie became panicked by this prospect, but outwardly she maintained her composure. She explained to her father that this was to be an intense six months of working with the *Doctors Without Borders* program. She adamantly maintained that she would not be able to spend any time with him.

"If I'm not working, I'll probably be sleeping," Natalie insisted. "I think this would be a great trip for all of us to have after my mission is over. After all, this is not the kind of trip you want to have without adequate time to see everything. Maybe we could do some ancestry research and visit places together with Mom. I bet you would be able to locate Grandpa's family if we had the time to do this right. I think you should postpone this trip until after my work is complete, Dad."

Mr. Romano was disappointed but persuaded to believe that Natalie made sense. "I suppose you're right, baby. But I still think it's a good idea. Let's not just give this lip service. Life has a way of changing your plans. Soon, you'll have a real job right here. You will be a married woman and life just gets in the way."

"We just won't let that happen," Natalie smiled. Natalie felt that her father was probably right. If he didn't go now, they likely never would. But in her predicament, one more little white lie on top of all the other whoppers hardly mattered.

Even though Natalie insisted that she would mostly be wearing a nurse's uniform and casual clothes, Mrs. Romano insisted they go on one last shopping spree. Mrs. Romano did not know that Natalie was pregnant, but she did know that Natalie was acting out of character. Why would she suddenly leave Jeremy, knowing that this could end their future plans permanently? Why the sudden altruism? Natalie never expressed any interest in working in this capacity before. It struck Mrs. Romano as odd, but she never questioned Natalie's motives.

Natalie's graduation finally arrived. The ceremony itself was a source of pride for Natalie and her parents. Nursing school is difficult. It takes long hours of grueling study and hard work. It involves homework and heartbreaking clinical work. All this culminates in a demanding nursing board exam. The pinning ceremony, dating back a thousand years, has been a long-held graduation tradition signifying that you are now a full-fledged nurse. The pin, once a symbol of Christianity, eventually evolved into a unique design that signifies the school from which one graduated. Both of Natalie's parents welled up when Natalie was pinned.

The day before Natalie left for Sicily, she and Regina had a girls' day out. It was a sad time for Natalie, knowing that after tomorrow her life would never again be the same.

"Regina, I must be out of my mind doing this," whined Natalie. "How in the world did I get to this point?"

"We are *not* going there again," snapped Regina. "You are doing the right thing. It all boils down to one thing: you are having a baby. You are not taking the life of this unborn child. You are giving to a good family a real live person who otherwise would have been wiped out of existence. How can you possibly think you are out of your mind or doing the wrong thing? This is really getting old, Natalie. You are my hero. This is absolutely the right thing to do and I want you to stop beating yourself up about this decision."

"Thank you, Regina. I need lots of reassurance right now. It's not like having a baby and giving it away is a small thing. I truly worry about how I will be able to handle the separation. I definitely will not renege on my promise to Connie and Mr. Santo, though. I'm constantly giving myself a pep talk to get through this ordeal. It helps that Connie encourages me to be part of the child's life, but I'm not sure how that will look. I know that Connie and Thomas will love and nurture the child, and I don't know how I will fit into their life. What am I? Am I an aunt, a friend of the family, or what? Will the child ever learn I am his or her mother? When will that happen? What about my own parents? Where will they fit in this picture? I have way more questions than answers."

This circle of people knowing Natalie's secret was expanding. If it expanded any more, then it would hardly meet the definition of a secret. Fortunately, except for Regina, everyone who knew of Natalie's charade had a vested interest in keeping the pregnancy and adoption quiet. Papa and Mama definitely were not about to tell anyone they were becoming grandparents. First of all, Mama did not want to tempt the saints. There was still plenty that could go wrong. Papa and I knew that if Natalie's parents ever found out she was pregnant, the whole scheme would be out the window. Connie and her husband did not want to rock the boat. They had a baby on the way that would be an actual part of the family, even if they were not the biological parents. The only other person who knew was Rocco, and he did not care about Natalie's drama and lived in Italy anyway. Everything really hinged on Regina's discretion, but Papa felt in his heart that Regina was on the side of the baby and wanted Natalie to be a mom. Regina knew that Natalie needed her friendship and trust and she was not about to throw that away.

Mr. and Mrs. Romano invited Jeremy out to dinner the evening before Natalie's departure to Italy. To celebrate the trip to Italy, Mr. Romano took everyone to Giacomo's Ristorante. They began with antipasto provolone cheese. Then, all feasted on Zuppa di Pesci with a side order of lobster ravioli. They shared a bottle of Sauvignon blanc. Natalie pretended to drink the wine, pouring it discreetly into her half empty water glass when no one noticed. Mr. Romano had a new guarded opinion of Jeremy. Where before he had readily accepted Jeremy as a prospective son-in-law, he now viewed him as unworthy for his daughter. Mr. Romano never explored the hypocritical nature of this attitude, considering his own dalliances, but he held the man who married his daughter to a much higher standard than he maintained for himself. Mrs. Romano had a more merciful view of Jeremy.

"So what will you do for all those months away from Natalie? I can only guess this move came as quite a surprise to you," said Mr. Romano. Mr. Romano was trying to glimpse some insight into Jeremy's character from his answer. Jeremy gave the politically correct response.

"Mr. Romano, I'm going to take this opportunity to really learn my job. Dr. Hanson always needs a radiologist on call to work weekends and at night. This will give me a chance to make some extra money and provide me with lots of experience. I've always tried to keep my personal time free for Natalie, but this is my chance to throw myself into my work as I try not to obsess about missing her."

It was a good answer. No one was able to detect from Jeremy's delivery that his answer was anything but sincere. No one cheered at Jeremy's response but solemnly gave him respectful, droll smiles. Mrs. Romano teased that she would be certain to visit Jeremy to keep him from being lonely. She expressed this sentiment in such a wry manner that Jeremy feared she might even be serious. This was Mrs. Romano's intention.

At the end of the meal, Mr. Romano said, "Let's take a stroll to Mike's Pastry Shop for some cannoli and biscotti."

"Thanks, Daddy," Natalie interjected, "but this is our last evening here for a while. I think Jeremy and I will go out for what's left of the evening."

"Of course you will," said Mrs. Romano. "Be safe and we'll keep the light on for you. Goodnight, Jeremy. Come on, Harry. Let's get that cannoli."

Jeremy shook Mr. Romano's hand and gave Mrs. Romano a gentle kiss and thanked them for dinner. As Jeremy and Natalie walked toward Jeremy's car, the Romanos left in the other direction.

"This is your last night, Natalie. What would you like to do?" asked Jeremy.

"I got us a room for tonight. I would like to give you a memorable send-off – something to remember me by," answered Natalie.

"Are you saying what I think you're saying?" Jeremy was shocked, nervous, excited, and anxious all at the same time.

Natalie was at that point where her values no longer mattered. She felt that she still loved Jeremy but was very conflicted. She would keep her secret. Making love to Jeremy now would not compromise any of her values. She was no longer a virgin, but he didn't have to know that. So Natalie carefully arranged a beautiful experience for what she felt was truly her first intimate lovemaking, where she was fully aware and committed to the rapture. If this was going to be her first passionate escapade, her first time to give herself to a man willingly, she would at least do it right.

Natalie had reserved a room at the Ritz-Carlton with a king-sized bed. She felt cheated that there was no plush rug in front of a fireplace but allowed that would be overkill, this being May. After a momentary embrace, full of promise, they made the Jacuzzi their first stop. Natalie had ordered champagne with the compulsory bowl of chocolate-dipped strawberries. She rationalized that one small glass would be all right vowing never to have another drink during her pregnancy. She made sure that her "first" time would be memorable. She packed an overnight bag containing her sexiest lingerie and the most enticing fragrances suiting her personal taste.

Jeremy was quite perplexed as to why this was happening. He could not understand Natalie's total reversal, compromising the values she averred for so very long. Why now, on the eve of her leaving for over six months to a remote section of a faraway country? At least Jeremy had enough restraint not to attack Natalie like a teenager in heat. He tenderly embraced her. He always loved inhaling the ambrosial scent of Natalie's soft, heaven-like hair. The excitement he derived from the aroma of that soft auburn hair was an overwhelming aphrodisiac, creating a tingling sensation throughout his whole body. It took all his control to keep in check the crazed beast erupting inside.

They kissed long, passionate kisses. Slowly he ran his hand along her side, her body, caressing her firm breasts. Her breasts were not large, fitting perfectly into Jeremy's hands. Jeremy felt that every feature of Natalie's body was perfect. Her wet body, shimmering in the soft light, made her look like a goddess to him. He lifted Natalie out of the Jacuzzi, careful to wrap her in the hotel's white, fluffy robe. In turn, Natalie held on tightly, her fingers clasped around Jeremy's neck as he transported her to delight.

Jeremy had a naturally athletic body that he kept in excellent shape. He had six-pack abs and well-developed biceps to complement his handsome face with its chiseled features. Natalie couldn't help thinking that this whole evening could have been treasured unmarred by the secret she kept from Jeremy. If Jeremy had just trusted her long enough, this moment could have been their vestal dawn, untarnished by reality. Their first time would not have happened for the wrong reasons. Natalie was afraid that her absence would be too much for Jeremy to bear, but she was hopeful that he would be there waiting for her when she returned. She hoped that Jeremy would keep his promise to her parents and fill his time working and waiting for their future together. The voice inside Natalie told her that if Jeremy could not wait for her when he saw her all the time, he would soon give in to his manly desires while she was away. Jeremy's libido drove most of his behaviors and this did not bode well for their separation. With all this in mind, Natalie's decision was still firm. After meeting Mr. Santo and the rest of Ricky's family, she was not about to change her mind about having this baby.

Jeremy hesitated as he lay Natalie on the bed. Stroking her arm softly, he asked, "Why this sudden change, Natalie?"

"Why not?" Natalie replied. "We are practically married, aren't we, Jeremy? Maybe we should get engaged first, but I know you've been waiting to get a good job. Well, you have one now."

"What about your desire to remain a virgin until married? That almost broke us up and now you totally reverse yourself. Boy, I'm confused, and I have no protection. You certainly wouldn't want to get pregnant now, just as you're leaving for Europe."

Natalie reassured Jeremy. "Jeremy, I'm a nurse, so you can believe me when I tell you that there is no way you can get me pregnant tonight. This is the best possible day for us to do this."

"This must have cost you plenty," said Jeremy. "Let me at least give you the money you spent on the room."

"I will not hear of it. This is my treat."

"I don't think so," exclaimed Jeremy with a mischievous grin. "This will definitely be my treat."

Natalie made the first move. She had firm evidence of Jeremy's excitement without even having touched him. Jeremy tried to control the sensation he got from being intimate with Natalie. It was unlike the lust he had felt with other women. This was a different fire, one of quiet, growing passion. The soft bristles of Natalie's pubic hair aroused Jeremy's being. He teased Natalie into excitement, exploring the outer lips of her most private erotic zone, careful not to penetrate too soon. But it was Natalie who guided Jeremy into her own warm, moist, welcoming passage.

"Am I hurting you, Natalie?" whispered Jeremy, considering that Natalie's first intercourse would be painful.

"Just be gentle," Natalie sighed.

They would linger as one, remaining fairly motionless, swaying imperceptibly. Jeremy knew that he had to get his mind on some faraway, meaningless thought because his heightened senses made it very difficult to control nature's urge. Defeated, he tightly grabbed Natalie, kissing her while rocking forcefully inside her, finally erupting while clinching her ever more tightly. There he and Natalie remained clenched as one until he finally slipped out of her warm tenderness and rested his head peacefully on her stomach. Natalie was satisfied in the knowledge that her real first time was rapture.

Chapter Six

Italian Vacation

"You got in very late last night – or should I say very early this morning? Did you have a good time with Jeremy?" Mrs. Romano had a wry smile on her face. "It's a good thing your flight to Sicily is in the late afternoon."

Papa had booked the flight to Catania with one connecting flight in Rome. This was the shortest flight Papa could find at a somewhat reasonable price. Still, between Papa, Mrs. Santo, and Natalie, the fare was about $3,500 using economy class. Papa, who was always money conscious, never considered the expense of the trip as an issue. He regarded this trip as an investment assuring the continuation of the Santo family. Papa felt that he couldn't put a price on securing his grandchild.

Natalie passed the day uneventfully. Regina spent several hours with her going through her luggage, putting last minute touches on her wardrobe. Mostly, Natalie packed light summery outfits. For show, she made certain to pack a few nurse's uniforms. She hated to waste the space, but she did not want to arouse any suspicion about the trip. In the afternoon, Jeremy came by to have lunch with the Romanos. Regina stayed for lunch, trying to study Jeremy's body language as his inamorata was preparing to leave for many months. Regina was biased against Jeremy, knowing how he had screwed Natalie over during his freedom period. She tried, partially successfully, to hide her disdain. She knew that Natalie still loved him and did not want to distress her with her own opinions of Jeremy's odious character.

About two hours before the flight, Mr. and Mrs. Romano drove Natalie and Regina to the airport. Jeremy would also see Natalie off, but he drove his own car, not wanting to subject himself to questioning by Natalie's parents on the return trip. He certainly did not want to hear anything Regina had to say unrepressed by Natalie's absence. Accounting for Boston traffic and overseas check-in, Natalie felt the entire two hours was needed.

Papa, on the other hand, dragged Mrs. Santo out three hours ahead of time. Mrs. Santo was accustomed to Papa's obsessive compulsion about being early, but it still aggravated her nevertheless. Papa would always say, "What if there is heavy traffic or the car breaks down or the lines at the airport are long?" They almost always ended up waiting an extra hour in the terminal, but at least Papa was comforted knowing he made the flight. Mama was also comforted knowing she did not have to listen to Papa hurrying her along every three minutes. After years of marriage, they both learned to tolerate each other's ways. I guess that's why they are still married after forty-plus years.

Papa also hated to wait. He didn't mind waiting at the airport or waiting at the cinema for the picture to start, but he hated waiting idly for Mama to leave the house. In truth, Mama did take forever. She would check the heat, check to see that all the doors were locked, and check every appliance in the house, and when she finally stepped outside the house, she would without fail always, and I mean always, go back inside again. Sometimes she would go into the bathroom or recheck things she wasn't certain she checked the first time. Then she had the irritating habit of reading things as she was about to leave. This could be mail, a news article that caught her attention, or just about any distraction that any sane person would consider unnatural. This had been the root of many arguments over the years, but Papa has learned to be tolerant. He now uses this time as an opportunity to listen to music or a ballgame or simply to rest in the car. He would always wait in the car because actually watching Mama go through her neurotic ritual would certainly drive Papa over the edge. This is also why he prepares everyone to leave at least an hour before time, knowing half that time will be wasted by Mama actually leaving the house. This was especially true on this day since Mama would leave her home for two weeks. I assured Mama I would check on the house every day. I said my goodbyes at the house, not wanting to be seen at the airport by any of the Romanos. I arranged to pick up Papa's car so he did not have to pay for long-term parking.

Sunday afternoon finally arrived, marking the start of Natalie's Italian adventure. At the airport, Papa introduced himself to the Romanos. He remained Dr. Valentino, since that name had brought him good fortune the first time he met Natalie. Natalie was close at hand to buffer Papa from her parents' questions. Mama remained in the background, posing as just another traveler. Fortunately, the meeting between Papa and the Romanos was short, lacking any probing questions about the trip. Natalie had made a point of substantially providing any background for the bogus trip. Anyway, Papa made a beeline to the security checkpoint, not wanting to converse with the Romanos. Papa has learned from years of experience that the less said, the better. You never know what people remember and pick up on as you bluster through with charming lies.

"Remember," said Natalie to her parents, "I will call you at least three times a week. I will e-mail you and send you pictures. It will be hard for me to answer the phone, so unless there is a dire emergency, just wait for me to call. I will try to call about five p.m. your time. This will be about 11 p.m. for me. I will call earlier on the weekends since you'll be home."

Natalie hugged and kissed her parents. Her brother had said his goodbyes two days before.

Natalie took Jeremy aside for their personal farewell. "Jeremy, I'll e-mail you every day. Like I told my parents, don't call me, because my schedule is likely to be crazy. Since I will be calling my parents and Regina and you, my overseas phone bills will be very high, but I'll call you as often as I can, probably late afternoon Boston time because of the time difference. I don't know how my schedule will look. I expect there will be some days off during the week, but they probably won't be on weekends."

The rest of the time Jeremy spent telling Natalie how much he loved her and what a special night they experienced just hours ago. Jeremy savored the last vestiges of Natalie's being. For the final time for many months, he inhaled the perfumed, soft, brown hair that always excited his passion. He tenderly kissed her lips. Her lips were a gentle, bewitching invitation that he was able to taste, knowing it would be too long before he was again satiated. The final inevitable moment came when Natalie had to release Jeremy's grasp and enter the sanctity of airline security and probing machines. "When I return, I will be yours forever, Jeremy. Wait for me."

Jeremy promised that he would. He promised that he would use this time to prepare a life for them. They both avoided speaking directly about marriage, only alluding to their life together forever. But no rings were exchanged and no official announcements were made. Natalie felt it was better this way, since her trust was badly shaken and the anguish of having to break an engagement was second only to divorce.

Once safely inside the departure terminal, Natalie's thoughts turned to other things. This was the real beginning of her self-imposed exile. Papa wanted Natalie to regard this trip as a happy farewell and the greatest adventure of her life. This was not mere rhetoric. Papa believed with all his heart and soul that each life was a new beginning of hope. He viewed every child as a new opportunity to improve the world. Papa would emphasize to Natalie that her decision to keep her baby was the absolute right thing to do. As Natalie, Mama, and Papa waited to board, very little was said.

Mama was the social torchbearer of the family. Papa could be charming when he had to be, but he greatly preferred his own silence.

Papa was anxious about the long flight ahead of them. He dreaded the prospect of using the airplane restroom and did everything he could to avoid it. Strategically, Natalie was to sit in the window seat and Mama in the middle. This ensured that if Natalie was chatty, it would be Mama conversing and not him. Also, being on the end gave Papa quick access to the aisle. He knew that he would need to make at least one pit stop, even if he didn't take a sip of water. This he knew from the last four years of living with the consequences of treatment for prostate cancer. Papa seems to be cancer free now, but he never misses an opportunity to remind us of his mortality. He says he is preparing us. I think he enjoys the sympathy and attention.

As hard as he tried, Papa was not able to sleep on the plane. He might have made it to a quasi-sleep, but his mind was attuned to every weird noise and the possibility of a terrorist attack. It was good that this was an uneventful flight. Knowing Papa as I do, I'm sure he would have put his white knuckles to use at the first sign of a threat.

Natalie and Mama talked for a while during the beginning of the flight. Mostly Mama asked Natalie about how her parents were doing and plans for the future. Mama tried to avoid a heavy discussion about Natalie's pregnancy and Natalie's boyfriend. Mama was always very pleasant and Natalie spoke to Mama with kindness and respect. It wasn't too long before both women fell asleep. Their biological clocks were approaching their normal bedtime and the drone of the jet engines coupled with the darkened cabin made sleep easy for everyone – except Papa, of course. Papa took this opportunity, about halfway into the flight, to use the vacant restroom. He had watched intently, and no one had used it for a while.

Papa tried to read but could never seem to concentrate on the words that seemed to be glued to the page as he tried to advance to the next sentence. He mostly pretended to be asleep, instead watching the in-flight tracker. As long as the plane seemed to be going forward, he felt somewhat reassured. He watched the plane follow the Canadian coast, passing Nova Scotia and then Prince Edward Island on to the northern Atlantic Ocean. This unsettled him, knowing there was only a great expanse of water below. He rationalized that this plane was over 37,000 feet high. Shit, that's over seven miles. The fall would kill them instantly and painlessly. But the time getting to the ocean would be an eternity. Papa did not want to think about this. He desperately tried once more to fall asleep, but anyone who bothered to look would see that Papa's hands were tightly clutching the armrests. His mind told him that holding on tight would not help if the plane descended rapidly, but the anxiety portion of his brain trumped the sensible part.

When the powerful Boeing jet engines finally slowed to a stop and the plane was at the gate, Papa was able to relax. "Let's go," Papa bellowed. "Hurry, we need to find the next gate and board the plane for Sicily."

Natalie was amused by the banter between the Santos. It was quite a departure from the way her parents spoke to each other. There was very little criticism or sarcasm exchanged between her parents. They would have arguments, as most couples do, but they were usually of a substantive nature. Natalie felt the raillery between Papa and Mama was somewhat frivolous and more a matter of normal discourse cultivated over many years. Papa was trying hard not to annoy Mama, but he could not seem to help it. Having watched them over the years, I believe he is trying to be more considerate and truly does it teasingly and not maliciously. That doesn't much matter to Mama, though, and depending on her mood she can become exasperated all the way to irate.

Papa was able to understand most of what was said as they navigated the airport. Italian was his first language, but it was his uneducated parents' southern Italian dialectic brand. Anyway, there are always enough attendants who are able to speak English. Europeans have a much greater propensity and mastery of foreign languages than Americans, probably due to the proximity of other countries with different languages. European schools made English readily available since it was the language of the airways, tourism, and diplomacy. Americans are either too lazy or too vain to try speaking a foreign language. In Papa's day, most immigrants abandoned their native tongue and many customs to become fully Americanized. By the time they hit the second generation, most of the Old Country was totally lost. It is that way for me. I wish I was able to speak Italian or any other language, but only English was spoken at home.

The remaining leg of the trip was a short ninety-minute jaunt. Papa had been keeping a secret from both Natalie and Mama. Papa was only planning to stay in Scordia with his cousin Rocco for about three days. Papa figured any more than that would drive everyone nuts, and you do not want to make people uncomfortable in Sicily. Papa made plans to rent a car and drive the length of Italy, ending in Milan. From there, he had plane tickets for the return flight. This would be Papa's one and only opportunity to visit the land of his ancestors and he was not about to spend two weeks in Scordia. It's not that this part of Italy wasn't beautiful, but he had an entire country to see.

Their Sunday departure ended in a Monday arrival. Rocco was there to meet Papa, Mama, and Natalie. Rocco knew that he was only going to be put out for a few days. I'm certain this fact greatly improved his disposition. Most people can tolerate a disruption in their daily routine if they know it will only last three days. Pictures of Uncle Rocco revealed that he had a round face and wore medium-framed wire eyeglasses. His face had a ruddy complexion, which surprised me, considering the amount of sunshine to which he was exposed. He was about eight years younger than Papa, but I wouldn't have guessed that if I didn't already know. Rocco's hair was almost all white but covered his head completely in a thin sort of way. Papa actually looked younger than his sixty-five years would indicate. He still had a mixture of dark brown and gray hair. The dark brown still maintained a slight advantage, but the gray was certainly catching up.

Rocco's English was not as good as Papa's Italian, but Rocco attempted speaking English for Natalie's benefit. Mama could mostly understand Italian, though her years of disuse made speaking the language challenging. Rocco's two sons were both married and living in Italy. One lived in Palermo and the other lived on the main part of the big boot in Salerno. Rocco and his wife, Maria, were left with a modest house with two empty bedrooms. Maria made these rooms suitable for guests. This meant moving things around a little, but she kept her computer and printer in the larger bedroom. Natalie stayed in the smaller bedroom that was still of sufficient size to suit her needs. The home was a two-story, box-like dwelling with a stucco exterior.

Rainbow-colored pastels splashed the houses, accentuated by vibrant landscapes, making the vicinity quite picturesque.

Maria still preserved vestiges of her younger days. She was now in her mid-fifties but maintained a bronzed complexion and dark hair. She was apparently a petite woman, although the years may have added a few pounds around her hips. Still, Maria was quite an attractive woman and very pleasant. Maria's English was slightly better than her husband's, thanks to the many American movies she'd watched and to her having been a good student in English class forty years ago.

It was now late afternoon and the travelers were content to relax for their first evening. Any sightseeing could wait until the next day. Both Rocco and Maria took time off from work to serve as tour guides for their American relatives. In the finest Italian tradition, Maria fed her guests beyond the needs of human consumption. They started with *capunata*, an eggplant dish consisting of a cooked vegetable salad. Numerous ingredients, including olives, carrots, green peppers, and raisins, were evident. Next was the rigatoni with meat sauce. Papa always called sauce "gravy" since that's what it was called growing up. The tinge of sweet tomato sauce brought memories from fifty years hence flooding back. If that wasn't enough, Maria brought out a platter of roast beef. Natalie did not want to appear rude, but she was already stuffed, not expecting the meat course. She managed two thin slices of the succulent beef marinated in its own juices. After feasting, they all retired to the small outdoor patio for espresso and dessert. The choices were *frutta Martorana, cannolo Siciliano,* and *granita.*

"*Basta*! Enough already," said Mama. "I am going to explode! Maria, you went too far, but we thank you sincerely. Everything was *delizioso.* Domani, you will take us to your favorite *ristorante* and it will be our turn to treat you."

"Grazie," said Rocco. "You are our guests and it is *non necessario.*"

"Nonsense," said Papa. "I only hope we can recover by tomorrow. We may not be able to *mangiare* for weeks after this meal."

Mama insisted on helping Maria clear and wash the dishes. Mama couldn't help thinking how this part of the meal was just like being home.

Natalie excused herself to call her parents, letting them know she had safely arrived. She told them she had only arrived a short time ago and was safely in her dorm. She stated that she did not yet have a lot to tell them, but she would call in a few days. She also texted Jeremy to let him know she had arrived and would call him tomorrow night about five o'clock Boston time. After her obligatory arrival notices, Natalie said good night and thanked Maria and Rocco with a hug. The older folks spent a half hour talking about how *bellissimo* Natalie was. Both Rocco and Maria knew the full circumstances of Papa's visit and were very supportive of their predicament. Papa said the trip and the dinner had knocked him out, too. Both Mama and he retired for the evening.

Tuesday morning, everyone drove to Catania. Catania is the largest city on the east coast of Sicily, about a forty-five minute drive from Rocco's house. Scordia was pleasant enough, but for visitors Catania had much more to offer. Papa, Mama, and Natalie at least had to stick their toes in the Ionian Sea. Rocco suggested that if they wanted to see the water, they should visit the Playa of Catania. The golden sandy shore and warm sea air made this a popular attraction for both Sicilians and tourists.

They arrived about eleven in the morning. Papa rented some umbrellas and chairs and they all soaked in the sunshine. They had only a few days to spend in Sicily, and there was too much to see in such a short time.

Papa hated the beach. He knew that he was in the minority in this regard. For Mama and Natalie's sake, he made the supreme sacrifice of going there without even complaining. Well, there was not too much complaining and only Mama picked up on his demeanor.

Natalie was really a good sport. Here she was, the guest of total strangers in a foreign country, chaperoned by Papa and Mama who, until a short time ago, had been unknown to her. She traveled thousands of miles to give credence to some story concocted by this man to whom she had entrusted her life. And yet, it really didn't seem all that weird to her. Natalie was family by virtue of the fact she was carrying Papa's grandchild. Natalie truly felt the caring and loving vibes emanating from these people who treated her with warm tenderness. She was understandably reserved but enjoyed the warm waters of Catania. She had a terrific frame of mind, considering her situation.

Natalie was not expecting to have an exciting time with four much-older companions. Where Natalie might want to see a bit of nightlife, Papa's day was basically over at dinnertime. Where Papa might like to see historical sites, Natalie would be more interested in the amusement park area in Catania. Natalie resigned herself to the idea that her indiscretion had cost her seven months of her life, to be spent as a human incubator for someone else's child. That whole deliberation between life and ending the pregnancy was waged and life won. Natalie's penance was banishment from home in an isolated albeit loving hermitage, therefore she was determined to enjoy Sicily, whatever the venue might be.

After about three hours on the beach, Papa suggested that everyone freshen up and head out for lunch. By this time it was slightly after two o'clock. Rocco suggested La Siciliana on Viale Marco Polo. Papa reminded Rocco and Maria that this was his treat. He wanted to avoid any embarrassment when it was time to pay the check. They all settled on the house specialty based on Rocco's recommendation. They ordered risotto with cuttlefish ink and fresh ricotta cheese. They all shared the *sarde a beccafico* or stuffed sardines and *calamari ripieni alla griglia.* Natalie enjoyed all of the seafood delicacies, but Rocco waited until they were all finished to tell Natalie she had eaten squid. Natalie was unaffected and said, "I need to look for this in Boston."

Papa was already starting to wind down, but they still had lots of sunlight left, even if Papa's candle was starting to burn out.

Rocco said, "I think a visit to Mt. Etna might be too much for a pregnant lady. We will take a look at the volcano in the car. It is so big to miss," said Rocco.

"That's fine," said Natalie, "but let's look around this city. There are beautiful churches, shops, and gardens. Let's take a walking tour."

Rocco started everyone on the Via dei Crociferi, an avenue that shows off eighteenth-century Baroque architurecture, where there is a never-ending, opulent line of religious buildings such as the Church of San Benedetto and the Church of the Jesuits and the Church of San Giuliano. In the heart of Catania lies the Piazza Duomo. The elephant stands as the symbol of the city. The city's cathedral with the Chapel of Sant'Agata looks out onto this square, where precious treasures are kept. There is also the Palazzo degli Elefanti, which is the city hall. Catania's most famous street, Via Etnea, starts from Piazza Duomo, where there are splendid Baroque buildings with lava dust façades and a multitude of shops and confectioners. Natalie made certain to take tons of pictures, especially the churches and Bellini Gardens. This would be proof positive that she was in Sicily enjoying her brief time away from the clinic she was supposedly serving.

After too much gelato and candy, everyone agreed to start back for Scordia. The time was approaching six o'clock. It did not take long for Natalie to realize that if you are a tourist in Italy, be prepared to do a lot of eating, a lot of walking, and a lot of singing. There was no shortage of Italian singers on the streets and in the restaurants. Natalie had to admit the first day in Italy was fun.

Natalie called Jeremy as promised at 11 o'clock.

"Jeremy, can you hear me OK?"

"Hello, baby. I hear you fine. Did you start saving the world yet?"

"No, not yet. My first day will be tomorrow. Today, another one of the girls and I did some sightseeing in Catania. Sicily is really colorful, with good food and nice weather. What can I really say after only one day?"

"Well, I'm glad at least you had this opportunity to see some things. Hopefully you will have other chances."

Natalie was more interested in what Jeremy was doing. She figured since she just left that he would try to act like a good boy for at least a while. "Do you miss me yet?" asked Natalie.

Jeremy replied instantly, "As if I wasn't going to miss you after you blew me away with your surprise at the Ritz-Carlton! How could you do that to me? I'm going to have to fly out to Sicily to see you now. I don't think I'll be able to last six or seven months. Maybe I can swing a trip by early summer."

"No! You can't do that." Natalie hadn't figured on this at all. "The trip here is very expensive and the lodging will cost a fortune. Anyway, my schedule is so crazy I never know when I will be pressed for duty. Please save your money for more important things like a honeymoon." Natalie and Jeremy always talked about their future and marriage without making the engagement official. Natalie wondered why Jeremy never made that commitment.

"Natalie, making love to you was the most beautiful sensual intimacy I will ever experience. Being with the one you truly love can only intensify this kind of feeling. Natalie, I hope you know that you are the only woman for me. I will wait, but it won't be easy."

"Jeremy, you surely know I always loved you. That's why it hurt me so much when you couldn't wait for my love. There's always so much to say, but this is costing way too much. What will you do tonight?"

"I worked all day and I'm tired. I'll probably fall asleep in front of the television watching the Sox."

"I'd better go, Jeremy. Goodnight, and remember, I love you. When I return, I'll never leave you again." This is truly what Natalie believed and hoped. She wished that Jeremy had not destroyed the trust she had in him.

"Natalie, you can never love me as much as I love you. Everything I do in the next few months will be to prepare for our future together. When you return, we will make that official. Good night, my angel."

That was the closest thing to a proposal Natalie had heard. It was like the promise of a proposal. Natalie was satisfied with that. A long-distance engagement to Jeremy might be too painful for Natalie under the circumstances. She was dealing with her pregnancy but even more with her trust issue.

"I'll call you in a few days, Jeremy. I may call on the weekend so I won't have to call so late. I may be too exhausted to stay up late. I'll know more after a few days at the clinic. Good night."

Natalie was first to hang up. She thought back to the nights when she and Jeremy would stay on the phone for hours, neither one wanting to be the first one to hang up. It seemed silly now, but love makes you do these things. Natalie was not able to play that game from Sicily. She hoped the nagging feeling she had about Jeremy only lingered because of what he did to her this winter. She knew that she had to rebuild her faith in Jeremy if they were ever going to make it. Natalie decided for her own peace of mind that she would have to trust Jeremy. However, she remembered what her government professor said about President Reagan when dealing with the Soviets: he would trust but verify. Natalie always felt that was a prudent policy. Natalie decided to use her personal spy to do the same thing. She called Regina.

"Hello, Regina," said Natalie in greeting. "We all arrived safely and I already had my first day of sightseeing in Catania. How are you?"

"The same as when you saw me two days ago. I checked your flight online and know you arrived safely. Did you think I could relax until I knew you had landed? I suspect there is something else on your mind for you to call me so soon."

"That's the problem right there, Regina. You know me too damn well," Natalie replied with a laugh. "OK then, I just got off the phone with Jeremy. I never told you this, Regina, but the night before we left I screwed the hell out of him."

"Natalie, you never cease to amaze me. I suppose you thought it would hold him until you returned," surmised Regina.

"Something like that, Regina. I also felt, what the heck am I saving myself for now? You know I always wanted to be with Jeremy."

"Was it what you expected?" asked Regina.

"Regina, that night was the closest I believe I will ever get to heaven without dying. It was absolutely perfect." Natalie gave Regina the entire experience vicariously. By the time Natalie finished, Regina was ready to jump the first man she saw.

"Wow," said Regina. "Now do you see what I've been telling you for the last umpteen months?"

"That was never the thing. You know that, Regina. It was always the virginity issue. Now, it doesn't matter about that. I guess I better stop beating around the bush. Would you object to checking on Jeremy's whereabouts every once in a while? I hate to put you in this position, but Jeremy basically told me that we would be engaged when I returned. I have the same gnawing distress. If he cheated on me when I was home, what's to stop him while I'm away? If he cheats while I'm away, will he cheat on me after we are married? What is it with me, Regina? Am I making too big a deal about this faithfulness thing? Maybe we should all be screwing everyone else and not worrying about it so much."

"That's bullshit and you know it, Natalie – especially for you. You could never condone that kind of relationship, much less fuck someone else and go home to Jeremy the next instant. Let's stop kidding ourselves about that. That's just not you. Hell, even I wouldn't want that kind of serious relationship, much less that kind of marriage. And I've had a pretty swinging time, if I do say so myself."

"Like I said, you know me too well. I could never really have the kind of love I need with Jeremy knowing I was not enough to keep him faithful."

"Don't worry, Natalie. I will be your own private CIA. I almost look forward to it. I always believed Jeremy was too fake or too into himself or something. For your sake, I truly hope he proves me wrong."

Natalie replied, "Not nearly as much as I do, Regina. Thank you for always being there for me. I will call back again by next week. Stay happy."

After her two phone calls, it was nearly midnight in Sicily. Natalie had enjoyed a long but wonderful day in Catania and sleep crept upon her, making her head heavy and her eyelids like falling iron curtains. She fell asleep in minutes.

The next morning, Wednesday, everyone awoke fresh and cheery. Rocco was happy knowing that he only had to entertain his American cousins for two more days. Natalie was still in the dark about Papa's plan to tour Italy. Natalie wondered how they would spend the next two weeks. She could not imagine sightseeing every day. Also, she was not sure about Rocco's having to go back to work. She knew Rocco had some time off, but how long?

Natalie asked, "Rocco, when do you have to get back to work?"

Papa interrupted. "Natalie, Mama and I decided to make a slight change of plans. We are only staying here today and tomorrow. Thursday morning we are leaving for a trip to Amalfi, Rome, Verona, Venice, and then finally Milan. Our flight back to Boston is scheduled for the Tuesday after next."

Natalie was inwardly pleased and excited about this surprise news. She tried not to show her elation, not wanting to hurt the feelings of her hosts. They had been very kind and welcoming and did not deserve any indignity.

"That's wonderful news," said Natalie. "But I will be very sad to leave Uncle Rocco and Aunt Maria after so short a stay."

Rocco and Maria were gratified hearing Natalie's words. Rocco said, "We too will be sad. Italy is a big country and there is lots to see. How can you come to Italy and not see Rome and Venice? I understand Papa wants to show you thanks for what you do. I am happy you feel good here. What do you want to do today? I think Palermo too far to go with short time."

"Rocco, would you mind taking us to Mineo?" asked Natalie. "I need to at least see the place where I'm telling everyone I'm working. Maybe I will be able to get a feel for the place. I could even talk to some doctors and nurses. Who knows? Maybe I will really want to work here some day."

Natalie said this not really believing she would work anywhere else but in the Boston area. She was a Bostonian through and through and could not imagine living anywhere else.

They packed the car and headed for Mineo. Although this wasn't a place that Rocco would choose for sightseeing, he understood Natalie's desire to know something about the town. It was only a short drive from Rocco's house and he had been there many times.

Natalie insisted that she be left to explore the facilities alone to get a feel for the mission she would have supposedly experienced. She didn't want to bore the others with her undertaking. Papa was not at all comfortable leaving Natalie alone. As a compromise, Maria volunteered to stay with her, mostly to interpret. Natalie happily agreed, knowing she would need an interpreter and Maria was the best one for the job. Maria had also been to Mineo many times and had nothing new to see except this facility.

Surprisingly, Natalie was given access to the buildings and grounds, simply because of her expressed interest as a nurse to volunteer in assisting the international support for these victims. Natalie was thoroughly screened, showing her passport and her nurse's pin. Neither Natalie nor Maria were seen as threats and they were allowed to speak to the medical staff. Natalie quickly learned that Mineo served as a refugee way station for displaced people from the fighting in northern Africa, mostly housing those Libyan victims from the civil war there. Other refugees were from Eritrea, Somalia, Sudan, and Nigeria. The Italian government faced greater challenges than they had expected in offering refuge. The medical staff treated mainly mental health issues, victims of gas poisoning, and victims of torture and sexual abuse. In addition to these problems, the refugees were mostly idle, without any constructive outlet for their own boredom. The authorities found themselves sitting on a powder keg of refugees who had been penned up for months.

Between Maria and herself, Natalie was able to construct a very clear picture of the situation, at least the outward appearance. The facility itself reminded her of World War II military prison camps she had seen in movies, with barrack huts and barbed-wire fences. She was not surprised to learn about riots in the facility.

Natalie was also able to speak to some of the refugees. One person complained that all he did since he arrived in Mineo was walk in circles. He felt like a prisoner. For two months he had been told that he would be released and get his papers, but nothing happened. Time passed and he received no word about his family. He worried about their survival, stuck in Nigeria without him. He said he had worried so much he was unable to sleep or eat.

Another survivor had escaped by boat from Libya. He told them this was his only means of eluding death. He was happy and grateful that Italy had received him from his narrow escape from dying. "Italy welcomed me with open arms and I felt alive again. Now, though, every day is the same. We have no access to news; we have nothing to keep us busy. I wonder why I am alive. If I die, no one will cry. And if I live, I am the only one who will care."

Natalie had her eyes opened in a few short hours. The problems went far beyond the physical treatments she had viewed as the reason for medical personnel's gifts of time and skills. To be sure, there were plenty of opportunities to treat the bodily trauma evident in these people, but the human condition was more far-reaching than she could have ever imagined. She was not sure that she herself had the dedication and unselfishness necessary to do this kind of work. She was thankful to have this opportunity to see firsthand what these dedicated doctors, nurses, and support staff do. She knew that this would be an experience she would never forget. She and Maria spoke to each other with their eyes and by holding hands and hugging each other. Very little was said. Very little could be said without sounding patronizing. There but by the grace of God go I.

Maria called Rocco and he returned to pick up the ladies. When questioned by Papa about the experience, Natalie gave a very brief, courteous response. Papa could tell by looking at Mama that he should not press the issue. Maria told them that these people were mostly from northern Africa and were living a day-to-day existence. "These refugees made the journey by boat," she said. "At least they are safe and I only hope they will be able to find the strength to begin again. Our government is trying to help them."

It was mid-afternoon and everyone was hungry. Rocco knew that there was not that much to see in Mineo. The Church of Sant'Agrippina was the main tourist attraction of the small town. The church was dedicated to the patron saint of the village and rebuilt toward the end of the seventeenth century, since an earthquake damaged its structure in 1693.

I laugh to think about Papa touring Italy and having to visit all these churches. It's the only time he steps inside a house of God, and the scenario is always the same. The women explore every statue and stained glass window, examining each carving, studying the texture of the wood and masonry. Papa takes a quick walk around and is outside in five minutes, waiting for the women to finish. Invariably, Mama asks Papa his opinion on the aesthetic beauty of the church and why he left so quickly. Papa always has the same answer: "If you've seen one old church, you've seen them all." I believe Papa had a secret fear of being in the church too long. Just in case he was wrong about this whole savior notion, he did not want to invite the ire of the Almighty.

Rocco took everyone to a restaurant on the Piazza dei Vespri. I will spare you the cuisine. Papa's obsession seems to be peppered with many sojourns of obligatory dinners and stopovers at old churches, piazzas, public houses, museums, etc. Papa would rather take a picture and study the site by reading about it on the Internet. He's glad to experience the ambiance and flavor of the places he visits because he knows that feelings are really the only things he will remember. The details of what things looked like, the paintings or sculptures, all are soon faded memories. Papa is forever asking Mama where they were when they saw one thing or another. I hate to say this, but I think Papa basically looks at his whole life as a journey ending in death without any possibility of everlasting life. This attitude prevents him from experiencing the highs and lows of life. Papa lives in constant fear that something bad will happen to those he loves. As long as Mama and his two children are safe and happy, Papa is truly a contented man. He has his own little pleasures to keep him satisfied and most people accept this and leave him alone. Papa is a selfish man by not sharing himself with others, but at his advancing age he chooses to be comfortable over being magnanimous. And yet, if you truly knew Papa, you would know he is a bighearted man in his own reticent way.

The short drive back to Rocco's home lacked a great deal of conversation. Natalie spent the time reflecting on what she had seen. She went into nursing to help people but also to have the skills necessary to find work readily. She rationalized that maybe someday she would be prepared to work at a facility like Mineo, but not now. Papa was thinking mostly about Natalie and how to keep her positive and upbeat. He sensed this trip to Mineo was a setback. Mama was Mama. She enjoyed the new sites in Mineo. She was spared the despair of the refugee camp. Mama is the kind of person who truly only needs family with her and being around people. The fact that Mineo was just a small Sicilian town did not matter to her whatsoever. Being with Papa on this trip was a treat for Mama. She has lived with him for over forty years and still enjoys his company. At home she is more alone with Papa in the house than she is by herself somewhere else.

Rocco said, "OK, one more day. Where we go tomorrow?"

"I have a lot to do tomorrow, Rocco. I need to book my hotels online, so I need to plan how far to travel each night and how long to stay in each place. I also need to rent a car for our trip and plan the rest of our holiday. So far, the only thing I've done is book our flight back home from Milan. Do you think I'll have trouble renting a car in Scordia?"

"Oh, si," answered Rocco. "I take you back a *aereporto domani.* You get car in Catania."

"Grazie, Rocco. I should have rented a car right away to spare you another trip to the airport. But could we get the car tonight so we can leave in the morning? I was hoping to get an early start for our trip."

"She's OK," said Rocco. "*Non è un grosso problema.*"

After they'd enjoyed Maria's light dinner of pasta and vegetables, Rocco drove Papa back to the airport to pick up his rental. When Papa saw his choices in rental cars, he was very upset. Most of Papa's choices were European or Japanese cars. Papa would not be found dead driving a "foreign" car, even though he was now in a foreign country. One of Papa's obsessions is buying American goods whenever feasible, but he is not wealthy enough to indulge his own principles. Sometimes he realizes that he must compromise his values when there is a substantial amount of money at stake. This is why most of Papa's clothing is made in China or Mexico or some other Asian or Latin American country. He hates supporting these companies that exploit child workers and offer ridiculous salaries to all workers, perpetuating their low standard of living. However, when he tries to buy an American-made shirt or trousers, he finds the price is out of sight. He wishes the government would increase the tariffs on all foreign goods so that Americans could compete with these unfair labor practices. Unfortunately, that would make everything we buy too expensive for most American consumers. So he settles. He buys American when he can and accepts the fact he must depend on many foreign-made products. But in cars, he always buys American. Even when the American cars where considered inferior to Japanese models, he would never buy a Toyota or Honda. It kills him to think that Deming, an American, taught Japan how to produce better cars than Americans. He feels the tide has turned and the American car companies are now respectable again.

However, his dilemma at the Italian airport was whether to rent a Fiat Panda for 657 Euros or a Ford Galaxy SUV for 1,952 Euros. The choice was not ideal, considering Papa's innate thriftiness. He rationalized that at least Fiat was Italian made and maybe some of his relatives would benefit from his purchase. Having to drive a five-speed standard transmission car after many years of driving an automatic would be challenging. Papa grew up in the sixties and seventies only driving a three-speed stick shift on the column, but he hoped that working the clutch would be like riding a bicycle. Papa rented the burgundy Fiat Panda 1.2. Rocco complimented Papa on his choice.

Papa laments that most American manufacturing has gone overseas because the corporate types are trying to make as much money for their investors as possible. Papa is not savvy in business, and that's putting it mildly. He foolishly believes that buying American products would mean more Americans are employed and therefore more Americans would have money to buy more American products. He doesn't understand economics and the effect labor costs have on the price of goods, not to mention the onerous tax structure to which corporate America is subjected. He has this prehistoric notion that what's good for Americans is good for America. He feels that if corporate America were not so damn greedy, America would ultimately benefit like in the good old fifties and sixties before the Kennedy assassination changed America forever. I understand that he is a misguided liberal from Massachusetts and I can only forgive his naïveté. After all, he is my loving father and treats me like a son. Thank God I was not brainwashed by his outlook on America First.

While Papa was out with Rocco, Natalie tried to watch television, but she couldn't understand what was happening. Though Maria explained what was said, it wasn't like the television Natalie typically watched, which was mostly reality shows and MTV. Mama asked Natalie if she wanted to go for a walk. Natalie agreed, if only to get away from the TV. She wished she had learned some Italian before the trip. Mama was sensitive to Natalie's plight and always tried to treat her with compassion. This was no stretch, since Mama was the most compassionate person on the planet. Mama told me later that it was Natalie who first broached the subject of me. I guess that since Natalie was carrying my baby, it was natural for her to be curious.

"Tell me about Ricky," Natalie requested.

"My Ricky?" answered a shocked Mama.

"Of course," replied Natalie.

Mama paused briefly before complying. Where would she start? The best thing to do, she thought, was speak from her heart.

"Well, Natalie, I think it is fair to say I may have indulged Ricky a little too much. Still, I believe he is not spoiled and a very good man. As a child, I would take him everywhere with me. I had to if I ever wanted to leave the house. We weren't real big on spending money on babysitters. I took him shopping, to friends, to the movies, to restaurants – we both loved going to the Chinese restaurant. When I was home, Ricky was outside. If it were summer, I would hardly ever see him. He would be out playing baseball mostly. In the winter, he would always find things to do. He is a very inquisitive boy. Maybe that's why he became a writer. Ricky has a master's degree in public relations. He does well but is looking to improve his position now that the economy is doing better."

"What about his girlfriends? Why did he never marry?" asked Natalie.

"He has had several girlfriends that I know about. At least three have been for a year or more. I know because I have met all of them and they have been to the house on numerous occasions. I don't think Ricky ever found the girl he wanted to spend his whole life with. It's too bad that you are going to be married," continued Mama, since Natalie brought up the subject. "Although he has never directly spoken to me about this, he did confide in his father. Papa has no problem sharing Ricky's confidential thoughts with me. He knows that I can keep a secret. Anyway, Ricky is really crazy over you. He told Papa that you were the most beautiful woman he ever saw. I can see that he is right."

Natalie couldn't help blushing a bit at this remark. "Believe me, Mama, Ricky has made no secret about his attraction to me. In fact, his behavior bordered on stalking."

"I can understand that, but it also surprises me. Another thing about

Ricky is his shyness. Two of his three girlfriends actually pursued Ricky. He is too afraid to ask girls out for fear of rejection. I think now at twenty-eight years old he is finally growing out of this fear. Please do not worry about Ricky. He is totally safe and harmless. A mother knows. It's only that you are probably the first woman that made Ricky's heart flutter. Look, Ricky told his father about how you got in this situation. I am not at all proud of the way he took advantage of your condition and for that I am sorry. I am only glad that you are doing the right thing by keeping this baby. As the years go by, you will continue to be in the baby's life, if that's what you want. And I know Ricky will be a very active 'uncle.' If your paths cross, please try to forgive Ricky for being a venal man. He really is enamored with you and will just need to learn to get over it. After you are married and move on, then Ricky will get the hint."

"Thank you, Mama. I'm glad you told me these things. I don't hate Ricky. Actually, Ricky is very handsome and the attention is flattering. The predicament he placed me in, however, is life changing. I have to accept some if not all of the responsibility. I let this happen to me through my own bad judgment and behavior. But I blame him, too. My mother says everything always happens for a reason. I never believed that before, but we make our own choices and must live with them."

Mama smiled at Natalie as they continued walking. Mama really liked Natalie. I have already told you how much Papa liked her. It would be very hard to lose Natalie when this is over.

Thursday morning on the first week of Papa's Italian vacation marked the beginning of the adventure. Papa was up at five a.m. and would have been on his way except for the fact that Mama and Natalie were still asleep. He told Natalie and Mama that they should leave very early but never really gave an exact time.

Papa would never wake Mama. He learned over the years that Mama was an angry bear when forced to hurry. So instead, he made a point of being a bit loud when getting ready. He washed up by returning to the hall bathroom five times, each time closing the bedroom door louder than usual. He packed his clothes hurriedly, banged the suitcases against the floor, and slammed the car doors when packing the Fiat.

Fortunately, Mama had packed the day before and only needed to put on the clothes she kept out for the trip, stuffing her nightclothes back in the suitcase. After an hour of banging suitcases and slamming doors, everyone was basically aroused from their slumber. It took another hour for Mama and Natalie to make an appearance. Rocco and Maria were early risers since Rocco was conditioned to start getting ready for work about 5:30. Maria was preparing a breakfast of sliced cured ham with a plain pastry, coffee, and fruit. Rocco was probably in his bedroom, quietly singing and dancing, throwing his arms up wildly and snapping his fingers with the knowledge that his guests would be gone in about an hour.

They all sat around the breakfast table. Everyone would say how wonderful it was to have met each other. Papa thanked his Italian cousin and made the usual obligatory invitation that he must take a trip to America and stay with them as their guests. Rocco said he hoped that he would be able to do that. Maria really wanted to take that trip but knew her husband well enough not to make an actual commitment. Natalie, looking beautiful for the car trip, was very gracious and thanked Rocco and Maria profusely.

By 8:30, they were out the door and ready to drive. The first stop would be Amalfi, after about a seven-hour trip of straight driving. Papa, ever the calculator, figured to himself that with stopovers and road conditions, it might be closer to nine hours. Papa always planned for the worst case. He was hoping to be in Amalfi by late afternoon with plenty of sunlight left to enjoy their first day on the road.

The first delay came in taking the ferry from Messina to Villa San Giovanni. Fortunately, the ferries departed about every twenty minutes, so the delay was only a short one. Mama hated going over water and Papa had to reassure her that the 2003 Staten Island ferry disaster was a fluke and an almost non-existent occurrence. He told Mama to enjoy the fresh air and the view as they made the short crossing. Papa knew there was actually a direct ferry from Messina to Salerno that made the trip in about seven and a half hours but figured having to comfort Mama for over seven hours would be more than his patience and nerves could handle. In addition, Papa was not much of a sailor himself, prone to motion sickness even when he sat in the back seat of a car. As it happened, they stayed in their car for the crossing and there was no view, unless you counted the trucks and other cars on the ferry. In a short twenty minutes, everyone was on the southern part of the Italian mainland. Getting off the ferry took as long as the trip. Fortunately, Papa was an excellent edger when it came to merging into one lane. This is a skill he had mastered over the years of driving in Boston traffic.

Chapter Seven

Immortality

Papa had been on his best behavior for quite some time, as he was in the presence of Natalie. This was a most unnatural state for Papa and it was just a matter of time before he became comfortable enough to be himself again. I believe Natalie got a kick out of the things Papa would say because they were so unlike the stoic and reserved manner in which her own father conducted himself.

"Well, Mama, we finally made it to Italy. Soon we will be back home to where my own sweet mother started out. I will spare you the honor of meeting any more of my relatives."

"It's hard to believe anyone would even want to leave this country," commented Natalie. "It's so beautiful."

"Yes, it is," Papa agreed. "Unfortunately, the beauty wasn't enough to overcome the hardships of life in southern Italy." Papa switched to his paternal lecture mode and continued. "Northerners dominated the government. Southerners were hurt by high taxes and high protective tariffs on northern industrial goods. Southerners also had much less land to cultivate, and the land they did have was plagued with soil erosion and deforestation. Plus, they lacked the coal and iron ore needed by industry. It was a little like America's conflict between northern and southern states, minus the slavery issue, except that southern Italians chose flight over fight.

"Natural disasters also rocked southern Italy during the early twentieth century," he continued. "Mount Vesuvius erupted and buried a town near Naples, then Mount Etna erupted. In 1908, an earthquake and tidal wave swept through the Strait of Messina right here where we took this ferry."

Papa glanced over at Mama, whose eyes had suddenly gotten large. "I neglected to tell you this, Mama, because I knew you would swear that the next one was coming today."

Natalie and Mama smiled, and Papa continued his lecture. "More than 100,000 people died in the city of Messina alone. All these things contributed to the people leaving for America, Argentina, and Australia.

After the second World War, lots of these people left for Canada to seek a better life, fleeing the war's devastation."

Mama said, "Papa, you are better than a history book."

"Natalie," asked Papa, "do you believe in fate?"

"I believe in God and I believe that God works in mysterious ways," Natalie responded. "To me, that's the same thing as fate."

"You are so right, Natalie. I believe that your coming into our lives just now is fate. Your father being Italian is fate. Our trip of a lifetime coming to Italy is fate. Mama and I would not have made this trip without your having met Ricky. Ricky saw you leave that clinic. Was that not fate? You were meant to be in our lives."

Papa looked through the rearview mirror to see Natalie's facial expression. He could tell she wanted to argue this whole fate theory but was too respectful or too polite to debate the question. Papa quickly changed the subject.

"Mama, aren't you glad we came here before we die?"

"Before we die, before we die, Mama retorted. "You've had us dying for the last twenty years now!"

"You know, Mama, that one day I will be right."

Papa could see Natalie suppressing a giggle. The corners of her mouth and eyes were clearly going up.

"Well, I guess you're right, Papa. That's why I insist that we start getting some coverage when I have to live alone. I do not want to depend on our children to care for me in my old age when you're gone."

Papa said, "At our age, that insurance will cost a fortune. Anyway, when I die, I foresee that you will die, too. I expect you to practice *suttee* and throw yourself on my funeral pyre just as the faithful Indian women did before they were contaminated by the corrupt influence of the British government."

Natalie could not control herself. She burst out laughing.

"Natalie, please," said Mama, "you will only encourage him. And God knows he does not need much encouragement."

Papa checked the map. Taking the *autostrade* E45 to A3 would probably be the best route. Not knowing the roads, this was his best option. Even though Rocco's son lived near Salerno, Rocco did not suggest Papa's stopping to see him, and Papa was glad the subject did not come up. Both Rocco and Papa had had enough relative hospitality. Papa found the autostrade to be akin to racing on the Daytona 500. To keep up with traffic, Papa had to drive anywhere from eighty to ninety miles per hour, and that was not kilometers per hour. It did make getting to places a lot faster, as long as you lived to get there.

Amalfi was the most beautiful place Mama had ever seen. The homes and apartments displayed the typical soft pastel colors for which Italy is renowned. There were some deeper shades of reds and oranges, but all were very tasteful. The entire landscape was terraced, with one row of buildings above the next. Papa wondered who lived on top of the mountain. It is an interesting fact of human nature that the more powerful and wealthy you get, the higher up you live. This is true for penthouses, for the hills of Beverly in California, or wherever. Papa wondered about getting up there in the winter but realized that snow is not an issue in Amalfi. There is occasionally a dusting on the tops of the Lattari Mountains high above the Amalfi Coast, but it has no lingering effect. The last such dusting was three years previous.

Mama was especially impressed with the older Italian women, who would definitely fit into women's plus sizes off the Lane Bryant racks. Many of these women looked to be well into their fifties, sixties and seventies, yet they were bounding up the terraces like Olympic athletes. Papa said it made him proud to be an Italian, even if these women looked like Bruno Sammartino. These same Italian women almost all started out as the most beautiful women on the entire face of the Earth. Papa knows this to be a fact and he dismisses any bias on this subject.

He noticed that Italian women might drink alcohol but do not get drunk. It would be in poor taste for an Italian woman to be seen sloshed. Mama herself almost always had one drink each day. It was usually red wine, packed with antioxidants. More than one would tend to make Mama tipsy. Maybe if she lived in Amalfi, she could increase her tolerance for alcohol.

One of the notable attractions of Amalfi is an alcoholic drink known as limoncello. Lemons are grown here from February to October and possess a unique sweetness that results from a combination of the volcanic soil, year-round warm temperatures, and a perfect amount of rain.

Papa also noticed that in Amalfi, Italian women do not drink sodas. It is not ordered at dinner because it would not go with the food anyway. Also, it makes you burp, which is frowned upon. Italian women dress well, but they have to be comfortable. They gravitate to the classic rather than the adventurous look. The women wear little makeup to avoid projecting the wrong look. Papa noticed that Italian women like to talk too loud and sometimes inappropriately.

Italian women make good mothers. This is a result of the importance the culture puts on family. Unfortunately, the men are often seen pinching women's asses, only hoping for an invitation free from the commitment to marry. All this Papa and Mama observed on the first afternoon in Amalfi.

Natalie wanted to call her parents and Jeremy to blurt out how beautiful she found the Amalfi Coast. She had to settle for calling Regina. Natalie was glad that she had at least one friend with whom she was able to share her secret.

Papa promised everyone that on Saturday, they would take a tour of the Island of Capri. Mama had to overcome her fear of boats but was willing to risk it for a chance to see the island. All Papa could think about was the Frank Sinatra song "Isle of Capri" from his *Come Fly With Me* album.

As advertised, on Saturday morning, Natalie, Papa, and Mama took a boat to Capri. Papa drove to Sorrento and they boarded. Papa confessed to me later that he hated that trip. He was getting seasick from the short, choppy ride to the island. Surprisingly, being on water didn't terrify Mama. I already mentioned her fear of drowning. Mama would always seek the nearest life preserver. I often wondered how she would react if she ever needed to use one. Knowing Mama, she would be too polite to fight the crowd scrambling for the lifejackets. Mama was just made that way and we have come to love her for her compassion. I think that's why everyone looks out for her. I have absolutely no doubt that in the case of an emergency Papa would've fought any mob to secure lifejackets for Natalie and Mama. These are things that go through your mind, even though you know the trip's short voyage is routine.

Everyone was impressed as they wove around the tunnels of rock formations and the clear blue water approaching the main island. Papa overheard some tour guide say this had been the scene of a James Bond movie. From the pictures I saw, they did look familiar, but I can't remember which movie. I would guess that it was *Thunderball.* It was at this location the boat stopped and let people actually go for a swim in the water. I couldn't imagine this ever happening in the United States. With the hurried nature of the boat schedule trying to make a buck and the possibility of someone drowning, Americans would never take a risk like that.

Papa was happy when he finally touched dry land. He said his head was dizzy and it took him about an hour to settle down. Papa insisted that Natalie and Mama go on and tour the island without him. They arranged to meet at a nearby restaurant at one o'clock. Papa is just as happy being on his own. He loves to study people, especially in a foreign country. It took him about ten minutes to determine that Capri was a big letdown. It was beautiful, of course, but merely a paradise for rich people. The shops were plentiful, all out to make a Euro. The food was good, but it was basically the same kind of food you would find anywhere in southern Italy. There were more terraces to climb and more flowers to see. Papa concluded that if he had a few thousand dollars to blow, it would be nice to rent a villa here for about a week.

Mama and Natalie were really getting to know each other. Mama told me that it would not be hard to love Natalie and she understood why I was so crazy about her. Mama was cool and sophisticated. She never tried to build me up to Natalie. That would have been too obvious. Mama only talked about me when Natalie asked questions, as she did in Scordia. Mama told me that Natalie would take her arm or walk hand-in-hand with Mama as they took in the sights. Natalie decided to forego wearing shorts and put on a bright, flowing floral skirt with a clean, white satin blouse. I'm so glad I wasn't there to see her. It would have driven me crazy. The pictures alone made me forlorn. My only hope was that Jeremy would blow this chance he had and that Mama would work her innocent magic on Natalie, making her realize that she had an opportunity to marry into a wonderful, caring family.

At lunchtime, they met at the restaurant. All Papa could think about was the return boat ride, hoping that his lunch would stay where it belonged. They spent the rest of the afternoon together, shopping and sightseeing. Having only a few hours, they stayed close to the Capri Piazzetta. Papa is always more interested in history than in buying things he doesn't really need. He convinced Mama and Natalie to visit the Museum of Villa San Michele. From there, they were able to get sweeping views of the entire Bay of Naples. All in all, it was another nice day in which Papa and Mama bonded with Natalie. If Natalie had to endure so much time with strangers, it was at least nice being on the Isle of Capri.

The next day they were off to Roma. It was a beautiful Sunday morning and Mama had to go to church before leaving. Papa was very happy that Natalie was enthusiastic about attending Sunday mass. Papa didn't go to church and made no pretense on the subject. However, church was a sanctuary for Mama and he encouraged her attendance and tried to accommodate her going when they were out of town. He even occasionally attended mass himself, only to keep Mama company. Natalie and Mama attended mass at the Amalfi Cathedral. Like most churches in Italy, it was old, a ninth century Roman Catholic structure in the Piazza del Duomo, dedicated to the apostle Saint Andrew. The only thing Papa remembered was that there were about a thousand steps leading to the doors of the cathedral. Papa could not help thinking how in the world would someone in a wheelchair get up there. Mama came back excited about the stained glass and statues.

Mama also learned that a wooden crucifix hanging in the liturgical area dated back to the thirteenth century. Another crucifix, this one made of mother-of-pearl, was located to the right of the back door. This crucifix was actually transported there from the Holy Lands. The sarcophagus of the Archbishop Pietro Capuano formed the high altar in the central nave with a painting by Andrea dell'Asta, "The Martyrdom of St. Andrew." The whole cathedral was decorated with Renaissance artwork of a religious nature, as were most things created during that period. Mama felt she was in the presence of a divine power. All churches had that effect on Mama, but especially those that she discovered in the old country.

Papa was glad when mass was over so they could start for Rome. He was always in a hurry to get somewhere and then was happier to leave. It was getting close to the time when he would be ready to get back to his own home and the comforts he'd built around him. When Mama was not in the kitchen or doing laundry or cleaning bathrooms or whatever, she would sit with Papa and watch what he watched. Papa would sometimes watch a ballgame on the computer without the sound and put something on the television that Mama enjoyed watching. Even though Mama had access to another high-definition television, she would stay with Papa. She said it was the only time she could be with him, if you don't count sleeping.

"How long a drive is it to Rome?" Natalie inquired.

"Have you ever driven to New York from home, Natalie?" Papa asked.

"I have gone with my parents, but my father drove."

Papa continued, "It's just about the same distance from here to Rome. I would say about three-and-a-half hours if all goes well. We should be in Rome by mid-afternoon."

"I cannot believe we've been in Italy nearly a week. The time has just flown by," said Natalie.

"Now you're experiencing how short life is from the perspective of an old timer. Being semi-retired, I speak from experience. When you're young and working, time seems to drag by slowly. That's because most people are in jobs that are packed with either boredom or stress. Even *you* will experience that, Natalie. I'm sure you're proud of being a nurse, but you'll still face tremendous pressure – avoiding mistakes, dealing with irate or irrational patients and demanding doctors and head nurses, and so on. Sometimes the time will zip by because you're engaged in something important and other times you'll just want to get home and relax, to get off your feet. The longer you stay in the job, the more routine it becomes. You'll have to be careful not to become careless or complacent."

Papa paused, but it was apparent he was not through with the lesson. "Being on vacation, like now, the time disappears. It's just like summer vacation when you are a kid and you can't believe school is starting already.

I'm sure you've experienced that on other vacations. Being in school for the past four years, you've probably felt like it would never end. One day, though, you'll look back and say how wonderful those years were. That's because you are young now, and your memories will be not so much of school, but of parties and friends and good times. For Mama and me, time keeps whizzing by like a rocket. We try to savor each and every day."

"Ricky told me that you were a philosopher," Natalie told Papa.

Mama interrupted her. "Natalie, I told you not to encourage Papa. That goes for his jokes, silly stories, and mostly his views on life, whether political or personal."

Papa ignored Mama's comment and focused on Natalie's remark. "Natalie, I am very flattered that Ricky would tell you that I was a philosopher. I used to be an old, stuffy, know-nothing trying to ruin his life. I guess now he is getting wise enough to see how brilliant his father really is. But I'm even more flattered that you would remember what Rick said about me. That means you were actually listening to him."

Mama jumped in. "Natalie is a sharp young woman, Papa. Don't think that just because she remembers a conversation in which your name was brought up she was fascinated by the prospect of meeting you. Don't listen to him, Natalie. Papa always thinks he is the most important person in the room."

Natalie was glad that Mama defended her from a potentially awkward moment. Papa was also glad that Mama helped him get his foot out of his mouth. I think that Papa is really frustrated that no one takes his views seriously. He doesn't even realize how much he influences his family and the clients he meets in his job.

"Enough," said Papa. "Basta! On to Roma!"

Now that the three travelers are headed for Rome, it's a good time to tell you about another one of Papa's obsessions. I say this because Papa made certain that they visited the Roman Colosseum. This was certainly one of the sites that Papa had to show everyone, but for Papa, he would prefer to visit the Oakland Coliseum or any other baseball stadium. Of course, in these stadiums you miss the pleasure of seeing gladiators slashing each other to death. In fact, the fans hardly ever yell "Kill the umpire" anymore. Papa made it his mission to visit every major league city to see a baseball game, dragging Mama along with him. He even took Connie with them to visit the Southwest before she was married. Connie still says it was the best trip she ever had in her life. They flew into Phoenix, drove to Denver and took in the sites, and then proceeded on to Las Vegas

On one trip, I even went along. We flew into Chicago to see the

White Sox and the Cubs. We took the river tour through the city to see the architecture of Chicago. We also took the famous gangster bus tour of Chicago. This is one tour I could have done without. Later, we visited the Chicago Science and Industry Museum and took a walking tour of the city. That may have been a mistake, because we found ourselves in a dangerous section of the city.

One day during our baseball trip, Papa drove hours from Chicago to Springfield to see Abraham Lincoln's home. I will spare you the details, but Papa also has a presidential birthplace and historical site obsession.

After Chicago, we drove to Detroit to see the Tigers mop up on the Yankees. All Red Sox fans hate the Yankees but secretly respect their great tradition of winning even though they stole Babe Ruth to finance their dynasty. We stayed at the Greektown Casino Hotel and it was a terrific place. Later we spent a day at Greenfield Village to see all the things that Henry Ford built and stole from other famous people. This includes the reconstruction of Thomas Edison's Menlo Park laboratory. I guess if you have enough money you can collect just about anything. Papa had to resign himself to collecting *New Era* baseball caps after visiting each ballpark. My personal favorite part of the trip was to a small little house converted into a recording studio called Motown. I confess that I inherited Papa's love of music and especially the old roots of rock and roll. Papa impressed me when the tour guide told the story of a group who recorded "Do You Love Me" because the Temptations were late for their recording session. The guide asked the tour group if they knew the name of that group. Papa, not wanting to look like an old nerd, waited until he saw that no one responded and yelled out, "It was The Contours." He was right, of course. There is not too much Papa does not know about fifties and sixties music. He can usually name that tune in three notes or less. I think that was my personal favorite trip.

If that wasn't enough, Papa continued driving east just to take me to see Niagara Falls. While in the neighborhood, we drove up to Toronto to see a Blue Jays game. There is so much more to tell about Papa's obsessions, but I know that I am digressing from Natalie's story back in Rome. I suppose I had better return there.

The trip from Amalfi to Rome was a pleasant drive and fairly uneventful. By this time, Papa was shifting gears without burning out the clutch. The most challenging part of the trip for Papa was using the Italian gasoline pumps. It took him about fifteen minutes to figure them out. They were not like the ones in Boston and Papa is a creature of habit.

Papa said he was amazed to see a vibrant city of Rome with an ancient setting containing the Colosseum, the Circus Maximus, the Pantheon, the hills, and other preserved sites tucked inside. Today this area is mostly a tourist attraction, with the Italians making a good living off the vacationers. Papa hated to be manipulated and the exploitation in ancient Rome was both blatant and aggressive. Most people accept this as part of the Rome experience and go with it, but not Papa. He kept his hands in his own pockets to guard against the pickpockets known to be scouring the area. Even the children are taught to steal here, posing as sweet, harmless kids.

Papa told me he almost had to come to blows over some pictures with this big man who probably could have picked him up and tossed him away. This parasite was very aggressive in demanding that Natalie take her picture with him for ten Euros. He was all decked out in the garb of a Hollywood gladiator. With the Colosseum as the backdrop, a picture with this Adonis would be a keepsake forever of one's trip to Rome. Papa figured that if this guy could get even twenty stupid foreigners to take his picture, and that's a conservative guess, he could rake in two hundred Euros a day. Let's give him an American five-day workweek and that adds up to a thousand Euros a week. This is not bad money for looking like Russell Crowe. Of course, you need to factor in that the job will only be there while you are young and beautiful. However, Papa did notice a few old gladiators who probably would not fare well if they really had to wield a trident or ball club. It's not that Papa's cheap – well, possibly a little – but he hated to be hustled out of his hard-earned money.

In addition, Papa was content to examine the Colosseum from the outside and not pay the exorbitant price to go inside for a tour. He could imagine that some tour guide would tell everyone about the construction of the Colosseum, the holding pits for combatants, how slaves were selected and treated, and so on – information he could get from a Google search online. Papa figured, why pay good money to see the inside of an old structure after visiting over thirty baseball parks. Now if there were some matches inside where people were actually killing each other that would be worth the price. No one from the three-person Santos tour group went inside. Natalie told Papa that she didn't have any desire to go inside and Mama usually went along with Papa unless it was something religious. They were all satisfied taking pictures from the outside and took a short walk to see the site of Circus Maximus. It was here that ancient chariot racing and horse racing took place. I would tell you that it was here that Ben-Hur had his famous chariot race, but Papa informed me that Ben-Hur was a fictional character that some Union officer created after the Civil War had ended. Between visiting the Colosseum, walking around the ancient section of Rome, and eating, Sunday was very pleasantly spent. According to Papa's itinerary, they would visit Rome on Sunday and Monday and then depart for points north. Papa, because of Mama's devotion to the saints, planned to stop off at Assisi for a short visit.

After dinner, they returned to the hotel. This was usually the time Natalie would call or Skype Jeremy. I'm sure it was hard for Natalie to suppress sharing all she had seen in Rome that day.

The next day, Monday, Mama insisted that they visit Vatican City. Mama told Papa that she did not come to Rome to see the Colosseum. She would visit the Vatican with or without him. Natalie was also excited to visit the Vatican. Papa assured Mama that they would all go to the Vatican together. Anyway, Papa said he had a few things to discuss with the Pope.

When they finally arrived at the Vatican, Mama was almost in heaven. Papa thought to himself that this must be a pretty good business. The statues alone must have cost multi lire. Of course, Papa understood that the overhead must be out of sight. Between all the security, keeping things looking clean, souvenir shops to staff, electricity, insurance, etc., this is not a cheap country to run. Papa wondered if any of his Sunday collection dollars found their way to the Pope's coffers. He suspected there was a small tribute but was not privy to the trail of funds. The Vatican doesn't really like to discuss financial matters since they intrude on the main mission of saving people's souls. Papa knew his soul was far beyond redemption. Mama still believes that she will be able to pull off a St. Monica miracle and convert Papa into a staunch believer of the Gospel before he retires from life.

Speaking of saints, Mama was captivated by the row of saints – I mean their statues, overlooking St. Peter's Square. Natalie was equally enthralled. She felt that her decision to keep the baby was blessed by the Holy Virgin. Finding her way to Vatican City just weeks after she had decided not to abort her baby was a sign that she had done the right thing. At the center of the square was an Egyptian obelisk, erected four and a half centuries ago. It took another one hundred years for Gian Lorenzo Bernini to design the square. Granite fountains constructed in the seventeenth century complete the feeling of reverence. The massive colonnades circling St. Peter's Square put man in his humble, infinitesimal place.

How could anyone possibly come to Vatican City and not see the inside of the Sistine Chapel? Even Papa could not pull the same trick he did at the Colosseum. After all, if Michelangelo could spend four years of his life on his back painting the ceiling, Papa felt that he could at least take a few moments out of his life to witness one of the greatest achievements in the history of art. Mama was determined to see the inside; seeing the Sistine Chapel from the outside was not an option.

Papa, Mama, and Natalie were crammed into a group with other like-minded tourists trying to get a glimpse of ethereal history. Papa sensed that even Mama might have felt more like an exploited tourist than someone fortunate enough to be in the sacred setting. The lighting was poor, the voice of the tour guide was muffled, and most felt more like sardines than pilgrims. Papa told me that this was one of the few times that he wished he was rich enough or famous enough to have a private viewing. He knew there was some real good stuff in the Sistine Chapel, if he could only see it for more than three seconds. Papa did sardonically notice that there was a prominently displayed gift shop in the Sistine Chapel. Papa was almost tempted to buy the red boxer shorts with the imprint of man's finger reaching out to touch God's finger for the reasonable price of $16.99. When Papa considered the very likely possibility of farting into the holy undergarment, he decided against the purchase. Instead, he took out his credit card so Mama could buy several Chubby Cherubs oval decals as souvenir gifts for her friends at home.

Having had enough of the Vatican, it was on to a very special place for dinner entertainment. Papa loaded everyone into the rental and it was off to Opera Ristorante. Papa, being a proud Italian American, did genuinely believe that Italy was the world's center of vocal achievement. The singers performing at the restaurant did nothing to change his opinion.

The restaurant featured both men and women singers. Papa said if you are looking to have a good meal in Rome, do not go to the Opera Ristorante. If you are going to Rome to hear opera, try the Teatro dell'Opera di Roma. But if you want to hear some good singing while you eat pasta, then the Opera Ristorante is the place to go. Papa laughed to himself when the singers belted out "Volare" and "That's Amore," but when in Rome… Anyway, the restaurant catered to dumb American tourists and everyone at least knew those songs even if they couldn't sing the words to "Nessum Dorma" or "'O Sole Mio" after they got past the "'o sole mio" part. Both Mama and Natalie were enthralled throughout dinner. Papa liked it too, but he could have done with less singing and more eating.

Monday was drawing to a close, and it had been a wonderful day visiting the Vatican followed by dinner and opera. Everyone was a bit tired, or should I say Papa was a bit tired. Papa's typical schedule is from six in the morning to about six at night. After that, he is basically useless, but he can persevere for special occasions. Being here with Mama and Natalie qualified.

Tuesday morning meant a short drive to Assisi. St. Francis, St. Anthony, and St. Joseph are Mama's three favorite saints. When Pope John Paul was canonized, he became Mama's new favorite. Mama believed that John Paul represented the best traits of a Catholic leader.

Papa was glad that he was still able to negotiate the walk up Corso Mazzini to Piazza del Comune. The medieval *palazzi* were beautifully preserved, featuring the Temple of Minerva. Minerva was the Roman goddess of music, poetry, wisdom, and lots more. After the spread of Christianity, most Italians figured Minerva's temple would be better suited as a church so it was converted. Papa was most impressed by the murals of vices. They were colorful and almost avant-garde depictions of the vices that man has displayed since the beginning of time. Being in the town of a saint meant Mama had to visit the Basilica of St. Francis.

The trip to Assisi would not have been complete without seeing another tomb. St Francis was buried in the thirteenth century and became the patron saint of animals and of Italy. What Papa liked about St. Francis was that he devoted his life to the poor. As I have mentioned, Papa is not the person to see if you want to discuss the spiritual aspects of human life. However, Papa is a self-proclaimed authority on the subject of religion. I think as death sneaks up ever so gradually, Papa is trying to find the same answers philosophers and scientists have been seeking forever. Papa really hates the big-shot televangelists with their television stations, universities, and expense accounts with the big bucks rolling in. Papa truly believes that money is the root of all evil. If you are a clergyman, then you should not be rolling in the dough. You should not be fornicating, embezzling, or preaching politics from the pulpit. Catholics seem to be better at this than most other Christian religions. Unfortunately, the celibacy thing creates its own problems for Catholic priests.

Francis was the son of a wealthy cloth merchant from Assisi but rejected his own comfortable upbringing to help those in need. It is said he received the stigmata, making him the first person to bear the five wounds of Christ. Papa is the most skeptical guy I have ever met. He always says that if you can't get two people to agree on a crime they both saw, how could you believe some account made by religious zealots over eight hundred years ago? In general, that's his whole take on the Holy Bible, too. Why didn't the historian Josephus say much about this man called Jesus? Why do people believe the accounts of four men who supposedly knew Jesus and yet waited many years after the fact to write their accounts? Papa suspects some kind of collusion or attempt on the part of these guys to profit from the new religion. "How can anyone prove anything in the Bible?" Papa says. Mama has a very simple one-word answer: faith. Can't you see God in the world everywhere? This is why Papa almost never argues religion with Mama or anyone else. You cannot possibly convince someone to change his or her beliefs. It is the same subtle process becoming a skeptic as it is becoming a believer. Papa does not have the desire or the inclination to fight that futile fight.

The body of St. Francis had been placed in a bronze urn and buried in a stone crypt in his hometown. Today, with the benefit of expert Italian metal polishers and stone restorers who worked day and night to renovate the tomb, St. Francis rests peacefully. His followers, the Franciscans from all over the world, celebrated the event. Tuesday drew to a close and the next stop was Florence in Tuscany. The Italy trip had less than a week left.

The drive to Florence was another two-hour trip. Papa made a conscious effort not to stay on the road for too long because of Natalie's pregnancy. She never complained and didn't seem to show any symptoms of morning sickness. Her appetite was good and so was her disposition, considering the circumstances. Mama insisted that Natalie sit up front next to Papa for the drive to Florence. Natalie did not put up much of a fight. Nobody likes to always sit in the back seat. Papa rarely does because of his tendency toward motion sickness. Mama asked Natalie how she was feeling.

"I'm fine, Mama. Thank you for asking."

Mama liked the fact that Natalie was calling her "Mama" without appearing at all uncomfortable. This was made easier by the fact that she called her own mother "Mom" or "Mother."

"Connie has made an appointment for you next Friday with an obstetrician she uses," said Mama. "If that's not OK with you, we can cancel and you may select your own."

Natalie replied, "This will be Connie's baby. If she selected this doctor, then I'm sure he or she will be good. Anyway, I don't know any doctors in Chelmsford."

"Can you believe that one week from today we will be back in Boston?" asked Mama.

"Don't rush it!" said Papa. "We still have Tuscany, Verona, Venice, and Milan left to see."

"I know, Papa. I will hate to see it end – but all things do eventually." Mama was even starting to sound like Papa.

Papa asked Natalie if she was enjoying her trip to Italy. Since Natalie was half Italian, he thought this country would hold a special place in her heart.

"I find all of Italy fascinating and beautiful, Papa. This is the most wonderful trip that I ever took. I only regret that I can never share it with my parents."

"Who knows? Life is unpredictable. Maybe one day you can," Papa replied. "Anyway, you can always share it with Regina and you know you can always reminisce with Mama and me." Papa asked Natalie what impressed her most.

Natalie thought for a few seconds. "I have been really amazed that everything here is so old and yet so beautiful. The churches, the art, the statues, the fountains, the streets, even the demeanor of the Italians appear old."

Papa was pleased with Natalie's answer. "It's good to hear a young person show appreciation for the old. When you are young, old is a foreign and abstract concept. I will share with you the wisdom of my years."

Papa was about to enter the world of his number one most omnipresent obsession – his obsession with death. Papa always reminded Connie and me that death for him is around the corner, and we should be prepared to deal with it. The truth is that both Connie and I were now old enough to support ourselves, and Mama and Papa were far more important to us than any financial support. They were our best friends and our emotional support. Papa articulated this when he spoke to Natalie. Although Papa never said these words to me, I was not surprised when Natalie repeated this conversation to me later.

"Natalie, I'm sure you have heard that being young is a state of mind. Frank Sinatra said that fairy tales could come true if you're young at heart. Well, maybe a little. When you lose your first parent, you lose your childhood. I was a child as long as my own father was alive. When he died, I had to become a man, even though I was already supporting a family. And when my mother died, then there was nothing left between the inevitable finality and me. This is the saddest emptiness you can experience, short of losing a child. I could not pretend to possess the strength it takes to bear that loss. I know this sounds morbid but I do not mean it to be, because I am totally at peace with all that life has in store. This is because I am immortal."

Papa paused, as if for dramatic effect, then continued. "I'm not immortal in the sense that I will die and go to heaven and see Jesus. This is Mama's belief, and this I am truly happy to say is your belief. I hope you always hold firm to that conviction and never waiver. For me, though, immortality comes in one of two ways. One becomes immortal by accomplished achievements in one's life. This is how George Washington became immortal even without children of his own. He was the father of our country. This is how Beethoven or Genghis Khan or Julius Caesar or even Jesus Christ became immortal. Or you become immortal through your children or your children's children. I believe that as long as you have a child or a grandchild alive, a small piece of you will live forever. This is partly biological but mostly otherworldly."

Papa looked over at Natalie. "You may have your mother's smile or your father's silly habit of shaking his head when listening to someone. You are a partial clone of your parents, diluted by time and breeding, but always a part of them will remain forever. It sounds ridiculous and I acknowledge this. How can I be anything like my great-great-great-great grandfather? I know nothing of his existence. And yet I know deep down that a small part of him is still in me. This is immortality."

Now Natalie understood what Ricky was telling her about his father and his obsessions. And yet, Natalie understood the breadth of Papa's compassion. He was an amazingly strong and positive man, complicated by his own feelings. Papa had a hard time concealing his sentimentality. A memory, song, or movie could make him cry, but he would try to conceal it by joking or laughing. Natalie knew she had made the right decision to have Papa's grandchild.

The depth of this man's deliberation on this subject of death amazed Natalie. I suppose Natalie shared the sentiments of most young people about older folks – because they are old, they must be somewhat senile or at least old-fashioned in their thinking. Natalie was surprised to learn that both Mama and Papa were very modern in their attitudes. I suppose that Natalie never realized that people growing up in the sixties saw lots of things and were really the catalysts for the attitudes most Americans share today.

"Natalie," Papa said, "you are too young to know it, but we are all dying some little deaths every day. When I was young, I would love to drive the car and could go to Florida and back and relish the trip. Today, the idea horrifies me. I could stay out all night and watch the sun come up. Now I'm up before the sun. You know that it is highly improbable that you could ever play baseball for the Red Sox, but when you reach a certain age, you despair over the fact that it would be a physical impossibility. Retirement, even for great baseball players, is a small death. Retirement in general is a terrific time in life, free of the pressures of work, but another small death. As we get older, we fail to produce melanin and the hair turns gray or white. Color it all you want. This is a small death of the cells in your body. It's worse for men as their hair slowly disappears."

He continued his monologue on death, lamenting the fact that once he'd had thick, black, curly hair. He went on to complain about dead skin cells, the loss of energy, and the loss of a sex drive.

These are all small deaths to Papa and he is obsessive on the subject. I am only scratching the surface, but you get the idea.

Chapter Eight

Sights of Italy

Papa made reservations to stay at San Gimignano for the night. The town was beautifully situated on top of a hill and clearly visible in the distance were its many towers. Today, thirteen towers remain from more than seventy built in the Middle Ages. Every well-off family built a tower to show its position of prominence. Only the richest families of merchants and moneylenders could afford these works of construction.

Papa, Mama, and Natalie once again ate dinner serenaded by an Italian crooner. This time the songs were more of the Italian variety Papa liked and less operatic. The restaurant wanted to provide an atmosphere of gaiety and merriment and the wine was flowing. Mama purchased a round, wrapped package of Marzolino cheese from one of the local shops. This cheese was featured in the region as a spring cheese, named for the month of March. Papa could not eat very much cheese and ice cream any more because of his stomach's reaction to lactose. This is another small death, Papa would emphasize when he was in one of his pity moods.

Natalie phoned Regina that evening, asking if Regina had seen Jeremy.

"Natalie, I am not spying on Jeremy every minute of the day," Regina replied.

"Of course you're not," said Natalie. "I mean, did you happen to see him out and about?"

"You have been away less than two weeks," Regina blurted, talking a bit loudly since she figured Italy was a long distance away. Let me handle this in my own way."

"I didn't mean to pressure you, Regina," answered Natalie. "Anyway, I know that Jeremy will wait for me without running after other women. I left him in a very good frame of mind when we said goodbye. I'm sure he will be working hard to save money for when we're married."

Regina heard the words coming from Natalie's mouth, but she could not help feeling unconvinced, either in her own faith in Jeremy or by Natalie's conviction. Regina welcomed the idea of becoming a spy for

Natalie. The time Regina saw Jeremy clubbing was quite by accident. Now she would leave nothing to chance. She would basically need to stalk him to see if he was behaving. Regina ended her conversation with Natalie promising only that she would do the best she could to keep an eye on Jeremy. Regina knew that undercover work would be difficult, especially since Jeremy recognized her, and that she might need to recruit some help. She also firmly believed that if Natalie heard any bad news about Jeremy, it should not be before she had a stress-free period to nurture the baby. She feared that any distressing news might have an adverse effect on her friend's pregnancy.

On Thursday morning, Papa drove the short distance to Firenze, known to Americans as Florence. Mama and Natalie both wanted to visit the Basilica of Santa Croce. This is the largest Franciscan Basilica in the world, housing sixteen chapels. Mama was certainly in her sanctifying glory, having all kinds of statues and frescoes and tombs and carvings to absorb. In Mama's mind, she was absorbing the Holy Spirit. Papa hated to tell her that these were stone and wood carved by some very talented medieval artists. To Mama and most other devout Catholics, these likenesses of saints personified the glorified soul of the Virgin Mary or Saint Francis or whichever saint was immortalized for eternity. Papa, as I mentioned, only saw the art. Rightfully so, he was awestruck by the magnificence of the renderings, but was quick to say that they were only an artist's interpretation. These statues were often taken from an illustration in some ancient book and created with artistic license without any solid basis. I have often heard him ask Mama how could anyone know what Jesus looked like. The image from the shroud of Turin, he would say, could be anybody. Mama never really listened to Papa and he never tried to draw attention to his belief. He learned early in life that being a heathen doesn't play well in most circles.

Papa did enjoy the history of the basilica. Buried within those walls were some of the greatest Italians in history, including Michelangelo, Galileo, Machiavelli, and Rossini. There were also monuments dedicated to people not actually interred there, including Enrico Fermi, Marconi, and Dante of Dante's Inferno fame. It was like an indoor cemetery for who's who in Italian history. Papa can never, and I mean never, listen to Rossini's William Tell Overture without welling up. He especially asks for silence as the slow prelude builds ever so calmly, erupting violently into the overture. Being from an earlier generation, this also conjures up visions of Tonto and the Lone Ranger galloping off in a cloud of dust.

Papa could only handle a small dose of the basilica. I believe that after being inside a church for more than an hour, Papa gets the shakes as if he were an alcoholic without liquor. In this case it was sort of reversed. He was bombarded with too much spiritual symbolism and if by some remote chance he was wrong about his belief in God, or lack of, he did not want to offend the creator by freeloading in his house.

Papa told Mama that he wanted to visit the Pitti Palace while they were in Florence. Natalie wanted to stay with Mama in the basilica. Papa said that later in the day he wanted to take a short drive to Pisa. He asked Mama how could they be so close to the leaning tower and not see it. He said that if they had a late afternoon lunch they could make it. They made arrangements to meet at the Trattori Baldovino in three hours.

This gave Papa the opportunity for some alone time. He walked over the bridge traversing the Arno to see the Palazzo Pitti. Papa's obsession for solitude had been greatly compromised constantly being in the company of Mama and Natalie. I say that knowing that he loved them both dearly. Papa was in his glory being alone and dealing with life at his own pace, at least for three hours.

Papa said the *palazzo* was the most beautiful building he had ever seen. It was entirely covered with art. The ceilings, the walls, and every room were a magnificent feast for the eyes. Papa thought, this is what art is supposed to look like. It's not some splotches of paint giving the impression of a face or tree. The artwork was not a bunch of lines and angles. Colors were bright or dark, depending on the mood of the scene or portrait. Raphael's Madonna was especially beautiful to Papa's eyes. He thought Raphael must have been a great artist because he only had one name, like Michelangelo or Cher. The Madonna proved Papa's point about the artist's rendering. Raphael had more Madonnas out in the world, so his images of Mary were the most admired.

The Medici family had bought the palazzo from Luca Pitti in the middle of the sixteenth century. For some reason, the name of the palace never changed to Palazzo Medici. Papa speculated it would be too confusing to change a brand name after so many years. That is probably why the Cleveland Browns play football in Cleveland, even though the original Cleveland Browns are now in Baltimore calling themselves the Ravens. It was probably wise not to call themselves the Baltimore Colts, since the original Baltimore Colts are now playing in Indianapolis. Anyway, the Ravens was a good choice for a name since Edgar Allan Poe had lived in Baltimore. Other than that, I can't imagine why they would call themselves the Ravens. If they were going to name themselves after a bird, the Orioles would have made more sense since the Oriole is the Maryland state bird. But that might prove confusing since the Baltimore baseball team is already called the Orioles. However, I seem to recall a time when there were two teams called the New York Giants playing both football and baseball in the city at the same time. Maybe that's why the baseball team moved to San Francisco. It proved too confusing having two teams in two different sports with the same name in the same city at the same time. And the real point is that it was probably wise for the Medici family to live in the Palazzo Pitti keeping some other family's name for their abode. It showed both reverence for tradition and class by the Medici clan. They probably had enough money and power that the name change was of no importance to them.

After Papa got his fill of the palace and all its artwork, he walked back to the north side of the Arno River to meet Natalie and Mama for lunch. At lunch, Papa did more listening about the basilica than he did talking about the palace. Papa found that the women were far more enthusiastic about their experiences and much more descriptive in the telling. Papa tried with some moderate success to hurry the ladies through lunch, pleading his case about seeing the Leaning Tower of Pisa before the sun went down. Papa had already reserved a room near Pisa at the Hotel Galilei. They departed after the brief visit to Florence and Tuscany for an hour drive to Pisa. They also left with a lifetime of memories.

Papa recounted later that they were barely out of the car when they were hawked by some young men trying to sell them postcards, miniature Pisa towers, caps, T-shirts, etc. These men spoke enough Italian and enough English to sell their wares. Papa learned that the hustlers were from Ethiopia, having migrated to Pisa to make a living. Papa figured it was easier to buy a little something than it was to avoid the barrage of salesmen. Papa bought an aqua blue cap with the Leaning Tower of Pisa emblem and some plastic elephants. It seemed his secretary at home was a collector of elephants. These elephants offered no distinction outside of the fact that they were purchased in Pisa. The cost was small enough that Papa succumbed to the pitch and at least he had something tangible to show for compromising his values.

Natalie was surprised to see the Leaning Tower close up. In her mind, she had always imagined the tower to be buried somewhere in the city, surrounded by other buildings. She had seen pictures, but they never seemed to show the surrounding area. Natalie was like an excited little kid. She had Mama take a picture of her holding up the tower to keep it from falling. Naturally, Natalie had to position herself the correct distance from the tower, placing her hands and arms in the exact right spot to give the illusion that she was keeping it from toppling over. This was not an original notion, based on all the other tourists posing for the exact same picture. Others would lean at the same angle as the tower, creating the illusion of parallel twin towers.

The tower itself had been constructed as a bell tower for the beautiful adjacent cathedral. Mama and Natalie were blessed with seeing another cathedral. Papa took a five-minute pass-through and returned quickly to the grounds. He felt that this could be the day the tower actually plummeted to earth if he remained too long inside God's house. I've already told you about Papa's obsession not to tempt fate.

The tower actually took nearly two hundred years to construct. It was built in three separate stages. Papa thought it was sad that no one who started the project or even their children got to see the completion of the tower. It was only fifty years ago that the Italian government stabilized the foundation of the tower to prevent it from toppling over. And twenty-five years afterwards, the bells were removed and cables added to the third level, anchored several hundred yards away. This had the effect of actually straightening the tower to its 1838 angle, aided by the removal of thirty-eight cubic meters of soil from underneath the raised end. The tower reopened to the public in 2001. This enabled the Italian government to recoup the cost of strengthening the tower and maintaining its integrity. For over twenty dollars a head, anyone could now get a bird's eye view of Pisa from the top of the tower. Papa did not encourage the women to digest that view. Papa, as I mentioned, did not like to throw his money away for a cheap thrill that he would soon forget. Anyway, Papa said he could get a better and longer-lasting view from the top of the tower by buying postcards or checking out other pictures. When Papa got home from his trip, he did an Internet search to prove his point and he was right. Papa saved himself over sixty dollars for a very unnecessary look at the same Pisa he could see up close and personal on YouTube. Papa was somewhat obsessed about not throwing good money away. Papa says, if he were a wealthy man, he would not mind spending his money flippantly.

Anyway, Papa said he went to the very top of the Empire State Building when he visited New York and it was much higher than the Leaning Tower. Even the Eiffel Tower at King's Dominion in Virginia was higher than this tower and Papa went to the top for the cost of admission. In truth, no one asked to see the view and they were probably aware that the money spent on a good dinner was a better use of Papa's funds. As I mentioned, Papa was frugal, but he really was not cheap. Like anyone else, he chose to spend his own money for things he felt were important.

After a good meal and a good night's sleep, they headed for Venice.

On that same night, I received a very unexpected call from Regina. She told me that she needed my help but I was not, under any circumstances, to reveal her request or what I may see to anyone. This included, above all, my parents and Natalie. The Natalie part was easy since she wouldn't take a call from me anyway.

"Ricky, I want you to do some spying for me," said Regina.

"How did you get my number and why would I want to do that?" answered Ricky.

"Like your number is a state secret. It's publically listed, you know. Anyway, have you given up on Natalie? Do you want her to marry Jeremy?"

"You know the answer to that, but why are *you* trying to break up Natalie and Jeremy? I thought you were her best friend," Ricky replied.

"Actually, I am not trying to break them up," said Regina, "but I need you to help me snoop on Jeremy. Natalie wants me to do this, but she's hoping I will verify that Jeremy has been faithful. I know she loves him and wants to trust him, but I don't think he is the dependable man Natalie deserves. Oh sure, he's handsome and has a good job and has a killer body, and –"

"That's enough! I get the idea," I interrupted. "But why me?

"That's easy," said Regina. "Jeremy doesn't know you, so you can watch him without arousing any suspicion. And you, more than anybody, have a vested interest in her relationship with him. If my suspicions are right, Jeremy is not sitting at home quietly watching television while Natalie is away."

I told Regina that I didn't have anything in particular to do that evening. She emphasized that she didn't want to upset Natalie during her pregnancy, so I was to keep my mouth shut about whatever I saw. Regina was very outspoken and demanding, but I admired her no-nonsense approach to things and her obvious devotion to Natalie. Her motives were honest and I sensed that she was hoping that I wouldn't find anything out about Jeremy that Natalie wouldn't want to know.

Regina drove with me to point out Jeremy's apartment and his car, then directed me to drive her back to her own car. She left without even saying thank you. I think she felt that she was doing me a favor and not the other way around. She was probably right.

I started watching Jeremy's car about eight that evening. I felt as if I were on a stakeout, like you see on those cop shows, and having my smartphone camera added to the whole espionage aura. This was a Friday night and if Jeremy was going to hit the clubs, this would be the night. About nine-thirty, he left his apartment. I couldn't see him well in the darkness, but the streetlight near his car illuminated the area. It looked to me that he wasn't dressed to go to the gym for a workout. Jeremy started out driving south on Interstate 93 and then onto Route 3. It was apparent that he was heading toward the Cape. As it turned out, he stopped at Plymouth and entered a bar on Court Street. We were about an hour's drive from Boston, and I suspect Jeremy figured this was far enough to remain undetected by people who might know him. The bar was probably selected for its unobtrusive location. I walked in about three minutes after Jeremy entered and ordered a draft beer at the bar. Jeremy sat alone at a table for two. At approximately eleven o'clock, a beautiful brunette with silky hair entered the bar and sat right next to Jeremy. This was definitely no chance meeting, because she greeted him with a long kiss – long enough for me to snap a few photos. Jeremy ordered a couple of drinks and they sat there talking quietly while the digital jukebox played several songs. Jeremy couldn't keep his hands off her and she laughingly tried to restrain him from his public display of affection. Jeremy appeared oblivious to anyone or anything but this beautiful creature. I know I'm prejudiced, but as beautiful as she was, she couldn't hold a candle to Natalie. I suspect that Jeremy didn't really care about that at this moment. He was clearly working himself up for some private entertainment. After only one drink, Jeremy and his lady friend left the bar, staying very closely attached to each other. I followed them out of the bar at a safe distance and once again followed Jeremy's car. They drove about five miles back north and entered an apartment building together. I assumed that this was where the young lady lived. I couldn't tell you anything about her other than what she looked like. I didn't know how Jeremy knew her and I am quite certain that I had never seen her before.

Having all the pictures I needed, I decided to drive back home. I suspect Jeremy was there for the duration and I did not intend to sit in the car all night until he decided to leave.

On Saturday morning, I awoke with a mild sense of euphoria. I felt like a child who got his way and wanted to taunt the grown-ups. I felt a sense of power. Knowledge is power and I knew that Jeremy was a cheating bastard and as soon as Natalie found out she would be done with him. In my mind I was running around the room shouting, "Jeremy is an asshole! Jeremy just lost Natalie! Natalie will be mine soon!"

Then reality set in. I was the only one who knew what happened. The Jeremy-was-an-asshole part was true enough, but his bad behavior was no guarantee that he would lose Natalie. Even if he did, the prospect of her turning to me was very remote. The fact that she was carrying my baby gave me a glimmer of hope that she might consider looking to me as a compromise companion. I knew that sounded pathetic and tragic, and I knew I was becoming my father, but my obsession was Natalie.

All this speculation was a lot like the old song by The Temptations: "It was just my imagination running away with me."

I had promised Regina that I would not say a word to anyone and I kept my promise. I sent the pictures I took of Jeremy to Regina's cell phone. It wasn't ten minutes before she called me. She didn't want to discuss this over the phone so she invited me to her apartment for breakfast. I was eager to hear what she had in mind. I picked up some cinnamon buns and arrived at Regina's in forty-five minutes.

"I knew that turd was up to no good," Regina exclaimed. "Do you know who she is?"

"First of all," I told her, "she's probably not from around here. Maybe Jeremy met her at work or maybe she was having X-rays at his clinic or maybe he picked her up one day. How the hell would I know? The question is, what are you going to do about it?"

I told Regina all about the trip out to Plymouth and the dive bar. I described how friendly they were and that this was definitely not his first time seeing her. I told her that I followed them to her place and left them there.

"I'm not going to do a damn thing until after Natalie has her baby. I told you that I do not intend to upset her now. If she knew what Jeremy was doing, I don't know how she would react. Maybe she would forget about all this baby business and tell him off. If I were you, Ricky, I would not risk having her lose this baby, either by choice or by stress."

I told Regina that it was never my intention to tell anyone about Jeremy. "Let her continue to live in fantasy land," I told Regina. "For all I care, she can continue to call him and talk about love and marriage. I want Natalie to be in a good frame of mind. In just a few days she'll be back from Italy and then Connie and her husband can take their turns spoiling her. They also have a vested interest in keeping Natalie and the baby happy and healthy."

Regina added, "When the time comes, I will tell Natalie all about Jeremy. I don't want her to ruin her life by marrying this ladies' man. It would only be a matter of time before he was out chasing other skirts. Believe me, I know his type. I also know Natalie – she let him back into her life once, but she will not do it a second time. Ricky, I appreciate what you did and I appreciate your discretion, even though I know you want to put the screws to Jeremy. Maybe during the next few months you could gather a bit more ammunition for me to hand over to Natalie. See if there are other women or if he spends all his time with this one."

I told Regina that I would try to check him out a few more times, but I didn't plan on making Jeremy my life's mission. "I've got my own thing going on, Regina. I don't expect to chase this guy around Massachusetts while he screws everyone he meets."

"Of course not, Ricky. I know you have more important things to do on the weekend."

For some reason, the sarcasm in Regina's words sounded like an insult. She probably thought that I was sitting around every day waiting for Natalie to come to her senses. Well, maybe there was a little bit of truth in that.

Saturday morning in Italy was sunny and warm as Papa and his ladies left for Venice. This leg of the trip was the longest, but Papa stopped in the middle for Natalie's sake. Natalie said that she wasn't feeling nauseous and she didn't think the trip was too long. Actually, counting the half hour they stopped for breakfast at about 10:30, they still made it to Venice by around one in the afternoon. Papa figured that they would spend the better part of two days in Venice. He reserved a room for two nights at the Hotel Canal Grande. Mama said the hotel was very charming and that the dinner accommodations were excellent. While a bit away from St. Mark's Square, they could take the vaparetto, or waterbus, everywhere. Papa preferred being away from the crowds.

Saturday afternoon upon arriving, they checked in to the hotel and immediately set out for St. Mark's Square. Mama and Natalie naturally made the Basilica San Marco their very first stop. Papa had to endure yet another church walk-through. In typical Papa fashion, it was a very fast self-guided tour. He was trying to avoid having the city of Venice sink into the Laguna Veneta. You can tell by now that Papa's habit is to say outrageous things for theatrical effect.

The church features multi-domed architecture. Influences from Byzantine, Western European, and Islamic architecture are all incorporated to display Venice's powerful seafaring past. Papa had to agree that the city of Venice perched on the canals was a beautiful place to visit. The square was attractive, but Papa didn't care for all the pigeons. He said he had enough of pigeons at city hall and Yawkey Way. But of course these were Italian pigeons, so they were much higher in the pecking order. The square worried Papa somewhat since restaurants and shops dominated it, the two businesses Papa tries to avoid in the real world.

When Mama and Natalie returned from what seemed like an hour tour of the basilica, they were ready for lunch. They sat down outside at the Café Florian for some pasta, a salad with lots of green olives, and a Coca-Cola.

Natalie and Mama were thoroughly impressed with the basilica. It seemed as if it were made of gold. In fact, gold or bronze dominated the interior. In typical medieval fashion, the several layers of domes and walls were adorned with statues or depictions of saints and warriors. The square within the church itself was the focal point for several altars, with a straight view toward the main altar farthest away. Papa pretended to listen, giving credence to the excitement in their voices, and nodded and smiled with reassurance that their descriptions were most evocative. I've seen that look myself more times than I can remember. Papa is always preoccupied within his own mind and thoughts and has acquired this technique of gratuitous listening. Sometimes his absence of concentration is discovered when he is asked for a response and must struggle to reconstruct the question. Mostly he gets away with it, but this is a very selfish aspect of Papa's behavior and not at all attractive. When Papa's mind once again returned to the enthusiastic sketch of the church's interior, he said that he wished he had stayed inside longer. Of course, Mama knew better than to believe that.

After the late afternoon lunch, Natalie made a suggestion. This wasn't typical of Natalie since she considered herself Papa's guest and didn't wish to impose on any plans he may have had. Clearly, though, Papa was pretty much winging it and had no definite plans. "Papa, between sitting in the car for four hours and sitting down for lunch, I feel it would do my body good to do some serious walking. Also, I think a good walk would be a terrific way to digest our food and see the sights a bit off the beaten path. Are you up for it?"

"Natalie, don't let our age fool you. I can jog two miles without stopping and walk another mile for emphasis. I do it on a regular basis. Mama here is in better shape than I am. The question is, are *you* up to it?"

Papa always felt that he was a born athlete and had a way of deceiving himself into thinking that he was in better shape than he was. The fact is, he could afford to lose a few pounds and exercised just enough to convince himself he was in good shape. However, a leisurely walk would not be too taxing for either Mama or Papa.

Natalie answered confidently, "Papa, I'm a nurse and know that exercise is good and necessary for a pregnant woman. I'm not a piece of glass about to break. I truly want to walk. I've let my whole exercise routine go since I've been in Italy."

"OK, then," exclaimed Papa, "I have the map of Venice right here in my pocket and I am an excellent navigator. Let's walk back to our hotel. It's about a two-mile walk. OK by you, Mama?"

"That's no problem for me," answered Mama. "I only wish I had put on my walking shoes, but these will be fine."

Knowing Papa, I'm sure he was glad to save the money for the water taxi. They were not cheap by taxi standards, considering the exploitation of tourists and high overhead for maintaining the boats. Walking the lanes of Venice was like a trip into the past. The old weathered buildings and the shops along the way left a lasting impression. Mama, in particular, was quite descriptive about Venice upon returning. I believe she enjoyed Venice as much as she did Amalfi, but they were totally different in charm and scenery. Leaving St. Mark's Square, they walked down Calle Dietro Ai Magazzini. I found out later this was literally the street behind the stores. There were a variety of artist displays, prints, posters, and merchandise for any tourist's delight. Mama purchased a canvas of the Venetian canals. Papa was more upset about having to carry the package than he was about the price. In retrospect, the water taxi would have been a lot cheaper. Papa offered to buy something for Natalie, but she kindly declined.

They walked past the Turkish consulate building and Santa Marta. They walked across one of the many archways bridging the canal. On their walk, before they reached the hotel, Papa saw the Italian publishing company Marsilio Editori. I never mentioned that writing is another one of Papa's obsessions. He unsuccessfully tried to publish at least two novels. The rejections affected Papa's enthusiasm to continue his writing, but I notice he still tinkers. Papa is a creative genius in his own mind that no one really appreciates. I think he figured that trying to get published in Italy while there would be a waste of time. He never entered the building.

Their walk home was over before they realized it. There was a festive area around the hotel and enough light to enjoy the warm Venetian evening. Papa had plenty of diversions for the evening. The Casino di Venezia was located right where they were staying. Mama knew that Papa would visit it, if only for the experience. In typical Papa fashion, he lost enough money to curse himself but not enough to cause him any grief. Papa enjoyed his occasional gambling opportunities but was not addicted to the thrill of it. Probably that is because he was too sensible to lose a substantial sum of money. Since he never learned to quit while he was ahead, he almost always walked away a loser, even if he started out on a winning streak.

It was six p.m. in Venice on a Saturday night and Natalie called Jeremy. It was only noon in Boston. Natalie had no idea of knowing it, but Jeremy was still in Plymouth with his female companion. When his cell phone rang, Jeremy quickly put on his pants and excused himself. Natalie's call had interrupted his slumber after a very late night of drinking and lovemaking. Jeremy quickly walked outside to take the call, knowing it was Natalie.

In reality, the conversation was a performance by two liars reassuring each other of their love and devotion. Natalie maintained her pretense about working for Doctors Without Borders and went to great lengths fabricating stories about her latest trials. Jeremy complained about how busy he was at the lab while professing his undying love to Natalie and hoping for her quick return. In fact, he asked Natalie to give up the whole idea and return home early. Natalie told him that her sense of responsibility and duty could not allow her to quit early. Although the conversation was all invented, their expressions of love for each other were genuine. Jeremy's display of love showed a total lack of commitment to Natalie. Natalie's deception was at least intended to keep Jeremy in her life. Neither lie was a basis for a future together.

Natalie's call to Jeremy was less than ten minutes, owing to the expense of it. Mama waited for Natalie and they explored the streets of Venice together without straying too far from the hotel. Mama refused to watch Papa gamble his time and money away frivolously. This was Mama's ultimate boredom. Mama and Natalie enjoyed a pleasant Saturday night together. Papa got the gambling bug out of his system and all was right with the world.

Sunday was their last day in Venice. They took the water taxi back to St. Mark's Square. The Bostonians walked out to take a good look at the Grand Canal. Almost immediately, a gondolier invited Papa to explore Venice for only 150 Euros. Let me repeat, one of Papa's main obsessions is not wasting money on things that he feels are frivolous. To me, this is a bit difficult to understand. How can you come all the way to Venice and not experience the "must do" event in the city? Papa explained to the gondolier that just a few years ago his whole family experienced the pleasure of a ride in a gondola while in Las Vegas, Nevada. How a gondola ride at The Venetian in Las Vegas compares to a gondola ride in the waters of Venice escapes me. I will admit that the gondolier in Las Vegas was a terrific singer. I suspect the talent required to get this job in Las Vegas is set at a higher standard than in Italy. I confess I do not know if there is a gondolier's union in Venice. Anyway, Mama did not appear all that upset about missing out on this opportunity. Then again, Mama is afraid of boats and being in the water for fear of drowning. I would bet that Natalie wanted to take the ride, but she never said so. Papa should have considered Natalie's feelings since Natalie hadn't been to Las Vegas. The gondolier walked away in a huff, cursing not-so-much under his breath as only an Italian tradesman can do. Papa was totally unaffected.

Having seen Venice, Papa escorted Mama and Natalie to Verona, which was on the way to Milan. As I mentioned, Papa tried to plan his trips as short jaunts for Natalie's benefit. Natalie had done a terrific job, with only a minor trace of nausea on one occasion. This trip was less than ninety minutes by car. Papa made a reservation for that evening at La

Grotta Hotel. It was not in the center of the city and Papa welcomed its quiet atmosphere. Verona's main distinction was Juliet's balcony from *Romeo and Juliet* fame. Shakespeare must have had a special fondness for Verona, since three of his plays were set there. In addition to *Romeo and Juliet,* he set *The Two Gentleman of Verona* and *The Taming of the Shrew* in this city. It interested me to hear that in Verona there was an actual balcony that Juliet supposedly used. This suggests that there actually was a real Juliet and the Capulets and Montagues were real families of Verona. I later learned that this play was based on some semblance of fact. Shakespeare was not the first writer to retell this story of two love-struck teenagers. William Painter authored *The Goodly History of the True and Constant Love of Rhomeo and Julietta.* Matteo Bandello had written a novella of the story in 1554, revising Luigi da Porto's *Guiliette e Romeo.* Even earlier, Masuccio Salernitano had recounted the story of the tragic young lovers in *Mariotto and Gianozza of Siena.* Italian traveling theatre companies performed the tragedy throughout Europe and England. There is so much we don't know about Shakespeare. Did he even write the plays that bear his name? In any event, it is a terrific story retold countless times in many disguised ways with some not so hard to discern. My personal favorite version is *West Side Story.* I tend to agree with Papa on this one. The acting, singing, costumes, sets, and especially Leonard Bernstein's music made this my favorite musical story of all time.

If I know one thing about Papa, it is that he is not a dirty old man or perverted in any obvious way. If he has any dark, dirty secrets, he certainly has me fooled. Having said this, I was surprised to hear Mama say Papa rubbed Juliet's breast. Of course I am speaking about the statue of Juliet in the courtyard in Verona. Papa swears that he is not depraved and that rubbing the statue's right breast in the hope of good luck has become tradition. Papa said that he really needed some good luck with Natalie soon returning home. He was truly worried that Natalie would change her mind and keep his grandchild. He knew, or at least believed, that he would have little part in the child's life if this happened. After spending two weeks with Natalie in very close proximity, he had grown to love her as a second daughter. He hoped that she would always remain in his life, even though Papa kept telling us that the grim reaper was not far away and he did not have much time left.

Natalie found Verona to be one of her favorite places in Italy. For Natalie, it was the simple, quiet history of the city. Natalie had recently seen the movie *Letters to Juliet*, making this visit much more special. Natalie was a romantic at heart. She felt that being here rekindled her own tender emotions and hoped that she and Jeremy would live the fairytale life that was taken from Romeo and Juliet over some misguided hatred. Natalie's body was in Verona but her thoughts were with Jeremy. She prayed that her last magical night with Jeremy was her first night of forever love. Natalie rubbed Juliet's right breast and the three of them left for the hotel to have some dinner.

Chapter Nine

Goodbye Milan

While Papa and company were in Milan for the next to the last day, Regina decided to pay a visit to Jeremy at work. Since Regina had promised Natalie that she would look in on Jeremy, she felt that this was a good way to do it. Anyway, Regina was dying to hear Jeremy's lies firsthand. She could almost predict what he would say but was curious to hear how deep he would pile on the shit.

It was nearly noon when Regina walked into Jeremy's lab. She was hoping to invite him to lunch in order to catch up. Regina was totally unprepared when she noticed that the same young woman that Jeremy visited in Plymouth was working in the lab. Although Regina had never seen this woman before, Ricky's photos were quite sharp and there was no mistaking the fact that this was the same person.

"Regina!" said Jeremy with a surprised tone. "What are you doing here? I hope you're not having a medical problem."

"No," said Regina, "I'm just checking on you. You know that Natalie made me promise to keep an eye on you to be certain you were a good little boy."

"That sounds like Natalie. But you needn't waste your time on me. With my heavy work schedule and trying to save money for our new life together, I have time for little else except sleeping. You can almost always catch me here or in bed asleep."

"Yes, I know that you like to spend lots of time in bed."

Jeremy figured that was a sarcastic remark, based on the time he broke it off with Natalie. He was quite sure that Natalie had been crying her heart out to Regina. But he pretended that this snide remark had no bite on him.

"And who is this attractive young lady working with you in the lab?" asked Regina.

"Pardon my bad manners. Kathy, this is Regina, my fiancée's very best friend. Regina, this is Kathy Furlong, a part-time inhalation therapist.

She's usually here three days a week."

"Nice to meet you, Kathy," said Regina. "I just invited Jeremy to lunch. I hope that you will join us. No one should eat alone." At least Jeremy let her know he has a fiancée, Regina thought. She was dying to get the scoop on her. She wondered why this woman would go with Jeremy out of town for an hour's drive, then ball him all night and come right back to Boston to work beside him.

"I think that would be nice," replied Kathy. "How about meeting in the cafeteria in fifteen minutes. I'm afraid that I don't have time to leave the building for lunch."

"Sure, that's fine!" said Regina. "That will give me time to visit the little girl's room."

Regina's first impression of Kathy was favorable, considering she was screwing her best friend's intended and knew it. She had a calm, pleasant disposition and spoke with an air of assuredness. Regina was anxious to get her story but had to avoid seeming too obvious.

At lunch, Regina paid more attention to Kathy than she did to Jeremy. Jeremy was a lying, cheating bastard and she knew that. Maybe she could get some insight into Jeremy's thinking by interrogating Kathy.

"That's a beautiful ring, Kathy," said Regina. "Does your husband work in Boston?"

"Jason is stationed at Hanscom Air Force Base. Right now he's deployed at Bagram Air Force Base in Afghanistan. Actually, that's about all I know. The Air Force is not really big on sharing their mission details or day-to-day activities. I think he's relatively safe but you always worry that something will go wrong. I worry about training accidents, I worry about ground-to-air missiles, and I worry about him being in the wrong place at the wrong time. Believe me, when you are the wife of a military man on deployment, you take each day as it comes. Right now he is about halfway through a ten-month deployment."

"I know you're really proud of Jason. I can hear it in your voice."

Regina truly felt that Kathy loved her husband and genuinely worried about his safety. She also wondered how she could be so pathetic as to run around on him while he was defending our country. Knowing Jeremy, Regina convinced herself that he probably charmed his way into her pants. He probably told her that they were both in the same boat and could comfort each other until their loved ones came back. She could only imagine Jeremy's smooth lines. First, he would move in on her by being all friendly and caring. Maybe they would have lunch together regularly. Then he would invite her out for an occasional movie or dinner, just to have something to do. He would give her a friendly kiss goodnight, the next time a little more passionately. Before she even knew it, Kathy would be eating out of his hand. She is, after all, a beautiful woman, alone and bored. Jeremy would convince her that they would be very discreet and careful. Why else would they meet in Plymouth, which is in the opposite direction from Hanscom?

Regina continued her interrogation. "Is your husband a pilot? Do you live on base? You must be very lonely without him. Do you come from around here?"

Jeremy, knowing Regina's busybody nature, was not all that surprised by her questions. He never suspected that Regina was on to his game. After all, he went out of his way to be very careful.

The big question Regina had that she couldn't ask was how the two of them ended up in an apartment in Plymouth. Regina assumed that Jeremy probably rented a nice condo for one night. Plymouth is a popular stop on the Cape Cod tour and this was still off-season. He was probably able to find something and avoid the cheap motel scene. They probably even spent the whole weekend there.

Kathy answered casually. "I met my husband in Virginia. He was stationed at Langley in Hampton and I was a student in the pre-health program at Christopher Newport. I'll spare you the details, but let's say that I knew right away that Jason was a special kind of man." Kathy took a bite of her salad before she continued answering Regina's questions. "Jason isn't a pilot. He's a combat system's officer. In the old days, you might've called him a navigator. We have nice housing on base. Between my work and base activities with the wives of other deployed airmen, I'm rarely bored."

Regina thought to herself, but when you *are* bored you sure have a great way to escape. Kathy seemed a decent person, except for the fornication with men outside her marriage and lying to cover it up. Why Regina would put most of the blame on Jeremy when he was still technically single only spoke to the total misgivings she had about his character. Regina then focused her cross-examination on Jeremy.

"How about you, Jeremy? You must be getting horny as hell waiting for Natalie to come home. What did you do this weekend? Did you take many cold showers?"

Natalie tried to discern any hint of guilt or hesitation in Jeremy's answer. Jeremy had become such an adept liar that she doubted if he would even fail a lie detector test. Kathy, on the other hand, appeared to glance askance at Jeremy, wondering what kind of story he would concoct. Regina suspected that Kathy was feeling discomposed having cheated on her husband and then lying about it, and then listening further to Jeremy lying about it, too. Kathy was probably wondering whether Jeremy truly loved his fiancée. But how could she cast any stones?

Jeremy answered in a confident, assured manner, which everyone at the table knew was a truthful answer – up to a point.

"Regina, considering I was away from Natalie, I had a terrific weekend. I got plenty of rest and I really enjoyed staying in bed past noon. This is something I'm rarely able to do when I have work. I was also able to watch the Red Sox. I think they can go all the way this year. It's hard not being with Natalie, but we left in a real good place. Those weeks away from her when we broke up proved to me that she's the only one for me. I'm not going to blow our second chance."

Regina was dying to expose Jeremy right then and there, but she didn't want word to get back to Natalie during her pregnancy. It was hard enough living away from home like an outcast without having to deal with Jeremy's betrayal a second time. So Regina bit her tongue as much as she was capable of doing.

"Well, from what I heard, you were able to locate replacements for Natalie pretty fast," Regina countered.

"Now you are confusing sex and love. These are two different things. A man can easily separate the two. I think for a woman it's a bit harder."

Jeremy just insulted Kathy, whether he knew it or not... But probably not.

Regina had a ready response for Jeremy. "I'd like to address your convoluted philosophy from the benign perspective of an unworldly female. Let us suppose that you and Natalie are madly in love, as you profess. You have convinced Natalie that you are worthy of a second chance, due to your undying devotion to her. Let's agree to this truth. If you discovered that Natalie was screwing one of the doctors in Italy to pass the lonely hours, would this upset you a tiny bit? I suspect it might because of what it says. It says what you don't know won't hurt you. It says variety is the spice of life. It also says this person to whom I pledged my life is not worthy of my promise."

Regina realized she was going too far. She paused and tried to divert her attack, yet without giving Jeremy any undue credit. "Anyway, I'm sorry, Jeremy, and you too, Kathy. I didn't set out to air your dirty laundry today and especially not in front of your colleague. Kathy is a married woman and knows what I'm talking about. The fact that she waits faithfully for her husband's return is proof enough of that. Kathy, Jeremy really is a terrific person. You probably know that because you work with him. I just get a bit ill-tempered when I think of how he hurt my very best friend in the world. Please forgive my bad manners."

Regina rose to leave. "I only came here to see Jeremy because Natalie made me promise to look out for him. I think she wanted me to see that Jeremy was not too lonely in her absence, but Jeremy can entertain himself without me hanging around. It was terrific meeting you, and I pray for your husband's safe return. He should be home before Natalie returns. Maybe we can all go out together one day."

"That would be nice," said Kathy. Regina hugged Kathy goodbye.

Regina had a playful smile when she said goodbye to Jeremy. "Be sure to behave yourself, Jeremy. You never know when or where I might pop up."

As Regina was walking out the door, she glanced back to see Kathy's facial expression, which was a combination of worry and shock. Natalie had introduced just enough innuendo to make Kathy feel uncomfortable. She imagined Kathy seeking reassurance from Jeremy that they had not been found out. Knowing Jeremy, Regina had no doubts that he would badmouth her as being an instigator. In her mind's eye, Regina could see Jeremy comforting Kathy and putting her fears to rest. If nothing else, Jeremy was charming and a very smooth operator.

Meanwhile, back in Italy, our three travelers were enjoying their last full day in Milan. They were ready to come home from the trip of a lifetime. To Papa, being away from his Red Sox, music, movies, Thursday night poker, and his basic solitude was an immense sacrifice, though I know that he would not have traded the experience for anything in the world.

Mama told Papa that she expected to see a performance at La Scala. Being a Monday, they were fortunate that there was a performance that particular evening. Unfortunately, it wasn't an opera, but a symphony performed by the Filarmonica della Scala, the house orchestra of La Scala. The performance started at eight p.m., but since their flight the next day was late in the afternoon, time was no issue.

The New Royal-Ducal Theatre alla Scala originally opened about the same time colonists were fighting the British in the streets of Concord. Mama said that the theater was huge, having close to three thousand seats. Mama and Natalie were excited to hear the symphony and I expect Papa was, too. Being in a fancy, high-class building steeped in tradition gives the average person a feeling of worth. Life, after all, needs these evenings to offset the myriad endless days of routine. The acoustics must have been scientifically designed, because Mama felt the total intensity of the marriage of instruments. She felt as if the performance was directed at her personally.

Papa had the sense that he had been directed to La Scala on this particular evening by fate. On the program, along with Pietro Mascagni's *Cavalleria Rusticana,* Giacomo Puccini's *Manon Lescaut,* and three other pieces, the orchestra played *Guillame Tell* by Gioachino Rossini. Papa could hardly believe his eyes, having purchased tickets not knowing what was on the program. And, true to form, Papa would very privately weep, trying to look unaffected, when the orchestra blasted from the slow melodious entrance into the very memorable overture.

So ended the last full day of Papa's, Mama's, and Natalie's memorable trip through Italy that had begun in a small Sicilian town with Papa's cousin Rocco. Tuesday was the day Papa dreaded. It wasn't that he was sad leaving Italy. Quite the contrary, Papa was anxious to return to his comfortable surroundings at home. It was simply that he dreaded the long trip back across the Atlantic. He was glad that he lived during a time when this trip could be made in twelve hours, counting the layover. He couldn't even imagine what a hell it must have been for his grandfather making the trip a century ago. And even that was a pleasure cruise compared to the shackled voyage below deck the Africans were forced to endure during the slave trade.

All three travelers boarded the plane, ready to return to the good old U.S. of A. The connecting flight to Paris was relatively short. Papa wondered why the Parisians were so unpleasant. In Italy, the attendants had been easygoing, friendly, and still efficient about checking on any possible safety violations. In Paris, the security personnel seemed to treat everyone as a potential underwear bomber. They absconded with Natalie's Fontanini musical snow globe with manger scene that played *Joy to the World.* Apparently, the snow globe contained too much water and it was obvious that rules had been broken. In Florence, Natalie had been greeted with "*bellissimo!*" when the attendant went through her bag and saw the baby Jesus. In Paris, the attendants were apparently too clever to be duped by such an obvious deception by this seemingly innocent American woman. I am quite certain that the snow globe ended up in somebody's display at Christmastime. Natalie was heartbroken over losing the sixty-Euros present she purchased for her mother. They went through the personal items so meticulously that Papa worried about missing the connecting flight home. Then, after all that, a second person went over the same stuff all over again. There were some anxious moments, but they made the flight.

The long trip home was a time of reflection and solitude, time to relive the last two weeks and contemplate the future. There was little conversation. Natalie sat by the window, with Mama in the middle and Papa on the aisle for his quick rush to the restroom.

Papa was overjoyed at the prospect of returning home. For one, he figured he would not be spending any more money on overpriced mementos or tour guides or general admission – or whatever. But more importantly, he would soon be back sleeping in his own bed, surrounded by all the sights and sounds that made his house a home.

Mama, on the other hand, was sad to return. She enjoyed escaping the day-to-day drudgery of being home. She hadn't cooked a meal or washed clothes or vacuumed or dusted or performed any of the household chores that consumed far too much of her day. She instead had a rare chance to experience life. She had seen where her grandparents lived and where the roots of Catholicism had taken hold and flourished. Nearly ninety percent of the people she met were Roman Catholics. This was a far higher percentage than she encountered at home. The food, the art, the churches, and the pastels of Italy would now be emblazoned in her mind forever. She hated to leave but knew that everything comes to an end.

Natalie was apprehensive about her arrival home. She was returning to six months of living with strangers. She was returning to six months of nurturing a living human being inside her body, one that she would ultimately hand over to this family. Although she was committed to the adoption, she worried about the emotional detachment she would experience when the time came. She worried about Jeremy's commitment to her. She had sacrificed to keep Jeremy in her life and wondered deep down whether he would come through. She struggled with the idea of living a life while keeping a secret of this magnitude. Would she be able to go on with her life as if nothing had happened? She knew that many young women gave up children for adoption and lived normal, happy lives, never seeing their child again. Would she be one of these women? She knew the Santos would be happy for her to visit with the child, but would that be too painful?

Everyone was sleepy, since they were still functioning on Italian time. Natalie slept the most but Mama was close behind. Since Mama sat next to Papa, she monitored his respiration and pulse with the cunning of a fox. Her gentle grip around his wrist was for no obvious purpose to Papa. Mama knew Papa's anxieties better than he knew them himself. She figured he would survive the trip as long as the turbulence was at a manageable level. At times, she even started up a conversation with Papa when she noticed his obsessive attention to the flight tracker.

"Look at that woman walking down the aisle," she whispered to him at one point. "I think she's French because I noticed her at the gate when we were boarding. She must be fifty-five if she's a day. And she's wearing black vinyl boots with a mini-skirt and a tight sweater. Who wears their hair that long at her age? I hope that you don't think I dress too young when I'm wearing my boots. You know that boots in Boston have a practical purpose and I always try to wear pants that look smart. Do you think I look too old for those boots I like to wear? I always felt they looked fashionable."

Papa had lived with Mama far too long to fall into that trap. She was fishing for a compliment. He didn't realize that she was also trying to keep his mind off the flight monitor.

"Not to me, Mama," he replied. "To me, you look like you are twenty-one years old. And I think you're once, twice, three times a lady."

"I'm not sure, Papa," responded Mama, "but I think you just insulted me."

Mama noticed a wry smile starting in the corners of Natalie's mouth. Apparently, Natalie had been eavesdropping and confirmed Mama's suspicions about Papa's left-handed flattery. Mama was not at all offended, knowing Papa's propensity for showing off his dry sense of humor.

When the plane landed, close to midnight Boston time, the airport was fairly desolate. There was little chance that anyone would notice Natalie's arrival in town. I made it a point not to pick them up, not wanting to make Natalie uncomfortable upon returning to her new life for the next six months. I can only imagine how she must have felt, arriving home but knowing that she could not resume her normal life. With the assistance of one of my friends, I parked Papa's car at the airport that afternoon and texted him the space location. This had all been prearranged.

Papa and Mama drove Natalie to their home. It was too late at night to drive to Connie's house in Chelmsford. While everyone was away, I had kept an eye on the house and adjusted the thermostat prior to their return. I also stocked the refrigerator and cupboards with enough food for a few days.

In the morning, Connie would pick Natalie up and drive her to her new home. Connie was a very sensitive and tactful person and would make Natalie feel as comfortable as possible under the circumstances.

Chapter Ten

Return to Reality

"Papa, thank you for the most wonderful trip I will probably ever have," said Natalie.

"Natalie, it was my pleasure and my honor – and I should say 'our' honor because I know that I also speak for Mama."

Papa had better say that, if he knew what was good for him. Mama hated when Papa got all the attention or all the credit for anything good that happened. She felt that it was her sacrifice that enabled Papa to become modestly successful in his career. She had put her own dreams on hold in order to raise their two children. Mama had wanted to become a nun and devote her life to God, but somehow Papa won her over and convinced her that God would be number one in her life, the children would be number two, and that he would be blissfully content to assume the number three position in her life.

Now that they had been together for over forty years, it was hard to fathom how these two people could survive without each other. Papa was what you might call a benevolent chauvinist. He felt he wore the pants in the family but was still genuinely wary and even guarded against upsetting Mama. This was because in Papa's eyes, Mama was an earthly saint. Mama tolerated so much heartbreak and disappointment from Papa's insensitive behavior and yet she always managed to forgive him. However, that forgiveness came at a price, because Mama had a memory like an elephant and would allude to Papa's past callousness completely out of left field. Papa never knew what stimuli crashed into Mama's head to make her remember feelings of anger or dejection; however, when the mood struck her, he felt her wrath for acts he had committed decades ago. He feigned ignorance over ancient history and protested that he lived in the present. He implored her to treasure the here and now. In fact, the present was much more comfortable than the turbulent past. Papa knew this and regretted that he had to be old to learn this lesson. Mama had been old in spirit at twenty-five with the beauty of an angel. Papa epitomized the old saying, "I wish I knew then what I know now." I believe Mama knew then what she knows now. Everyone lauded Papa for his great breadth of knowledge and wisdom, but Mama was blessed with perspicuity at a very early age.

Papa continued. "Natalie, please forgive my boldness in saying that in a few short weeks we have come to love you as a daughter. I realize that Mama and I are influenced by the fact that you are the mother of our grandchild, but that's only a small part of it. You are a beautiful woman caught up in a very unfortunate situation, and you made the conscious decision to honor life against all of your other interests. Oh, sure, Regina and I were relentless bullies, but it was ultimately your decision. Mama is the best judge of character on the globe and you have won her over completely. Today is May 26 and you leave for Chelmsford to live with strangers until late December. You will miss Thanksgiving with your family and possibly Christmas. Please consider us your temporary family. Mama and I already think of you as our daughter."

Natalie smiled and blushed slightly. "Thank you," she replied. "I feel very safe and comfortable with our arrangement. I know Regina will visit and I'm sure Connie and Thomas will be terrific hosts. But Papa, you know better than anybody what it feels like being home in your own surroundings. That will be absent for me for over six months. And all those months of waiting around while I incubate a child only to hand it over will feel like an eternity."

She saw a look of concern pass over Papa's face and quickly added, "But don't get panicky. I will not renege on the promise I made."

"I appreciate your honesty and commitment," Papa said. He straightened, preparing for one of his philosophical treatises. "Before Connie gets here, let me pass on my discovery of time that only many years of living can teach. Time is the relentless host of mundane existence that is interrupted by brief moments of joy or happiness. When one looks back over decades of life, it is these moments that are remembered. The rest is a blurred afterthought of the routine with no significance. I am often amazed when I contemplate how I got to be sixty-five. I know that I worked and interacted with people and sold my product and swallowed my pride in order to earn a living. I had to do that to survive. What I didn't do, and this is the regret of my life, is to treasure those early years with my children. I wish I had provided Mama with more happiness. I am trying to do that today, but it is harder now because the youthful energy and excitement of springtime has waned. My point is that if you treasure each day, treating it as a gift, it will be a glorious time for you. If not, the time will be an endless drudgery that years hence will become a dead zone in your mind's eye. It will become a composite awareness of anguish that will have the effect of wasting a precious part of your life. You will remember being uncomfortable, miserable, lonely, and sad. I beseech you to treat this time as a gift from God."

Natalie nodded as Papa continued. "And no matter what you say, this child will always be a part of you. You know that we encourage you to be an active participant in his or her life. When the time comes, this child will know you as his or her biological mother. We have no intention of harboring a secret to keep this child deceived. The reason I have such a poor memory of the past is because I lived in a world of commonplace workday banality. Mama's elephant memory is the consequence of giving thanks for the time she gave and made for her children and other people. Your state of mind will make the difference in how quickly this time passes. It could drag on forever or it could zip by like a flash. I confess that the three months I spent at boot camp at Parris Island felt like an eternity. And now, looking back, I know that I benefited from it nonetheless. All time has this possibility."

The next morning, Connie drove Natalie to her home in Chelmsford. She and Thomas had prepared the spare room for their special guest. The bed was new, with a queen-sized mattress. The closets and drawers had been cleared out, making the room solely Natalie's domain. Thomas had a high-definition television mounted on the wall across from Natalie's bed. Two chests of drawers, a desk, two nightstands with lamps, and a mirror remained in the room for Natalie's use. Natalie had exclusive use of the hall bathroom with tub and shower.

"Natalie, this is your room. If you want to change the curtains, bedding, redecorate, move furniture, whatever, just say the word. You have your own laptop. Our wireless network is at your disposal. We also have a phone in your room with a separate phone number from ours. Sometimes it is just better using a landline. You could call Regina or businesses from here if you wish. I wouldn't call your parents or Jeremy from this line. The number is not blocked. Have I missed anything?"

"Thank you, Connie," said Natalie. "I don't expect to stay buried in here. I hope we can eat together and watch shows in the den sometimes."

"All the time," Connie corrected. "You have free rein of the house. I just wanted you to know that you have your own private place, too. Life goes on. You will have dirty clothes to wash, special things you might want to cook, or whatever it is you want to do."

"Leisure time will be a new thing for me," Natalie said, as a gentle smile flitted across her face. "I'm not sure how to deal with it. I've been studying, going to class, or spending time with Jeremy. I'll need to figure this whole new freedom thing out."

"Oh, I almost forgot," said Connie. "Friday will be your first doctor's appointment. I use the same doctor and find her very thorough and extremely caring. Of course, you could select any doctor you want. Papa said he would assume any medical expenses you incur."

"I'm sure your doctor will be fine, Connie. I'm still on my parents' medical insurance or I would gladly use that. I'm sure that if they saw statements from the doctor, the gig would be up. This will cost Papa several thousand dollars out of his pocket."

"Believe me," retorted Connie, "this will be the best money Papa ever spent. He sees having this grandchild as a blessing. He would pay ten times the cost if necessary."

"May I invite Regina to stop by on Saturday?"

Connie answered, "Of course. This is your home and you can invite anyone you want."

"Unfortunately, Regina is the only one I really trust with this secret, but she's been my best friend forever and she'll be more than enough company. I'll probably need to give you a signal to come rescue me from her, though. I love her and all, but she can be a real pain at times."

"Sorry, Natalie," Connie said with a smile. "You'll need to do that dirty work all by yourself."

When I was certain that Natalie had left for Connie's, I paid a visit to my parents and got the firsthand account about the Italy trip. Not surprisingly, it seemed that they went on two different trips. The one thing they could agree on was that Natalie was a terrific lady.

Papa asked, "Why didn't you come earlier so you could see Natalie?"

"Papa, I will not insinuate myself into her life. She wants to marry this Jeremy guy and has made it very clear that it is a source of anguish to even look at me. I'm not saying that I'll never see her again. That seems unlikely, considering the situation. However, I won't cause Natalie any more stress than she already has."

Papa, seemingly knowing the future, interjected, "Well, it's only a matter of time and Jeremy will be out of the picture."

"What makes you say that? Do you know something I don't?"

I wondered if Natalie had discovered the truth about Jeremy's two-timing tête-à-têtes from Regina. I had believed that Regina would stay quiet, if only to protect Natalie's pregnancy during the first trimester.

"No," said Papa, "but I know the type. She will eventually dump that bastard and I expect that she will turn to you for comfort."

"Now you are really dreaming," I protested mildly, wishing that could be true.

"Be patient, time will prove me right."

Time again. Papa's favorite obsessions were making everyone feel the gloom and doom about the relentless march of time and his approaching demise.

Papa continued. "You are still too young to understand the impact of time. Time is not only a road to old age, but it is also a healer. Natalie will discover that Jeremy is wrong for her and her feelings toward you will soften. Her child will trigger a connection with you that cannot be denied. She has already cemented that bond with Mama and me."

I thought Papa was caught up in his own fantasy world. He lived in fantasyland most of the time. It must have been because *The Wonderful World of Disney* conditioned him at a very early age. Perpetuating the precious Santo name has always obsessed Papa. This, he said, was his immortality.

"Papa, when this child is born, it has a fifty percent chance of being a girl. Then the Santo name will be lost in marriage. Even if it's a boy, the child will be christened with Thomas's last name, not Santo. Why this neurotic need to keep the child in the family?"

"Listen to yourself, Ricky," Papa bellowed. "This is your child! How could you bear to see your own flesh and blood lost out there, not knowing his or her future? That's all I'm saying. You'll be able to stay in this child's life, if only as 'Uncle Rick.' And I very strongly suspect – no, I know – that Natalie will not be able to stay out of the child's life either. I only worry whether she will back out on her promise to give this baby to Connie. She claims with conviction that a baby would change her life and she doesn't want it, but I have gotten to know Natalie. Parting with this child will not be easy for her."

"Don't worry, Papa. You still have me as an insurance policy. I should be good for at least ten more babies. There's plenty of time."

I had unknowingly waved the red cape in front of Papa.

"There is less time than you think," Papa wailed.

"Papa, you have always been harping to everyone about time. Frankly, this obsession is tiresome and outright morbid. I can't remember when you didn't tell Connie and me to prepare for your impending doom. You are in better health now than most men twenty years younger than you. You can't seriously believe that you're dying," I asserted.

"That proves my point in a way. When I hit fifty, a light bulb went on inside my mind's long, dark tunnel leading down into forever. That was fifteen years ago and you were only thirteen so it seems to you I was gloom and doom forever. That really wasn't that long ago, and it seems like yesterday to someone of my years. I often watch a movie from twenty years ago. The actors are still acting today and most look pretty good. Some have even remained top box office stars. Then it hits me – twenty years ago! How is that possible? I think it's even worse when I listen to my sixties station on the radio. I hear a song and I am right back to my teenage years. How could it be possible that this song is over half a century old? I was just listening to it down at Revere Beach with a little dark-haired Italian girl the other day. That's time's effect."

I shook my head and smiled, a here-we-go-again look in my eyes, but Papa continued. "Oh, sure, I remember when I was a young man hearing old people say time flies and it's over in a flash. That has no meaning when you are young and looking at fifty years in front of you. It's funny, last year I saw an old friend when I went to a Red Sox game with your mother. My mind had a picture of my friend when he was eighteen years old. It was a vivid image emblazoned by all the many times we played ball, chased girls, had parties – well, you get my meaning. When I saw him after all these years, he was a bald-headed, wrinkly old guy I did not recognize. But then magically, as we started talking, he slowly transformed into Bobby again. And now when I think of my friend, I still see the young Bobby, even though I know the old Bobby has moved into his skin. Learn from my years of experience, Ricky. You may not realize it, but I am the best friend you will ever have. I only want the best for you, even if you disagree."

Papa got a distant look in his eyes. "I know this is my problem," he said. "I tend to impose my values and desires on you when you have your own life to lead and have no kind of schedule at present. You really must develop a plan of action that includes career and family and then make it happen. These things should not and cannot be put off. When the baby you are having finishes high school, I will be either dead or into my eighties and probably wishing I was dead. Believe me, high school graduation is not that far off. Do you get it?"

"Okay, Papa," I assured my father, "I get it. But please put a lid on all the doom and gloom. It's really depressing for us to think of you not being here. It will be bad enough when the time comes without your reminding us every ten minutes."

I really started to understand how my father was wired. He still didn't realize that my goals were quite different from his. If I never had a child to raise, I believed that would be fine. Maybe I would feel differently in ten years. Maybe in ten years I would have missed my opportunity. Papa always believed that having children was a young person's job. If you were too old when you became a parent you might miss out on your own second childhood. That would be very unfortunate.

Then I left the home of my childhood and returned to real life. I was so blessed to have my childhood home to go back to. It was a comforting retreat whenever things were getting too heavy, but it was nice to leave it, too.

"Well, Mama, once again we are home alone. That was quite a trip. This is an experience that we'll never forget. You've had a long voyage and I know you don't feel like doing anything right now. Neither do I. So let's go to our favorite Italian restaurant for dinner. Then tomorrow we'll unpack."

"Good idea, Papa," said Mama. "I suppose leaving all these suitcases around for one more day won't hurt. Let me get myself together and I'll be right there."

Papa knew what that meant. He would have at least a thirty-minute wait, so he went inside to catch up on his favorite recorded shows. Papa rarely went out when it meant that he would be home very late. In fact, he hated to drive when it was dark. He also knew that Mama would begin unpacking as soon as they returned from dinner and that tomorrow she would spend the entire day doing laundry.

"You know, Mama, I'd like to be back home by seven-thirty to catch the Red Sox game."

Mama laughed. "I can recall when you stayed out past ten o'clock. Remember? There was a time when you and I would stay out all night just making out and talking. Anyway, why are you spending money on this DVR if not to watch shows later? I promise I will not tell you the score before you watch the stupid game."

"Sure, but when we stayed out late it was to rescue you from staying in that prison of a home you had. Now you're living exclusively with me. You should be in a hurry to get home."

"Right, so I can watch you watch a ballgame or a movie. No thanks, I would rather stay out and see actual live people."

At dinner, Mama was showing signs of drowsiness. "Papa, you know it's eleven o'clock at night in Italy. Our bodies are ready for bed now. I hope you don't become upset if I fall asleep."

"Do you mean to tell me that I will have to carry you out of the restaurant?" Papa retorted.

"Why are you so silly?" Mama chortled. "You know I mean after dinner I will probably conk out. You are the silliest man I ever knew."

"Damn! How could you think of going to sleep? This will be the first time in weeks that we will be alone and in our own bed. I took Viagra before we left and was really expecting to get lucky tonight. I didn't feel right jumping you in those Italian hotels with their thin walls with Natalie on the other side. And now you tell me you're tired."

"Papa, you haven't even touched me in over three months and now all of a sudden you want to make love. Is this another one of your attempts to blame me for not being interested?"

Mama was able to read Papa like a book. Papa had a great desire to make love but it was a desire driven from memories of years ago. The truth is that since the removal of his prostate gland, Papa's sex drive was next to nil. He had the mental desire but was lacking the physical. Mama had her own physical issues and never seemed overly concerned with the want of lovemaking. She was just glad that Papa caught this slow-growing cancer early. Papa's life was far more important than being able to make love. She would be content with caresses and kisses. This was probably true even before the lovemaking ended. But Papa was really frustrated by the loss of his manhood.

"You know, Mama, only three short years ago I could have repopulated the entire city of Boston, given enough available young women. And now, I couldn't repopulate a ghost town with one new life. I must tell you that this hurts my pride more than words can express."

In Mama's eyes, Papa remained a handsome, virile man. She had lived with him for over forty years and he would always be her lover and protector. I only wished that I could find a love that strong for myself. I feared that my mother and father's love and devotion toward each other had set the bar so high that I could never attain it. That is the love I felt for Natalie, but it was a one-way love affair.

Upon arriving at Connie's house, Natalie immediately began personalizing her new room. That meant hanging all her clothes in the empty closet and filling up the drawers. She also took over the hall bathroom with her toiletries. She put out her family pictures and, of course, Jeremy's picture. It sickened me knowing that every morning this would be the face she woke up to. I had an urge to sneak into her room and tear up or burn the picture, but that would tell Natalie that her privacy had been violated. I preferred that she not realize that I had sneaked into her room simply to smell her pillow.

On Friday, Natalie went with Connie for her first doctor's appointment. Dr. Connors was an attractive woman in her early forties. She had been in practice with a medical group that specialized in obstetrical care for twelve years and had developed a reputation as a very competent and caring doctor. Before she examined Natalie, as a first-time patient, she conducted an interview with her. Dr. Connors sensed Natalie's uneasiness and assured her that she took the doctor-patient confidentiality very seriously. She also told Natalie that her concern was for the baby's and her safety and she was in no way judgmental about the circumstances of the pregnancy. Natalie already knew this but was happy to see that Dr. Connors was insightful enough to recognize her apprehension.

Natalie said, "Dr. Connors, I'm from Boston but currently live with one of your other patients, Connie Salvino. I just recently received my BSN in nursing and have had training in prenatal. I just never expected to be a patient quite so soon."

"That's terrific," interjected Dr. Connors. "And what about the baby's father? Why are you not sharing this blessed event with him?"

"I don't want to give you the wrong impression, Dr. Connors. I am over twenty-one years old and was still a virgin until this baby was conceived. In fact, I have only had coitus twice in my entire life. The first time with the father of the baby and the second with my fiancé."

"That does complicate your life," added the doctor. "Are you certain that this baby is not your fiancé's?"

"Yes, I am very certain since I already knew I was pregnant when I had sex for the second time. I figured at that point, what the hell. I will spare you all the details of why I am here only to say that Connie will be adopting this baby. The baby was conceived on Saturday, March 20. I am not quite sure of the time since I was not really that involved."

Dr. Connors appeared concerned. "I must ask, Natalie. Were you raped?"

"No, Dr. Connors, "I was wasted, mad, and hazily aware of what was happening to me. I guess you could say that my defenses were down but I let this happen to me. I was not raped."

"Okay, then, let's go check you out."

After the examination, Dr. Connors confirmed what Natalie already knew. Dr. Connors told Natalie that the due date was on or about December 21.

"Did you want a Christmas baby, Natalie? This will be a wonderful present for Connie and I expect you will discover for you, too. Everything looks fine and I will prescribe your diet and vitamins. Until about September, I want to see you once a month. But call if there are any problems and I will see you immediately. After that we will meet twice a month until you deliver. Do you have any questions?"

"No. Thank you, doctor," said Natalie. "This is exactly what I expected you would say. Thank you for your concern. Connie told me you were a terrific doctor."

Natalie left the doctor's office feeling relieved. In her mind, this was the official start of her gravidity. Today was June 4 and she had six and a half months to nurture this life growing inside her.

On Saturday, Regina drove up to Chelmsford to spend most of the day with Natalie. Regina told her she'd have to leave by five, since she had a date later that evening. Natalie was jealous but tried not to show it.

The friends left Connie's house to go shopping and have lunch. There was little or no chance of running into anyone they knew. Natalie had spoken to her parents and Jeremy before Regina arrived just to be sure that they would not be going anywhere near the area that day. As the reality of Natalie's intention set in, she began to question her decision to exile herself in the company of strangers until wintertime. She was beginning to feel lonely and isolated even though Connie and Thomas bent over backwards to make her comfortable.

"Maybe you were right all along, Regina," Natalie confessed. "You told me I should just face the music and let my parents know the truth. I was so afraid of losing Jeremy forever; I let my shame cloud my common sense. I still think I did the right thing, though, because Jeremy would definitely leave me if he knew I was pregnant. Have you seen Jeremy anymore since the last time we talked?"

It was all she could do to hold her tongue. Regina was positively committed to telling Natalie the truth about her loving fiancé, but she would wait until the baby had been born or at least until miscarriage was an unlikely result of the upsetting news. At this early stage of her pregnancy, telling Natalie could result in anything from a miscarriage to a deliberate abortion. Considering the fact that Natalie gave her promise to Papa and accepted his gift of two weeks in Italy, that likelihood was very slim.

"Natalie," replied Regina in her typical bossy way, "I saw him just that once. I have a life, too. Do you expect me to shadow his every move?

"Don't get so huffy about it," replied Natalie. "You are my best friend and right now you are my only friend. I just wanted to be sure that I wasn't wasting all my time living in a make-believe world trusting that Jeremy would be faithful to me. You know better than anyone how hurt I was by Jeremy's behavior after our breakup. It caused me to do the most foolish thing in my life and now God is punishing me."

"Please get real. God has a lot more important things to do than punishing you for getting laid. If God didn't intend us to get laid, he would not have made it feel so good. And like I told you, Jeremy was busy working. He seems to be fine and is trying to make some money for your marriage. I know that he misses you terribly and can't stand being away from you. The very idea that you finally screwed him before you left made him realize how much you love him."

"You mean you discussed our last night together with Jeremy?" Natalie asked, her shock apparent in both her voice and her face.

"Of course not. I meant he would be a fool to leave you after that show of devotion. Where in the world would he ever find anyone as beautiful, smart, and loving as you rolled up in one package? I would love you myself if I was into women."

Natalie only laughed, knowing that Regina bordered on nymphomania and her interest in the female sex had no erotic components attached. She was a lifelong friend to Regina and if she knew nothing else, she did know that.

Natalie and Regina shared a very pleasant day. When Regina left, it felt to Natalie as if a friend paid her a visit while she was confined to prison but now the cell door closed behind her again.

While all this was going on, I decided to do a bit more spying on Jeremy. It seemed I was obsessed with this Jeremy character, but evidently it was really Natalie that drove my callow behavior. I would never reveal Jeremy's indiscretion to Natalie personally. That would be a blatant act of treachery on my part and not the endearing quality I wished to present to Natalie. Therefore, I had to be a sneaky bastard about it. I was a bit better prepared this time. I brought along the high-quality digital camera from work. In my capacity as public relations officer, taking pictures and sometimes video is part of my job. I guess you could call me somewhat of an expert. I was glad to see that all the classes I took on media presentation in college finally came in handy as a spy. I thought that maybe I had missed my calling, but considered the fact that private eyes probably need to put themselves in dangerous positions, carry a gun, and have fights, etc. – at least that's what the detectives do on television – I would stick to my regular day job.

Jeremy set out for wherever he was going at about eight o'clock, except this time he didn't seem to be bound for the Cape. When it became apparent that he was heading back to his workplace, I figured that he was working a late shift or something. I decided to wait around a little while before leaving. Jeremy parked in the employee section of the parking lot but never left his car. This was curious. I often sit in my car waiting for a special song to end before I leave, but Jeremy waited over ten minutes. I was baffled until I saw Kathy walking toward Jeremy's car. She quickly opened the passenger-side door and furtively entered the car. I did not see her kiss Jeremy or even show signs of acknowledging his presence. I had my telephoto lens and was able to get a decent shot, even in the dim light. I assumed that this would be an overnighter a bit closer to Boston and not a weekend rendezvous. It was already Saturday night and Jeremy had to work on Monday. I didn't know his work schedule, so that was only guesswork on my part.

This time, instead of driving south, Jeremy took his lady friend north to Saugus. It was far enough out of town that he would probably be safe from peering eyes. He stopped at Chisholm's Motor Inn, bypassing any attempts to romance Kathy before taking her into the room. I figured by this time, romance had been replaced by raw sex. They both understood the situation and were by now past any pretext of flirtation. Jeremy went in alone to get a room. He wore a baseball cap, I supposed, to make him look less recognizable in case the infidelity police were tailing Kathy from the Air Force base. The motor inn was very unassuming. If I were to hazard an opinion, I would say mostly frugal family men watching their budget and other guys playing out Jeremy's lustful fantasy frequented this wayside. From the few minutes I watched, I saw some evidence of this. Jeremy and Kathy hastily entered their room. Kathy carried a small bag similar to a carry-on and Jeremy had what appeared to be the refreshments. They pulled the shades low and closed the drapes tightly. However, I did get a fairly clear zoomed in video of Jeremy and his escort. This was now the second piece of evidence. I shared it with Regina the next evening.

I went to Regina's apartment about six. She was showing the effects of an entertaining evening the night before. By the time we met, she was recovered enough to have a lucid conversation. She started by telling me that she had visited Natalie the day before.

"Did you see Natalie when she returned with your parents?" asked Regina.

"No. I'm trying real hard to be cool about this whole scheme and I didn't want to impose myself into Natalie's space," I said. "Frankly, I don't get this whole thing. Just tell Natalie that her boyfriend is a dirtbag and let her move on. Here, you can show her these photos and this video. She asked you to keep an eye on him anyway."

"I told you that I am not going to tell Natalie about this while she is carrying the baby. At least not until the baby has fully developed and Natalie is out of danger of having a miscarriage."

"Well, I think that we are doing her no favors by concealing this evidence," I countered. "Who knows, Natalie might decide to give up this whole pretext and go back home to have the baby."

"Don't say that too loud," Regina cautioned. "It wouldn't take much for Natalie to do just that and keep the baby. Your father would go ballistic, and you and your family might never see the child again. She might even decide to have the abortion now. There is still time. So I recommend that you keep your mouth shut. We both want Natalie to have the baby. I just know in my heart that this baby will be a comfort to Natalie one day. She will always thank God that the child was born and she didn't kill it. I truly believe that. A strong, loving force will surround this child, no matter what."

"Okay," I relented. "You know Natalie better than anyone and I can't argue with you. I don't know why, but I just have a feeling that something is in the air, and this whole program concocted by Papa will blow up. Call it male intuition, but something's going to happen."

"Well, if you had women's intuition, you'd realize that Natalie will be fine. She'll have a few tough months, but between your family and me, we'll get her through. Maybe you can even visit your sister once in a while. That's not so unusual, is it?"

I confessed that it was infrequent at best. I never took the time to drive all the way out to Chelmsford to see my sister. Anyway, she often came to Boston to see Mama and Papa and that's when I would drop in to see her.

"I think you're right, Regina," I added. "It's perfectly natural for a brother to visit his sister. I really should be doing more of that. And anyway, Natalie doesn't know I never visit Connie. I'll need to call Connie and tell her to keep her mouth shut about that. Connie will definitely get it."

Chapter Eleven

Unexpected Turn

On the first weekend in June, I paid a visit to my folks' house. I tried my best to visit them every week, usually on the weekend. Papa gave me his typical "How are you doing? Is everything OK?" If I answered in the affirmative, which I always did, he went inside and left me alone. Unless I made the effort to engage him or to sit and watch television with him, we might not see each other my whole visit, until it was time to say goodbye. Sometimes I took Mama out for lunch or to see a movie. I always picked a movie with a simple plot because she got lost in the new complicated Hollywood adventure films. A chick flick or light comedy was good, as long as the gratuitous sex and profanity was kept to a tolerable level.

When I got to Papa's house, he was reading the news online. I always got a kick out of being a spectator watching my parents interact. After all these years, they said whatever came into their minds, without really thinking about the other's feelings. Papa particularly liked stories about religion and reading the obituaries of famous people. This fed two of his favorite obsessions. I was a bit surprised when Papa asked Mama about the new pope. He really tried to be respectful of Mama's strong faith and belief in God, but sometimes he became a little devilish in a playful way.

"Mama, are you aware of the fact that Pope Francis canonized Pope John Paul II and Pope John XXIII?"

"Of course," said Mama. "Unlike some people in this house, I go to church every Sunday and hear about such things."

Papa wondered out loud, "Do you think this new pope might be setting a precedent so that when he dies he will be canonized?"

Mama exclaimed, "Absolutely not! This pope has recognized the goodness and purity of these two great men and seeks their just reward."

"Lots of people are good and pure and they are not made saints. Aren't they supposed to perform some miracles to become saints?" Papa queried.

"They have performed miracles," Mama insisted.

"What were the miracles, Mama? You seem to know a lot about this subject."

"Oh, I believe they cured someone," Mama said casually.

"In that case, don't you think Oral Roberts should have been canonized?" Papa said, baiting her. "Anyway, I think that Pope Francis is going to waive one of the miracles for Pope John Paul II. I don't believe it should be harder to get into Cooperstown than to become a saint. Being a saint is a pretty big deal. It means statues, new churches named, hometown museums – you know, the works."

"Papa, I should know better than to discuss anything resembling faith with you. You are the most cynical person I ever met. But I have not given up on you. You will see the light one day."

"Here's a truly sad and tragic story. A young man lost his battle against a very rare disease. I can remember seeing this same story in a *Ripley's Believe It Or Not* book I took out in elementary school. It's funny how these things stick with you all these years. In very rare cases these young children grow, and look like they are aged when they might only be in their teens. As you might suspect, they heartbreakingly succumb to this disease at a very young age."

"That is heart-wrenching," she agreed. "It's always tragic when parents lose their children." Mama is the world's most ardent supporter of loving kindness toward children and animals.

"I'm fortunate, Mama. I have the opposite problem. You know, I have the same malady that Benjamin Button had. Now that I've reached sixty-five, I'll be getting younger. You may have noticed that since I reached my last birthday I appear to be younger and better looking. It will be very sad for me in twenty years when I'm in my forties and you will be – well, let's just hope that you will be. The only thing that I really dread is becoming a baby again and then, poof! You know, you just can't win in this life."

Mama, almost ignoring Papa's fantasy, said, "I really feel sorry for you." Mama mostly paid no attention to Papa's childish delusions. He would occasionally say something remotely funny by accident but more often his stories were juvenile attempts at humor.

Then Papa read that the Preakness Stakes was coming up soon. He knew Mama was very interested in the Kentucky Derby, since she'd had her very first mint julep when they had visited Churchill Downs. Personally, Papa felt the drink was far too bitter. Papa preferred sweeter drinks like those fruity Hawaiian concoctions. His favorite drink was rum and Coke – only hold the rum. Papa mentioned that the California-something horse that won the Kentucky Derby had a chance to win the Triple Crown.

Mama said, "I wished that Rosie Napravnik had won that race and become the first female jockey to win the Kentucky Derby."

Papa laughed. "A woman come in first? I believe she came in last. Look it up. What's the good in being the first female jockey if you're going to be last? Hell, I could be last and I never rode a horse."

"Sure, but you're not a woman, so it wouldn't be a first. Maybe you could be the first 200-pound jockey to win. Now that would be a first. You could be the fattest jockey to ever win the Kentucky Derby."

Papa wanted to blare at Mama, "Bang, zoom, straight to the moon, Alice!" But he didn't. He let Mama have the last word. Mama usually had the last word.

On a much more serious note, Papa wanted me to remember that today was his father's birthday. Maybe his corny attempts at humor masked the real melancholy that was in his heart. I was only about seven years old when my grandfather died, but I remember him. Papa would always force me to spend time with my grandparents. I didn't realize how important that was until I was much older and it was too late. My grandfather could only speak Italian so it was very difficult for me to understand him. You would have thought that he would have picked up English living in Boston as long as he did, but he never made much of an effort. Papa would always translate any business or legal issues that periodically arose. My grandmother survived my grandfather by a couple of years. I think that once he died she felt her own life was practically useless. She lived to serve my grandfather and never really had a life of her own. She was a tough but caring woman, from what I can remember.

Papa said with some sadness, "Today my father would be 104 years old."

It's not as if we have a lot of 104-year olds walking around, I thought. I was bracing for another discourse by Papa on his favorite obsession.

"Papa died twenty-one years ago. If I had been born when my father was twenty-one, then I would be at the age he died right now. I'm glad he had the foresight to wait until he was nearly forty to have me. Anyway, that's no guarantee for anything. I could easily drop dead this afternoon."

Mama and I looked at each other with that familiar here-he-goes-again look. We should have anticipated this today. Papa's father's birthday is like his New Year's or countdown to doom.

Mama spoke up. "Your father was a very heavy smoker and got practically no exercise for the last twenty years of his life. I'm surprised that he lived as long as he did."

"That's my point, Mama. Life is totally unpredictable. I hold on to my father's longevity as a life preserver in the sea of unknown perils. If nothing else, my father did live a very active life. He worked hard as a laborer until he retired at sixty-five. I never saw him drink alcohol. I believe that's because he abused the stuff when he was young. He almost never ate meat. He ate lots of lentils, eggplant, pasta, some fish, and other good stuff like that. He would only drink water. Isn't that odd? I never saw him drink soda, juice, beer, or anything outside of an occasional single glass of wine. His weight was never a problem, as long as I knew him. And here I am overweight. I eat far too much crap. I eat too many potato chips, too much ice cream, too much meat, too much of the wrong things. I try to avoid it but I am weak. This will be my undoing."

Mama tried to be reassuring. "Papa, you look better now than most men fifteen years younger than you are. You can still jog miles, and you still do more pushups than most thirty year olds. Just keep working on that food problem. You will be fine."

"You have always been my biggest cheerleader, Mama, but I know I'm getting old. I was surfing the channels last night and noticed this story about Katy Perry. Who the hell is Katy Perry? I've heard of Gaylord Perry, Jim Perry, Perry Como and Perry Mason, but who the hell is Katy Perry? Apparently she is a big, big star. Did you ever hear of her, Mama?"

"Of course I have, Papa. Everybody on the planet has heard of her. I can't believe that as much as you read and watch television you haven't heard of her until now."

Papa looked embarrassed. "I guess she does not run in the same circles as those things that interest me."

"Of course not," said Mama. "All you watch are reruns of *Columbo, Gunsmoke,* and *Matlock*, and occasionally you will enter this century by watching *Monk*. News flash, Papa: *Monk* is now in reruns, too. If not those, you are watching movies starring Frank Sinatra, Elvis Presley, or Marilyn Monroe. None of those actors are making any new movies."

I wouldn't say a word. Mama was doing just fine without my input. It didn't really matter. Papa was not about to change. He was stuck in the past and enjoyed it there. And yet, he was very well versed on current events and the news of the day. I just think shows like *Entertainment Tonight* and any kind of reality show he tuned out.

"I watch lots of current shows," argued Papa.

Mama answered, "Let's not count Red Sox games, ESPN, or the news as current shows. If you take those out of the equation, the average age of movies or television shows you watch is 1968."

"Well, maybe you're right, Mama. Ricky, your Mama is right. I want you to go down to the video store and rent *Katy Perry: Part of Me*. They mentioned it in the piece I saw about her."

"I hate to tell you this, Papa," I said. "There are no more video stores. Blockbuster closed its doors. You could try Redbox, but I doubt if they would have it. But you are in luck, Papa. We can watch it on Netflix streaming. I have an account and we could connect through your Blu-Ray."

"Oh, never mind," said Papa. "The Red Sox game is starting. Maybe another time."

"All right, Papa, another time."

I said goodbye to my parents and set out for home.

Papa developed a very deep-seated set of values to go along with his obsessions. I say this only to help you understand that they have influenced Connie and me. However, as any semi-observant person can see, the values of the parents do not necessarily become manifest in the child. In particular, I refer to divorce. You don't need to look very hard to find people divorcing today with their own parents married for forty or fifty years or more. The arguments for these divorces are usually pretty good. Why should I stay in a loveless marriage? We have grown apart. I was too young when I got married. Man was not meant to stay with one woman his whole entire life. There are about a million more reasons. I thank God that Mama and Papa have stayed married. However, I think life today is much more complicated, with more temptations, more distractions, and more open avenues and opportunities for infidelity than ever before. I acknowledge that infidelity is not the only reason for divorce, but it is a biggie.

The little voice inside my head heard Papa's words on this loud and clear. You made a vow before God, church, and family. How can that be taken lightly? If you get divorced, you will find another woman, fall in love again, and then after a few years the same exact bullshit will occur that ruined your first marriage. No, Papa would correct himself. It's really not the same bullshit – it's different bullshit with a slightly different stink. Then he goes on to lay a guilt trip on any parent who divorces when a child is still at home. Now you must send your beloved children to stay with an ex-husband, a stepmother, and step-everything else. How can they possibly love your children as they love their own? Why would you want to waste the few precious years you have with your children, spending those years as only a part-time father or mother? He painted a really bleak picture of divorce. Papa maintained with ferocious certainty that no matter how bad things were, losing your children was ten times worse. Put your energy into making your marriage work. You loved this woman for a reason. Recapture the feeling, Papa would say. Things change in life, so you change, too. Treat your wife with love and respect and you will overcome nearly all obstacles that arise.

You are probably asking yourself why I'm going off in this direction. It's because of Jeremy and Kathy. Without boring you with all the details of my spying, let's just say that I have gotten pretty good at sleuthing. I have even been able to entice others to eavesdrop on Jeremy and Kathy when they were out in public. There was this one girl in particular who doubled as my date and co-conspirator. I think she enjoyed the excitement attached to spying on a married woman having an affair. As an extra benefit, it made her horny as hell when Jeremy took Kathy off to his secret rendezvous. I almost felt as if I was cheating on Natalie myself, except I forced myself to go on living in the real world, and not in my fantasy world where Natalie loves me.

I have learned that Jeremy was falling in love with Kathy. Whether it was a line or factual, I wasn't able to determine. Then I asked myself, why would Jeremy talk about love with Kathy when he knew that she was married and that her husband would be returning in a few months? Why would he encourage Kathy to reciprocate if he was so devoted to Natalie? It made me both furious and frustrated. I wanted to bust in and confront Jeremy on the spot but restrained myself because of Regina. She held firm to her belief that telling Natalie could be injurious to the baby. Personally, I didn't buy it, but God forbid I should be wrong. It just wasn't worth the risk. What was worse, Kathy told Jeremy that she hadn't been married that long and only knew her husband a few months before they married. She told Jeremy that she fell in love with the uniform and the excitement of going to different places. Instead, she discovered that being a serviceman's wife was like being fitted with a chastity belt for long periods of time. Kathy told Jeremy that she needed a full-time man. This sure sounded like someone headed for a divorce. Maybe I should have told her what Papa thought about divorce. Of course I wouldn't, because Kathy might very well be the answer to my prayer for getting rid of Jeremy. I would much rather that Jeremy self-imploded. Trying to explain to Natalie how we knew Jeremy was cheating would not be a pleasant or dignified thing to do, even though she did ask Regina to check on Jeremy.

Jeremy received an unexpected call from Mrs. Romano one evening during the second week in June. No one really enjoys getting calls from the in-laws. The fact that Jeremy was not even an in-law yet made it worse. Add to this Jeremy's conflicted feelings arising from his new romantic attraction to Kathy and the call from Natalie's mom became quite objectionable. Mrs. Romano invited Jeremy to dinner on Saturday. She felt an obligation to Natalie not to ignore Jeremy during her daughter's absence. It would also give Mr. and Mrs. Romano an opportunity to talk with Jeremy alone. Mrs. Romano could not remember being with Jeremy outside of the company of her daughter. She knew the reason for Natalie's breakup with Jeremy and was also wary of Jeremy's character. Jeremy could not think of a worse way to spend Saturday. He already had a beautiful getaway planned for the weekend with Kathy.

"That would be terrific, Mrs. Romano. I'd love to see you and Mr. Romano this weekend. Is it possible that we do this on Friday instead? I have to work this Saturday."

I knew from Jeremy's habits that he picked his new girlfriend up on Fridays to have more time with her. If he had the typical Saturday or Sunday dinner invitation, his weekend of lovemaking would be ruined. Hell, he could pick Kathy up Friday after the dinner. Kathy would understand. His only fear would be getting caught in a lie if someone checked on him Saturday at the hospital. This was unlikely and a risk he would be willing to take.

"I think we can manage Friday. Will seven o'clock work for you? Good." Mrs. Romano had another more important question to ask Jeremy during dinner.

Jeremy must have discussed the change in plans with Kathy, who looked forward to being with Jeremy as much as he did. Kathy was still cautious, however. From what I can infer, she made friends with other wives at the base and did not want to be seen in public with a man. She would make excuses about working on the weekend or visiting relatives. The fact that she did not have any really close friends made her time off base less of a problem.

When the fateful day came for dinner, Jeremy arrived with a smile and a box of pastries from Mike's. Jeremy remembered Mr. Romano's fondness for cannoli. Mrs. Romano had the house looking festive in spite of the fact there was no particular holiday any time soon. She prepared codfish and fried clams accompanied by linguine and a variety of vegetables. The Boston cream pie for dessert made Jeremy's cannoli superfluous, but Mr. Romano still managed to eat two desserts, not wanting to offend Jeremy. Quite naturally, they mostly discussed Natalie and how they all missed her. They brought up Natalie's sudden and surprising decision to make this trip right after graduation. The Romanos tried to avoid the subject of marriage, not wanting to appear presumptuous. Mrs. Romano asked Jeremy about work and how he spent his free time now that Natalie was away. Jeremy was far too clever to fall into that snare. In fact, he anticipated that question and had a prepared response. Mr. and Mrs. Romano appeared satisfied with his answer and with the evening in general. And then Mrs. Romano dropped the bombshell.

"Jeremy, how would you like to visit Natalie in Sicily? We were thinking about surprising her in September. It's very hot in Sicily, but at least in September it should be bearable. September is about the halfway point in her mission. I think she would be thrilled to see us after being there four months."

Jeremy was totally taken aback. "But don't you remember that she specifically told us that she would be very busy every day. We can't even call her. She has to call us. This would be a very big expense and we might not even be able to see her."

"That's true," Mr. Romano responded, "but she can't be working twenty-four/seven. Even if we only see her a few hours a day, that would be fine. And I'm sure that if the administration knew we were visiting, they would give her at least one day off. Anyway, we have always wanted to visit Sicily and we would have time to vacation and see the sights."

"Wow! This I never expected when I came for dinner," said Jeremy. "That sounds great and I would love to go but I really just started at the hospital. I wouldn't be able to take time off so soon. Even if I could, it would cost thousands of dollars for the trip. I'm saving every penny for when Natalie and I get married."

"That's terrific. You keep that money and let us take care of your flight, your room, your meals, and anything else. Consider it an early wedding present." Mr. Romano was very persuasive.

Perhaps Jeremy realized that he didn't really want to go. Perhaps he didn't want to use or take an advance on his vacation time. More importantly, perhaps he realized he didn't want to leave Kathy for even one week. I don't know if he considered telling the Romanos that he might not even marry their daughter, but even he probably knew that this would be a terrible way for Natalie to find out.

"Thank you so much, Mr. and Mrs. Romano. This is very generous. In fact, it's too generous. It would really be awful seeing you go through all this expense for me. God forbid, what if something should happen before or after you spend all this money?"

"What could happen?" Mrs. Romano said abashedly. "Is there something you need to tell us, Jeremy?"

"Of course not. I only meant what if there was an emergency at work and I couldn't leave. What if Natalie decides she wants to stay in Sicily because she found her calling and decides to call off the wedding? What if she fell in love with a handsome doctor?"

"Jeremy, I hate to tell you, but I think the hospital can manage a few days without you. And Natalie loves you. Do you know something I don't?" Mrs. Romano's suspicions about Jeremy were getting confirmed.

"Of course not," said Jeremy. "Let me call you early next week about this. I can't make a commitment without talking to my boss."

"Certainly," Mr. Romano replied.

The shock over, everyone exchanged pleasantries and said their goodbyes. Mr. and Mrs. Romano discussed Jeremy's reaction. In typical fashion, Mr. Romano saw nothing unusual. Mrs. Romano was much more insightful. Knowing Jeremy's recent penchant for "romance," she had a bad feeling about his degree of commitment and love for Natalie.

Jeremy immediately drove to meet Kathy at their prearranged location. His head must have been swimming from the events of the evening. How long could he lead Natalie on, knowing he would never marry her? He knew that on Monday he would call the Romanos and decline their invitation. He would use work as an excuse, blaming his boss for not giving him any time off. Right now all he wanted was to be with Kathy.

Kathy left her car in the hospital parking lot, where it would be safe from vandals or suspicion. Jeremy picked her up and they drove to their romantic hideaway in Saugus. Learning what happened between Jeremy and Kathy after these events occurred, I can only imagine their conversation.

"Did you have a nice dinner with your in-laws?" Kathy asked.

"Don't be funny," Jeremy responded. "That was the weirdest and most uncomfortable dinner I've ever had. Do you know that they invited me to go with them to Italy, all expenses paid?"

"That's unbelievable! How did you handle that one?"

"I told them that it would be impossible, but they just had an answer for every excuse I made. I was able to hold them off. Monday I will definitely call them and tell them my boss refused to give me the time."

Kathy pensively replied, "Jeremy, here we are ready to destroy Natalie's life and Jason's life and run off to be together forever. Do I have that about right, Jeremy?"

"You make it sound so tawdry, but yes. I love you, Kathy, and want to spend my whole life with you."

"Correct me if I'm wrong, Jeremy. Didn't you tell Natalie that same exact thing? And didn't I promise to forsake all others and be with Jason until death do us part?"

"I will admit that Natalie and I have an understanding about getting engaged when she comes back but meeting you has proven to me that would be a mistake. How could I marry her when I love you?"

"And how could I marry you when I'm married to Jason? Should I reward his patriotism by divorcing him the minute he returns safely? I guess that when I am alone with my thoughts, I just don't like myself."

"I absolutely get it," Jeremy replied. "Don't you think that I called myself a bastard for what I'm about to do to Natalie? Love is a very intimate and quiet feeling that eats away at your soul. I tricked myself into thinking I loved Natalie because she is beautiful, a wonderful person who is caring, attentive, and charming. Should I go on?"

"It sounds like you are an idiot to give that up," said Kathy.

"That's my point, Kathy. Even with all that, I think only about you. What we have is special. It's intimacy and it's natural. I can say and do things with you that I could never do with Natalie. Natalie is a bit of a prude and meeting you aroused a fire in me that will burn for at least sixty more years. Where is this coming from? The other day you told me that you married Jason to escape your humdrum life. You said you really didn't know him all that long before you married."

"All this is true and I confess to being totally confused after meeting you. Don't you ever ask yourself if we aren't using our attraction for each other to expel the deserted, empty, lonely feeling we have inside right now? One thing cannot be denied. You and I are both very sexually attracted to each other and have a great time in bed. I wonder if this is love or great sex? What if you or I had to leave for a few months for whatever reason? Could you be true to me if I left? Could I? Isn't that the definition of love?"

Jeremy was certain. "I know that I could. I have proven that. I stayed with Natalie for nearly two years, never having sex with her. And believe me, you know that was not my idea. I stayed with her because I really thought I loved her. Things have changed. It's not just the separation. I waited for her before but I can't since I met you."

"That's an interesting side of you I never would have believed. Look, Jeremy, I love you too and want to be with you. But I have to know if I would still feel this way after Jason comes home. I can't imagine loving you less. I want to convince myself that it's more than Jason's absence making me love you."

"Then I should let you welcome Jason home. I should sit home and imagine him fucking you while I wonder if I will ultimately win the big love fest contest. Don't you know that would torture me? Do you want me to run back into Natalie's arms and pretend that these weeks with you have been a way to mark time until she returned?"

"This is much harder for me, Jeremy. I am married and Jason has done nothing but care and fight for me. I am only expressing my feelings. We have a couple of months to explore them before Natalie and Jason return. In the meantime, I want to be with you. I'm glad you're not going to Sicily. It would be hard for me to find another lover to take your place in only one week."

"Very funny. Let's forget all this for now. It's right that you told me how you feel. I was blinded by my own selfish desire to be with you and I still hold on to that desire. You're right. Time will tell what happens. It always does," said Jeremy.

The brutally honest soul-searching from Kathy in no way altered her weekend with Jeremy. Their lovemaking convinced her that they had something very special. Jeremy already knew that. The difference between Jeremy and Kathy is that Kathy thought with her head and Jeremy thought with his dick. She knew that the excitement would inevitably subside into routine. If she left her husband for Jeremy, then Jeremy would be the new husband. Lovemaking would no longer be a forbidden, electrifying thrill. It would always be desirable, but without love the feeling would ebb like the tide of passion, like it always does in time. Kathy knew that before she left Jason, she should wait for his return and play the dutiful wife in every way. If Jeremy could not deal with that, then it was too bad.

On Monday afternoon, Jeremy called Mr. Romano to apologize that he would not be able to go with them to Sicily. He explained that his boss was not able to give him the time off in September. It was company policy that employees had to work there for at least six months before they could access their vacation leave. He assured Mr. Romano that he tried to persuade his boss that he would have those six months by October anyway. He added that his boss was a stickler for the rules and he didn't want to set a precedent. Mr. Romano was very gracious and said he totally understood.

Secretly, Mr. Romano was happy for two reasons. Without Jeremy taking up all his time with Natalie, they would have a much more memorable vacation. Second, and just as important to Mr. Romano, he could save the thousands of dollars in hotels, food, and airfare that he promised Jeremy. Mr. Romano told Jeremy that he would make his apologies for him to Mrs. Romano.

Mrs. Romano said to her husband, unflustered, "That doesn't surprise me one bit. Couldn't you tell that Jeremy was taken aback when we sprung the news of this trip on him, Harry? He never wanted to go in the first place and he was just stalling for time until he could find a way to bow out gracefully."

"Kathryn, think about what you're saying. He is offered a free, all-expense-paid trip to Sicily to see the woman he loves. What young man in his right mind would pass that up?"

"That's what I love about you, Harry. You live in your own little fantasia. It is so easy to put something over on you because you live in la-la land. This fact has really served me well over the years. Remind me to tell you about it one day."

Mr. Romano let his wife have the last word. It wasn't so much that he wasn't up to the verbal repartee, but he knew that she was right.

The next day, Mrs. Romano called Jeremy's boss at the hospital. She was not in the habit of trying to catch a person in a lie, but this situation had her convinced that her intuition was unclouded. She had no trouble finding the man's number in the hospital directory and left him a message to call at his earliest convenience.

"Hello, is this Kathryn Romano?"

"Yes, thank you for calling so quickly, Mr. Holden. I'm actually calling for some information on your vacation policy. I understand that your employees are not permitted any vacation time until they have worked there six months. Is that correct?

"Not exactly," Mr. Holden replied. "Employees earn one vacation day per month of service. If they work here six months, they have accumulated six vacation days."

"So if someone worked there five months, they would be entitled to five vacation days. Is that correct?" asked Mrs. Romano.

"That's right. Why are you asking?" Mr. Holden inquired.

"We were considering taking Jeremy Quinn with us to see his soon-to-be fiancée in Italy in September. I was wondering how many days of leave he would have. Did Jeremy discuss this vacation with you?"

Unsuspecting, Mr. Holden answered, "No, he hasn't. But he should have five days leave by then. In fact, if he needed more, I'm sure we could work something out. I don't expect Jeremy to leave us, and even if he did, he would simply be docked those unearned leave days. We're pretty flexible around here."

"Thank you so much for your time and responsiveness. And please don't mention our conversation to Jeremy. We may not even be able to make this trip and I would hate to disappoint him. You know how young lovers are."

"I totally understand, Mrs. Romano. I can almost remember being young and in love myself. You have my promise that I will not mention this to Jeremy."

Mrs. Romano thanked Mr. Holden and hung up the phone. Now that her suspicions were confirmed, she wondered what it all meant. She was reluctant to rub her husband's nose in this news. He had a tendency to fly off the handle and make things worse than they really were. She was also reluctant to confront Jeremy with his own lie. It would make her seem distrustful of him while also putting him on the defensive. She would have to think about the wisest reaction.

While Jeremy was having dinner with the Romanos that Friday evening, I was visiting my parents, taking advantage of my weekly free meal. I still liked Mama's cooking better than anything I could prepare or find at a restaurant. During baseball season, I liked to sit and keep Papa company while he watched the Red Sox game. After the game, I typically went out and started my evening, unless I had a date and needed to leave earlier. Even though I only lived a few miles from Papa and Mama's house, it was not unusual for me to stay the night. I still had my old room and Mama always kept it ready for me as if I still lived there. This was a very comforting feeling. I believe that if it didn't appear unmanly to live with your parents at my age, I would still be there today. Of course, there were major disadvantages in not having your own place when it came to entertaining the ladies. For that reason alone I had to move out, but I could have used the money I would have saved in rent.

My bedroom was on one end of the hall, and my parents still slept together in the master bedroom on the opposite end of the hall. The bathroom was in the middle. I started to notice that Papa would always get up during the night to use the bathroom, sometimes twice. I had the unfortunate nature of being an extremely light sleeper and knew this was a recent change in his habits. The change could directly be pinpointed to the time that his prostate gland was removed. This occurrence saddened me as much as it inconvenienced my father. It was another indication that his life was approaching a new and possibly final chapter. I found myself lying in bed worrying that Papa would soon be gone and out of my life. This sad but inevitable fact preoccupied my thoughts. The years of Papa's obsessing about his death started to play with my psyche. Yet Papa was still a very strong man. I hate to admit this fact, but I would never want to take him on in single combat. It would be embarrassing for a man in the prime of life to be bested by a man of his years. He was blessed with a powerful frame and had about forty pounds and four inches on me. Why I inherited Mama's DNA was a matter of genetics.

I would often lie in bed and imagine the feeling of being without this man, though aware of the selfishness of it all. I no longer needed Papa in the sense that I was dependent upon him for sustenance, but I still needed Papa to be in the world for my sense of emotional security. I know that I was preparing myself in my own way for his eventual final goodbye.

About five years earlier, a friend gave me a black necktie. I resolved never to wear that tie until the time came for Papa or Mama's funeral. I put it on my tie rack and looked at it each time I readied myself for work in the morning. There have been other funerals of people I knew at work or older relatives since I received this tie, but I never put it on. It was as if keeping this accessory on the tie rack would stave off death itself. As it turned out, that tie stayed put where it belonged for twenty-five years. My worrying about Papa's return of cancer or labored breathing or subtle loss of mental faculties continued a very long time. It was long enough to prepare me mentally, but that's a subject I will discuss in more detail later.

I already mentioned Papa's obsession with collecting digital music. He eventually arrived at the point of accepting that the storage of MP3 files was sufficient. He no longer felt the compulsion to make CD backups of every file. I may have mentioned that he organized songs either by artist or year and burned CDs of them. He was only up to the J's when he questioned his own sanity in doing this. I believe this coincided with his purchase of an iMac computer, because he finally found a computer that he felt was dependable enough to store and organize his music. He still maintained backups of his files but finally trusted other sources like external backups and companies that kept his files in cyberspace. This saved him lots of money, since he no longer had to buy blank CD ROMs, labels, storage cases, cabinets, and ink, but it mostly saved him time. He literally had 978 Academy Award movie soundtracks on CD dating back to 1934. He made an additional 983 CDs of top 100 songs for recording artists from Billboard's top 100 songs from 1955-2007. This took up lots of space in his music room. He had shelves and cabinets to store all this music. He also had twenty-eight boxes of vinyl 45s, 236 long-playing albums, and another 169 commercial CDs. His decision to store his music digitally became a matter of practicality. If not, he would need another room, which Mama was adamantly against. She put her foot down whenever she noticed that Papa's music, DVDs, or VHS tapes were making their way into bedroom or living room bookcases. This was not a fight that Papa was willing to wage because he knew Mama, as accommodating as she was, would win this battle.

I really get a kick out of listening to Mama and Papa discussing a life that preceded my existence. I was fortunate to grow up in a home filled with music from another era. Papa's stories, music, and movies introduced me to a history of which most people my age are ignorant. One time when Papa was working on his "L" songs, he mentioned to Mama that this particular song by Steve Lawrence in 1962 was one of the first songs he learned all the words to by heart. He proceeded to prove that a half-century later he could still remember all the words. Papa had a decent voice and mostly sang in tune but gave himself far too much credit as a crooner.

Mama said, "It's too bad that Roman Polanski and Woody Allen didn't listen to that song and take it to heart."

The song was "Go Away Little Girl," and not knowing the details of the reference, the remark flew over my head. Later I had to check Wikipedia in order to "get it."

"You're right, Mama," he replied, "but at least Donnie Osmond listened." Apparently fourteen year-old Donnie Osmond covered the song. He must have been having lots of trouble with an adoring ten-year-old.

This Saturday morning, I left after breakfast. I had nothing pressing to do, but I resisted the urge to visit my sister Connie. Of course, it was Natalie and not Connie that I wanted to see. Then totally out of the blue, Connie called me to ask if I would like to pay a visit. Connie was a good sister. She knew that I never drove to Chelmsford to visit. But she also knew that Natalie didn't know that.

Chapter Twelve

June

I arrived at Connie's house about noon. This was a calculated arrival time since I already had breakfast at Mama's house and would be ready for lunch soon after I arrived. If nothing else, it would afford me the opportunity to gaze at Natalie. I tried to be inconspicuous and stare at her without her noticing. This wasn't easy since Natalie still considered me a stalker and was on guard against my examination. In fact, I know that I caught her once or twice taking a quick peek at me. I wasn't sure if she was checking me out as a potential mate for life or just wary of my ogling her and sending me a message to stop it. I suspect the latter.

Natalie was about two and a half months pregnant by then. I had more than a casual interest in her condition. Connie protected Natalie against all danger like a mother bear. I never spent much time around pregnant women, but I've heard the expression, "she's glowing." That expression did not apply to Natalie. Natalie was not glowing – she was on fire. Her skin was smooth and even-toned with a bronze sheen exaggerated by the warm June sun and her Mediterranean roots. The Irish in her was manifest in her shimmering auburn hair that now seemed to take on a tawny luster. Her cheeks were rosier, as if the blood in her face was perfectly positioned to make her look illuminating. The only failing was in eyes saddened by her circumstances. If she had welcomed this pregnancy, I know she would have attained a look of perfection. I hoped against all hope that she would cherish this time of nurturing life. The fact that this baby would not ultimately be hers made the circumstances doleful.

I purposely didn't engage Natalie in conversation, not wanting to insinuate my presence into her private world. I imagined that my being here made her feel uncomfortable. I wanted to break the ice and speak with her but waited for Natalie to make the first move. As it turned out, my patience and strategy were ineffectual. Natalie never uttered a word to me and that included the words "hello" and "goodbye." At least I had the gratification of hearing her soft, ethereal voice. Connie engaged Natalie in conversation about how she felt and her plans for the upcoming week and asked her if there was anywhere she wanted to go. I believe that Connie did this more for my sake.

Thomas asked me how I was doing, which gave me the opportunity to talk about my work and what I did for fun. I told Thomas that I was going with a few friends to Vermont for some hiking and camping next weekend. I also spoke about visiting Papa and Mama last night and leaving their house this morning. I thought I detected some perking of Natalie's ears during this exchange. It was as if Natalie restrained herself from asking how they were doing. God forbid she was to inquire about them to me. That would involve a civil chat, which Natalie was not prepared to do. All in all, lunch was fairly uncomfortable. We had little to talk about, since my presence put Natalie in a reticent mood.

I considered inviting everyone out for a drive or a movie or to see Butterfly Place. I especially thought visiting Butterfly Place would be a pleasant diversion for a pregnant lady, to put her in the right frame of mind. I helped Connie take lunch plates in to the kitchen and shared my idea, which she liked. However, when she invited Natalie, extolling the virtues of Butterfly Place and the desirability of getting out of the house for an excursion, Natalie declined without a reason. She excused herself after lunch and hid away in her room.

I got the hint and only stayed about three hours with Connie and Thomas. I actually wanted to leave the moment Natalie placed herself in isolation, but for appearance's sake I remained there a suitable amount of time. At least I established the fact that I actually visited my sister on occasion. If I arrived there some day in the future, it would not necessarily mean I stopped over for the express purpose of pursuing Natalie's affection.

On a hunch, I decided to return to Boston by way of Saugus. I suspected that Jeremy and his new love might return to the Chisholm Motor Inn, and I was right. The location was convenient to both Boston and Hanscom Air Force Base, and I suspected that by now Jeremy was more interested in lovemaking than he was in being cautious. Jeremy's weekend ritual appeared to be spending time with Kathy. Regina told me all about Kathy and of course I had seen her myself on previous occasions. It was approaching dinnertime, and since I basically don't have a life, I decided to park where I could get a good view. Jeremy paid little attention to me the one time we met at Natalie's house for dinner, but since he might remember what I looked like, I tried to disguise myself by wearing a hat and sunglasses. I was a bit more concerned about remaining parked in my car for any length of time. I didn't want the clerk to come outside to ask me what I was doing.

Fortunately, Jeremy and Kathy left for dinner about forty minutes after I arrived and no one had approached me. They drove a short distance to Jimmy's Steer House. Knowing that the restaurant is not the spot for a quiet, leisurely dinner, I surmised that Jeremy was anxious to get Kathy back to the room.

Fortunately for my espionage purposes, the hostess seated them at a table beside the bar, where an empty barstool awaited my company. They chatted about the menu before their conversation yielded anything that I found of interest.

"Kathy, are we OK?" I overheard Jeremy ask. "I mean, you sounded really conflicted the last time we spoke. Have you had a chance to do some soul-searching?"

"I thought of little else, Jeremy, but I see you at work and I continue to spend all my free time with you in bed. It's hard for me to get a perspective."

"So what does that mean? Are you thinking of quitting work?" Jeremy's voice took on an impish tone. "Then I will be monopolizing only your free time. I think that's a terrific idea because at work I am always wanting to grab you and make love to you behind the X-ray machine."

Kathy whispered, "What's the other alternative?"

Her tone lacked the playfulness that Jeremy was trying to encourage.

"I know that you're not thinking about leaving me," he said, his voice taking on a confidence that seemed forced. "What we have is far too good."

"Of course that's what I think about," said Kathy. "I think about it constantly. I tell myself that this is crazy. We are playing with other people's lives here. And then I pick up the phone to tell you that I am not coming but grab my car keys instead. I am too weak to leave you."

"That's not weakness," Jeremy assured her. "That's passion, desire, and love."

"It's interesting that you wrapped my feelings together in that particular order because ultimately the first one burns out, the second wanes, and if this is to be forever we're really left only with the last."

Jeremy smiled and said, "How do I love thee? Let me count the ways."

"Please don't," interrupted Kathy. "First of all, you probably only remember the first line and I would hate to see you embarrass yourself. But passion is there somewhere, only it's not used in the lustful way you behave. But that's fine. I really like the way you display your passion. I think that Elizabeth Barrett had a lustful streak in her, too. She probably wanted some good loving so she married this guy Robert Browning who was six years younger than she was. How old are you anyway, Jeremy?"

"I'm old enough for you, but more importantly, I am young enough for you. Let's go back to the room. You're making me horny."

Their food arrived and they ate in silence. I pivoted my stool a bit so I could watch the dastardly little lovebirds. Kathy's eyes were on her food, occasionally wandering around the room, but Jeremy's eyes roved no farther than Kathy – primarily focusing on the cleavage that her low V-neck shirt did little to hide.

"It's time for dessert," Jeremy said seductively when Kathy finally lay down her fork.

Kathy smiled and signaled the server. Her smile disappeared. I followed her eyes and saw that an airman in uniform had just entered the restaurant. Kathy hung her head low and turned away from the officer. As soon as he and his party were seated, Kathy got up and left, her face averted – leaving Jeremy to pay the bill and wonder why she'd left so quickly.

Regina arranged to visit with Natalie that Sunday. Natalie told her that would be great, because she was dying to get out of the house. Of course, that meant as long as I wasn't part of the getting out scenario. Natalie would apparently prefer being incarcerated if the alternative was going out in public with me. Natalie and Connie went to church on Sunday about ten o'clock, and Regina arrived about twenty-four hours after my unwelcome arrival the previous day.

"Where would you like to go, Natalie?" Regina asked.

"I'd like to go to Butterfly Place. Ricky Santo mentioned it when he was here yesterday."

"Then why didn't you go with him yesterday?" Regina probed. "He would do anything short of murder to take you out with him."

"Me go out with *him*? Have you lost your mind, Regina?"

"Have you really taken a good look at Ricky?" Regina queried. "He is a really good-looking guy, he earns a fairly decent living, and he has two terrific parents whom you have come to care about. You told me that Connie and Thomas are good people. He adores you more than any woman deserves, and you ask if *I've* lost my mind. I should be so lucky to have someone love me so much."

"I already have someone who loves me more than he does" Natalie replied. "I have Jeremy."

Regina managed to control herself. She really wanted to blurt out to Natalie what a total bastard her fiancé was and she had the pictures to prove it. But Regina simply told Natalie that Ricky loved her more than she could ever imagine.

"How could you possibly know how much Santo loves me?" inquired Natalie. "Do you see him now?"

"No," lied Regina. "I was there when all this went down. I remember everything about Ricky and especially how much he worshiped you."

"You mean how much he stalked me. I don't want to talk about Santo anymore."

"OK." Regina surrendered. "And why do you want to go to Butterfly Place?"

"You remember when Janet got married last summer in Revere? They had this whole butterfly theme and when they said their vows they released a boxful of butterflies."

"Of course I remember," said Regina. "I remember how the butterflies just lay there in the box and did nothing. I was getting embarrassed for the happy couple. I remember talking to Janet's father, who complained that he spent over $200 to buy some stupid butterflies only to throw them away."

"That's a typical man for you," said Natalie. "I thought it was beautiful. After a few taps on the box all, well most, of the butterflies covered the bridal area. I really thought it was a beautiful way to fly off and start your life together."

"How is it possible that we have remained best friends all these years, Natalie? You and I have totally different ideas about life and love. You see beautiful butterflies and all I see are creepy caterpillars that suddenly grew wings. All I can see is the gross part. We disagree on having sex, Jeremy, Ricky, abortion – should I continue?"

"Well, Regina," said Natalie with a mischievous smile, "I think I'm coming around to your way of thinking when it comes to sex. And I never approved of abortion, not really."

"Only when it comes to you," argued Regina. "Do you think that maybe I'm right about Ricky, and that Jeremy is a two-timing loser who will break your heart one day?"

"Oh, shut up, Regina. Let's go and see the butterflies."

Upon returning to Boston, Regina made a point to stop by and see me. I'm convinced that she wanted to give me hope that Natalie would one day turn to me. She told me that Natalie mentioned my being there the previous day and then proceeded to relive her day spent with Natalie in detail. She especially emphasized that Natalie wanted to go to Butterfly Place, even if it wasn't with me. Regina was fast becoming my biggest ally.

Mrs. Romano was building up to a fever pitch level of excitement. She was energized by the thought of seeing her daughter again and had always wanted to see Sicily, even though she was Irish. She also wanted to surprise her daughter. She knew that Natalie would try to dissuade them from making this trip, since she had been quite adamant about not having any time for socializing. Mrs. Romano couldn't believe that Natalie would be occupied all the time. It wasn't as if the Romanos would be sitting in the room until Natalie was available. There was a lot to do in Sicily as a sightseer. Mr. Romano spoke terrible Italian, but he knew enough to survive.

Saturday afternoon, Mrs. Romano called Jeremy. Her timing must have been right, since Jeremy picked up the phone right away. "Hello, is that you, Mrs. Romano?" answered Jeremy.

Mrs. Romano, though knowing that Jeremy had lied about asking his boss to take time off from work, decided not to entrap him. If she intended to do this, it certainly would not be over the phone. "Yes, Jeremy. How are you today?"

"I couldn't be better," Jeremy said with a smile. Mrs. Romano detected something impish in his tone, but she had no way to suspect what Jeremy really meant or to envision the tousled bed sheets or the woman wrapped up in them.

"Have you spoken to Natalie since we spoke about the trip to Italy?" Mrs. Romano asked.

"Yes, of course," said Jeremy. "We speak every week and sometimes twice a week."

"Did you mention our plans about visiting?"

"No," replied Jeremy. "You gave me the impression that your plans were tentative and that they may have been a surprise."

"You are exactly right, Jeremy. That's why Natalie loves you so much. You are so insightful and brilliant." Kathryn Romano was masterful at hiding the sarcasm that lay behind her words.

"Please, Mrs. Romano. It didn't take a clairvoyant to figure that one out, but thanks anyway. If this is a surprise, your secret is safe with me."

"Thank you, Jeremy," said Mrs. Romano. "It *is* a surprise, as you surmised. We'll probably leave sometime in September. I know it must seem like forever for you, but Natalie will be home by Christmas. Are you sure that you can't arrange time off from work?"

"I really wish I could. You must know how much I miss Natalie," Jeremy said. I suppose he was a master of sarcasm as well.

"Of course I do," said Mrs. Romano. "I was young and in love myself, you know. Stay well, Jeremy. I hope that we can see each other again soon."

"Goodbye, Mrs. Romano. I look forward to that." Jeremy hung up, a look of relief on his face.

With the question of Natalie's knowing about their plans to visit Sicily resolved, Mrs. Romano figured it was time to start planning their trip. She still refrained from telling her husband that Jeremy had lied to them about his work preventing him from going on this trip.

Mr. Romano's relief about not spending the money to pay for a third person on this vacation was short-lived, since Mrs. Romano suggested they invite their son, Rob, to take the vacation with them. She thought that it would be a nice memory, one last family adventure together. It was a small consolation for Mr. Romano, knowing at least it was his own son and not Jeremy he was supporting.

When Rob got the news about their secret trip to Sicily, he was surprisingly agreeable to the idea. He would have no problem getting the time off from work and was excited by the prospect of visiting somewhere, anywhere. Mr. Romano was basically a workaholic and thrifty all his life, and the family had taken few trips. Rob reminded his mother of Amanda Knox and the trouble an American single lady could find in Italy. Kathryn Romano was upset by her son's words but staunchly refuted any such notion. She asserted that Natalie would be working on a humanitarian mission and not taking drugs or consorting with the Sicilian Mafia. The idea of Natalie lying about her plans never entered Mrs. Romano's mind. Natalie was always very truthful and compassionate. That's why she became a nurse and that's why she went to Sicily. Rob agreed with his mother, acknowledging that Natalie was Little Miss Perfect Child. He said this with the natural resentment an older sibling has for an adored younger sister. The truth is, Rob actually felt protective of his sister and would never have any harm come to her if he could prevent it.

Mrs. Romano coordinated the trip. They would leave on Tuesday, September 7, and return the following Friday, September 17. She booked their entire stay at the Castello Camemi in Vizzini, Catania. Her research revealed that this was a decent place to lodge and not too far from where Natalie was staying. It was still a thirty-minute drive from the refugee facility at Mineo, but Mrs. Romano had been unable to find anything closer that was satisfactory. She had about two months to plan the perfect trip, and with the help of a travel guide, she proceeded to do just that. Mr. Romano had little interest in the planning and left the entire vacation in his wife's hands. The truth is that he would've preferred to stay home and make money instead of spending it in a foreign economy. Mr. Romano figured from September to December was only another three months. Natalie was a big girl and he could wait to see her. That's what he told everyone, but deep down Mr. Romano missed his daughter even more than his wife did. If that weren't true, he would have put up a battle to stay home.

The month of June is typically pleasant in New England and this June was no exception. For Natalie, June was a month of waiting, waiting for the life inside her to grow. Connie and Thomas continued to attend to her every need, even though the attention was disconcerting to her. She continued her pretense of being in Sicily by e-mailing, texting, and calling home on her bogus telephone. The phony stories and photos from Sicily made Natalie's fabrication all the more convincing. As he promised, Cousin Rocco mailed Natalie's prewritten letters to her family and to Jeremy every week. Rocco always made certain to include pictures to support the illusion of whatever Natalie wrote. Natalie's handwritten letters and envelopes left no doubt as to their authenticity. Natalie always initiated the call home, praying that no one would call the mission. She continued to assure everyone that things were going well. She asked God to keep her family safe during her time of incubation so they would have no occasion to call her. This was her greatest fear. Had she known what her mother was up to, a new fear would creep into her concerns. She worried that God was not in the business of helping people keep their lies closeted.

My last visit to Connie's house was very disheartening to me. I knew without a doubt that Natalie was not waiting with bated breath until she saw me again, and she made it unmistakably apparent that she did not welcome my presence. She didn't even have the decency to say hello or goodbye. It was just sinking into my thick head that Natalie abhorred the sight of me. This saddened me beyond words because the chances of mutually taking part in our child's life appeared slim to none. I knew that Connie and Thomas would be the actual parents, but they made it clear to Natalie that she could be an active participant in her child's life. There would be no secrets about the adoption or who the natural mother or father were when the child was old enough to understand.

I never wanted to settle for love, but time was not my friend. Most young, unmarried women can only wait so long before they give up on a guy and cut their losses. This would probably be a good time to introduce you to Marion. Marion and I were – well, I'm not really sure what we were. I did know a few things. It was probably more accurate to say I believed I knew a few things when it came to Marion. I truly believed that Marion loved me very much. She said things to me and dropped not-so-subtle hints that led me to this conclusion. Marion insisted that I meet her mother and we actually spent an entire day with her. Marion wanted us to drive out to Canobie Lake Park to meet her. I'm one of the few people who actually hate amusement parks but I agreed to go because it seemed very important to Marion. I get motion sickness very easily and I hate being ripped off for a five-dollar soda and a seven-dollar hot dog. But I went. I had a terrible time and, what was worse, everybody else probably had a lousy time, too, just because of me. I got really sick on the Psychodrome. The ride is very well named since you need to be somewhat psycho to purposely rattle your brain bone, which in my case is attached to the stomach bone. I was actually trying to turn the wheel counter to the direction Marion was spinning it to slow down the supersonic revolutions. I lost the contest and that basically took me out of commission for the next two hours.

Marion's parents were divorced and she lived with her father. Her father and I have never had a conversation of any substance. I sensed that he would rather have been somewhere else when I was around, which was not often. Marion and I usually met somewhere. There was an immediate attraction between us. I hate to admit it, but that attraction was obviously more one-sided on her part. I'm not saying that I thought Marion was unattractive but that she wasn't really my type. I recognized that this was an irrational feeling on my part. Marion was always terrific toward me.

She had an older married brother and another brother living on his own. Marion was the baby sister and her brothers felt the need to protect her from any male predator. I think she told her brothers that they'd better not give me a hard time, because they really never gave me too much grief.

Marion and I were about the same age, which meant that she was already an old maid at twenty-eight years old. Marion was extremely athletic and was a parks-and-recreation director. She was adept at most sports. She played tennis much better than I did, but that's not really saying much. I avoided playing tennis with her. I would take her on in bowling because I had a better-than-even chance of beating her in a three-game match. When it came to winter sports, I didn't even try. I didn't skate or ski or generally do anything that exposed me to prolonged periods of cold. This is why I knew Marion loved me. None of these things mattered to Marion. She was content just to be with me. If that meant sitting in a dull movie or going to a party with my friends or taking a drive or doing some boring sightseeing, Marion was fine.

Marion was of Swedish descent. She had long, naturally straight hair. If you have seen a Swedish girl before, you know what a towhead looks like. Marion was the perfect height for me. When standing in the same direction with my arms around her waist, my nose came to the top of her head. This is the perfect kissing height while standing and we did quite a bit of standing-up kissing at the beginning of our relationship. It wasn't very long before we graduated to lying-down kissing. I have been out with lots of girls and although I am not what you would call a "playa," I have had enough women to develop a sense of what is typical from the female perspective. Marion was not typical. Marion was almost always the sexual aggressor. This was a very bizarre sensation for me because I always have to work so damn hard to get laid. Maybe it's me. Everyone tells me that women today are very liberated and out for themselves. Until I met Marion, though, I was never able to find that kind of woman. Marion would explore parts of my body with excessive pleasure, without any desire to specifically satisfy her own need, often continuing the quest until I was totally spent. I think Marion was on to something. When she attacked me for round two, I was able to sustain my sexual appetite for a much longer period of time and that's when Marion and I would spend a long period of time being whole.

Another reason I knew Marion loved me was that she did not want to be with anyone else. If Marion was one of those liberated women, then she was unique in that I was the only man with whom she wanted to be liberated. I knew this because she was always available for me and me alone. When making love, we would talk about love without saying the words. A man always says "I love you" to a woman when he's about to come, but Marion actually asked me why I didn't. I know she felt hurt by the fact that she let the words slip from her own mouth once. What could I do? I had to say the words back if only to preserve Marion's dignity. Neither one of us said the words again. I get that Marion is waiting for me to make the next declaration, but I have not yet felt the compulsion.

I told you that Papa was obsessed with old music. As a result, he even managed to get me interested in his music. I found myself listening to the sixties or seventies station on my XM radio. For most dates, I would put on the music of today. But when I was with Marion, I didn't feel the need to change from my preferred station. Marion really jarred me when an old Ronnie Dyson song came on the radio. She looked at me and said the song was written just for me. This song was written well before Marion was born – 1970: "If you let me make love to you, why can't I touch you?"

The sad thing is that Marion felt the distance I was trying so hard to disguise. I was torn and hoped that this night would not be our last. From that moment I knew that I had better get in touch with myself. I knew that I would miss the way Marion would brush up close to me, softly clinging as if to say, "Why can't you please love me?"

I wondered why love had to be so damn complicated. Why couldn't I love this striking flaxen goddess who so obviously adored me? What the hell was the matter with me? Why wasn't she my type? What made Natalie, a woman who made no secret of the fact that she detested the sight of me, my type?

I thought about marrying a Swedish woman whose ancestors came from the Norse land. My ancestors came from the warm climes of the olive groves. I thought about children and wondered whose genes would predominate. I almost felt the need to review the Mendel chart. Then I told myself that this is America. In a few decades we'll all be mongrels where none of us will really know our origins. That's what my rational self said. I only wished that I could feel that way in my heart. I was terror-stricken by the idea that I was about to let the woman who worshiped the ground I walked on walk out of my life for some fantasy to which I clung. I continued to hang on to Marion, hoping to mask my feelings better. Marion was looking deeply into my heart and I knew she did not like what she saw, no matter how much she loved me.

That same Saturday, Papa and Mama spent the evening doing what they typically did. Papa was sitting in his man cave watching his big screen and Mama was checking her Facebook and e-mail on the iPad, which Connie and Papa had chipped in to get for her.

Mama said, "We're behind two episodes of *The Young and the Restless.* Let's watch that."

"*The Young and the Restless*?" replied Papa. "All you're going to see is a bunch of people eavesdropping on each other's conversations. I never saw so much important business conducted in a coffeehouse or the athletic club. These are supposed to be rich people. Don't they have an office?"

"Don't be foolish, Papa. How else can the show let the audience know what's going on?"

"And what's the deal with all these people dying and coming back to life?" added Papa. "Carmine Basco was shot to death by that Baldwin kid and here he is again alive in some witness protection thing. I remember that Cane Ashby was murdered at some church – but no, that was really his twin brother. And do you recall when Malcolm Winters plunged to his death after crashing off a bridge in Kenya only to return a few years later to yell at his brother for not finding him? What was that about? And there was Katherine Chancellor who died in a car crash. But no, that was Marge, her exact double. I guess they couldn't find her twin sister. At least when she died for real they didn't go searching for another exact double. I'm glad of that because Katherine could never be replaced, even though Michael Learned did a nice job standing in for a few episodes when Jeanne Cooper was ill. I remember seeing Jeanne Cooper in an old Frank Sinatra movie from 1967 called *Tony Rome.* She played the part of a skid-row bum and I was disappointed, hoping to see the beautiful young Jeanne Cooper. Now we have Cassie showing up, who died years ago because Sharon is a nutcase. I guess ghosts must age in heaven because Cassie looks a lot older now than when she died. That must mean we have some really old-looking spirits in heaven. Let's not forget John Abbott, who pops up once in a while as his son's conscience. I think John died in 2006, but at least his ghost looks well."

"For someone who doesn't enjoy watching the show, you remember more things than I do," Mama said with a chuckle. Mama had a good point and Papa was caught.

"I'm a man. How do you expect me to watch these commercials selling soap, snacks, and old-age ailment remedies?"

"The fact is, you don't watch those advertisements anyway, even though I'd really like to see what's out there these days. You zip through all the commercials," said Mama. "I couldn't pry the remote from your hand with a pair of vice-grip pliers. And when you seem to fall asleep, you're up like a flash if I reach for it."

"And why not," answered Papa. "Our lives are way too short to be watching some Yoplait Greek yogurt commercial when it's a beer that I really want. The show is thirty-six minutes long without the commercials and not the whole hour I would have to sit through. I just saved us twenty-four minutes of our precious lives."

"Thanks," said Mama. "I can put the time to good use folding the laundry. It doesn't get done by itself."

Papa said, "Let's compromise. If you watch the news with me, I will watch your soap with you."

Mama agreed, wanting to watch the news anyway. She knew Papa was bullshitting. He looked forward to watching *Y & R* more than she did. Papa's commentaries on the news and about the soap opera were annoying, but that was Papa.

"It looks like Jay Leno is retiring again, or was he forced out?" commented Papa. "Isn't ten billion dollars enough for him to stay retired? He must really like his job to keep at it so long. I don't think he or Walter White will ever have enough money. I sure wish I enjoyed working that much. I'd be satisfied with a small monthly income so I could never work again."

Then Papa felt compelled to opine about the black teenager shot to death in Wild West Palm Beach, Florida, for not lowering the sound of his rap music as requested. The young men in the car gave this man some lip, which must have been very threatening to him because he shot the boy to death. The alleged murderer was standing his ground, as Florida allows. "I wonder what would have happened if the young men in their car stood their ground and shot the man," Papa opined. "I suspect that the story would've had a much different outcome than the George Zimmerman trial for shooting Trayvon Martin."

Mama retorted, "Do you remember when you blasted your Frank Sinatra music with the windows open when you were driving through a poor section of town last summer?"

"Well, I had to do that," said Papa. "I couldn't hear my song above some hip-hop being boomed out of some bouncing black convertible."

"You're lucky they didn't shoot you, Papa. You're always pushing the envelope. I just wish you would do it when I wasn't there."

"It's no fun without an audience. Anyway, I was just doing my thing. I think the street enjoyed the finale of *New York, New York.* I doubt if they hear much of old blue eyes in Roxbury."

If the news wasn't bad enough, Papa had to sit through the commercials since it was a live news show. Papa complained about the Rosetta Stone claim to teach him a foreign language the natural way. He told Mama that he must be really stupid, because even after hours and hours of listening to the French discs, he was still not able to understand one bit of *Camille Claudell.* Mama said he didn't really care about learning French. He just had a thing for Isabelle Adjani. Then Stephen Baldwin came on, telling Papa that people who used the whitening strips for their teeth look an average of thirteen years younger. Papa told Mama that he had better not try those strips because people would wonder why a twenty-five-year-old man was living with this old lady. Papa got tired of watching commercials and turned on *The Young and the Restless.*

When it was over, Papa said, "I think we still have one more episode to watch to catch up." Mama smiled and told him to put it on.

Chapter Thirteen

July

July marked the fourth month of Natalie's pregnancy, and Connie and Natalie made their scheduled visit to Dr. Connors' office. Natalie allowed Connie to be totally involved in all aspects of the doctor's examination and follow-up consultation. Connie watched Natalie for signs of reneging on her promise to give the baby up for adoption. So far, she saw no indication of that.

"Your baby is now in its fifteenth week of development and weighs about three and a half ounces," said the doctor. "Hair on the head, eyebrows, and eyelashes are starting to appear by now."

"If the baby weighs only a few ounces, then why have I gained eight pounds? No, never mind," said Natalie, "I know the answer to that."

"Being a recent graduate of nursing school, I expect you know pretty much the whole process you will be experiencing," continued Dr. Connors.

"Knowing what to expect and feeling the changes in your body firsthand are two different things. But you have children of your own, Dr. Connors. You know exactly what I mean."

"Of course I do," said Dr. Connors with a smile, "and this is your actual little living and growing part of you inside. The changes in your body are far more intimate and not some author's textbook description of what you should expect."

"Isn't that the truth! I do see the swelling in my abdomen, but I can still hide the fact that I am pregnant to people who don't know the situation."

"Things are proceeding very well. Connie, you must be taking good care of this young lady. Remember, Natalie," added the doctor in her professional voice, "move slowly when you get up from sitting or lying down to avoid feeling dizzy. Keep taking your vitamins and continue your exercises."

Connie assured the doctor that Natalie was taking terrific care of herself. Connie couldn't help feeling somewhat jealous of Natalie's nurturing experience. She was grateful that Natalie was so committed to the baby's good health and future happiness, but at the same time felt that she was missing out on this emotionally charged, hormonally crazy period of development. She privately worried that Natalie's motherly instincts would supersede her genuine intention to give this baby a good home in the family of the child's father. The fact that Natalie never considered Ricky anything but a sperm donor concerned her. Ricky had no contact with Natalie whatsoever since she'd basically ignored his presence the month before.

The next day, Ricky decided to join Papa and Mama on their drive to Chelmsford. There was no sense wasting gas and Ricky hoped Papa would be a buffering influence on Natalie's disdain for his existence. Connie hoped that Papa's presence and enthusiasm would help Natalie's disposition and support her choice to give the baby up for adoption.

Papa was in rare form during the trip to Connie's house. He combined two of his favorite obsessions into one argument. Papa's disdain – and that word may be mildly exaggerated but fairly accurate – for the Japanese and his love for Red Sox baseball collided head on. Papa was discussing how great the Red Sox have been since 2004 when they crushed the Curse of the Bambino by sweeping the Yankees four straight games after falling behind in the playoffs three games to none. I already mentioned that, since being a Yankee in Little League, I have always been a fan of the pinstripes, but not nearly to the neurotically maniacal extent that Papa is a fan of the Sox. The Yankees' loss in 2004 even hit me as a sad end to the Red Sox's penchant for blowing it in the end. Personally, I enjoyed watching the Red Sox screw it up just one more time. Papa would go ballistic if the subject arose of Bill Buckner's miscue in the 1986 World Series, especially since it was to the Mets of New York. Before that, in 1978, Bucky Dent's homerun in the 1978 playoff game at Fenway Park dashed Red Sox hopes for the American League East pennant. It was a devastating blow in the face of a Red Sox double-digit lead for first place that year. It was really fun for me to watch the Sox lose year after year, but I was really too young to enjoy the full extent of the agony shared by Papa and his older diehard friends. I would never rub the Red Sox collapses in Papa's face because it hurt him way too much and he was heartbroken enough without my adding more pain. Now that the curse is over, they're playing better. Maybe Papa should move to Chicago and start rooting for the Cubs. That will never happen.

"I'm glad we have a terrific closer in the Sox," said Papa. "He makes it an eight-inning game. I only wish he wasn't Japanese. We showed them how to make good cars and electronics, we introduced baseball and golf to them, and how do they repay us? They bomb the hell out of us!"

"Papa," interrupted Mama, "that happened way before these things. Japan has been a good friend to us for many years."

"A good friend? Does a good friend talk to our leaders one day and then sneak in like the cold shadow of death and obliterate our air bases the next? With friends like that, who needs enemies?"

"What did we do?" I asked him. "We dropped an atom bomb on not one but two large cities, killing and maiming something like 200,000 people. That includes women and children. What kind of people are we?

"They got exactly what they deserved. Those sneaky bastards."

Papa was getting hot just thinking about it. I really had a tough time understanding his hatred for the Japanese because he really was a very tolerant person. Papa hated all forms of injustice and discrimination, and I never heard him tell even one Polish joke in my whole life. But this event really affected him and he wasn't even alive when it happened. He was born very shortly thereafter.

"How do any children deserve that, Papa?" Mama asked. "That was a horrific act by our government."

"Know your history, people! When the Japs attacked Pearl Harbor, we were not at war with them. We were discussing peace with their government while they were planning to destroy our Pacific defenses. Not only that, we later dropped millions of leaflets warning the Japs to surrender or face the most powerful bomb known to man. Even after Hiroshima, this warning was not enough to stop those samurais. Germany had already surrendered and they still kept coming. What was Truman supposed to do? Should he have let thousands more American military men die because of the Japanese banzai mentality? Let them all commit hari-kari, those devious bastards. Now we pay these people millions of dollars to play our baseball game. I just don't like it."

"This attitude is no better than keeping the Negroes out of baseball until the late forties," I told Papa. "If you want the game to be of the highest caliber, you need to let the best play the game. That's only fair and right."

"I know you're right, Ricky, and I accept it. By necessity, I will still buy Japanese Blu-Rays and I had to break down and buy a Samsung Smart TV because all the other televisions were just too damn stupid. And I will still root my heart out for the Sox and hope that my guy closes out the game. But don't ask me to like it and definitely do not ask me to buy a Japanese car until December 7, 2041. That's when my hundred-year boycott will end."

"I doubt if you will be driving then, Papa," Mama said with a smile.

"Exactly my point! Now look at those damn Yankees. They go get

Hideki Matsui and he becomes the World Series MVP in 2009. But he's gone now, so they hire this pitching phenom, opening the bank like he was Babe Ruth. They hired Ichiro Suzuki, probably the best hitter in baseball these past ten years. It's a good thing Seattle had him in his prime. They hired a top-notch pitcher from the Dodgers a while back. Before you know it, the Yankees will need to move their franchise to Osaka to save transportation costs. Beating up on the Yankees will be all the more satisfying."

"Papa, I think you need to get over yourself," said Mama. "The war has been over for seventy years now. The Japanese have been a good ally to us for a long time. That's what we do. We help nations rebuild so they do not become another Germany like after World War I. And what about Italy? They were Japan's allies." Mama had decided enough already about the Japanese. She'd heard it all before and tolerated Papa's irrational hatred. Papa knew it was time to shut his mouth on the subject.

Papa, Mama, and Ricky arrived at Connie's house about one in the afternoon. Papa never stayed too long, so I figured we would be home by dinnertime. Papa and Mama were happy to see Natalie again. They hadn't been to Connie's house since they all returned from Italy. This was my first opportunity to witness Natalie's interaction with Papa and Mama. I sensed her genuine affection for them, born from unhappy circumstances but cultivated by their close bonding in Italy. I was happy to see this, for it boded well for the future of our offspring.

"How have you been, sweetheart?" asked Papa.

Papa had a tendency to call everyone sweetheart, mostly because he could never remember anybody's name. In Natalie's case, it was a sincere and heartfelt greeting for the mother of his burgeoning grandchild. I have no doubt that Papa remembers Natalie's name as well as he does his own.

"I'm very well, thank you, Papa. How are you doing?"

"Whenever I am in your luminous presence, how else can I be but restored? You have the power to make all my ailments disappear. I think that's why you must be a terrific nurse."

Natalie chuckled. "Mama, your husband is incorrigible. I don't know how you put up with him all these years."

"Papa has always flirted with pretty girls as long as I've known him," Mama replied. "The disturbing thing is that I could see the ladies were taken by his good looks and charm and I admit that it more than worried me. Now, I think he is pretty much harmless, so I let him have his trifling without too much concern. I figure after all these years, if he leaves me now, it will be his loss."

"So what are we going to do?" I asked. "Anyone up for lunch somewhere or a movie or a trip to Franklin Park Zoo?"

"Let's save that last one for after the baby's born," said Connie. "I've prepared a nice lunch for everyone. Let's just sit around and catch up a bit. It seems we're always going somewhere or doing something that gets in the way of enjoying each other's company."

I know this was an idea Papa loved. He could save money, since he was always the one to foot the bill for everyone. More importantly, Papa was wearing down, and too much walking around tired him. He had seen his share of zoos and museums and movies and parks and churches for a lifetime. He was happy to sit and spend some quiet time with his three favorite ladies in the world.

During the chicken salad with apples and walnuts portion of our meal, I had the shock of my life. Natalie actually asked me how my work was going. It just so happened that I had won an award that previous week.

"Thank you for asking, Natalie. I do some occasional freelance writing for a local Cambridge paper, and it just so happens that I won first place for The New England Press Association award for investigative reporting."

"That's terrific," said Natalie.

"Yes, that is terrific!" followed Mama. "Why didn't you even tell us?"

"To tell the truth, I forgot. It's really great and it will look good on my résumé, but it totally slipped my mind that I hadn't told you or Papa."

"We're really proud of you, Ricky," said Papa. "I don't know where you get your writing skills from. I only know where you don't get them from."

I was almost glad that I had forgotten to tell Mama and Papa. It made me come across as more humble. I was proud of that award. I beat out literally hundreds of entries covering a year's time. I sneaked a peak at Natalie and discerned a small trace of a smile. She was probably secretly glad that her baby's father wasn't a total illiterate.

But that was the last word from Natalie directed at me. We all spent a lovely afternoon around Connie's picnic table in their backyard. The weather was pleasantly warm for July, not stifling hot. As predicted, Papa wanted us on the road by five o'clock, probably so he could get home for the Red Sox game.

Regina called to speak to Natalie just as we were leaving. She told Natalie not to make plans for dinner because she was coming there to take her out. I heard Natalie gabble that she'd just had lunch a short time ago. She accused Regina of trying to get her fat. I deduced from Natalie's response that Regina teased that she was too late and that ship had already sailed. Regina apparently told her that she would visit anyway and then they could have a late dinner.

It was only about an hour after Papa, Mama, and I left Connie's house that Regina arrived. She tried to visit Natalie every week, knowing that she was really the only friend Natalie had who could visit her.

Being almost the time of the summer solstice, the days were long and three hours of sunlight still remained in the day.

Natalie greeted her with a hug. "You really don't need to visit me every single week, Regina," she said. "This isn't exactly prison here at Connie's house. Anyway, we had visitors this afternoon."

"You must mean the gorgeous Ricky Santo. I bet that made you horny."

"Very funny," mocked Natalie. "You know that I will pretty much ignore Ricky when he visits his sister. In fact, Connie is usually the one who visits her parents in Boston. They've only visited once since I've been here. Ricky has been here twice."

"And I will bet you anything that he never visited Chelmsford before you arrived," conjectured Regina.

"Perhaps, but I can always hide out in my room when he visits. Maybe I can't stop him from calling, but I can ignore him whether he is here or in Boston," said Natalie.

"One day you will find out that Ricky is the one who loves you, not Jeremy. Ricky is the one who will love your child, not Jeremy. Ricky's family is the family that will treasure you, not Jeremy's family. I really don't know Jeremy's parents, but I imagine they could never love you like Papa and Mama."

Natalie confirmed that Jeremy's parents were divorced and Regina smiled and said, "Why doesn't that surprise me?"

At about nine o'clock, Regina drove Natalie to the local Applebee's for dinner. She was fortunate that the booth farthest back was available. Natalie sat with her back to the door and Regina sat facing the front, just on the off chance that someone came in that she knew. Regina and Natalie had mostly mutual friends. Regina told Natalie that it was totally unlikely that someone they knew would be in Chelmsford, and certainly not to eat at an Applebee's restaurant when there were probably five other Applebee's locations on the way from Boston. Regina told Natalie that no one goes out of his way to eat at a chain restaurant. Natalie was happy to get out of the house and always happy to talk to Regina, even if she was a bit pushy at times. Natalie knew that she could never ask for a better friend than Regina.

Regina couldn't resist telling Natalie that she was giving up a terrific date with every potential of getting laid, just to be with her. Natalie knew that Regina had every other night of the week to explore her steamy side.

It was 9:30 p.m. at Bagram Air Force Base when Jason Skyped Kathy as arranged. Jason initiated the call. "Hello, baby. Here I am again. How do I look?"

"Handsome as ever," said Kathy. "How is it going over there?"

"Now you know I don't want to talk about that. What if I said it was great over here? Could you believe that? What if I told you we were nearly shot down this week? Would you really want to know that?"

"Were you nearly shot down?" exclaimed Kathy.

"Not that I'm aware of," said Jason. "Anyway, that's not why I called. I wanted to remind you that I love you and miss you. I'm still thinking that our group will be relieved before Thanksgiving. Can you learn to cook a turkey by then?"

"Oh, Jason. I love you, too. I have been so lost without you. I'm glad that I have my work to keep me busy. I count each day until we're back in each other's arms. And I will ignore that turkey remark. Did you marry me for my cooking?"

Jason looked around to see if anyone was listening and whispered, "No, I married you mostly for the sex."

"And how is that working out for you? Maybe you should consider a career change," teased Kathy.

"Well, now that you mention it, these months away from you has given me that exact same idea. At least the Air Force has trained me well. I feel that I'd be able to get a job fairly easily. And your being a medical technician means you could work near any hospital in the country. At least until the babies start coming," said Jason nonchalantly.

This comment stopped Kathy cold. Here was Jason fighting for his country and risking his life while she was discussing dumping him with her lover. In fact, she planned to meet Jeremy that very evening. Kathy started to question her whole psychological state. What the hell was she doing with Jeremy? Maybe she was using him as he was using her – waiting for his fiancée to return. In any event, it was more wrong for her than for Jeremy. She was married. Could she believe Jeremy loved her more than Natalie or was that just a line to get laid while he was waiting for Natalie's return? Kathy was confused and conflicted.

"Kathy, are you still there? I see you but can't hear you."

"I'm here, Jason. Your talking about babies sent my mind reeling."

"Well, I think about it a lot and can't wait to start trying," said Jason. "I think some other guys are waiting to use this computer. I'll check in again next week. Love ya, babe."

"I love you, too, Jason. Please stay safe for me."

Knowing how her affair would devastate her husband tormented Kathy. She rationalized that her fling was nothing more than a temporary diversion. She dismissed Jeremy's professing his love for her as a game he was playing to make her infidelity more palatable. She always took precautions to prevent her secret from being exposed. She always stayed pretty much to herself on the base intentionally, to remain anonymous from prying eyes. At work, she tried very hard not to encourage Jeremy's vexing sexual advances for fear that someone would unriddle the signs. When meeting Jeremy, she was careful to select spots off the beaten path, like Plymouth or the motor inn, where she could remain anonymous save the brief stretch from car to room. It was mostly those short intervals of time when she joined Jeremy in a restaurant that worried her. In these instances, she would never act lovey-dovey toward Jeremy and she discouraged his compulsive grabbing of her ass. She let Jeremy know her feelings about public displays of affection and he actually did try to behave himself. If anyone saw them, it could be construed as one colleague having dinner with another. As unlikely as that sounded, at least it was somewhat plausible. When Jeremy called to confirm that evening's rendezvous, Kathy was wavering.

Her phone rang and she answered distractedly.

"Hi, beautiful. Same plan? I'll meet you at the mall about seven and then you can join me to drive to Chisholm's."

"Jeremy, I just now finished Skyping Jason in Afghanistan and now you want me to screw him and screw you. This whole idea is becoming more and more distasteful to me."

Jeremy, always the charmer, told Kathy, "I don't want you to screw me, Kathy. I want you to make love to me. As for your husband, I already told you that I totally agree that you should continue to keep him positive while he is stationed overseas. I can only pretend to imagine what it must be like for him. I have no desire to have him know that we intend to get married. Neither of us wants to be responsible for what may happen to him over there. He's dealing with enough as it is."

"Did I ever once tell you that I planned to leave Jason after he got back? He was talking about starting a family with me just a few minutes ago."

"Well, yes, in a way you did," answered Jeremy. "You told me that you really didn't know your husband all that long before you were married and he was deployed. You told me that you wanted basically to escape from your previous life. I read that to mean that you didn't really have time to develop the kind of love for him that we have now for each other."

"I think you'd better learn to read, Jeremy."

"I am a very good reader, thank you. Well, are we on?"

Kathy was as weak for love as a dieter was for a piece of Boston cream pie. "OK, Jeremy. I'll meet you at the usual spot. But let's please not make this out to be anything more than it is. You're not bullshitting me. I know I am your temporary diversion while Natalie is away and that's fine with me. You're my diversion, too. Let's stop making this about love."

"Kathy, I do love you. I have never really felt this way about anyone before and that includes Natalie. I can't believe you don't feel like I do. No one could be that good an actor for so long."

Kathy started doubting herself. She doubted her feelings for Jeremy as well as her feelings for Jason. Not having Jason home gave Jeremy a distinct home-field advantage. What she didn't doubt was that Jeremy made her feel wonderful. He was tender and a good lover. And she was in constant need of affection. Maybe it was her need from childhood, affection that she had missed from her own father.

"Goodbye, Jeremy. Make sure you are really clean. I prefer putting only clean things in my mouth before I get really dirty."

Jeremy picked up Kathy at the mall as they had arranged. Driving separately to the motel created one set of problems. They would have two cars to park instead of one. That probably would not have been a problem unless the motel clerk decided to check cars against the sign-in registrations. Another problem was that the odds of someone recognizing one of the cars would double. This was also unlikely unless someone was looking to spy on Kathy or Jeremy in the first place. Driving together was not without its risks either. If they rode together and someone spotted them, it would be very difficult to explain. Jeremy tried to drive extra carefully, not wanting to get a ticket or, worse, have an accident.

Jeremy and Kathy spent about two hours in the motel before they decided to have dinner. They both put off dinner, having more of an appetite for each other than for food. They were like two dogs in heat and barely had enough self-control to wait for their room. Suffice it to say, they were very happy to see each other, as evidenced by their affectionate greeting. In fact, Jeremy was a bit too anxious to show his fondness toward Kathy. But, being young, he was able to revivify his rapture in about forty-five minutes. Kathy did not seem to mind the interruption, knowing from past experience that Jeremy was well worth the wait. Jeremy also had a way of keeping Kathy hot until he was able to spring up again.

After the second, more elongated session, both Jeremy and Kathy were bestially sated and turned their attention to satisfying a different hunger, one they had not even noticed until the climax of their recent activities. Jeremy and Kathy intended to spend the entire night together so having dinner was a prerequisite to some late-night frivolity.

Having nowhere particular in mind to go, Jeremy drove north on

Broadway and then headed west on Interstate 95. Thinking it would be better to drive north, Jeremy got off the interstate and headed north on Middlesex Turnpike. After about forty minutes, Jeremy's hunger eclipsed any need to mellow. Kathy was of a like mind. They spotted an Applebee's and decided to go in. It was about ten o'clock.

Regina could scarcely believe her eyes – Kathy and Jeremy were waiting to be seated. It took all the restraint she had not to show her shock. Fortunately, she and Natalie were finishing up their own dinners. She noticed they were seated in a different wing of the restaurant. That at least was a good thing, but Regina needed to move quickly in order to leave before Natalie or Jeremy saw each other. Regina was also worried that Jeremy or Kathy might spot her. Regina insisted on taking the check, leaving the tip on the credit card. She got up, not even asking Natalie if she needed to use the restroom.

"What's the big hurry?" asked Natalie.

"Would you forgive me if I told you that I lied before?" fibbed Regina. "I didn't really give up a hot date tonight. I just pushed it back to midnight. I think I had better get started for Boston."

"Now that sounds more like the Regina I have come to know and love. Why didn't you just say so to begin with?" inquired Natalie.

"I didn't want you to feel that I put our friendship on the clock. I really expected to have dinner earlier than this, but I knew you had a late lunch."

"You know better than to keep those silly secrets from me," said Natalie. "Of course, let's go."

Regina grabbed Natalie's arm to position her to her left, knowing that Jeremy was seated on the right. Regina turned her face away from Jeremy's section, always being certain to block Natalie from view. Jeremy did glance up at the front entrance as they were leaving, but not expecting to see anyone he knew, especially Natalie, he did not recognize his prospective fiancée only a few yards away.

The next day, I received a surprise visit from Regina. She filled me in on the whole near miss, explaining to me that Jeremy sat a few yards away from them as she hastily escorted Natalie out of the restaurant. Regina told me how she spent most of that evening with Natalie, talking me up. Regina told Natalie I was everything she ever needed and that I would be the only way for her to keep the baby. Regina insisted that Connie would never agree to adopt the baby if she married me. She told Natalie how handsome I was and that she would be a fool to go back to Jeremy after he cheated on her. Regina told me that girlfriends like to hear that their BFF thinks their guy is a hunk. It's an ego thing. Of course, to my face,

Regina told me that I was really nothing special. Her wry smile gave her away, however. I believe Regina was secretly hot for me. But then again, I think all women are hot for me in the fantasy world I built for myself.

Chapter Fourteen

August

August marked the fifth month of Natalie's pregnancy. As usual, Connie and Natalie made their scheduled visit to Dr. Connors. Connie privately shared with me that these few months of waiting for Natalie's delivery were like eternity. She wondered how time could pass so quickly during the routine of everyday living and drag on interminably waiting for a child to be born. I mentioned that if it seemed long to her, she should imagine how it must feel to Natalie.

"How are you feeling, Natalie?" probed Dr. Connors as she poked here and there.

"I feel very well, all things considered," answered Natalie. "I haven't really felt the baby move or anything. Should I be concerned?"

"There you go again," said the doctor. "You know that it's still early for that, but I would not be surprised to hear you tell me about some kicking the next time you visit. Your baby is less than five inches long right now and from the ultrasound everything looks perfectly normal. Your baby is only about three and a half ounces. So don't worry about feeling him or her punch you yet. It's coming soon. I see that you have gained seven pounds, but on you it looks good. Don't be surprised if you notice an increasing appetite. That's perfectly normal. As they say, you're eating for two now."

Connie did not ask the doctor any questions for fear of seeming overly possessive of the baby that would ultimately be hers. Connie, ever the sensitive female, noticed a perceptible melancholy in Natalie's demeanor. Natalie was by nature a very upbeat lady, but Connie continued to fear that the months of confinement, knowing her baby would be surrendered in the end would result in an unhappy consequence. Natalie was satisfied that all was going well and thanked the doctor as both Connie and Natalie scheduled an examination for September. For Connie it would be her annual gynecological exam.

Connie insisted on buying Natalie lunch before returning home. Connie genuinely enjoyed Natalie's company, even if she sensed a slight feeling of despair in her. She tried very hard to keep Natalie amused and positive. Connie also wanted to buy Natalie some new things to wear to accommodate her growing waistline. Natalie balked at the suggestion, but Connie was adamant. For a change of scenery, Connie drove Natalie a few extra miles to shop at the Maternity Boutique in Dracut.

Natalie returned to Connie's home with two new pants and three new tops. Connie was pleased, assuring Natalie that she was the most beautiful mother-to-be in the country. Connie hoped that Natalie took the compliment in the spirit it was intended.

Thomas arrived home shortly after Connie and Natalie. Even though it was summertime, Thomas had contracted with the school system to conduct psychological screenings for those students scheduled for a special education evaluation. August was a fairly busy month for Thomas, but he was able to take some time off to be with Connie and Natalie. Thomas even suggested that they take a few days or a week to spend at the Cape. Natalie feared that this would be too risky, knowing her parents and some of her friends often went there during the summer. Natalie agreed to spend a few days at Hampton Beach in New Hampshire, on the condition that Regina was able to get away to join her. Regina almost never turned down Natalie's invitations and this was no exception. She usually took vacation in August anyway and being with Natalie was more important to her than any other way she could imagine spending the time.

It was the second week in August and Papa asked Mama if she wanted to take a trip to Chelmsford to see Natalie and Connie, as it had been a month since their last visit. Mama reminded Papa that they had left for the beach in New Hampshire and wouldn't be there. Papa considered driving to the beach with Mama but felt they might be imposing. He wasn't really a beach person anyway and the drive was more than two hours one way, and he'd had his share of driving in Italy. So Papa and Mama put off their visit.

They found it hard to believe that three months had passed since their trip. Mama told Papa that going to Italy was wonderful, but she would die happy if they could visit Hawaii before it was too late. Papa reminded Mama that they had been to every major city in the United States over the past twelve years.

"It was very nice visiting all those cities," Mama said, "but that was your thing, Papa, not mine."

"What do you mean? Didn't we mostly do sightseeing, visit churches, and see shows? What about Fisherman's Wharf and Niagara Falls and the Chicago River Tour and the San Diego Zoo and Hollywood? Do I need to go on? And I went to mass every Sunday with you when we went on these trips. That was a very big sacrifice for me. The baseball games were only a slight diversion and you seemed to enjoy the atmosphere. I remember your remarking about the sushi at Dodger Stadium and Boog's Barbecue in Baltimore and I know you liked Ivar's Seafood and Chowder in Seattle."

"Yeah, yeah, yeah," said Mama, "but be honest. Those trips were planned by you and for you to see your ballparks. It was nice that you threw a few crumbs my way, but I would like to see Hawaii before I die. That is what will make me happy."

"So you want to see Hawaii before you're dead," bellowed Papa. "That will make you happy! But when you're dead you won't even remember being happy, so what's the difference?"

"I'll know I was happy in the afterlife," countered Mama.

Papa argued, "If you actually make it to the afterlife then you'll be in heaven and that will be the ultimate happiness. Going to Hawaii will be like taking a trip down the block. If I were you, I'd forget about Hawaii and really focus on that afterlife. I believe that once there, you'll be able to take all kinds of trips. Maybe if you die before I do, I'll go to Hawaii and then you can be with me as my guardian angel. We would save money that way. But please give me a sign that you're with me just in case I meet a young woman."

Mama knew Papa like a book. Now that she had planted the seed about going to Hawaii, Papa would make it his mission to see that the trip happened. However, it would have to be next year or later. As long as Natalie was with child, Papa would not leave. He had confidence that all he had done to create in Natalie an atmosphere of trust, splashed with a degree of guilt, would work for everyone's benefit. Papa was genuinely sincere about the wrongness of Natalie's decision to abort this child. Now that she had committed to the baby's life, he had to remain a presence until his or her arrival and somewhat beyond.

I made a crucial decision in August. We all know that there are turning points in our lives that can alter the path we take for the rest of our days. Robert Frost wrote a whole poem about it. I came to that fork in the road the August before Natalie was to deliver our child. I doubted that Natalie would ever truly be mine. They say all's fair in love and war, whoever "they" are. Was it fair that Natalie loved a two-timing bastard like Jeremy, while my heart languished in despair over this young woman whom I barely knew? But I did know her in my soul. Papa and Mama adored Natalie and that was validation that this feeling I had for Natalie was untainted. She touched my heart. Connie adored Natalie. The brief time I spent with

Natalie was of no importance. I knew the first time I met her and we made love that she was the perfect divine match to my being. I had always felt this gnawing sensation that a part of me was missing until Natalie's caress stilled the pain.

Then there was Marion. It was becoming increasingly apparent that these same feelings I had for Natalie, Marion had for me. If I devoted myself wholly to Marion, as she deserved, I would be saying goodbye to any chance that Natalie would turn to me. I convinced myself that my love for Natalie was so absolute it would permeate the recesses of her heart. My love would overpower her unwillingness to see me as her one true love and we would finally be together. Then I realized that those same thoughts were Marion's toward me and I must break her heart. I never wanted to hurt Marion. She was a beautiful woman deserving of my love. Then the realization hit me that I was Natalie's Marion and Natalie would break my heart one day. And yet, until the next several months of Natalie's life played out, I was helpless to abandon this image my mind had mused.

In wrestling with this life-altering decision, I had to ask myself, "Are you certain that you don't love Marion?" I put the question to the ultimate test. If another man picked up the pieces and showed Marion the love I had been unable to deliver, would I be tormented? If another man made love to Marion, taking the place that was rightfully mine, could I bear the suffering loss? The answer honestly derived was that I could. This convinced me that I had to stop feeding Marion's hopes of a future with me. There is absolutely no way to end a viable promising relationship without causing pain. I knew that Marion was all class and that she would never reveal the depth of her heartache. The welling up in her eyes was far too much for me to bear. I kissed her softly, not wanting to say anything further. I had said it all and no words of consolation could mitigate the dejection. Marion asked that I not walk her inside and I was grateful for that.

My only selfish hope upon leaving, now that Marion was free of me and back on the dating circuit, was that none of my friends would ask her out. I could deal with a strange guy becoming her new lover, but a friend would be totally different. There were many times in my life when a friend of mine broke up with an attractive girl whom I secretly desired. But I would always deny myself. I have invariably had the do-unto-others mentality in this regard. A real friend would never ask you if it was all right to date your ex after you broke up. He should intuitively know that it's positively not all right, even if your manly pride says that it is. That question should never be asked. When it is, then you know not only have you lost a girlfriend, but you also have one less friend in the world. I could not abide that kind of friend. I only hope years from now that I will not look back in sorrow over having lost the one woman who ever truly loved me.

The whole breakup with Marion was very depressing to me. When I'm depressed, I tend to do one of two things. I either find a place to be alone and sulk or I visit Papa and Mama. I chose the latter, since seeing Papa was the next best thing to being alone. As it turned out, Rev. Kenneth Scott stopped over to see Papa, too. The friendship between Rev. Scott and Papa is one that truly defies logic. They met each other over thirty-five years ago when Papa was a struggling insurance salesman. Rev. Scott was a new pastor in town looking to cover his church at a better rate. In talking to each other, they realized they had a great deal in common. They were both diehard Red Sox fans and loved old music. Rev. Scott was impressed with Papa's knowledge of rhythm and blues songs from the 1960s and was in awe of Papa's knowledge of history and cinema. Papa was amazed at Rev. Scott's skill at chess and checkers. He was unbeatable. Rev. Scott knew every tidbit of fact pertaining to black history. He was extremely articulate and very loquacious, but mostly Papa admired Rev. Scott's commitment to things he believed in passionately.

Over the years, starting in their younger days and continuing today, Rev. Scott and Papa would meet for golf or bowling. They were extremely competitive. They attended milestones in each other's lives and were often called upon to speak on each other's behalf. Their friendship defied logic, because Papa was not at all religious, and Rev. Scott had devoted his life to the service of God. Papa did have black acquaintances; however, he had no black friends. The one exception was Rev. Scott, who was his best friend in the world. Looking at their culture, religion, lifestyle, and personalities, one would expect that these two had nothing in common, and yet they were kindred spirits. They often did not speak or see each other for months at a time, and yet their bond was such that one could anticipate the other's next move. They have both suffered life's misfortunes and were there to see each other through the rough times. I believe it is accurate to say that these two men loved each other.

Once a year, Papa and Rev. Scott drove to Yankee Stadium when the Red Sox were in town to catch a couple of games. They always stayed on Long Island and caught the train to the stadium. It was actually cheaper than driving there, considering tolls and parking, but mostly far less of a hassle than trying to fight the traffic. During the day, they drove to Bethpage State Park to play golf. Rev. Scott told everyone that he played the Black Course before Tiger Woods won the U.S. Open. He neglected to mention that he shot on the wrong side of 100. Papa enjoys playing the Green Course.

Papa often repeated his favorite Rev. Scott story, a tale I heard more times than I can count. Papa and Rev. Scott were in a mall because Papa wanted to buy a pair of pants. I will omit the store's name because Papa said the actions of this employee are hopefully not an indictment of the store's policies and it would be unfair to brand them such. Papa was bumming it. He wore blue jeans and a sweatshirt and was sporting a three-day beard. Rev. Scott, coming from a funeral, was "clean," as he would say. He wore a black three-piece suit with mirror-shined black shoes and looked sharp. The saleslady placed Papa's pants in the bag and they proceeded to leave. The very second the two men left the store's front gate area, an embarrassing loud blaring buzzer alarm was tripped and two guards came flying out. Here we had Papa, looking like a vagrant, holding the bag, and which person do you think the two guards stopped and questioned? Rev. Scott was flabbergasted. Papa immediately spoke up, holding the bag in an attempt to deflect any further harassment of his friend. As it turned out, Papa produced the receipt and the guards saw the theft detector that the saleslady had neglected to remove. It continued to be a funny story they enjoyed retelling, both knowing it was a sad commentary of the state of racial profiling in America. Rev. Scott was very aware and guarded on the subject of race but still displayed a faith in human nature. I think that's one of the main things Papa admired about Rev. Scott.

I spent the next two hours listening to Rev. Scott and Papa reminiscing about past adventures to Yankee Stadium or times of friendly competition on the golf course. They bandied on nearly oblivious to me as a non-involved onlooker. This was just the diversion I needed, being near my father listening to his familiar soothing voice rambling on with boastful trivia. It helped lessen my anguish over leaving Marion, though it was only a temporary respite. Losing Marion made me more resolved to fight for Natalie. I had to find a delicate way to win Natalie's love without completely alienating her. This was not going to be easy.

It was the last weekend of August, and I convinced myself to visit Connie for the sole purpose of speaking my mind to Natalie. Even though it was killing me to keep silent about her two-timing boyfriend, I was determined to keep my promise to Regina not to expose his affair. I didn't really think this news would shock Natalie into a miscarriage, but neither did I wish to upset her and test my belief. I called Connie in advance so she knew to make herself scarce when I arrived. I greeted Connie and Thomas and they quickly excused themselves, saying they needed to pick something up at the store for dinner. I was surprised that Natalie didn't insist on joining them, because she was basically stuck with me. She could have disappeared into the safe haven of her room, but she remained. After the typical pleasantries, I basically laid all my cards on the table.

"Natalie," I said, "I've made no secret of the fact that I really like you. In fact, with just the smallest encouragement – well, you know what I mean without my saying the words."

"Yes, Ricky, I know. I practically needed to issue a restraining order against you."

"I hope you know that I am not unstable, even though you do drive me a bit crazy." I watched for a small smile from Natalie and convinced myself she was trying real hard to suppress it.

"Ricky, I'll be married in a few months and you will have a new baby in your family. I feel that I've been more than generous about this whole unfortunate situation. I don't want to have this conversation with you.

"OK, Natalie. But just know that there is still a lot of time left before you get married, and things happen. Believe me when I say that when it comes to Jeremy, 'He don't love you like I love you. If he did, he wouldn't break your heart.'"

"Are you kidding me?" laughed Natalie. "Do you think that you can lay some old Tony Orlando lyrics on me and I will swoon for you?"

"How do you even know that song? Tony Orlando had a number one hit with that about forty years ago!"

"Actually, I got to be a Telma Hopkins fan from watching the sitcom *Half & Half* so I Googled her to see what other shows she was in. When I saw that she was a singer in *Dawn*, I was curious about her songs. From that I started downloading *Tony Orlando and Dawn's Greatest Hits*. I actually like their songs, even though they are a bit hokey. And what about you? You're not that old."

"If you grew up in Papa's house, you would have been saturated with old songs. I recommend Jerry Butler's rhythm and blues version. It didn't reach number one, but it's way better. You also might want to try the blue-eyed soul version by The Righteous Brothers. They call it 'He Will Break Your Heart.'"

"I'm shocked," Natalie said. "You really know your stuff when it comes to old music."

"Papa is obsessed with top 100 pop music. He gave me a two terabyte hard drive containing every top 100 song from 1955 to 2007. It would take a lifetime to hear them all, but I'm willing if you are. This has been interesting, but somehow we got sidetracked from what I was saying at first."

"If it looked like I was trying to change the subject, maybe you should take the hint."

It was then that Connie and Thomas returned. I was glad I got my feelings off my chest, even if Natalie didn't profess her undying love for me. I felt that we got to know each other a little bit more in that brief time together. If nothing else, we were able to have a civil conversation and share our mutual interest in music. I felt that was a start.

Chapter Fifteen

September

September was the month when the proverbial shit hit the fan. This was Natalie's sixth month of pregnancy and things were changing in her psyche. She could really feel her baby now. It was a growing part of her, both physically and spiritually. She experienced changes for which her medical training never prepared her. She was now clearly pregnant to anybody having a clue. This was also the month Natalie's family would greet her with a memorable surprise visit in Sicily. Mrs. Romano was especially excited to see her daughter after more than a four-month absence. Mr. Romano had to confess that he really missed his little girl. Natalie continued her pretense by texting and calling Jeremy and her parents on their planned regular schedule. Kathy was still in contact with her husband in Afghanistan and knew this would be the last month of his deployment. She still faced Jeremy's pressure to leave her husband, but she was still unconvinced of Jeremy's commitment, not to mention the torment she felt about betraying Jason. Papa always said that things have a way of working themselves out. I suppose it must by necessity, but this was one dirty mess to work out.

Regina dropped by the first Sunday in September to pay her weekly visit. Natalie was especially glad to see Regina, the only person on Earth in whom she could confide – and Natalie had lots of unburdening to do.

"Regina," said Natalie, "I've had enough. What in the world is the matter with me? I am carrying this baby, who is my own flesh and blood, and now I will just say to Connie, you can have the baby. I am out of my ever-loving mind. What am I, a child? My father will just have to accept the fact that his little girl is not a child. His little girl had sex, big deal. He will have to deal with it. I know my mother would be devastated if she knew I was giving up this baby."

"Didn't we have this same exact conversation months ago? Didn't I beg you to keep this baby for yourself? But no, you wanted an abortion. Thank God you didn't go that far. And now after all this time you want to keep the baby yourself. You take a trip on Papa's money. You give hope to Connie and Thomas, living off their good graces because of a promise that you made. I'm not saying that you are wrong to want to keep your own child. What I'm asking is, did you consider how this broken promise would impact them? At least you didn't have a legal contract, but that's because Papa trusted you to keep your word. He'll probably be broken up about this as much as Connie and Thomas."

"Of course I thought of those things. I am certain my father would reimburse Papa and Connie for their expenses," said Natalie.

"You know this is really not about the money," argued Regina. "Believe me, Natalie. I'm on your side. I should have predicted this would happen, but you were so damn sure of yourself and your feelings. I think you've had way too much time to think."

Natalie began crying softly. "I don't want to hurt Connie. She and Thomas have been terrific. I don't want to hurt Papa and Mama. They've been wonderful to me and I really believe they love me, and not just because of the baby. Oh sure, that's how it began, but now they treat me like a real daughter. I hate having to do this to them, but it's my baby, isn't it?"

"There are lots of ways to answer that question," said Regina. "It is your baby. But isn't it also Ricky's baby? And didn't your solemn promise make him or her Connie's baby? There is no simple answer."

"You always tell it like it is, Regina. I wish that just once you would give me the answer I want to hear. I won't make any immediate decision. I'll continue to be the incubator. This week I have my doctor's appointment. Dr. Connors knows everything about my situation. I feel very comfortable confiding in her. In fact, she has encouraged it. I'll wait before I start destroying people's lives. But I really appreciate your bluntness, Regina. That's why you're a true friend. I know you tell me what's in your heart without malice or envy. I really love you, Regina."

The two friends embraced a long time.

The next Friday, Natalie and Connie had their doctor's visit. For Natalie, this would be her last monthly appointment. Doctor Connor wanted to see her twice a month starting in two weeks. For Connie, it was her regular annual checkup. Connie went in with Natalie, as she always did.

"Natalie," said Dr. Connors, "I'm very pleased. Everything is progressing perfectly. You must be resting and taking good care of yourself."

"You know my situation, Dr. Connors," answered Natalie. "I have nothing much else to do but take care of myself. I'm not working and have no stress to speak of. I only leave Connie's house for shopping or an occasional meal."

"In any event, things are looking great. Why don't you wait outside while I examine Connie?"

Connie was waiting in the outer office at Natalie's urging. Natalie told Connie that she had a personal question to ask Dr. Connors unrelated to her physical condition or the baby. Connie wondered what to make of this request but took a seat looking uneasy. "Before I leave, Dr. Connors – I'm starting to have second thoughts about giving my baby away. You said I could discuss anything with you, even if it's personal. Have you ever treated women in my situation?"

"OK, Natalie. I'm your doctor and I want you to have a healthy baby. But now you are touching upon some personal and legal issues."

"There really aren't any legal issues," replied Natalie. "Connie, Thomas, and I have an understanding. I always had every intention of living up to my promise, but now I feel differently."

Dr. Connors could feel Natalie's anguish and said, "I've treated young women in your situation. I've even treated women who were surrogates, knowingly carrying a baby to term for another couple. I'm not going to tell you that you're right to want to keep your baby, nor do I think you're a terrible person for reneging on your agreement. This is totally your decision and it would be unethical for me to become your conscience. I will say that carrying a baby inside you changes things, and you wouldn't be the first woman to change her mind about giving her child up for adoption. My best advice to you is to talk to Connie about your feelings. It would be unfair to hit her cold if you decide to keep this child. I expect it will be a shock to her. She has been very supportive of you during your entire pregnancy. Give it a bit more thought, and if you do decide to keep your baby, then you must talk to them sooner rather than later."

"You sound a lot like my friend Regina. OK, then, thank you, Dr. Connors."

Dr. Connors felt unsettled when seeing Connie right after Natalie's revelation. Being the professional that she was, though, Dr. Connors proceeded to do her job, maintaining her typical amiable disposition. In examining Connie, Dr. Connors began to suspect that this would be more than a routine examination. Dr. Connors asked Connie if she'd had her period recently. The doctor noted some tenderness and swelling in Connie's breasts. Connie also indicated that she has been urinating a bit more frequently and did experience some queasiness at times.

"Actually, I did miss my period this month. I figured I was late and it would come eventually. I've totally resigned myself to the fact that pregnancy isn't a possibility for me, so I really didn't think much about it.

Do you know something I don't, Dr. Connors?"

"Let's not jump to any conclusions. Now go inside and pee in the cup."

Dr. Connors made Connie's pregnancy test a priority and had the preliminary results in short order. She followed the urine test with a sonogram. Then, with a wry smile, she told Connie that she was pregnant. She drew some blood as a third test, but it would take a day or two for the lab results.

"I can't believe this!" Connie exclaimed. "I had totally given up on ever having my own baby. It must be true that adopting a child improves your chances of having a baby!"

"Let's not start making those kinds of claims just because you became pregnant. Sometimes it simply takes longer," said Dr. Connors with a smile. "The fact is, the number of people who get pregnant after pursuing adoption is the same as the number of people who get pregnant after ending infertility treatments. Planning to adopt a child does not improve your odds in the least."

"Whatever the case, I can't believe this," beamed Connie. "This is terrific news, but now it looks like I will have two babies in less than a year. I didn't bargain for that."

"How do you think Natalie will take the news?" Dr. Connors asked.

"Let me discuss this wonderful dilemma with Thomas. I'll tell Natalie as soon as we wrap our heads around this news. Thank you so much, Dr. Connors. You are terrific!"

"It's not like I did this to you." The doctor laughed. "Remember everything I have been telling Natalie. I will spare you the whole lecture since you've just been through it with her. But take this information and read it carefully. And do what it says. I'll see you next month – go make an appointment."

Returning to the waiting room, Connie's eyes met Natalie's.

"You must have had a good checkup," said Natalie. "You look relieved."

"Yes, Natalie. It was a terrific checkup. It may have been the best checkup I ever had. Are you ready for some lunch?"

Connie grabbed Natalie's arm with a new sense of confidence and left the office.

That evening, Connie called Papa and Mama and asked if they could visit tomorrow. She told them that she had some news that she preferred to deliver in person. She asked if Mama would call me to join them tomorrow. An invitation to see Natalie was an invitation to paradise. I was at Papa's house early the next day and we all drove there together. Mama and Papa were concerned, thinking something was wrong with Natalie's baby, or that Natalie had changed her mind about the adoption. Papa fussed at

Mama for doomsday notions about why they were summoned. I drove, using Papa and Mama's car. It had satellite radio and the station was set to sixties on six. I'd never presume to change the station. Actually, I enjoyed hearing the two of them reminisce whenever a song played.

When "Paper Roses" came on, Mama asked, "Isn't that Linda Ronstadt?"

Mama was really good at knowing the lyrics to old songs. In fact, I would put her right up there with Papa, and maybe even better. But Papa was nearly unbeatable when it came to knowing which artist was singing and for naming that tune in three notes.

"No," said Papa. "Believe it or not, that was Marie Osmond. She must have been something like fourteen years old when that song was a hit." Papa knew the year was 1973 and was quite certain that the song was a top 10 hit on the pop charts.

"Are you sure that isn't Linda Ronstadt?" insisted Mama. "I'm pretty sure that she's the singer."

Papa said assuredly, "No, Mama. That's not Linda Ronstadt and as far as I know, I don't believe she even recorded the song, but I'm not sure of that. It's funny, but I just saw a show of Donny and Marie Osmond on the Biography Channel. They both had quite a ride and dealt with financial problems, anxiety, and other things. I think they both did very well at overcoming these issues. It must be that Mormon upbringing."

"I think Marie Osmond had eight children," said Mama. "She looks pretty good for having all those kids."

Papa responded, "Now *that's* a Mormon thing for sure. Those people love sex and making babies. The women are encouraged to pop out the babies. I wasn't surprised to hear about all those kids Marie had. In fact, ever since Romney lost the 2012 election, I believe the New Era started advocating for Mormons to have lots more children and for the young people to move their families to Florida, Pennsylvania, and Michigan. This way, the Republicans can win those close states and impose their values on every one else. I believe they're grooming John Huntsman or Mitt Romney's sons to make a run for president in a few years, so they need to have about ten kids from each woman. It's not like the Mormon men need any extra encouragement."

"Now you're just being ridiculous," said Mama. "Why are you so silly?"

Papa always enjoyed teasing Mama with his exaggerated notions. I'm not so sure that he didn't half believe what he was saying.

"Getting back to 'Paper Roses,'" said Papa, "you may have confused Linda Ronstadt with Anita Bryant. I believe Anita Bryant was the first singer to make this song a hit back in 1960."

Mama didn't even realize that Anita Bryant sang the song.

"Now that's one I never heard before," I said. "Who's Anita Bryant?"

Mama informed me that Anita Bryant was a former Miss Oklahoma but was probably better known for her outspoken views against homosexuality. "Anita Bryant was the spokesperson for the Florida Citrus Commission. She was able to lead a charge to repeal an ordinance in Dade County that prohibited discrimination against people based on sexual orientation."

"And she won," interrupted Papa. "This was perfectly logical. Conservative Christians believe homosexuality is sinful. These loving Christian people did their best to stop this 'homo disease' before all the children turned queer. They even called it 'Save Our Children.'"

"This sounds like the opposite of loving thy neighbor," I said.

"It's OK to love thy neighbor as long as thy neighbor is a woman and you're a man."

"What if the woman's married?" I added sarcastically.

"That's definitely taboo," said Papa, "unless you're a Mormon. I think it's OK to love any number of neighbors if you're Mormon."

"She must be really frustrated today. We have gays getting married and gays in the military and gays receiving government benefits from their spouse. How does she handle this?" I enjoyed stirring the pot just to hear Papa's response.

"I believe she moved to Russia," Papa said. "I haven't heard much from her for many years."

At least listening to the oldies and listening to Mama and Papa's reminiscences made the hour-long trip go by quickly. It was a diversion from the apprehension we all had over Connie's mysterious invitation. If Natalie decided to renege on her promise for Connie to adopt her child, Papa would be devastated. On this point, Papa and I shared a mutual uneasiness.

When we arrived, we sensed an air of anticipation from Connie and Thomas. They greeted us and invited us to sit in the living room. Papa, Mama, and I sat on the sofa and Connie sat in the cushioned chair. Thomas pulled out a dining room chair, leaving Natalie the recliner that was not in the reclining position.

"I suppose you're wondering why I asked you all here. I am going to give you some news that only Thomas knows. I haven't even told Natalie what I'm about to say. You know that Natalie and I had doctor's appointments yesterday. Natalie is doing very well. The doctor says things are looking great."

"That's wonderful," said Papa, "but you could have told us this over the phone."

"That's true," replied Connie, "but I wanted to see your face when I told you that I was pregnant."

Everyone sat in stunned silence. I especially made a point of looking at Natalie. I could not discern whether this was welcome news or not. Did Natalie feel this news would take the attention away from her own baby? Mama was the first to display her pleasure. She ran over to Connie, embracing her with a bear hug and a kiss.

"That's wonderful," Mama exclaimed. "I always knew God would bless you, sweetheart. I prayed for it."

"That's great, sis," I said. "I guess I'll have to get used to being called 'Uncle Rick.'"

Papa added his congratulations and Connie elaborated on the details. She said that it was very early in her pregnancy and the baby's due date was April 11.

"This doesn't change anything really," Connie added, "except now we'll need to buy two of everything. Two cribs, more clothes, a double stroller, and things like that."

Natalie seemed to be thrown off guard. It took her a while to say anything, but when she did it was very revealing.

"How can you do this, Connie? When my baby is born you'll be nearly five months pregnant. How will you have the energy to take care of a newborn? What's going to happen when you are eight months pregnant and you have to carry a three-month-old baby around? This doesn't sound good. Don't misunderstand me, Connie. I'm thrilled that you're having a baby. In fact, this is the best news I ever heard. This is great!"

Natalie's excitement was genuine if not somewhat confusing. Why did Natalie display such happiness knowing that Connie's baby would drastically change everything? Natalie must have known that Connie's own baby would now assume first place in Connie's heart. Thomas, being a man, would totally feel the pride of fatherhood with his own child to the detriment of Natalie's baby. And yet, I saw a gleam in Natalie's eyes that I hadn't seen before. It was as if Connie's news had set her free, but I didn't know why until Natalie revealed her intentions days later.

"Don't worry, Natalie," said Mama. "I'll be here for Connie. In fact, if Thomas can put up with me, I'd be happy to move into the guest room – on a temporary basis, of course. And Thomas will be here. He can lift babies and change diapers and do all those things. He wouldn't be the first father to care for his children."

Natalie left it at that. I suspected that she had something more to say but had decided to wait. Maybe she wanted to think about the ramifications of this new development. Maybe she wanted to speak to Connie and Thomas in private about some concerns she had. Whatever the situation, Natalie was very happy for Thomas and Connie. Of course, Papa, Mama, and I were ecstatic. We spent the next two hours making plans for the baby's life and laughing about how the fickle finger of fate has a way of showing up when it's least expected. It was a great day.

After we left, Natalie called Regina, asking if she would visit on Sunday. Regina snapped back at Natalie. "Am I not there every weekend without fail? Have I missed even one weekend?"

"I know you've been here for me," Natalie affirmed. "There has been a new development here and I really need to speak to you. I prefer to do it face to face."

"I expect a late night. It *is* Saturday, you know. It's still date night for the rest of us. I'll be there about one or two. Have a nice lunch waiting for me."

Natalie had a restless sleep. She kept seeing visions of a new baby and she was right there in the middle of her own thoughts. Her mother was helping by allowing Natalie to get some rest. Natalie planned to stay home with the baby for the first few months. She expected that between her own mother, Mama, and childcare, she would be able to work after that. She didn't want anyone to be overly burdened by caring for her baby. She knew Mama would be happy to care for her grandchild without any reservations, but Natalie felt it would be unfair to take advantage of Mama's good nature. Anyway, Natalie was now determined to raise her own child and Mama was the grandmother, not the child's mother.

The next day, Regina arrived as promised. She was stunned by the news of Connie's pregnancy. Natalie asked Regina if this changed anything. Regina had been a strong advocate of Natalie's keeping her promise to Connie and Thomas.

"Are you kidding me?" exclaimed Regina. "This changes everything! God must have looked down on you and blessed your soul. Now Connie will have her child. The fact that it is her own child will be that much sweeter. I expect Papa will be somewhat upset. He strikes me as a man who would only be happy with ten grandchildren."

"That shouldn't matter. I'm totally open to the idea of Papa and Mama seeing their grandchild. I even dreamt about it last night. They will be involved in all facets of the child's life. Ricky is another matter. I can't see any legal joint custody arrangement. After all, this is my baby and Ricky will have no rights where he or she is concerned. I feel that Ricky should be able to participate in the child's life, but from a distance."

Regina pointed out the obvious. "Are you planning to deceive Jeremy by making him think that he is the father? If so, how would you explain the Santos being so involved in the child's life? You seem to be making a choice here, either Jeremy or the baby. You could marry Jeremy as you planned and have him raise the baby, believing it is his. If you tell him the truth, he would never accept this child and we could kiss your marriage to him goodbye."

"I'll worry about that tomorrow," proposed Natalie.

"OK, Scarlett," mocked Regina. "But tomorrow will be here before you know it. What's next?"

"I only know two things for sure," said Natalie. "Tomorrow I'll tell Connie and Thomas my intention to keep the baby and return home. I'll pack up and leave on Tuesday. Do you think you would be able to take the day off from work and help me move?"

"You know I will," Regina assured her. "Are you calling your parents to tell them the whole story? I would love to be there for that one."

"This isn't the kind of thing you can explain on the phone. Stay with me Tuesday and we'll confess the whole sordid story. I really need you there for moral support."

"Natalie, you and I have had enough tales of true confession to deal with today. Just don't be surprised to find a few more in the coming weeks. Wait until your parents and Jeremy get into the act."

Regina still felt compelled to tell Natalie about Jeremy's unfaithfulness, but this didn't seem like a good time. At least Natalie seemed strong enough to handle Jeremy's cheating. The baby was healthy and Natalie was in a good place, both mentally and physically. The news about Jeremy could wait until another day.

Natalie wanted to talk with Connie and Thomas after Regina left, but had second thoughts about spoiling their big evening. Both of them would go to work the next morning, so Natalie's announcement would have to wait until Monday afternoon.

This would give her most of the day to pack. It's not as if she had a whole lot of things to pack. Most of the baby furniture would remain in the room for Connie's baby. Connie and Thomas had purchased some clothing for Natalie, and Natalie had kept the receipts and could reimburse them. She couldn't reimburse them for their kindness and understanding. She could only dedicate herself to being generous and warm to them in the future. As her baby's aunt and uncle, Natalie expected that her child would still be a part of their life in some way. After all, Connie's child and Natalie's child would be cousins. She had no intention of denying that fact and imagined the cousins playing together and remaining close friends as they grew.

The next day, Connie and Thomas went to work in a very beatific frame of mind. Natalie, sitting at the kitchen table drinking a cup of orange juice, wished them a good day. While packing, Natalie rehearsed in her mind over and over how to deliver the crushing news to her guardians. The clock ticked away slower than molasses in January.

Finally, Connie arrived home, though without Thomas. She drove separately from Thomas on most days since their schedules usually had them in different locations. Natalie and Connie greeted each other pleasantly, but Connie sensed disquiet in Natalie's manner. When Thomas arrived home slightly after five o'clock, Natalie was relieved and anxious at the same time. She directed them both to sit down in a serious tone that was not typical of her demeanor. They complied without saying a word.

Natalie got off script a bit. Even though she had been practicing all day, the words seemed to come out differently when the time came. She had to adjust her prepared speech to harmonize with the feel of the moment as Connie and Thomas listened intently to her heartfelt words. Natalie started by telling them both how wonderful they had been to her and how she could never really repay them. She evinced genuine happiness for the wonderful news of their upcoming blessed event. Natalie's emotion was sincere, clearly not feigned. Then she dropped the bombshell. She told them both that she had decided to keep her baby. She told them that she had wrestled with the decision even before Connie became pregnant, but now the situation made her announcement less harsh. She prayed that they would not hate her. She assured them that she'd had every intention of giving her baby to them and would have kept her promise were it not for the news of Connie's pregnancy. This last part Natalie said not really believing her own words. The truth is, she didn't know what she would have done and thanked God her decision was made easier. She also asked Connie not to tell Papa, because she felt that was her responsibility.

Unbeknownst to Natalie, Connie and Thomas felt relieved that Natalie had made this decision, although they didn't tell her. They had discussed the difficulty of raising two babies at the same time. People have twins all the time, but Connie and Thomas were older first-time parents and glad not having to face the challenge. Thomas was especially thankful. He never really wanted to raise another man's child. All Thomas had thought about during Natalie's time with them was seeing Ricky and knowing that his child was Ricky's child. Thomas had felt a self-imposed responsibility to adopt because he was not man enough to father his own child. Some men are fine with adoption, but Thomas saw it as a failure of sorts. On top of that, Thomas, always the practical one in the family, had considered the financial burden of raising a second child. He felt guilty about having this attitude, so he hadn't shared it with Connie.

Connie felt differently. She had developed a nurturing disposition by watching Natalie's baby grow, believing this would be her baby. She had totally accepted the idea of being a mother. The biological aspect was secondary to the maternal attachment that she'd developed for what she passionately considered her child. With all that, Connie was disappointed with Natalie's decision, but accepting. The fact that Natalie now felt a motherly instinct was understandable. The knowledge of her own pregnancy helped mollify Connie's loss. Connie embraced Natalie, telling her she understood and would not question her decision. Thomas had the good sense to keep his mouth shut, nodding and smiling to Natalie with his eyes.

The next day, Tuesday, Natalie said goodbye to Connie, promising that they would always be joined as family and that they would see each other often. Thomas stayed home to help Natalie move her things. At about eleven o'clock, Regina arrived with a borrowed van. Thomas made short order of loading boxes of clothing, souvenirs from Italy, and personal items that Natalie had used to make her room seem more like home. Natalie insisted on leaving any gifts or baby presents that she had accumulated over the past five months.

In less than an hour, Regina and Natalie were ready to hit the road. Thomas hugged Natalie goodbye, knowing that his home was once again his private domain. It was a good feeling.

"How did your parents take the news about your coming home?" Regina asked as they merged onto the highway. "Did you get into the details with them?" She had no idea that Natalie hadn't spoken to her parents about coming home.

"Do you think that I should have told them on the phone that I'm pregnant and on my way home?"

"Why the hell not?" asked Regina. "At least they would know you were coming and it would give them some time to absorb the shock. Now the news and the sight of you will overwhelm them. I hope no one has a heart attack."

"Stop being so dramatic, Regina. Why is it that you and I never see eye to eye on how to approach a problem?" questioned Natalie.

"And has it ever occurred to you from past history that I am always right? Why don't you listen to me?"

"That's just it. I always do listen to you. If I had my way, I would never have had this baby and I would never have left Jeremy, my home, and the job I had waiting for me."

"You're forgetting also that you would not have had this baby that you decided to keep when there was a good family waiting to adopt him or her," added Regina.

"All right, enough," fretted Natalie. "Before I go home, make a detour to see Papa and Mama. I will call ahead to let them know we're coming. I feel compelled to tell them about my decision. To have them hear it from Connie would be cowardly. But I want you with me for moral support."

"That's the second sensible thing you said in the last six months," said Regina.

"OK, I'll bite," responded Natalie. "What was the first?"

"That's when you decided to keep your own baby," Regina replied with a smile.

When Natalie and Regina arrived at Papa's house, Mama had already set out some cold cuts with fruits and vegetables. They knew something was very wrong by the mere fact that Natalie was now in Boston and not safely hidden away with Connie. I will spare you the rehash of Natalie's decision as she related it to Papa and Mama. Papa, especially, listened in stunned silence. Natalie assured Papa that she would pay him back for the plane ticket to Sicily and all the meals and gifts they had given her.

As always, Papa spoke the sentiments for Mama and himself. "How can you think of paying us back when you have repaid us one thousand times over already? We have met and loved the most beautiful bella donna in the world, if you will forgive my redundancy. You are still having our grandchild, whether the child lives with you or lives with Connie. Oh sure, I'm sorry that the baby will not be directly in our family, but you have got to know the baby will be forever in our hearts. When I think back to what might have been, I can only rejoice now."

"You will let the child be in our life, no, Natalie?" Mama asked.

"Of course, Mama. This child will have two sets of loving grandparents. We will make this work somehow, though right now the future looks very hazy to me. But one thing I know for certain: you and Papa will be an integral part of the child's life."

Natalie was beginning to cry over the uncertainty she faced. Papa instinctively hugged Natalie, saying that they understood better than anyone the maternal need she experienced to care for the child. Papa told Natalie that in a few months time he and Mama would be grandparents twice over and what could be better than that? Natalie apologized for any grief she might have caused, then begged their pardon, noting that she had to get home. She told Papa and Mama that her parents were totally clueless about the events in her life and were sure to face a tremendous shock. Papa guaranteed the startling news would melt into joyous celebration and that she should not fear anything. Papa, as always, reassured Natalie.

Natalie had completed several major tasks. She informed Connie and Thomas of her decision to keep her baby. She solicited Regina's help to move and to speak with Papa and Mama – that went much better than she expected. The two hurdles left would be seeing her parents and Jeremy.

She was still uncertain what to do about Jeremy. Would she lie to him and have him believe the baby was his or would she tell the truth and probably lose him forever?

She would think about that tomorrow. It was time to face the music with her parents. It was her father's reaction that gave her the most concern, but she reminded herself that she was an adult. She was a modern woman living in the twenty-first century. Over forty percent of babies were born to unmarried women. What was the big deal? It's not like her father would attach a scarlet letter to her nurse's uniform. All that being true, Natalie could only see her father's face of disappointment and hear all his admonitions covering her entire lifetime about keeping herself pure in the sight of God and maintaining her own and her family's honor. Thank goodness Regina was there to hear her fears and to tell her that they were bullshit. "Your family will be thrilled after the initial shock, and if they're not, screw them," Regina had admonished her.

It was nearly two p.m. when Natalie and Regina pulled into the driveway. Natalie looked at Regina, holding her hand, and said, "Wish me luck."

"Do you want me to go in with you?" asked Regina.

"Would you mind? Maybe the tirade will be less violent if you're there."

"You are really driving yourself into a frenzy! Now chill. I'll come in with you. I've come with you all this way. Do you expect me to leave you now?"

"Anyway," said Natalie, "my father's probably at work now. I don't see his car in the driveway. That will give me a chance to break the news to my mother first."

Natalie opened the front door, stepping ominously into the entranceway. Not hearing any sounds, she stepped into the living room and then the kitchen. With no sign of her mother, she yelled out several times. She checked every room of the house, discovering they were alone, then went out to the garage to look for her mother's car.

"That's really strange," declared Natalie. "Both my mother's and father's cars are right here in the garage. How can that be?"

Natalie nervously called her mother's cell phone and got no answer. Then she called her brother's cell phone, thinking that he might know where they were. Again, there was no answer. Finally, in desperation, she called her father's cell and got the same result.

"Regina, something is terribly wrong here. No one is answering the cell and they are all going straight to voicemail. I could understand my father and brother – they never answer their phones – but not my mother. And their cars are here! What's going on?"

"Take a step back, Natalie. Call your father at work. At least his secretary will be there. It's his business, for Christ sake."

"Of course, I wasn't thinking straight," Natalie said gratefully.

Regina sat down on the easy chair while Natalie sat on the sofa to call her father's office. Regina could only hear Natalie's part of the conversation.

Regina saw a look of incredulity cross her friend's face and heard her say, "You mean my family all left for a vacation this afternoon?"

"That's right," said Helen, "I made the travel plans myself. They are probably on the tarmac as we speak and preparing to take off. I must say, Natalie, you sound like you're right here. The cell phone reception is phenomenal from Italy."

"Where did they all go?" Natalie insisted.

"Well, I'm not at liberty to tell you that. Your father swore me to secrecy."

"That's ridiculous," roared Natalie. "I'm his daughter. He didn't mean to include me if he wanted to keep his vacation spot a secret. Now tell me where they are!"

"I'm sorry, Natalie. I really can't tell you anything. But don't worry. I know for a fact that your father will call you the moment he lands. He told me so himself."

"This is all very mysterious," said Natalie, shaking her head in exasperation. "Thanks, Helen. I didn't know what to think when I saw their cars and couldn't reach them. I suppose there's nothing left to do but wait. Goodbye."

Regina ordered Natalie to go inside and relax as she carried her suitcases into her bedroom. She told Natalie that she was going home and asked her to call after she spoke to her parents. She also made Natalie promise not to tell Jeremy she was home until next week. Regina assured Natalie that there were good reasons for her to make this request, but she would not elaborate. Natalie could only promise Regina that she wouldn't let Jeremy know she was home. She had faith that Regina only had her best interests at heart, whatever her reasons. Natalie gave Regina a big bear hug and thanked her for being the best friend that anyone could ever have. Then she went into her bedroom and enjoyed a nap, sleeping on her own bed for the first time in many months.

After a brief nap, Natalie got up to rummage around the refrigerator for something to eat. Her mother had pretty well cleaned out all the food, so nothing would spoil while the family was away. Not wanting to leave the house, Natalie opened up a can of soup and made herself a tuna fish sandwich. That was plenty. She spent the rest of the evening on her laptop and watching television. She expected a call from her father when the family landed, as Helen had promised. By ten o'clock, she gave up waiting and went to bed. The day's excitement had taken its toll and she was very tired. Natalie slept soundly in her bed, soothed by the familiarity of her own surroundings. At slightly after four o'clock in the morning, Natalie was awakened by the sound of her cell phone ringing on the night table next to her bed.

"Hello, Natalie. Guess who this is?" said her father.

Natalie responded drowsily, "Daddy, is that you? Why are you calling me at four o'clock in the morning?"

"What are you talking about? It's after ten. Oh, I see. You think I'm calling you from Boston at four a.m."

"No, Daddy. It's four a.m. here and I was sleeping."

"How can it be four in Sicily? We're all here in Sicily and it's after ten in the morning and it's a glorious day. We can't wait to see you. Your mother is so excited I think I need to give her some pills. Are you working now? If you are, that's OK, because we're still at the airport. I got a rental car. I think we're a little more than an hour's drive from where you are. If you can't get away for a few hours we could check out the hotel and get some lunch. When can we see you?"

Natalie was astonished. She had been startled out of her deep sleep, jumped to her feet in the middle of her Boston bedroom, and she finally got it. Her parents' vacation was to Sicily. That's why all the secrecy. That's why Helen was so hush-hush.

"Daddy, you're not an hour's drive from where I am," Natalie said, her voice heavy and scratchy. "Actually, I'm more than 4,000 miles from where you are. It's four a.m. and I was sleeping here in Boston in my room in an empty house. I wanted to come home and surprise everyone."

"Surprise everyone!" Mr. Romano blurted out. "You sure surprised me to the tune of $20,000! Why in the world would you come home without telling us? And why did you come home? You were so certain that you would be here until December!"

"You can yell at me if it makes you feel better, Daddy, but why didn't you tell me that you were coming to Italy? I thought we had an understanding that I would be way too busy and you were not to visit. It's you who tried to surprise me and now it backfired."

"Oh, it's all your mother's fault," bellowed Mr. Romano. "She's the one who instigated all this. I was perfectly satisfied to wait three more months to see you when you came home for good. And why are you home? Did something happen while you were here? All your letters and phone calls led us to believe that things were going very well. Something is not right, Natalie. What's going on?"

"How long are you planning to be there, Daddy?" asked Natalie.

"We have a return flight a week from Friday," grumbled Natalie's father.

"Well then, you, Mother, and Rob enjoy your vacation and don't worry about me. I assure you that I am perfectly well. It's far too complicated and way too expensive to discuss why I am home now. Just don't worry and have a great time. I'll call Mother in the next day or two and I'll see all of you when you get back next week."

Natalie sounded normal enough to her father. The money was already spent for hotels and airfare so complaining about it now would do no good. Mr. Romano explained the shocking news to his wife and son. They had no choice but to enjoy sunny Italy for a week's vacation. Mrs. Romano's woman's intuition told her that Natalie was in some kind of difficulty, but saying anything to her husband could only make their stay fractious. Mrs. Romano was determined to have a good vacation in spite of the drama. She would talk to Natalie later.

Natalie went back to sleep. It was a restless sleep, disturbed by the baby's relentless kicking and the persistent thoughts of her parents' surprise visit. She convinced herself that only truly loving parents would bear the expense and make the effort to go all the way to Sicily to visit, especially when she planned to be home in a few months. She took solace in the fact that her parents and her brother were together on an unforgettable vacation. It was unforgettable for more reasons than one.

When she finally did awake about eleven that morning, she called her mother. Mrs. Romano was able to establish, at least in her mind, that Natalie had some news that she wouldn't reveal on the phone. This discovery didn't take a rocket scientist to uncover, since Natalie said as much. It was what Natalie didn't say that aroused Mrs. Romano's maternal suspicions that there was something very serious going on in her life.

Natalie was anxious to see Jeremy now that she had returned, but she was still unsure of what to do about her obvious change in appearance. She loved Jeremy and wanted to marry him, so the obvious thing to do was tell him that the baby was his. This idea had several complications, the biggest of which was that she would be lying for a lifetime. What if Jeremy learned the truth after they were married and he had bonded with the child? That wouldn't turn out well. How could she include this child in the Santo family's lives as she had promised? She couldn't say to her child, "These are your grandparents," without the child asking questions when he or she got older. Natalie knew that Papa especially couldn't keep up this pretense, and she had no right to ask him. The only thing Natalie could think to do was to press her confidante for yet another two cents' worth. Of course, Natalie didn't know that Regina's assessment would be tainted by the knowledge that Jeremy was a spurious bastard and not worthy to breathe the same air as his supposed fiancée.

It was Wednesday and Regina was at work. Natalie planned to discuss the matter with her that evening. When they finally got together, Regina reminded Natalie that she'd promised not to contact Jeremy until next week. Natalie couldn't understand why she couldn't see Jeremy, but Regina convinced her that she had a very good reason without telling Natalie what that reason was.

Regina was stunned when she learned that Natalie's parents were in Sicily. Regina blamed herself for not checking in with the Romanos, if only to keep her pulse on any suspicions that they may have had. Natalie told her not to blame herself. Natalie's parents had apparently been zealously determined to keep this Sicily trip a secret, and Regina was the last person her mother would have told. Regina knew that was right. She told Natalie that she should rest up until Friday, when she would take her out for dinner. Regina asked Natalie for a shopping list of things she wanted to have in the house to eat and whatever else she needed. Natalie told Regina that she was not incapacitated and was fully capable of shopping on her own. Regina implored Natalie to stay hidden just a few more days, because she didn't want anyone to discover she was home quite yet. As usual, Regina got her way.

Chapter Sixteen

Natalie's Return

The week's calendar revealed that autumn had arrived, which coincided with Natalie entering her third trimester of pregnancy. On Thursday, Natalie made her next doctor's appointment. The group to which Dr. Connors belonged also had offices in Cambridge. Natalie hated to leave Dr. Connors, but driving back and forth to Chelmsford for her more frequent appointments didn't make sense.

With Natalie back in town, Regina and I conspired to have Natalie catch Jeremy in the act. Regina felt that Natalie's pregnancy was no longer in danger, since she was in her last trimester and living at home. She believed it was time that Natalie had a reality check. Regina loathed Jeremy for the two-timing cheat he was. A picture is better than a thousand words and Regina was dogged in her determination to paint a picture that revealed Jeremy for exactly what he was.

On Friday night, I followed Jeremy and Kathy. They went to the same motor inn they had frequented for the past few months, exactly as Regina and I expected and, quite frankly, what we were hoping. I texted Regina, "They r there," and she did the rest.

Regina ushered Natalie out the front door and into her car, saying, "You've been home for three days now and it's time you left your haunt. Can you believe your parents! Oh my God! They'll be back one week from today, right?"

"Yes," Natalie responded, nodding. "I actually spoke to my brother this morning. I figured he was the least likely to give a crap about my not being there. He says my parents are mostly over it now and seem to be having a good time. Rob says he loves the food and sunshine. Mostly he went on about how beautiful the women are in Sicily. They all have glistening black hair and clear dark skin and not a single throwaway in the lot. Of course, Rob has a tendency to exaggerate and glamorize things a bit too much; however, having been there myself, it's mostly true."

Natalie and Regina spoke about less serious things like work and

Regina's love life until Natalie realized that they were driving quite a distance. Natalie questioned this, but Regina ignored the question and started discussing Jeremy. Natalie again inquired why Regina was so set against her seeing Jeremy. Natalie confessed that she wasn't certain whether Jeremy would even want to have anything to do with her once he saw her pregnant. She told Regina that she loved him so much that she prayed he could accept the situation and marry her anyway and be a father to her child.

Regina responded, "I think all your questions will be answered very soon. We're almost there."

"Almost where?" queried Natalie.

Natalie pulled into the Chisholm Motor Inn, spotting Jeremy's car. "Does that car look familiar to you, Natalie?"

There was absolutely no mistaking the car. Jeremy's vanity license plate left no doubt that it was his. At this point, Regina showed Natalie pictures saved on her phone revealing the indisputable truth covering several months of Jeremy's infidelity from Plymouth to only a few weeks ago all clearly marked with date and time.

Natalie felt the heat rising to her face. "Did you enjoy your free license to spy on Jeremy and put me in a shameful situation?" asked Natalie, staring at the car and avoiding eye contact with her friend.

"You have done nothing shameful," insisted Regina. "I am your best friend in the whole world. Do I need to prove that to you after all we've been through, especially these last six months? You can't marry Jeremy and I had to show you what kind of man he is. He says he loves you and wants to marry you. He says he's going to be working hard to save money so you two can be married when you get back. He's working hard, all right. He's probably working hard this very minute."

Natalie was fighting back the tears, not wanting to show Regina how much this hurt her. It seemed that everything in her life was coming unglued. She had held out some small glimmer of hope that Jeremy would tell her that he loved her no matter what. She imagined him saying that he was the one who screwed up and that he accepted all the blame for her pregnancy. She could plainly hear Jeremy say that he loved her without conditions and would be proud to be her baby's father. Instead, she felt her whole world crashing down. She told Regina to drive her back home.

"You wanted to see Jeremy, didn't you? Let me text him to come out to meet you. I don't know about you, Natalie, but I would love to show that bastard up for what he is."

"Why are you being so mean to me, Regina? Don't you even know this is killing me? Didn't I just pour my heart out about how much I prayed that Jeremy and I could somehow make this work? And now you want to show him up! You won't be showing him up, you'll be tearing my insides out if I have to see him now with both of us confronted by the ugly truth. Let's go home. I do *not* want to see Jeremy."

Regina was surprised by Natalie's reaction. She had clearly underestimated the shock effect this would have on her. Regina couldn't understand that type of love, probably because she had never loved anyone that much. But even so, she didn't regret revealing to Natalie the kind of man she would be marrying. If he could do this now, supposedly in the throes of passionate love for Natalie, he would most certainly be a philandering, good-for-nothing husband. Regina convinced herself she had positively done the right thing. Natalie would understand that too, once reality hit her. Natalie and Regina drove home in silence, except for Natalie's whimpering, which sounded like anguished screams to Regina's ears.

Natalie slept very well that night, probably due to the mental exhaustion and her unconscious desire to repress all thoughts of what had transpired the previous evening. In the light of day this bright Saturday morning, she once again was forced to face the facts of life. The baby was apparently very upset about his or her future, as it rumbled around, sloshing in Natalie's secure, insulated womb. Natalie sat silent on the soft easy chair for over an hour, nibbling on some darkened toast, lightly buttered, occasionally sipping some herbal tea, now passing from hot to barely lukewarm.

Natalie had many options for dealing with Jeremy. Regina recommended telling him to go fuck himself and never seeing him again. Natalie felt that option was not painful enough for him. He would simply go out and find a substitute. After all, Jeremy never seemed to be lacking for attractive women with whom to while away the hours. Natalie felt used and abused by Jeremy after loving him for so long. She even began to doubt his so-called faithfulness during the two years he professed to love her. She thought back to the several times that Jeremy couldn't see her for one reason or another. All along, her unquestioned, misguided trust in Jeremy raised no alarms. She simply believed whatever excuse Jeremy offered without question.

Natalie decided to see Jeremy face-to-face, without confronting him with the recent knowledge she had. She called Jeremy about half past ten that morning, but he didn't answer. Why would he answer? she asked herself. He was probably working his morning riser as she dialed. The unanswered call and that stupid ringtone of "Can't Hold Us" by Macklemore and Ryan Lewis using only the "ay, ay, ay" part of the introduction with its pounding drumbeat only pissed her off more. She hung up and sent him a text message instead: "R U Up? Home now call me."

As Natalie guessed, Jeremy was in no position to answer the phone. When things finally settled down, he checked his texts and exclaimed, "Oh, shit! Does this mean she's home home or home in Sicily?"

Jeremy held Kathy and asked, "What if she is home, here? Are you willing to commit to me now? Are you ready to tell your husband that your marriage is over so that we can always be together? He will be home in a few weeks."

"Nothing's changed, Jeremy. I will not dump Jason now or when he gets back to Hanscom. If things don't feel right after he returns and you still want me, well maybe. We'll see. But right now I cannot do this to him. How many times do I have to say the same thing? If your fiancée is home, maybe it's for the best."

Jeremy snapped. "She's not my fiancée – yet! These months away from her have changed me! You have changed me. I can't see spending my whole life with Natalie after you. I know she's special, but I find her to be way too clingy. You're a woman, she's still a child."

"You'd better call her back. I'll go into the bathroom and get ready. Don't worry, I'll be quiet."

Jeremy called Natalie, surprised to find that she was indeed home in Boston. "What in the world are you doing home? I know that your parents went to Sicily to see you. They even asked me to go with them, all expenses paid."

"And you turned them down?" Natalie asked. "What does that tell me?"

"It's nothing, baby. I just couldn't spare the time. You know that I've been saving money like crazy for us. I knew it would only be a few more months."

"Still," said Natalie, "you could have spared one week just to be with me."

"So why are you home?" Jeremy persisted.

"That's something we need to discuss in person. Do you want me to come over now?"

"No, no!" Jeremy said, barely hiding the panic in his voice. "Actually, I went to the gym to work out and I just started. I'll drop by your house in a couple of hours."

Natalie told Jeremy that she would be waiting anxiously for him and couldn't wait to see him. She was learning very quickly how effortless it was for Jeremy to lie. Even when she knew he was lying, she almost believed the sincerity in his tone. Natalie got up to make herself beautiful while waiting.

Jeremy arrived at Natalie's house a little before three. He wanted to make sure that he was fresh and clean when he saw her, leaving no traces of being with Kathy only a few hours before. He hoped that Natalie was not looking for sex, because he was worn out from being with Kathy all Friday night and Saturday, though he figured he would be up to the challenge if necessary. He assumed that Natalie would be horny after being away from him for six months. He was very sure of himself.

"Come in!" yelled Natalie. "The door is open."

Natalie was sitting behind the kitchen table when Jeremy walked in the door. He walked in the house slowly. He had almost forgotten how beautiful she was. He was thinking that he was a fool wanting Kathy and all her complications when Natalie was right there, waiting to be his. As beautiful as Natalie was, though, Kathy's whole being – her temperament, her sexuality, her sense of humor, and the feelings she aroused – made him want Kathy more than ever. He was playing another game with Natalie. He decided not to burn any bridges with her until Kathy had committed herself to him. Natalie was quite a consolation prize. She was a consolation prize most men would have considered the grand prize.

"Why are you just sitting there?" Jeremy asked in greeting. "Stand up and give me a kiss."

Natalie hesitated, rising languidly as Jeremy stood over her. With his eyes fixed on Natalie's, he tenderly embraced her, not seeing or even feeling the obvious changes in her body. He broke off the kiss, enveloping her with both arms, eyes still shut as he was drawn to the familiar tingling aroma of her soft auburn hair. As his hands moved over her body, caressing her breasts and her hips, he sensed the change in Natalie's body for the first time.

"Natalie? What's this?" Jeremy was in total disbelief.

"Jeremy Quinn! I thought you worked in a hospital lab and had some medical training," teased Natalie.

"How did you get pregnant?"

"Do I need to explain how this happened?" asked Natalie mockingly.

"How far along are you?"

"Somewhere in the neighborhood of six months," replied Natalie.

"I can remember your words almost verbatim when we were together at the Ritz-Carlton. You said there was no way that you could get pregnant that night. Hell, this changes everything. Why weren't you more careful? You, more than anyone, should know when it's safe to have unprotected sex," railed Jeremy.

Natalie responded, choosing her words very carefully. "That particular night was a night that it was impossible for you to get me pregnant. You must be an extremely virile man, Jeremy."

Jeremy didn't even remotely consider the possibility that Natalie had gotten pregnant by another man. He was so cocksure of his own star quality and, more than that, Natalie's wholesomeness. He knew Natalie's baby was his without even questioning her about it. Jeremy's whole world changed that very instant. Whatever else Jeremy was, he wasn't soulless. This baby was his responsibility and he would make the baby legitimate. Nothing else entered his mind. He never asked where she had been these past several months or if her parents knew, or anything else. He continued to ramble about how much he was not prepared for this right now and Natalie sat listening, quiet and seemingly obedient.

"How soon can we get married?" Jeremy demanded to know. "We don't need to have a big wedding. I have no great desire to include my parents. They've been divorced forever and I rarely speak to either one of them. You can invite your parents and brother and we could have a simple civil ceremony. I'm sure that would suit your father, having put out God-knows-how-much for this mock vacation."

Natalie never tried to steer Jeremy away from his fatuous conception of her conception. She nodded in agreement with everything Jeremy said, finally adding, "Don't worry, Jeremy. I'll take care of the whole thing. My parents will be home next Friday and we'll go from there. By the beginning of November, this whole wedding thing will be a memory. I think you need some time to yourself. Go home and don't worry about a thing. Don't come over later and don't call me. We were going to be married eventually anyway. Perhaps it's simply a bit sooner than expected."

As soon as Jeremy left, Natalie sat alone with her thoughts. Knowing Jeremy as she did, she had predicted his reaction accurately. She felt pleased with herself at getting Jeremy to propose so quickly. The news was exciting, and only one other person could appreciate the moment. She called Regina. Regina dropped everything and rushed over to see Natalie as if on a 911 call.

"Oh, girl, did you tell him?" Regina burst out when she came in the door.

"There was no need to tell him, Regina. He does have eyes, you know."

Regina shot back, "Did you tell him the baby wasn't his? How did he take that?"

"I didn't tell him anything. I never told him the baby was his and I never told him the baby wasn't his. He convinced himself that he was the father without my saying a word. I hate to contradict Jeremy. He takes correction so poorly, you know."

"That's just brilliant," Regina scoffed. "Did you think that maybe the fact that this child wasn't his might come up? Oh, I don't know, maybe in the next thirty years or so! Do you plan to keep Ricky and Papa concealed over the next couple of decades? Maybe you should rethink this approach."

"Jeremy proposed to me on the spot. In about five or six weeks I will be Mrs. Jeremy Quinn," said Natalie with a dreamy-eyed looked on her face.

Regina, who had been standing to project an ominous pose, suddenly sat down. "Natalie, have you lost your friggin' mind? Wasn't that you with me last night at the Chisholm Motor Inn? Didn't we both see Jeremy's car? I'm sorry that I was unable to get a picture of Jeremy with his dick up Kathy's ass, but I am fairly certain they were not there to play checkers."

"I know what he was doing," Natalie assured her, "but Regina, Jeremy is a passionate, fiery man. You can't expect him to act like a monk for seven months while I go off leaving him alone. Now that I'm back, he's mine."

"First of all, that's total bullshit," shrieked Regina. "Do you not care about faithfulness and devotion? Because believe me, Jeremy will be out playing the field while you are laboring in the delivery room. I take that back. He will probably wait a few hours so he can pretend to 'be there for you.' I have to question my own sanity. I have known you since we were little girls and I never would have believed this attitude from you. What happened to your sense of pride?"

"Maybe I've become more realistic since becoming a woman," Natalie replied.

Regina, never one to give up easily, asked Natalie if she might want to drop by unannounced for lunch with Jeremy on Tuesday. Regina figured this would be a great opportunity for Natalie to meet Kathy. Regina didn't know what kind of reaction to expect from Natalie, who had now become a total stranger to her.

"You want me to see the woman Jeremy's been sleeping with, don't you, Regina? Well, I think that might be interesting. You are coming with me, aren't you, Regina?"

"You bet your life," sassed Regina. "I wouldn't miss this luncheon for anything. I can't wait to see what's going to be on the menu."

Regina continued trying to talk some sense into Natalie, to no avail. She concluded that either Natalie had an incredible fear of being an unwed mother with an illegitimate child or her love for Jeremy was beyond her comprehension. She truly could not grasp either case. This was the twenty-first century in liberal Bean Town. The days of Hester Prynne were long gone. As for her loving Jeremy, the Natalie Regina knew would have tossed him out the door with the garbage. It was mind-boggling and Regina left miserably defeated.

Regina was overwhelmed by disbelief. She did the only thing she could think of – she called me. Understand, Regina never calls me unless she wants something. It's usually some reconnaissance and surveillance where I am placed on stakeout or enlisted to employ other devious methods that may be considered illegal in the Commonwealth of Massachusetts. But I do it willingly, hoping that the ends will justify the mean – the end being Natalie's removing Jeremy Quinn from her life. When I heard that Natalie and Jeremy were now on the fast track to be married, I was despondent. How could she be so shallow?

Regina and I exchanged incredulities about Natalie's behavior until the senselessness and futility of our conversation became painfully apparent to both of us. I always held out some small glimmer of hope that Natalie would eventually want to raise her baby with the child's father – me. I truly believed that Mama and Papa were a positive selling point and part of the overall package. I was forced to man up and I didn't like it. I thought about Marion and how I let the one woman who truly loved me get away. If I went crawling back to her now, I could see only two scenarios and one was worse than the other.

I decided to brood that Saturday. I have gotten to be an excellent sulker. On Sunday I decided to go with Mama and Papa to visit Connie. Being with my family after a whole day of gloom was moderately therapeutic. At least Papa was always good for a laugh. Also, if I didn't at least see Connie to congratulate her further on the exciting news about having a baby, she would know I only visited her to see Natalie. She knew that anyway, but I felt obliged to at least pay Connie this initial celebratory visit. I drove on the way there, taking Papa's car.

As usual, the satellite radio was tuned to the oldies station, and "Boogie Fever" by the Sylvers came on. Mama commented that she was amazed that so many Boogie songs had been played that week. I've mentioned that Mama didn't usually know the artists, but she was terrific about knowing the songs and lyrics. She told Papa that she'd heard "Boogie Shoes," "Boogie Down," and "Boogie Wonderland" during the past week. Papa, always the showoff, said there are millions of Boogie songs and proceeded to name them all.

"Mama, don't you remember 'Boogie Woogie Bugle Boy' from the forties? I always liked The Andrew Sisters' version because of the war and all, but Bette Midler did a good job on the remake. Then you got 'Boogie Child,' by the Bee Gees, and 'Birth of the Boogie,' by Bill Haley & His Comets, and 'Boogie Oogie Oogie,' by Taste of Honey, and 'Boogie Woogie Man,' by Paul Davis and –"

That's when Mama stopped him. "I know you're not going to mention all one million. I got the point. There are many Boogie songs. Thank you, Papa. I was only saying that for a long time I never remember hearing any Boogie songs and then all of a sudden they seem to be everywhere."

"And what about 'Boogie On, Reggae Woman,' by Stevie Wonder?" continued Papa.

"OK, enough already," interrupted Mama. "You've made your point. No more. There is one song that I really like about Broadway but I don't know who did it."

Mama should have stopped while she was ahead, but Papa bellowed, "Please, Mama. Let's get your Boogies and your Boogaloos straight. You're talking about 'Boogaloo Down Broadway,' by Fantastic Johnny C, not 'Boogie Down Broadway.'" Papa commenced singing the song to prove his point.

"Why should you care? You shake the same thing and move the same way no matter what kind of dance song is playing."

Papa retorted, "I'm still trying to perfect my moves."

"Let me know when you do and I will call *Dancing with the Stars*. Oh, never mind. I forgot you are not a star."

Papa said, "Everybody is a Star," to which Mama replied, "That's a *sly* answer and wouldn't get you on the show."

Of course, Mama was referring to the old song by Sly and the Family Stone, and with that she had the last word. Mama usually had the last word.

Connie was excited when we arrived, knowing that Mama would be making a fuss over her and Papa would be very proud in his own dispassionate way. I added my congratulations to Thomas and Connie. We chatted for a long while and had lunch together. After eating, Mama and Connie went into the living room to talk girl stuff. Thomas excused himself, stating he had fallen behind at work and had several psychologicals to write. This, I had no doubt, was true. Most people not in education have no clue how much work teachers and other educators do outside the school building. It drives me nuts when I hear people say how easy teachers have it with all their vacation and short working hours. How I would love to see them handle all these children, parents, instruction, administration, and God only knows what else crops up during a typical day. I know I could never do it. Anyway, Thomas probably would have found another excuse not to spend the next hour or two with Papa and me anyway. Thomas is decent enough, but we have very little in common.

Having Papa to myself, it was the ideal time to tell him what had transpired the day before between Natalie and Jeremy. Papa was visibly shaken by the news. I know that he had always held out hope that Natalie and I would ultimately find our way to each other and be a real family. In true Papa form, he quickly composed himself. I felt a Papa teachable moment coming.

It's funny. When I was young, Papa barely spoke to me about anything of consequence. But as an adult, I find Papa sharing his experience and wisdom much more often. I was grateful and it made me feel closer to him.

I was crushed when Regina told me of Natalie's plans to marry. Even though Natalie made it perfectly clear we never had a future, I always believed that there was a miracle due. Maybe I had seen *West Side Story* one too many times. All Sunday, while with my family, the awareness of loss smoldered. By Monday, I could take it no longer. Knowing that Jeremy was working and Natalie's parents were away until the end of the week, I summoned the strength to call Natalie. I needed to confront her for my own peace of mind. Natalie surprised me by inviting me over that morning. I called in late to work and made a beeline to Natalie's house.

After the not-so-pleasant pleasantries, I spoke sternly to Natalie for the first time ever and said, "Natalie, have you lost your mind? Jeremy is the last person in the world you should marry. He will not respect your vows, if he even takes them."

"Maybe I should marry you instead. Is that what you think, Ricky?"

"That's really not why I came here," I said. "But you could do worse. Your child would have a real father who loves him. It would take no effort on my part to love his mother either. Do you intend to spend your whole life lying to Jeremy and your child? How do you intend to explain my presence in his life? Do you expect to pretend Mama, Papa, and I do not exist? You know that we can't let that happen."

Natalie probed further. "Are you saying that you plan to go to Jeremy to expose the truth about the baby's paternity?"

"My family is not the least bit interested in interfering in your happiness, no matter how bizarre your concept of that emotion might be. However, we do not wish to be excluded from my child's life."

"I have given this some thought," offered Natalie. "It would be an easy matter for Papa, Mama, and you to be involved in the child's life. I would introduce you as close friends of my parents so your presence at their house or even mine would be natural. Your friendship could blossom into a very close one without raising much suspicion. Heaven knows that Jeremy will be absent working or playing most of the time anyway. Jeremy is the least observant and least doubting person I ever met."

"That's terrific," I said. "So you intend for me to act as your child's uncle or something and not his father. You want me to deny the fact that

I am the real father to my own child. How would you like that if the roles were reversed?"

Natalie sat silent for several moments. She finally said, choosing her words carefully, "Ricky, I totally understand your feelings. I have felt the love you and your parents have for this baby from the moment we met. I have even felt your intense fondness toward me. I purposely put you off, not wanting to encourage you to believe that we might be married ourselves one day. I know what kind of man Jeremy is. *I want you to trust me now to do what is right for me.* I venture that when the next few weeks pass, you will appreciate my actions and motives. Please bear with me and I promise that your child will be a vital part of your life."

To me, Natalie was speaking veiled, unintelligible words. It was as if she were telling me something of a cryptic nature but it was up to me to riddle the riddle. At least it was something. Natalie was not the cold, aloof woman she had presented to me every other time we spoke or met. I left feeling that Natalie had a mission that did not include harming the Santos in any way.

Jeremy saw Natalie that Monday after he finished working. Most of the time Jeremy spent talking about the plans he was making for his baby. It surprised Natalie to hear Jeremy's fervor. Where she expected Jeremy to feel trapped and tied down, he displayed the opposite reaction – not entirely because of paternal love, but also masculine arrogance. This baby was proof of Jeremy's potency at a time that Natalie said it was impossible for her to get pregnant. His little swimmers were determined barnstormers on a mission and would not be denied. Natalie suspected that Jeremy's own family life played a major role in his wanting to be a good father. His own father treated Jeremy as an occasional guest outside the circle of his new family. While the child was still in the womb, Jeremy spoke to Natalie of lifelong commitments. She heard his words but saw the image of his making love to other women. She wondered if she was deluding herself by believing one who lies so effortlessly.

After a couple of hours, Natalie told Jeremy that she was feeling a bit uncomfortable and needed to rest. Jeremy said he would sit with her until she dozed off. He did and quietly left.

The next day, Regina and Natalie surprised Jeremy at work for lunch. Natalie purposely neglected telling Jeremy they were coming, wanting their visit to be a surprise. Regina was hoping that by Natalie actually seeing the woman Jeremy was ravishing, she would put a face to Jeremy's betrayal and come to her senses about marrying the cad.

"Natalie!" said Jeremy. "Why didn't you tell me last night you were coming here for lunch? I could have made special plans."

"I wanted to see where you worked," Natalie said with a coy smile, "but I didn't want to disrupt your day. We could have a quick lunch in the cafeteria. Regina said that's what you normally do."

"Good ol' Regina," said Jeremy with a mocking grin. "Yes, she has been here before."

"Why don't you invite Kathy to join us?" Regina suggested. "It was so nice meeting her last time."

Regina saw Kathy in the clinic and waved her over to join them. Regina introduced Natalie to Kathy. The meeting was awkward for both women, but a bit more perverse for Kathy, knowing she had been screwing Natalie's intended and believing that she had no clue about it. At lunch, mostly the girls chatted, led as usual by Regina's prying. She got Kathy onto the subject of her husband, who was scheduled to be home in about three weeks. Regina appeared theatrically charged by the news of Natalie's nuptials and declared what a wonderful husband Jeremy would be. All the while, Jeremy was solemnly shamefaced, glancing askance at Kathy, knowing that a few days ago he was begging her to leave her husband to marry him. Kathy felt as if Natalie was staring a bit too intently at her, which gave her an uneasy feeling. Kathy convinced herself that it was only her guilty conscience that made her feel this way, believing that there was no possible way Natalie could have known about their affair. Kathy was very glad when lunch was over and felt unclean receiving a tender embrace from Natalie when they parted.

"I'm really sorry that you had to get caught up in this lunch," apologized Jeremy, taking Kathy into an empty lab. "I had no idea they were coming here."

"Your Natalie is totally gorgeous," Kathy responded. "I doubt if you ever really expected to leave her. It was extremely upsetting being in her presence. And when were you planning to tell me she was home, and pregnant, and that you were about to be married? Please do not invite my husband and me to the wedding. But you know? I'm almost glad it happened this way. I have been telling you for two months that we couldn't be married, even though I admit that I was tempted. All this has made the whole thing a non-issue. I will stay with my husband, you will get married, and may we both have a great life. And it goes without saying that our plans for this weekend are on indefinite hold."

Jeremy looked deeply in Kathy's eyes and said, "I still love you. I don't know how I can bear being close to you without – well, you know."

"In that," said Kathy, "I totally agree. When I can settle on some plans, this will not be a problem. Working together now would be impossible. I'm glad Jason will be home soon. Having him home will make things a lot easier. I'm sure that I'll be able to find something to do closer to the base."

"You know you'll never find anyone who makes you feel like I do," Jeremy said. He winked at her, then turned and walked away.

The next few days were routine. Natalie stayed home and everyone else went to his or her respective jobs. I wanted to visit Natalie, but I'd already said my piece and really had no reason. Well, I did have a reason, but it seemed to me a one-sided love affair. Jeremy continued to visit Natalie each evening after work to cuddle. I was embittered by his presence in Natalie's life, but more inflamed by the thought of his influential presence in the life of my child. More and more that idea motivated me to take some drastic action and tell Jeremy that his whole newly found devotion to Natalie was based on a depraved lie. For very selfish reasons, I restrained myself from acting on the impulse. I knew that this fitful action would result in my own undoing with Natalie, but, more distressing, would jeopardize any future with my own child. I decided to take a wait-and-see attitude and trust the fact that Natalie's cryptic words from our last meeting might prove propitious.

Friday finally arrived, the day that Natalie had dreaded with optimistic anticipation. This was the day her family would return. In the intervening months, since Natalie's initial dread of bringing a baby into the world, she had changed from a scared little girl, fearing her father's disappointment and wrath, into a rational adult, facing the consequences of her grownup sexuality. Still, the uncertainty of her father's reaction caused her anxiety. Deep down, Natalie lamented her lost resolve to marry as a virgin, but she soberly faced the consequences.

When her family opened the door to enter the house, Natalie's genuine happiness at seeing them after such a long absence overcame all her hesitations. It was as if her own weighty problems had made her forget how much she missed them and needed them in her life. Taking the offensive, Natalie spoke first.

"Now you can see why I wasn't in Sicily," said Natalie penitently. Natalie knew that her parents would question all the e-mails and phone calls from Sicily. They would be wondering where she had been the past five months. They would assume that Jeremy was the father and that he willfully kept the secret from them. Natalie, now being a master of deceit, felt the necessity to tell her family half-truths, always careful not to blatantly lie. She did this to safeguard her own secretive scheme, which was unknown to everyone else, including Regina. Natalie explained that she had a friend with relatives in Sicily who agreed to forward copies of her e-mails. She described how she sent this person a batch of handwritten letters to mail periodically, giving the illusion that she was there. She told her parents that she stayed with a friend and had terrific prenatal care. All this, minus some major details, was fundamentally true.

Mrs. Romano intuitively felt that Natalie was concealing a much deeper darker secret. She heard what Natalie didn't say as much as what she did say. Knowing her husband's propensity for flying off the handle, she kept her mouth shut and asked only the basic questions that she knew her husband would ask.

"Why did you feel the need to run away?" she asked.

"The truth is," Natalie replied, "it was my original intention to abort the pregnancy. Then I was persuaded to put the child up for adoption. I never wanted you or Daddy to know I got pregnant. Then, I felt this life inside me and I just couldn't go through with it. Daddy, I'm sorry. I never meant to disgrace you or disappoint you."

Mr. Romano was still in a state of shock. He stood there staring at Natalie in a stupor, trying to wrap his mind around this startling disclosure. Finally, he approached Natalie and embraced her.

"You haven't disgraced me. You have made me very proud. If you had aborted this child, then I would have been devastated."

Harry Romano had no idea the efforts it had taken to prevent this from happening.

"I expect that Jeremy will do the right thing by you, yes? I would hate to go out and buy a shotgun."

Natalie avowed that Jeremy didn't know she was pregnant until a few days ago. She told her parents that when Jeremy found out, he proposed on the spot. Natalie explained that under the circumstances, she didn't want a fancy wedding and planned on a simple ceremony in early November. Mrs. Romano endorsed Natalie's plans, feeling there was something yet to be revealed. The Romanos were exhausted by the news and weary from the long trip from Europe. After a necessary rest, there were still many unresolved issues that Mrs. Romano wanted to discuss. Natalie didn't tell her parents the real truth of her child's paternity, fearing that their involvement would unhinge her own guarded plans.

This period of time from the end of September until the second week in October passed slowly. It was on the second Friday in October that Kathy announced to Jeremy that it would be her last day at work. Jason would be back from Afghanistan in three days and she would dedicate herself to his adjustment to being back home without the constant fear of death. She made her boss promise that he would not throw her any party or tell anyone that she had submitted her resignation. In fact, she had offered her resignation the same week Natalie visited for lunch.

Kathy was conflicted by having Jeremy as her lover. The devil on her left shoulder beckoned her to leave her husband and stay with Jeremy. She knew that the chemistry they had would be hard if not impossible to find again. The short time she'd spent with her husband failed to compare to the rapturous magic she had with Jeremy. It was Kathy's angel on her right shoulder who prevailed. A delicately sublime voice told her that Jeremy's love was transient and not really love but lust. She knew that Jason was her future. He was a man of substance and character. But in order to avoid the temptation Jeremy constantly posed, she had to leave quickly without giving Jeremy time to change her mind. Jeremy begged her not to quit. He enticed her with gentle strokes and played upon her attraction for him. He promised that her staying married and his upcoming nuptial did not signify an end of the special love they shared. The temptation was powerful but Kathy was firm.

She knew that she had made the right decision to leave that job. It would only take a bad day at work or an argument with Jason to cause her to find solace with Jeremy. Kathy left and never looked back.

Chapter Seventeen

Twenty Years Later

Papa proved to me that being obsessed about things was not all bad. Until the very end, he still consumed most of his day with music and movies, though it was mostly new stuff. He lived long enough to see every Academy Award movie ever made that was still in print. Papa lived long enough to see the 100th Academy Awards presentation, and that's a lot of movies. He left me as his legacy a digital library of music so large that I would be unable to hear it all in my lifetime, but I try. Because he hated the new music so much, he branched out. That was no big surprise. Papa hated the grunge sound and repetitive dance beats of the 1980s. He really hated the hip-hop and rap music of the 1990s and 2000s. And the techno music of the 2020s, where melody was replaced with invented cyber instruments, drove him crazy. To maintain his sanity, he continued to amass the top-ranked albums of his day. "His day" meant anything from when he was born in the late forties until about 1980. Papa recently celebrated his eighty-fifth birthday, and even though I could see that he'd aged, he never appeared old to me. I saw only the strong, witty person who stood in my corner for my entire life. I am so fortunate to have had this man in my life for forty-eight years.

Papa's greatest fear, not having my child in his life, never materialized. Natalie had a son and she named him Joseph after Papa. Papa's real name was Joseph Santo but everyone who loved him just called him Papa. My son Joey had no choice but to be in Papa's life. Papa guided his grandson more closely than he did me. I knew that he was busy while I was growing up, so I have long since forgotten any resentment I may have felt.

Connie's daughter is a charming but independent young lady of twenty years. Terry is a few months younger than Joey. The two cousins see each other occasionally, no thanks to me. The hour's drive to Chelmsford doesn't help, on top of the fact that I am usually too tired or too lazy to drive the distance. At least Connie tries to make the effort once or twice every month.

Papa's zest for life, the spark that lit my own life and Connie's, started to smolder. Three months ago, Mama passed away quietly in her sleep. Papa was thankful that Mama left us without any apparent pain or suffering. He asked Connie and me to handle all the funeral arrangements. I knew it was because he couldn't bear the grief and finality of putting Mama to rest, though he said it was since he was too old to be running around everywhere. I could see that Papa was losing the will to go on without Mama. He stated to me without my prompting that he had lived long enough. He told me that no one can live forever and he'd had a terrific life. I could feel my own heart breaking because I knew that he was giving up. When I lost Mama, I felt the unbearable pain that comes from losing the one person who has always given unconditional love. The emptiness inside me when she died left a resounding void of anguish. Now I faced losing both Mama and Papa. I faced my loss of childhood. As long as Papa and Mama were nearby, I felt comforted. I would now be forced to grow up. My guardian angels had to say goodbye.

It was during the last week of Papa's life that he wanted to see Connie and me and his two granddaughters. I mentioned Connie's daughter, Terry, but I neglected to add that I too had a daughter, Amelia.

When we arrived, Papa was sitting up and showed signs of his old self, which I had not seen in the three months since Mama passed away. I felt an eerie, almost ominous sensation watching Papa with his granddaughters. They were old enough to respect his feelings, knowing that he was alone now, but they were still young ladies and probably wanted to be anywhere else but stuck in the house with a timeworn old man. I was proud of the girls' maturity, but not really surprised, knowing how much they truly loved their grandfather.

It was on the next day that Papa asked to see Joey alone. This was very surprising, since Joey had started sleeping at Papa's house since Mama passed away. He could have spoken to Joey whenever he wanted. Joey wasn't thrilled about living with Papa, because he found it a bit creepy; however, he didn't complain too much. Joey would always check on Papa before he went to bed. At night, he would listen for Papa's eventual trip to the bathroom. Fortunately, Joey's college was within commuting distance. During the day, Joey would either be at school, with his friends, or home to eat. Papa always had someone else come in to check on him during the day.

Joey balked about wasting a Sunday to be with Papa when he could be spending the time with his friends. I know that I laid a guilt trip on my son, explaining that Papa would not be around forever and that he should be proud to know that Papa expressly asked to see him. It didn't take much convincing, and Joey and I drove together to Papa's house. I sat in the living room as Papa spoke privately to Joey in Papa's den.

I must confess to my curious need to eavesdrop. Papa carried on a mostly one-sided conversation. It must have seemed odd to Joey, because Papa was saying things out of the blue, unprompted by any comment or gesture made by Joey. Papa would answer questions that were never asked or make observations about life as if recalling his past and retelling it to himself in the person of Joey. This alone made me think that Papa was descending into his own thoughts and using Joey as his sounding board, as the youngest standard-bearer of the Santo legacy.

"Don't think that I am stupid because I am old. That is a very common belief of young people. I know because I had that same belief. Old people are much wiser than you can imagine. I concede that the energy and quick mental faculties of the young account for most of the great accomplishments made for society, but it's really the wisdom of the old that keeps life on an even keel. Learn to hit to right field. When you take half the field out of play it greatly reduces your chances. Look at the great hitters who used the whole field. Look at today's great hitters like Jaime Juarez, Nelson Thomas, or Jackie Roland. They all use the whole field. Look at the great hitters from my era, like Wade Boggs, Ichiro Suzuki, Pete Rose, and Tony Gwynn."

Joey interrupted. "What about Derek Jeter?"

"Forget Jeter," Papa muttered, "he was a Yankee all his life."

"You forget, Papa, I'm a Yankee fan."

"God forgive you, Joey. You have been brainwashed by your father just because he played for the Yankees in Little League. Let me remind you that we live in Boston. It is sacrilegious to root for the Yankees. Forget that for now. I have something more important to tell you. You don't even realize that right now, right this minute, you are living the very best years of your life. Nature has cursed the youth with this thing called hormones. Young men your age only seek one thing: sexual gratification and relief. And you know what I'm talking about. I'm not asking you to suppress these feelings. That would be unnatural. But listen to this – use your youth to develop your body and especially your mind. Do you think I always looked old as I do now? Of course not. I was young too once and even better looking than you are now. We are all dying a little bit every day – even you. It is imperceptible to yourself or those around you. You will know what I mean if you ever see your high school friends at a reunion after not seeing them in ten years. Passing milestones will mark your life. You graduate one day, get a good job, marry, have children, anniversaries, and on and on. They will pick away slowly and you will look back and ask where the time went. You will notice a gray hair or a new ache or, God forbid, find your hair deserting the front lines during your time of greatest need. My point is that time sneaks up on you. Pick something you are passionate about right now and work toward that goal. And I mean right now. Too many young folks are trying to find themselves at your age. That's total bullshit. By the time they find themselves they discover that time has already passed them by. I hate to say it, but even twenty-five years old can be too late. Look at those successful young folks today like the actors or singers you admire. Many were focused as children to get where they are now. You say that you really enjoy music, but you know that you are not especially gifted? That's OK; learn all you can about the science of sound. Learn about the production of sound and sound waves and sound editing and those other things I don't even know about. Learn to use the technology of sound. And I only use this as an example. It could be anything. Only, do it right now while your hormones are raging and your energy's at its peak. Do not subscribe to the philosophy of have fun now and buckle down later. Have some fun now but really buckle down now, too. You're a terrific kid and I am blessed to have you in my life. You almost weren't here. Did your father or mother ever tell you that story?

"No," said Joey, "but now you've got to tell me."

Papa's response was confusing and a non sequitur. "I won't be with you much longer but I have no sadness because I have lived a full and happy life. Whether you believe in God or not, life is good. Unless there really is a hell. There are lots of really good people who don't believe in Jesus, and I would be very disappointed in God if he punished them just because they happened to be born in China or India. Do you think that all the Muslims are headed for hell because they don't believe in Jesus Christ? How about the Jews? What if we are wrong and we're the infidels? The point I'm trying to make is to believe whatever the hell you want; just be good to people and take care of your family. Look after your parents for me. I'm so happy you're here. You have no idea how close you came to being a waste product. Ask your mother about that one day. I really think it's important you know, because I never want you to make the wrong choice if the situation arises. But please, for God's sake, wait until I'm dead. If she knew I told you, your mother would kill me."

That is when Papa forced my hand. At this point I had to join the conversation if only to avoid the confusion or any dire thoughts of doom and gloom that Joey might be imagining. I told Joey that I never really intended to get into this with him, but I would rather tell him than have him think the worst.

Papa settled back and looked at me with a supportive smile playing around his lips, while Joey looked at me expectantly, his eyebrows drawn together in puzzlement.

"I'm sure that you're clever enough to realize that your mother and I were married six months after you were born," I began. "You never questioned that, but I knew that it would be a topic of conversation one day. Whatever you do, Joey, do not tell your mother that I told you this. She would never admit to herself that you might figure out what happened twenty years ago."

Joey promised, adding that he would never want to embarrass his mother and that this is exactly why he had avoided bringing up the subject. He admitted that ever since he could do the math, he knew there was a story.

I thought to myself that it might have been better if Joey had seen his friends that day, but there was no going back. I proceeded carefully, bending the truth where necessary. After all, Joey wasn't there twenty-one years ago, and I am under no legal or even moral obligation to tell him every detail. Then, at the worst possible moment, my wife and daughter walked into the house. This shouldn't have been a big surprise. Papa loved my wife in a way that could never be disguised. He never told her that he did, but it was understood, almost from the moment they first met. I could have been a tiny bit jealous because Papa often ignored me totally in her presence, but instead his affection for her warmed me all over. Since Mama shared Papa's love for my wife, it was never an issue. The mother-in-law thing that people joke about never existed in our family.

By the way, Natalie is Joey's mother. But you already knew that. You may not have known that Natalie is also Amelia's mother. Natalie and I have been married for twenty years. That's the story I was about to disclose to Joey.

"Hello, my two sweet loves." I greeted Natalie and Amelia.

"That can only mean I walked into something heavy. What is it?" Natalie was smiling, so I knew she hadn't overheard anything.

"Papa was just having a man-to-man with your son and I overheard him tell Joey that he almost wasn't here. I know that Papa's memory is not what it used to be, so I thought I would just set the record straight."

"Oh, Papa!" exclaimed Natalie. "Why in the world would you even bring that up? That's not something you discuss with your grandson."

"What's the big deal?" asked Papa, honestly questioning the import of his action.

I jumped in again. "The big deal is that this is private and if we wanted this to be a warm and fuzzy family story, we would have told it by now. Anyway, I was just about to get into it, so you and Amelia might as well sit down."

"Mom," Joey said, "don't you know that Amelia and I figured out that I was born before you were married? I mean, so what? You've been happily married to Pop for twenty years now. Who cares? Unless there is some deep dark secret you are hiding. Am I adopted? Is Pop not my father? Is that why you have been so hush-hush all these years?"

"Absolutely not," I snapped. "And I have a paternity test to prove it if you ever doubt that."

Natalie could not believe her ears. She couldn't imagine that I could blurt out such a thing. But now that I had said it, I had to find a way to take my foot out of my mouth. You must consider that after my indiscretion involving Natalie, in our previous life, this fudging of the truth to our children for the purpose of maintaining the saintliness of their mother is pardonable.

"Why in the world would you need to take a paternity test?" Joey pursued. "Were you involved with other men when I was born, Mother?"

I burst in, not wanting Natalie to answer that most embarrassing question for her own children. Knowing Natalie as I do, she was likely to tell the truth. The truth for me has always been an illusion anyway. Search your own memory. We have all internalized our own truths from recollections tainted by selective memory. If American or world history were based on truth rather than what some author wrote in the history book, our heroes today would be poor examples of uprightness to be emulated by the young.

"Absolutely not!" I bellowed. "The truth is that I was very ungentlemanly. I plied your mother with drinks, having met her at a friend's party. Your mother was not in the habit of drinking and became intoxicated. I take the blame for being very vulgar because I took advantage of the situation. Your mother cried to me later that she had never done anything like that before, and I confessed to having some doubts. When she told me that she was pregnant, I insisted on a paternity test. Your mother fleetingly considered ending the pregnancy, but instead, well, you're here aren't you, Joey? It took me over a year of groveling and courting your mother, but six months after you were born, she finally agreed to marry me."

I think Natalie was relieved that I slightly disfigured the truth, and she made no attempt to correct anything I said. Papa was uncharacteristically silent. I know that Amelia and Joey were satisfied with the explanation.

"Is that all?" Joey responded. "I was afraid that I was about to learn some ugly, dark family secret. As parents go, you two aren't all that bad. I'm glad you finally told us the truth, Pop."

The truth? You may be curious to learn the truth about the paternity test. There was one taken, but not at my request, nor Natalie's. The question of paternity was never an issue for Natalie or me. We both knew that I was the father. It was also never an issue for Jeremy, because he had always believed that Natalie was a virgin and faithful to him. His ego could not allow the possibility of anyone else being his baby's father. It was the evening before Natalie and Jeremy were to be married. Natalie went to Jeremy's apartment and told him that she wanted to show him some pictures. Jeremy assumed that these were pictures that Natalie had taken during her self-imposed exile. She pulled out her memory card and inserted it into a slot on Jeremy's smart TV. There, in gorgeous color, were Kathy and Jeremy greeting each other with a passionate kiss at a bar on Court Street in Plymouth. Then Kathy and Jeremy were entering an apartment in Plymouth. The time and date were clearly visible on each picture of the slide show. These slides were followed by numerous images of Kathy and Jeremy entering the Chisholm Motor Inn. The dates and clothing worn by our lovers left no doubt that there were multiple romantic escapes. Jeremy sat stunned. His reaction was not one of remorse or penitence, but anger.

Jeremy roared, "You show me this now on the eve of our wedding? Were you purposely waiting to expose my misbehaviors as some sort of avenging triumph? How could you spy on me like a sleazy weirdo? I know that you could never do this on your own. Did Regina put you up to it? Did you spend good money to have me followed? That would have cost you a fortune."

"Yes, Regina got these pictures for me. She had a friend follow you at my request. I wanted to trust you again but you had a lousy track record. Why are you acting so hurt and offended? You lied to me straight-faced over the phone and in person while all the time you and Kathy were banging away."

Jeremy, dropping his voice fifty decibels, said, "I'm sorry, Natalie. I'm only flesh and blood. How could you leave me alone all those months? Well, never mind – I know the reason now, but it made no sense to me when you first left. Didn't you know that I would stand by you and the baby? We would already be married if only you had told me the truth when you found out that you were pregnant. Don't you know how much I love you? How much I have always loved you?"

"You sure have a funny way of displaying your affection toward me, Natalie responded. "I can just hear you with Kathy now, telling her how much you love *her*. I can hear you telling her how much you worship the ground she walks on and that you never loved me like you do her. I expect you had it all planned for her to leave her husband so you two could get married."

Jeremy was shocked to hear his own words bounced back to him. "How can you possibly believe what you are saying? Did you bug my rooms, too? I never told Kathy that I loved her. We both knew that this was a temporary thing. Kathy would never leave her husband, and I would not want to hurt you for the world. I know that I've said that before, but it's true. But why do this tonight? You have been home over a month. Is this some sadistic way to hurt me for what I did? Think about what you are doing. We will have a child next month. I want to be the child's father. I can't believe that you want to raise this baby alone and deny his father. Please forgive my indiscretions and stay with me always. We are meant to be together and to be a family."

"Are you marrying me only because of this baby?" Natalie questioned. "What if this was not your baby? Would you still marry me?"

"Don't be ridiculous. Of course this is my baby. You forget that I know you better than you know yourself."

Natalie repeated herself. "That's no answer. Would you marry me knowing this was not your baby? Would you love the baby and me for my sake alone? Would you forego your pride and macho vanity to be with me forever?"

"I am not going to dignify such a preposterous ploy with a response. I already told you that I would always love –"

"I'm still not hearing an answer so I will take that as a 'yes.' I will marry you tomorrow, Jeremy, but it's only fair to tell you that you are not the baby's father."

Jeremy looked as if an arrow had pierced his heart. It was not the sting of Cupid's dart but a fierce penetration inflicted by torment.

"Why are you deliberately lying to me? I know that you are incapable of breaking your own sacred vows. Did you suddenly start having sex with all the men in the city? That's just not you, Natalie, and we both know it."

"Then marry me, Jeremy. But remember, I expect you to love this baby as if it were your own."

Jeremy studied Natalie's face. "You're playing me. I hurt you deeply and now you want to hurt me back."

"The choice is yours. You can marry me safe in your belief that this is your baby, or not."

Jeremy spoke carefully. "There is a third option. We can have a paternity test done before we marry. Is that what you want, Natalie? Do you want to postpone our marriage until after the child is born, making him or her a bastard, or do you want to confess now that this is my baby?"

"I have already told you that this is not your baby, Jeremy. The choice is really yours. If you love me enough to marry me knowing this, I will marry you tomorrow."

Jeremy responded in exasperation, "How and when did you get

pregnant? Please tell me that much."

Natalie replied calmly, "That is none of your fucking business, Jeremy. Maybe you should have been following me, after you decided to break up."

Jeremy knew that when Natalie used profanity, it was serious. She used the f-word very strategically and almost never. "OK then," said Jeremy, "we will wait for the paternity test. I do not want to take the chance of raising another man's child."

That was all Natalie had to hear to finally internalize the fact that Jeremy did not truly love her. This knowledge was painful to accept but still had a liberating impact. That was how I got my foot in the door to be with Natalie. To quote Papa quoting Rick Blaine, "I think this was the beginning of a beautiful relationship" between my baby's mother and me. And this is the reason why I have a copy of a paternity test, thoughtfully paid for by Jeremy Quinn. Natalie had neither the doubt about my being the father nor the inclination to waste her money on an unnecessary paternity test. However, Jeremy insisted on the test, still believing he was the baby's father. Natalie was only too happy to cooperate, if only to prove to Jeremy that he was not the father. Watching Jeremy's face drop when he read the results was a small justice for Natalie. That, plus to fact that Jeremy had to pay for the test since he insisted Natalie was lying about the child's paternity. I hated the idea of having to use this paternity test to prove to my own son that I was his father. As it turned out, Joey never asked to see it.

I believe that winning Natalie over was a product of my good fortune and circumstances. It is an undeniable fact that most things in life occur purely by chance. Both my being in the club the same time as Natalie that evening and benefitting from Jeremy's shallowness aligned my stars. To paraphrase one of my idols, although I was too young to actually watch Yogi Berra play in person: finding the right woman is 90% luck, and the other half depends on whether you can stop her from seeing what a jerk you are during the time you spend together. I really feel that the turning point in our relationship was that day I went to see her after she'd returned to her home from Connie's house. I remember her exact words: "I want you to trust me now to do what is right for me."

I've asked Natalie if she had intended to dump Jeremy all along, pretending to want him to marry her, but she never answered the question, electing to play coy. I decided to believe that Natalie purposely toyed with Jeremy as a cat holding down a mouse with one paw while precariously swiping at the mouse's whiskers with the other. Once she found out that Jeremy was cheating on her, I would bet anything that she became resolute in her decision to dump him hard. This intent she never even shared with Regina.

I deliberately omit the circumstances that led to our marriage. Suffice it to say, the birth of Joey was a blessed event that brought Papa, Mama, and me even closer to Natalie. The Romanos were extremely open to our visiting the baby. I would go so far as to say they were encouraging. Mr. and Mrs. Romano wanted their grandchild to be raised by a mother and father. Papa said he never believed in the notion of a modern family. Stepfathers and stepmothers only muck up the family harmony. Papa would say the split-time inane concept of sharing the child was an absurd notion, although Papa totally understood the dynamics. Papa felt that no matter whom you marry you are going to experience ups and downs but you need to suck it up and stick it out for the sake of the family. He would always be quoting Frank Vecchio from *Lovers And Other Strangers*. "You stupid kids today, ... don't know what to do with yourselves, you get a divorce, for kicks." Papa was obsessed about staying married. I always thought that it was easy for Papa to stay married because he had Mama. The truth is, they had tons of problems while married. I think they were just committed to making it work. I must have been indoctrinated living with Papa, because I have to agree with him.

In any event, during those cold winter months in Boston, Joey's first memories were of Natalie and me holding him and keeping him safe from the big bad outside world. He learned the faces of Papa and Mama as well as the Romanos. Mrs. Romano virtually pushed Natalie out the door, demanding that she go to a movie with me if only to get a few hours break from caring for the baby. I am sure that Mrs. Romano cherished her time alone with baby Joey. I would often catch her smelling his soft curls, smiling from the aroma of his new, downy, brown angel hair. During the next several months, Natalie became discernibly more comfortable with me. And I was able to think of her as a beautiful woman, and not as that porcelain goddess image I had that prompted her to consider issuing a restraining order against me. It took a short six months for Natalie to agree to marry me, making our family united. The story of our next twenty years, I will spare you for now.

It was on a Monday twelve weeks to the day that I received that dreaded call from Joey. The phone had an ominous ring and I sensed bad news. I realize the ring of the telephone does not change for good news or bad. Our phone had not even been programmed for distinctive rings, but I had anticipated this inevitable call ever since Mama left us. I could see that Papa's will was dispirited. Without Mama to listen to his silly jokes and attend to his frivolous requests, he felt useless. His reason for living had died with Mama. He could no longer reach up to the top shelf to grab a box for her. She was not there for him to open a stuck jar lid or medicine bottle with childproof caps. He remembered a million little things that made him cry in private when he thought no one was looking. He never expected to outlive Mama and dreaded the prospect of life without her. I heard him tell Mama a thousand times, when I die, do this or do that. As if Mama had the energy to find a new boyfriend after Papa had taken every ounce of love from her except the unlimited tenderness reserved for her children and grandchildren.

Joey told me in a trembling voice that Papa didn't get up this morning. Joey would always say goodbye to Papa before he left for school. Joey tried to rouse Papa to no avail. Papa's body was cool and Joey knew that he was gone. Joey called 911 prior to calling me. The EMTs could not find any vital signs but tried to revive him by performing CPR. After a few moments, the futile attempts were suspended.

Papa spent the last thirty years of his life obsessing about death, but I knew his secret. He actually never felt as if death was imminent. Talking about death was a game for him to prepare himself for a much, much later rendezvous with eternity. It really wasn't until Mama died that death had a looming presence and a welcoming face. Sadly, Papa did not expect to see Mama again in some afterlife. He welcomed the respite from a grief he was never, ever to transcend. I was glad that I was not present at the end. I know many people find it comforting to be present at the end. I could not even fathom the idea of waiting and watching for death to take Papa from me as I looked on in horror. I can now take some comfort in the fact that Papa went to sleep at night and "woke up dead." Papa would always say that he wanted to wake up dead ...not knowing everything was over.

For those of you incredulous with disbelief about Papa's certitude, you must understand that Papa's convictions about life ending on Earth upon death are as firm as those of you believing death is the beginning of everlasting life. Both you and Papa may believe what you accept, but the truth is, no one really knows. They only have faith, and sometimes, unflappable faith that their belief is the only truth.

None of that really matters to me. With the possible exception of Connie, no one could ever feel the loss of Papa's life as deeply as I do. To most friends and neighbors, Papa's passing will be a sad occurrence followed by "Thank God he got to live a full life." I know that's true, but it does not lessen my grief one scintilla. I am most abashed by the selfish thoughts relentlessly flooding my mind. The loss of Papa signifies the loss of my youth, even though at forty-eight years old I am hardly a baby. I am now the older generation, as I assume the role of next in line. It's a degenerate outlook in the face of my losing the two people I have loved the longest in my life. I know that even in years to come, I will long for Mama's caress, which never failed to warm my heart. I will remember Papa's gruff words, unmasking the hidden tenderness behind them, and long to hear them again.

I will find some way to keep Papa and Mama's home. To sell it, no matter how much we need the money, would be far too painful. That house, not some gravestone, is the true earthly monument to the people who gave me everything I ever needed. Anyway, where in the world would I store all of Papa's worthless long-playing vinyl albums? If I threw them all out, as Natalie will undoubtedly suggest, I fear that would upset the balance of the universe. Papa would be so distressed that he might break the Curse of the Dough Boy from the great beyond and cause the Red Sox to win another World Series before the predestined twenty-second century. On behalf of Yankee fans worldwide, I could never allow that to happen, even if it meant my being responsible for lots of dusting of shelves.

When it came time to lay Papa to rest, I was fortunate that Connie, Natalie, and Thomas took charge. Of course, the burial plot had already been purchased, right next to Mama's. Connie sat down with the funeral director and selected a coffin, made the necessary transportation arrangements, and prepared the schedule. The funeral director made certain that all preparations were covered and finalized. I had given Mama's eulogy, and asked Connie if she would prepare one for Papa. Having buried Mama only three months earlier, I was incapable of going through that ordeal again. I was barely able to hold myself together then. A second trial would have found me totally overcome with grief. Connie agreed to speak about Papa without reservation. This took a great burden off my mind. Here was a man of eighty-five years who lived a productive and full life. This was a time to celebrate that life and thank God for all the ways he touched those around him. It was not the time to have a middle-aged man choking on his words, crying like a little girl. It would have been quite inappropriate under the circumstances, and would have proven most embarrassing for me.

I was amazed to learn that Connie had such insight into Papa's private façade. I always believed that Papa had fooled everyone, with the possible exception of Mama, about his true self. Connie told stories about Papa primarily for the benefit of those in attendance who had only a superficial understanding of Papa, the guarded person. Papa was viewed as a grumpy old man and had a tendency to scare people off, especially during his later years. I knew that this behavior did not embody the real Papa that few people understood. To my surprise, Connie got it. Connie told about the times when she backed out of Papa's driveway straight into his front left fender. This happened on two different occasions, and Papa was furious and then more furious. He let Connie know what a careless woman driver she was and threatened to call Motor Vehicles in order to have her license revoked. So what did he do? Both times he had her car fixed in order to save Connie from the $500 deductible and avoid any possibility of an insurance rate hike. Then Connie told of the time that I was stuck in New Haven when my car overheated. I made the mistake of trying to drive my car three miles to a gas station. I fried my car's engine and had a blown head gasket. I called Papa about midnight for help. After five minutes of lambasting me for my stupidity, he told me to stay where I was and not leave. In about two hours, Papa found me and we spent the night in a motel. In the morning, he sold my car for junk because it was not worth fixing. All the while Papa was lecturing me, he was also looking for a car lot. Before the day was over, Papa bought me a more-than-decent used car. Connie went on to explain that Papa, underneath his public brusque exterior, was a generous and giving person. I always knew that, never realizing that Connie did too. Connie struck me as being almost afraid to upset Papa, avoiding any kind of confrontation with him.

I had always believed that Papa's gruff outward demeanor was a defense mechanism. My aunt, now deceased, told me that Papa was forever doing favors for people. She said Papa never minded helping his friends and relatives, but they started taking advantage of his good nature. She said Papa had to be played like an instrument and Mama was always the best musician.

I was glad when that day ended. I had to suffer through Papa's interment. The pain of watching the coffin lowered into that bleak, dark hole was excruciating.

I have heard it said that when it comes to finances, even the closest siblings could become bitter enemies. Papa was barely put to rest before Connie and I were at odds about money. I never would have believed this ill will could erupt between Connie and me. I told Connie of my intention to keep Papa and Mama's house and her reaction was tantamount to setting off a keg of dynamite.

Connie erupted. "Do you have any idea how much that house is worth? Papa and Mama have lived there for over fifty years. It is probably worth ten times more than it was when they built it. Papa has maintained the exterior of the house completely. There is a new heating and air conditioning system, new carpeting and hardwood floors, and new kitchen cabinets. Papa even remodeled his bathroom two years ago. You may be independently wealthy, Ricky, but I'm not. I took out a second mortgage to pay for Terry's college education, we have two cars to pay off, and we have let things go unrepaired for too long already. I cannot afford to have that house sit idle, deteriorating because you have some sentimental attachment to it. Man-up, Ricky, we must sell that house. And who do you suppose will be paying the property taxes and upkeep of that house? I won't!"

I explained to Connie that this was more than a house. This was our childhood home where we shared a lifetime of experiences. This house was Mama's curtains and the breadbasket shade of paint on the dining room walls. This was Papa's lifetime of books and music. Memories are fine, but the tangible touch and smell of our home was priceless.

Natalie could see that this hostility with Connie would not end well. She suggested that we both sleep on it. There was no reason that a decision had to be reached that very day. Determined, as I was to keep the house, Connie was resolute in her conviction that it needed to be sold.

I realize that I have not discussed the last twenty years of my life with Natalie. The crazed need I displayed two decades ago for Natalie has not really diminished. I love her more today than ever. She has been my faithful partner in life, and I know that she has come to love me as well. Natalie is to me what Mama was to Papa. I shudder to think what my life would be without her. She may have married me for Joey's sake all those years ago, but she has let me know in a million subtle ways that she loves me – and in some not-so-subtle ways. This is why when Natalie suggested a solution to our problem; I knew she did it for me. It was an obvious, almost too apparent solution that my mindset prevented me from seeing.

Natalie simply stated, "Ricky, let's buy the house ourselves. Connie is right. Neither of you could afford to keep that house. Let's sell our house and buy Papa's house. It would really be like buying half a house since fifty percent of the house is yours anyway. We have built up substantial equity in our own house after living here sixteen years. Let's take that money and use it as a down payment on a new mortgage for the fifty percent we owe Connie. I would not be surprised if we had lower monthly payments than we do now. We would have a better house in the end. It's a win-win solution."

I knew that Natalie loved our house. This was truly Natalie's home, having all her loving touches throughout. I would always defer to Natalie about every household decision, no matter how big or small. Now she was willing to forsake all those things she cherished for me. That, to me, is the definition of love. And the moving after sixteen years would not be a fun experience. But there was no other way to avoid my clash with Connie. With Natalie's blessing, we agreed to sell our house and buy Papa and Mama's house.

Another year has been torn from the calendar, and Natalie and I are firmly entrenched in the boyhood home of yours truly. Connie has to admit that it gives her great pleasure to occasionally visit the old homestead, but far less pleasure than the windfall she received from selling the house to me. I leave you as I sit here in Papa's den. I expect that to me it will always be Papa's den and I am simply the latest caretaker. I look around and see all the vinyl 45-RPM records and long-playing albums and ask myself, was it possible? Did he sit here and listen to each of those records? Then I spy his bookshelves containing the biography of every president of the United States, lined up starting with Washington. I ask myself, could he really have read all those books? Papa had a practice of writing the date when he completed a book on the inside jacket cover. He often included a summary of the book and an update on his family's life at that point in time. Then I focus on another section of books. One day, starting about sixty years ago, Papa began reading the books from the St. John's College Great Books program. It took him a lifetime to complete. Papa used to tell me that if you're going to do something, pick away at it slowly. In time, if you are lucky to live long enough, you will finish what you started. Papa was very lucky.

On separate bookshelves, Papa kept copies of the Academy Award-nominated movies that he was not able to find in a digital format or online. They were either on VHS tape or DVDs. Papa still had the machines in working order to play them. I pulled *The Vagabond King* from 1930, starring Jeanette MacDonald, Dennis King, and Lillian Roth, off the shelf. I then realized that one hundred years have passed since that movie was made. I believe that except for those lost and out-of-print movies, Papa watched every single Academy Award film. He made it a point to watch one movie each day. That amounted to nearly 11,000 movies in thirty years, and Papa did this for nearly fifty years. That's a lot of movies to watch. I wonder if he could remember any of them. I have always believed that Papa's obsessions kept him alive for all those years. He always had something else to look forward to – until Mama died, that is. Without Mama, he had no one to share his enthusiasm, even if it was the pretend variety usually indicated by his wife.

The hour was late, and Natalie joined me in Papa's den. Whenever Natalie cuddled close to me on the sofa, with the lights out, and the soft sound emanating from my Bose system, I felt a peaceful contentment indulge my entire body. Natalie's naturally perfumed figure after her taking a bath was erotic to my senses, but it was a quiet oneness of a spiritual non-sexual gentility. For some reason, I was drawn to an old album from the year 1965. The record was nearly seventy years old. Papa always kept his records in pristine condition, carefully using a vacuum record cleaner after each and every play. I almost felt Papa's spirit guiding me to this designated spot, surrounded by a wide variety of music from rock and roll to jazz to the soundtracks of his life. Then, as if begging to be pulled out, I am summoned by *More Greatest Hits* by The Dave Clark Five. I remember a particular cut on this album that today no one would ever remember. But I know Papa liked this song. Even in 1965 it was only a modest hit. In the years following, it was rarely, if ever, played on the oldies station. Today, the music from that era has died with the teenagers from that bygone time.

I put the record on softly, but not too softly. It was necessary to obtain the full effect of the bass. Then the song played, "Come Home": "As I write this letter today, tears start fallin' from my eyes … I remember things we used to say, And the ties that bind our love. Only one thing I want to do … Come home … Long as I know I'm comin' home to you."

I knew that instant that I was home. I wondered if Papa might not have been wrong about the afterlife, because I could swear I felt his presence in that room. I hoped that Natalie could not see the tears fallin' from my eyes. That's another reason I like to keep the room dark.

About the Author

Philip Iovino is retired from serving the public school education systems in New York and Virginia. He has a bachelor's degree from the State University of New York at Cortland and a master's degree, an advanced degree, and a doctoral degree in Educational Administration from the College of William & Mary in Williamsburg, Virginia. He has experience as a teacher, principal, State Department Specialist, Head Start Director, and school superintendent in Virginia. Iovino is a veteran of the United States Marine Corps Reserves (1971-1977).

Iovino includes reading the classics among his many passions. Beginning with the *Iliad* nearly thirty-five years ago, the author has been nurtured on a steady diet of religion, philosophy, politics, history, science and drama. Iovino also has an extensive collection of popular music and owns every Top 40 song from 1955-2000. The author currently resides in eastern Virginia with his wife of forty-two years, Christina Marie. His oldest daughter is an attorney in Miami, Florida, his second daughter is a Substance Abuse Counselor in Virginia, and his son recently completed his master's degree in journalism from Emerson College in Cambridge, MA.

www.ingramcontent.com/pod-product-compliance
Lightning Source LLC
Chambersburg PA
CBHW050515260626
47157CB00004B/1328
9781939930507